Praise for *The*

"Davis's delightful str
on full display. . . . Sl

—Carmela Ciuraru, *San Francisco Chronicle*

"One can read a large portion of Davis's work, and a grand cumulative achievement comes into view—a body of work probably unique in American writing, in its combination of lucidity, aphoristic brevity, formal originality, sly comedy, metaphysical bleakness, philosophical pressure, and human wisdom. I suspect that *The Collected Stories of Lydia Davis* will in time be seen as one of the great, strange American literary contributions, distinct and crookedly personal."

—James Wood, *The New Yorker*

"Small as they may be, these stories ought not to be underestimated, for they are the brave, bighearted works of a literary titan. . . . There's a lot going on in Davis's fiction. She merges forms in a way that feels radical and exciting."

—*The Oregonian*

"Be prepared for moments of beauty that are sharp and merciless. . . . We are in a period in literary history when accuracy, clarity, and faithfulness seem transgressive. But that—shorter, faster, more changeable—is only culture. Davis . . . answers to a higher god."

—Susan Salter Reynolds, *Los Angeles Times*

"Davis delivers one thrilling experience after another—dozens of them—because she rarely allows artifice to trump clarity. She is a fun read." —Darren Sextro, *Kansas City Star*

"Davis approaches the short-story form with jazzy experimentation." —Jan Stuart, *The New York Times Book Review*

"Lydia Davis is one of the few undebatably singular prose stylists alive today. She has invented a genre entirely unto itself—a form combining the precision and economy of poetry, the wry storytelling of short fiction, and a clear-eyed and surgical inquiry into the nature of existence itself. I push her books on everyone I know."

—Dave Eggers, author of *What Is the What* and *Zeitoun*

"Lydia Davis's short stories are perfected economies, witty devices, precision-made, primed to release intelligence, philosophy, hilarity. They celebrate the thinking universe while they redefine the possibilities of the form. There is no other writer quite like her."

—Ali Smith, author of *The Accidental* and *Girl Meets Boy*

"Davis is a writer who really knows how to work in miniature. . . . More than seven hundred pages of bedazzlements . . . Davis's highly burnished sentences [are] crisp, self-questioning, hedged in by doubt. They get to the heart by way of the head. And they remind us that, in the hands of a writer as gifted and precise as Davis, even the tiniest of stories can change how you view things."

—John Powers, *Vogue*

"You read Lydia Davis to watch a writer patiently divide the space between epiphany and actual human beings first by halves, then by quarters, eighths, sixteenths, and into infinity. . . . Few are better than Davis at representing thought on the page. . . . Davis's lapidary prose is above all a monument to her perceptual intelligence."

—Zach Baron, *Seattle Weekly*

"Davis's short stories burrow deep into your mind. . . . Davis, heir to the shredding wit and poignancy of Dorothy Parker and the shrewd surrealism of Donald Barthelme, is a master of the quick switch, the sneak attack, the end run. The rich spectrum of her daring short fiction can now be fully and luxuriously appreciated in this generous collection. . . . Whatever the focus, Davis's incisive, rightfully celebrated stories snap us awake with their topsy-turvy yet dead-on perspective." —Donna Seaman, *Booklist*

"Lydia Davis writes fractional, microscopic, and wholly addictive stories. Really, there's no one like her."
—Catherine Holmes, *The Post and Courier* (Charleston, South Carolina)

"Twenty-five years ago, I was house-sitting for Francine Prose. A voice mail (remember those?) came in from Lydia Davis, thanking Prose for her response to *Break It Down*. I looked around the house and found the galley. I read it, and I reread it, and I reread it; it got me through that long dark winter, and it dramatically influenced the book I was then writing. I've kept reading Davis's break-it-downs with near religious devotion; she has utterly altered how I think about writing, and she has gotten me through innumerable long dark winters." —David Shields, author of *Reality Hunger*

"Davis's masterful sentence style and peculiar perceptiveness make each work unmistakably distinct. . . . A testament to a writer who continually pushes the bounds of short fiction, and who brilliantly defies categorization."
—Kimberly King Parsons, *Time Out New York*

Also by Lydia Davis

NOVEL

The End of the Story

STORIES

Break It Down

Almost No Memory

Samuel Johnson Is Indignant

Varieties of Disturbance

SELECTED TRANSLATIONS

Madame Bovary: Provincial Ways by Gustave Flaubert

Swann's Way by Marcel Proust

Death Sentence by Maurice Blanchot

The Madness of the Day by Maurice Blanchot

The Spirit of Mediterranean Places by Michel Butor

Rules of the Game, I: Scratches by Michel Leiris

Rules of the Game, II: Scraps by Michel Leiris

Hélène by Pierre Jean Jouve

The Collected Stories of

LYDIA DAVIS

The Collected Stories of LYDIA DAVIS

Picador

Farrar, Straus and Giroux
New York

 Printed in the United States of America. For information, address Picador, 175 Fifth Avenue, New York, N.Y. 10010.

www.picadorusa.com

Picador® is a U.S. registered trademark and is used by Farrar, Straus and Giroux under license from Pan Books Limited.

For information on Picador Reading Group Guides, please contact Picador.
E-mail: readinggroupguides@picadorusa.com

Grateful acknowledgment is made for permission to reprint the following material:

"Worstward Ho," copyright © 1983 by Samuel Beckett. Used by permission of Grove/Atlantic, Inc.

In "The Walk," quotations from *Swann's Way* by Marcel Proust, translated by C. K. Scott Moncrieff and revised by Terence Kilmartin, copyright © 1981 by Marcel Proust, used by permission of Random House, Inc.; quotations from *Swann's Way* by Marcel Proust, translated by Lydia Davis, copyright © 2002 by Lydia Davis, used by permission of Penguin Books Ltd. and Viking Penguin, a division of Penguin Group (USA) Inc.

"Extracts from a Life" is adapted from *Nurtured by Love* by Shinichi Suzuki, and is used by permission of Exposition Press.

The tale in "Once a Very Stupid Man" is adapted from the traditional Hasidic story recounted in Martin Buber's *The Way of Man,* and is used by permission of Citadel Press.

"Lord Royston's Tour" was adapted from *The Remains of Viscount Royston: A Memoir of His Life* by the Rev. Henry Pepys, London, 1838.

Samuel Johnson Is Indignant was first published by McSweeney's Books.

Designed by Jonathan D. Lippincott

The Library of Congress has cataloged the Farrar, Straus and Giroux edition as follows:

Davis, Lydia, 1947–
The collected stories of Lydia Davis.— 1st ed.
p. cm.
ISBN 978-0-374-27060-5 I. Title.

PS3554.A9356A6 2009
813'.54—dc22

2009025451

Picador ISBN 978-0-312-65539-6

First published in the United States by Farrar, Straus and Giroux

20

Contents

SAMUEL JOHNSON IS INDIGNANT (2001)

BREAK IT DOWN

(1986)

Story

I get home from work and there is a message from him: that he is not coming, that he is busy. He will call again. I wait to hear from him, then at nine o'clock I go to where he lives, find his car, but he's not home. I knock at his apartment door and then at all the garage doors, not knowing which garage door is his—no answer. I write a note, read it over, write a new note, and stick it in his door. At home I am restless, and all I can do, though I have a lot to do, since I'm going on a trip in the morning, is play the piano. I call again at ten forty-five and he's home, he has been to the movies with his old girlfriend, and she's still there. He says he'll call back. I wait. Finally I sit down and write in my notebook that when he calls me either he will then come to me, or he will not and I will be angry, and so I will have either him or my own anger, and this might be all right, since anger is always a great comfort, as I found with my husband. And then I go on to write, in the third person and the past tense, that clearly she always needed to have a love even if it was a complicated love. He calls back before I have time to finish writing all this down. When he calls, it is a little after eleven thirty. We argue until nearly twelve. Everything he says is a contradiction: for example, he says he did not want to see me because he wanted to work and even more because he wanted to be alone, but he has not worked and he has not been alone. There is no way I can get him to reconcile any of his contradictions, and when this conversation begins to sound too much like many I had with my husband I say goodbye and hang up. I finish writing down what I started to write down even though by now it no longer seems true that anger is any great comfort.

I call him back five minutes later to tell him that I am sorry about all this arguing, and that I love him, but there is no answer. I call again five minutes later, thinking he might have walked out to his garage and walked back, but again there is no answer. I think of driving to where he lives again and looking for his garage to see if he is in there working, because he keeps his desk there and his books and that is where he goes to read and write. I am in my nightgown, it is after twelve and I have to leave the next morning at five. Even so, I get dressed and drive the mile or so to his place. I am afraid that when I get there I will see other cars by his house that I did not see earlier and that one of them will belong to his old girlfriend. When I drive down the driveway I see two cars that weren't there before, and one of them is parked as close as possible to his door, and I think that she is there. I walk around the small building to the back where his apartment is, and look in the window: the light is on, but I can't see anything clearly because of the half-closed venetian blinds and the steam on the glass. But things inside the room are not the same as they were earlier in the evening, and before there was no steam. I open the outer screen door and knock. I wait. No answer. I let the screen door fall shut and I walk away to check the row of garages. Now the door opens behind me as I am walking away and he comes out. I can't see him very well because it is dark in the narrow lane beside his door and he is wearing dark clothes and whatever light there is is behind him. He comes up to me and puts his arms around me without speaking, and I think he is not speaking not because he is feeling so much but because he is preparing what he will say. He lets go of me and walks around me and ahead of me out to where the cars are parked by the garage doors.

As we walk out there he says "Look," and my name, and I am waiting for him to say that she is here and also that it's all over between us. But he doesn't, and I have the feeling he did intend to say something like that, at least say that she was here, and that he then thought better of it for some reason. Instead, he says that everything that went wrong tonight was his fault and he's sorry. He stands with his back against a garage door and his face in the light and I stand in front of him with my back to the light. At one point he hugs me so suddenly that the fire of my cigarette crumbles against the garage door behind him. I know why we're out here and not in his room, but I don't ask him until everything is all right between us. Then he says, "She wasn't here when I called you. She came back later." He says the only reason she is there is that something is troubling her and he is the only one she can talk to about it. Then he says, "You don't understand, do you?"

I try to figure it out.

So they went to the movies and then came back to his place and then I called and then she left and he called back and we argued and then I called back twice but he had gone out to get a beer (he says) and then I drove over and in the meantime he had returned from buying beer and she had also come back and she was in his room so we talked by the garage doors. But what is the truth? Could he and she both really have come back in that short interval between my last phone call and my arrival at his place? Or is the truth really that during his call to me she waited outside or in his garage or in her car and that he then brought her in again, and that when the phone rang with my second and third calls he let it ring without answering, because he was fed up with me and with arguing? Or is the truth that she did leave and did come back later but that he remained and let the phone ring without answering? Or did he perhaps bring her in and then go out for the beer while she waited there and listened to the phone ring? The last is the least likely. I don't believe anyway that there was any trip out for beer.

The fact that he does not tell me the truth all the time makes me not sure of his truth at certain times, and then I work to figure out for myself if what he is telling me is the truth or not, and sometimes I can figure out that it's not the truth and sometimes I don't know and never know, and sometimes just because he says it to me over and over again I am convinced it is the truth because I don't believe he would repeat a lie so often. Maybe the truth does not matter, but I want to know it if only so that I can come to some conclusions about such questions as: whether he is angry at me or not; if he is, then how angry; whether he still loves her or not; if he does, then how much; whether he loves me or not; how much; how capable he is of deceiving me in the act and after the act in the telling.

The Fears of Mrs. Orlando

Mrs. Orlando's world is a dark one. In her house she knows what is dangerous: the gas stove, the steep stairs, the slick bathtub, and several kinds of bad wiring. Outside her house she knows some of what is dangerous but not all of it, and is frightened by her own ignorance, and avid for information about crime and disaster.

Though she takes every precaution, no precaution will be enough. She tries to prepare for sudden hunger, for cold, for boredom, and for heavy bleeding. She is never without a bandaid, a safety pin, and a knife. In her car she has, among other things, a length of rope and a whistle, and also a social history of England to read while waiting for her daughters, who are often a long time shopping.

In general she likes to be accompanied by men: they offer protection both because of their large size and because of their rational outlook on the world. She admires prudence, and respects the man who reserves a table in advance and also the one who hesitates before answering any of her questions. She believes in hiring lawyers and feels most comfortable talking to lawyers because every one of their words is endorsed by the law. But she will ask her daughters or a woman friend to go shopping with her downtown, rather than go alone.

She has been attacked by a man in an elevator, downtown. It was at night, the man was black, and she did not know the neighborhood. She was younger then. She has been molested several times in a crowded bus. In a restaurant once, after an argument, an excited waiter spilled coffee on her hands.

In the city she is afraid of being carried away underground on the wrong subway, but will not ask directions from strangers of a lower class. She walks past many black men who are planning different crimes. Anyone at all may rob her, even another woman.

At home, she talks to her daughters for hours on the telephone and her talk is all premonition of disaster. She does not like to express satisfaction, because she is afraid she will ruin a run of good luck. If she does happen to say that something is going well, then she lowers her voice to say it and after saying it knocks on the telephone table. Her daughters tell her very little, knowing she will find something ominous in what they tell her. And when they tell her so little then she is afraid something is wrong—either their health or their marriage.

One day she tells them a story over the telephone. She has been downtown shopping alone. She leaves the car and goes into a fabric store. She looks at fabrics and does not buy anything, though she takes away a couple of swatches in her purse. On the sidewalk there are many blacks walking around and they make her nervous. She goes to her car. As she takes out her keys, a hand grabs her ankle from under the car. A man has been lying under her car and now he grabs her stockinged ankle with his black hand and tells her in a voice muffled by the car to drop her purse and walk away. She does so, though she can hardly stand. She waits by the wall of a building and watches the purse but it does not move from where it lies on the curb. A few people glance at her. Then she walks to the car, kneels on the sidewalk, and looks under. She can see the sunlight on the road beyond, and some pipes on the belly of her car: no man. She picks up her purse and drives home.

Her daughters don't believe her story. They ask her why a man would do such a peculiar thing, and in broad daylight. They point out that he could not have simply disappeared then, simply vanished into thin air. She is outraged by their disbelief and does not like the way they talk about broad daylight and thin air.

A few days after the assault on her ankle, a second incident upsets her. She has driven her car down at evening to a parking lot beside the beach as she sometimes does, so that she can sit and watch the sunset through her windshield. This evening, however, as she looks over the boardwalk at the water, she does not see the peaceful deserted beach that she usually sees, but a small knot of people standing around something that seems to be lying on the sand.

She is instantly curious, but half inclined to drive away without looking at the sunset or going to see what is on the sand. She tries to think what it could be. It is probably some kind of animal, because people do not stare so long at something unless it has been alive or is alive. She imagines a large fish. It has to be large, because a small fish is not interesting, nor is something like a jellyfish that is also small. She imagines a dolphin, and she imagines a shark. It might also be a seal. Most likely dead already, but it could also be dying and this knot of people intent on watching it die.

Now at last Mrs. Orlando must go and see for herself. She picks up her purse and gets out of her car, locks it behind her, steps over a low concrete wall, and sinks into the sand. Walking slowly, with difficulty, in her high heels through the sand, legs well apart, she holds her hard shiny purse by its strap and it swings wildly back and forth. The sea breeze presses her flowered dress against her thighs and the hem of it flutters gaily around her knees, but her tight silver curls are motionless and she frowns as she plunges on.

She moves in among the people, and looks down. What is lying on the sand is not a fish or a seal but a young man. He is lying perfectly straight with his feet together and his arms by his sides, and he is dead. Someone has covered him with newspapers but the breeze is lifting the sheets of paper and one by one they curl up and slide over the sand to tangle in the legs of the bystanders. Finally a dark-skinned man who looks to Mrs. Orlando like a Mexican puts out his foot and slowly pushes aside the last sheet of newspaper and now everyone has a good look at the dead man. He is handsome and thin, and his color is gray and beginning to yellow in places.

Mrs. Orlando is absorbed in looking. She glances around at the others and she can see they have forgotten themselves too. A drowning. This is a drowning. This may even be a suicide.

She struggles back over the sand. When she gets home, she immediately calls her daughters and tells them what she has seen. She starts by saying she has seen a dead man on the beach, a drowned man, and then she starts over again and tells more. Her daughters are uneasy because she becomes so excited each time she tells the story.

For the next few days, she stays inside her house. Then she leaves suddenly and goes to a friend's house. She tells this friend that she has received an obscene phone call, and she spends the night there. When she returns home the next day, she thinks someone has broken in, because certain things are missing. Later she finds each thing in an odd place, but she can't lose the feeling that an intruder has been there.

She sits inside her house fearing intruders and watching out for what might go wrong. As she sits, and especially at night, she so often hears strange noises that she is certain there are prowlers below the windowsills. Then she must go out and look at her house from the outside. She circles the house in the dark and sees no prowlers and goes back in. But after sitting inside for half an hour she feels she has to go out again and check the house from the outside.

She goes in and out, and the next day too she goes in and out. Then she stays inside and just talks on the phone, keeping her eyes on the doors and windows and alert to strange shadows, and for some time after this she will not go out except in the early morning to examine the soil for footprints.

Liminal: The Little Man

Lying there trying to sleep, a little light coming through the curtain from the street, she planned things and remembered things and sometimes just listened to sounds and looked at the light and the dark. She thought about the opening and closing of her eyes: that the lids lifted to reveal a scene in all its depth and light and dark that had been there all along unseen by her, nothing to her since she did not see it, and then dropped again and made all that scene unseen again, and could anytime lift and show it and anytime close and hide it, though often, lying sleepless, her eyes shut, she was so alert, so racing ahead with what she was thinking, that her eyes seemed to her to be wide open behind the closed lids, bugged, glassy, staring, though staring out only into the dark back of the closed lids.

Her son came and laid out three large gray shells on her thigh, and the visitor, sitting close to her on another hard chair, reached over to take up the middle one and look at it—an oval cowrie, with white lips.

The moment when a limit is reached, when there is nothing ahead but darkness: something comes in to help that is not real. Another way all this is like madness: a mad person not helped out of his trouble by anything real begins to trust what is not real because it helps him and he needs it because real things continue not to help him.

Her son out on the terrace is dropping a brick over and over again on a plastic gun, breaking it into sharp pieces. The television is on in a room behind a closed door. Another woman comes out with her hair wet and a towel wrapped around her saying suddenly and loudly to him, That's bad, stop it. Her son stands holding the brick, with fear on his face. She says, I was beginning to meditate and I thought the house was falling down. The pieces of red plastic shine on the painted clay around his feet.

How it works: Sometimes there is a thought that becomes a dream (she is laying out a long sentence and then she is out on Fourteenth Street laying out a long piece of black curb) and the mind says, But wait, this isn't true, you're beginning to dream, and she wakes up to think about thinking and dreaming. Sometimes she has lain awake a long time and the stroke of sleep comes down finally and softens every part of her body at once; then her mind notices and wakes because it is interested in how sleep comes so suddenly. Sometimes her mind won't stop working in the first place and won't stop for hours and she gets up to make a warm drink and then it is not the warm drink that helps but the fact that action has been taken. Sometimes sleep comes easily, but almost right away (she has been sleeping ten minutes or so) a loud noise or a soft but offensive noise wakes her and her heart races. First there is only inarticulate anger, then her mind begins working again.

•

Coughing, her head up on three pillows, warm tea beside her; or on another night a limp, melting rag of wet kleenex across her forehead.

She slept by her son on the beach; they lay parallel to the line of water. The water lapped up in sheets over the sand and drained off. People moved, took positions nearby, walked past, and the sound of the ocean was enough of a silence so that the two slept peacefully, the lowering sun on the boy's face, grains of sand on his neck, an ant running over his cheek (he shuddered, his hand unclenched and then clenched again), her cheek in the soft grayish sand, her glasses and her hat on the sand.

Then there was the slow uphill walk home, and later they went into a dark bar to have dinner (her son nearly asleep bowing over the polished wood) and because of the dark, the crush, the noise, the violent noise, so that they seemed to be swallowing some of all the noise and darkness with their food, she was dizzy and confused when they walked out into the light and the silence of the street.

She is lying in the dark going through some complex turns to get to the point where she can sleep. It is always hard to sleep. Even on nights when it will turn out not to have been hard she expects it to be hard and is ready for it, so that maybe it might as well have been hard.

That night long ago there was nothing more to be done. She lay in a room crying. She lay on her left side with her eyes on the dark window. She was eight or nine, or so. Her left cheek on a soft old pillowcase covering a small old pillow with the smell in it still of old people. Near her, perhaps over against her, under her right arm, her stuffed elephant, nap worn off, trunk creased this way and that. Or more probably tonight, pillow tossed aside, elephant tossed aside, perhaps she has been lying on her right cheek staring at the light that runs under the door and shines on her floorboards, putting a hand down into the draft flowing across the floor; it has been a night of hoping the door will open again, there will be a relenting somewhere, the light will flood in from the hall, white, and against the white light a black figure come in. When the mother is gone at night she is gone very far away, though on the other side of the door, and when she opens the door and comes in, she comes directly to the child and stands at a great height above the child, light on half her face. But tonight the child has not been watching the door, she has her face to the dark window and she has begun crying hopelessly. Someone is angry; she has done some final thing for which there is no forgiveness tonight. No one will come in, and she can't go out. The finality of it terrifies her. It is a feeling close to a feeling she will die of it. Then he comes in, almost of his own accord, though he is not real, she has invented him, he comes in for the first time standing there above her right shoulder, small, soft, self-effacing, something come to tell her she will be all right, come into being at the limit, at the moment when there was nothing ahead but darkness.

She was thinking how it was the unfinished business. This was why she could not sleep. She could not say the day was over. She had no sense that any day was ever over. Everything was still going on. The business not only not finished but maybe not done well enough.

Outside, a mockingbird sang, changing the song often, every quarter minute or so, as though trying parts of it.

She heard him every night, but was not reminded every night but only now and then of a nightingale, which also sings in the dark.

The mockingbird sang, and behind it was the sound of the ocean, sometimes a steady hum, sometimes a sharp clap when a larger wave collapsed on the sand, not every night but when the tide was high at the time when she lay awake in the dark. She thought that if there was a way she could force a kind of peace into herself, then she would sleep, and she tried drawing up this peace into herself, as though it were a kind of fluid, and this worked, though not for long. The peace, when it began to fill her, seemed to come from her spine, the lower part of her spine. But it would not stay in her unless she kept it drawn in there and she could not go on with that for long.

Then she says to herself, Where is there some help in this? And the figure returns, to her surprise, standing above her right shoulder; he is not so small, not so plump, not so modest anymore (years have gone by) but full of a gloomy confidence; he could tell her, though he does not, but his presence tells her, that all is well and she is good, and she has done her best though others may not think so—and these others too are somewhere in the house, in a room somewhere down the hall, standing in a close line, or two lines, with proud, white, and angry faces.

Break It Down

He's sitting there staring at a piece of paper in front of him. He's trying to break it down. He says:

I'm breaking it all down. The ticket was $600 and then after that there was more for the hotel and food and so on, for just ten days. Say $80 a day, no, more like $100 a day. And we made love, say, once a day on the average. That's $100 a shot. And each time it lasted maybe two or three hours so that would be anywhere from $33 to $50 an hour, which is expensive.

Though of course that wasn't all that went on, because we were together almost all day long. She would keep looking at me and every time she looked at me it was worth something, and she smiled at me and didn't stop talking and singing, something I said, she would sail into it, a snatch, for me, she would be gone from me a little ways but smiling too, and tell me jokes, and I loved it but didn't exactly know what to do about it and just smiled back at her and felt slow next to her, just not quick enough. So she talked and touched me on the shoulder and the arm, she kept touching and stayed close to me. You're with each other all day long and it keeps happening, the touches and smiles, and it adds up, it builds up, and you know where you'll be that night, you're talking and every now and then you think about it, no, you don't think, you just feel it as a kind of destination, what's coming up after you leave wherever you are all evening, and you're happy about it and you're planning it all, not in your head, really, somewhere inside your body, or all through your body, it's all mounting up and coming together so that when you get in bed you can't help it, it's a real performance, it all pours out, but slowly, you go easy until you can't anymore, or you hold back the whole time, you hold back and touch the edges of everything, you edge around until you have to plunge in and finish it off, and when you're finished, you're too weak to stand but after a while you have to go to the bathroom and you stand, your legs are trembling, you hold on to the door frames, there's a little light coming in through the window, you can see your way in and out, but you can't really see the bed.

So it's not really $100 a shot because it goes on all day, from the start when you wake up and feel her body next to you, and you don't miss a thing, not a thing of what's next to you, her arm, her leg, her shoulder, her face, that good skin, I have felt other good skin, but this skin is just the edge of something else, and you're going to start going, and no matter how much you crawl all over each other it won't be enough, and when your hunger dies down a little then you think how much you love her and that starts you off again, and her face, you look over at her face and can't believe how you got there and how lucky and it's still all a surprise and it never stops, even after it's over, it never stops being a surprise.

It's more like you have a good sixteen or eighteen hours a day of this going on, even when you're not with her it's going on, it's good to be away because it's going to be so good to go back to her, so it's still here, and you can't go off and look at some old street or some old painting without still feeling it in your body and a few things that happened the day before that don't mean much by themselves or wouldn't mean much if you weren't having this thing together, but you can't forget and it's all inside you all the time, so that's more like, say, sixteen into a hundred would be $6 an hour, which isn't too much.

And then it really keeps going on while you're asleep, though you're probably dreaming about something else, a building, maybe, I kept dreaming, every night, almost, about this building, because I would spend a lot of every morning in this old stone building and when I closed my eyes I would see these cool spaces and have this peace inside me, I would see the bricks of the floor and the stone arches and the space, the emptiness between, like a kind of dark frame around what I could see beyond, a garden, and this space was like stone too because of the coolness of it and the gray shadow, that kind of luminous shade, that was glowing with the light of the sun falling beyond the arches, and there was also the great height of the ceiling, all this was in my mind all the time though I didn't know it until I closed my eyes, I'm asleep and I'm not dreaming about her but she's lying next to me and I wake up enough times in the night to remember she's there, and notice, say, once she was lying on her back but now she's curled around me, I look at her closed eyes, I want to kiss her eyelids, I want to feel that soft skin under my lips, but I don't want to disturb her, I don't want to see her frown as though in her sleep she has forgotten who I am and feels just that something is bothering her and so I just look at her and hold on to it all, these times when I'm watching over her sleep and she's next to me and isn't away from me the way she will be later, I want to stay awake all night just to go on feeling that, but I can't, I fall asleep again, though I'm sleeping lightly, still trying to hold on to it.

But it isn't over when it ends, it goes on after it's all over, she's still inside you like a sweet liquor, you are filled with her, everything about her has kind of bled into you, her smell, her voice, the way her body moves, it's all inside you, at least for a while after, then you begin to lose it, and I'm beginning to lose it, you're afraid of how weak you are, that you can't get her all back into you again and now the whole thing is going out of your body and it's more in your mind than your body, the pictures come to you one by one and you look at them, some of them last longer than others, you were together in a very white clean place, a coffeehouse, having breakfast together, and the place is so white that against it you can see her clearly, her blue eyes, her smile, the colors of her clothes, even the print of the newspaper she's reading when she's not looking up at you, the light brown and red and gold of her hair when she's got her head down reading, the brown coffee, the brown rolls, all against that white table and those white plates and silver urns and silver knives and spoons, and against that quiet of the sleepy people in that room sitting alone at their tables with just some chinking and clattering of spoons and cups in saucers and some hushed voices her voice now and then rising and falling. The pictures come to you and you have to hope they won't lose their life too fast and dry up though you know they will and that you'll also forget some of what happened, because already you're turning up little things that you nearly forgot.

We were in bed and she asked me, Do I seem fat to you? and I was surprised because she didn't seem to worry about herself at all in that way and I guess I was reading into it that she did worry about herself so I answered what

I was thinking and said stupidly that she had a very beautiful body, that her body was perfect, and I really meant it as an answer, but she said kind of sharply, That's not what I asked, and so I had to try to answer her again, exactly what she had asked.

And once she lay over against me late in the night and she started talking, her breath in my ear, and she just went on and on, and talked faster and faster, she couldn't stop, and I loved it, I just felt that all that life in her was running into me too, I had so little life in me, her life, her fire, was coming into me, in that hot breath in my ear, and I just wanted her to go on talking forever right there next to me, and I would go on living, like that, I would be able to go on living, but without her I don't know.

Then you forget some of it all, maybe most of it all, almost all of it, in the end, and you work hard at remembering everything now so you won't ever forget, but you can kill it too even by thinking about it too much, though you can't help thinking about it nearly all the time.

And then when the pictures start to go you start asking some questions, just little questions, that sit in your mind without any answers, like why did she have the light on when you came in to bed one night, but it was off the next, but she had it on the night after that and she had it off the last night, why, and other questions, little questions that nag at you like that.

And finally the pictures go and these dry little questions just sit there without any answers and you're left with this large heavy pain in you that you try to numb by reading, or you try to ease it by getting out into public places where there will be people around you, but no matter how good you are at pushing that pain away, just when you think you're going to be all right for a while, that you're safe, you're kind of holding it off with all your strength and you're staying in some little bare numb spot of ground, then suddenly it will all come back, you'll hear a noise, maybe it's a cat crying or a baby, or something else like her cry, you hear it and make that connection in a part of you you have no control over and the pain comes back so hard that you're afraid, afraid of how you're falling back into it again and you wonder, no, you're terrified to ask how you're ever going to climb out of it.

And so it's not only every hour of the day while it's happening, but it's really for hours and hours every day after that, for weeks, though less and less, so that you could work out the ratio if you wanted, maybe after six weeks you're only thinking about it an hour or so in the day altogether, a few minutes here and there spread over, or a few minutes here and there and half an hour before you go to sleep, or sometimes it all comes back and you stay awake with it half the night.

So when you add up all that, you've only spent maybe $3 an hour on it.

If you have to figure in the bad times too, I don't know. There weren't any bad times with her, though maybe there was one bad time, when I told her I loved her. I couldn't help it, this was the first time this had happened with her, now I was half falling in love with her or maybe completely if she had let me but she couldn't or I couldn't completely because it was all going to be so short and other things too, and so I told her, and didn't know of any way to tell her first that she didn't have to feel this was a burden, the fact that I loved her, or that she didn't have to feel the same about me, or say the same back, that it was just that I had to tell her, that's all, because it was bursting inside me, and saying it wouldn't even begin to take care of what I was feeling, really I couldn't say anything of what I was feeling because there was so much, words couldn't handle it, and making love only made it worse because then I wanted words badly but they were no good, no good at all, but I told her anyway, I was lying on top of her and her hands were up by her head and my hands were on hers and our fingers were locked and there was a little light on her face from the window but I couldn't really see her and I was afraid to say it but I had to say it because I wanted her to know, it was the last night, I had to tell her then or I'd never have another chance, I just said, Before you go to sleep, I have to tell you before you go to sleep that I love you, and immediately, right away after, she said, I love you too, and it sounded to me as if she didn't mean it, a little flat, but then it usually sounds a little flat when someone says, I love you too, because they're just saying it back even if they do mean it, and the problem is that I'll never know if she meant it, or maybe someday she'll tell me whether she meant it or not, but there's no way to know now, and I'm sorry I did that, it was a trap I didn't mean to put her in, I can see it was a trap, because if she hadn't said anything at all I know that would have hurt too, as though she were taking something from me and just accepting it and not giving anything back, so she really had to, even just to be kind to me, she had to say it, and I don't really know now if she meant it.

Another bad time, or it wasn't exactly bad, but it wasn't easy either, was when I had to leave, the time was coming, and I was beginning to tremble and feel empty, nothing in the middle of me, nothing inside, and nothing to hold me up on my legs, and then it came, everything was ready, and I had to go, and so it was just a kiss, a quick one, as though we were afraid of what might happen after a kiss, and she was almost wild then, she reached up to a hook by the door and took an old shirt, a green and blue shirt from the hook, and put it in my arms, for me to take away, the soft cloth was full of her smell, and then we stood there close together looking at a piece of paper she had in her hand and I didn't lose any of it, I was holding it tight, that last minute or two, because this was it, we'd come to the end of it, things always change, so this was really it, over.

Maybe it works out all right, maybe you haven't lost for doing it, I don't know, no, really, sometimes when you think of it you feel like a prince really, you feel just like a king, and then other times you're afraid, you're afraid, not all the time but now and then, of what it's going to do to you, and it's hard to know what to do with it now.

Walking away I looked back once and the door was still open, I could see her standing far back in the dark of the room, I could only really see her white face still looking out at me, and her white arms.

I guess you get to a point where you look at that pain as if it were there in front of you three feet away lying in a box, an open box, in a window somewhere. It's hard and cold, like a bar of metal. You just look at it there and say, All right, I'll take it, I'll buy it. That's what it is. Because you know all about it before you even go into this thing. You know the pain is part of the whole thing. And it isn't that you can say afterwards the pleasure was greater than the pain and that's why you would do it again. That has nothing to do with it. You can't measure it, because the pain comes after and it lasts longer. So the question really is, Why doesn't that pain make you say, I won't do it again? When the pain is so bad that you have to say that, but you don't.

So I'm just thinking about it, how you can go in with $600, more like $1,000, and how you can come out with an old shirt.

Mr. Burdoff's Visit to Germany

The Undertaking

Mr. Burdoff is lodged in Cologne for the year with a petty clerk and family in order to learn German. The undertaking is ill conceived and ill-fated, for he will waste much of his time in introspection and will learn very little German.

The Situation

He writes to an old school friend in America with great enthusiasm about Germany, Cologne, the house he is staying in, and his lofty room with its excellent view out over a construction site to the mountains beyond. But although his situation seems novel to him, it has actually been repeated many times before without spectacular results. To his old school friend, it sounds all too familiar: the house cluttered with knickknacks, the nosy landlady, the clumsy daughters, and the loneliness of his bedroom. The well-meaning language teacher, the tired students, and the strange city streets.

Lassitude

Mr. Burdoff is no sooner established in what he considers a productive routine than he falls into a state of lassitude. He cannot concentrate. He is too nervous to put down his cigarettes, and yet smoking gives him a headache. He cannot read the words of his grammar book and he hardly feels rewarded even when by a tremendous effort he manages to understand one construction.

Liver Dumplings

Mr. Burdoff finds himself thinking about lunch long before it is time to go down to the dining room. He sits by his window smoking. He can already smell the soup. The table in the dining room will be covered by a lace tablecloth but not yet set for lunch.

Mr. Burdoff is gazing out at the construction site in back of the boardinghouse. In a cradle of raw earth three cranes bow and straighten and rotate from side to side. Clusters of tiny workmen far below stand still with their hands in their pockets.

The soup will be thin and clear, with liver dumplings floating in it, spots of oil on the surface, and specks of parsley under the coil of rising steam. More often than not, the soup will be followed by a thin veal cutlet and the cutlet by a slice of pastry. Now the pastry is baking and Mr. Burdoff can smell it. The sounds he has been hearing, the many different heavy engines of the cranes and bulldozers grinding down below, are muffled by the sound of the vacuum cleaner beyond his door in the hallway. Then the vacuum cleaner moves to another part of the house. At noon the machines down below fall quiet, and a moment later through the sudden silence Mr. Burdoff hears the voice of his landlady, the squeaking of floorboards in the lower hall, and then the festive rattle of cutlery. These are the sounds he has been listening for, and he leaves his room to go down to lunch.

The Class

His language teacher is pleasant and funny, and everyone in the class has a good time. Mr. Burdoff is relieved to see that although his comprehension is poor, he is not the slowest in the class. There are many unison drills out loud, and he joins in with gusto. He takes pleasure in the little stories the class studies so painfully: for example, Karl and Helga go on a sightseeing trip that ends with a mild surprise, and the students appreciate this with waves of laughter.

Hesitation

Mr. Burdoff sits beside a small Hawaiian woman and watches her very red lips as she describes with agony her travels in France. The hesitation of the members of the class as they attempt to speak is charming; a fresh innocence endows them as they expose their weakness.

Mr. Burdoff Falls in Love

Now Mr. Burdoff feels a growing attraction to the Hawaiian woman, who has moved to a seat directly in front of him. During each lesson he stares at her lacquered black ponytail, her narrow shoulders, and the lower edge of her buttocks that delicately protrude through the opening at the back of her chair within inches of his knees. He hungers for a glimpse of her neatly crossed legs, her ballet slipper bobbing as she struggles to answer a question, and her slim hand as it writes, regularly traveling out across the page and then withdrawing again from sight.

He is enchanted by the colors she wears and the objects she carries with her. Every night he lies awake and dreams of helping her out of a serious difficulty. Every dream is the same and stops just short of the first kiss.

His love, however, is more fragile than he knows, and it dies in a moment the day a tall and sumptuous Norwegian woman joins the class.

The Advent of Helen

As she enters the room, swinging her hips around the crowd of silent students, she seems to Mr. Burdoff magnificent and unwieldy. No sooner has she pulled in her hip to accommodate the writing arm of a chair on one side than her low-slung breast on the other side dislodges the chignon of an angry woman from Aix. The students make some effort to shift out of her way, but their chairs are bolted together in threes and they cannot coordinate their efforts. A slow flush crawls up Helen's throat and cheeks.

To Mr. Burdoff's delight, she pushes past his knees and settles in the empty seat next to him. She smiles apologetically at him and at the class in general. A mingling of warm smells drifts from her armpits, her throat, and her hair, and Mr. Burdoff instantly forgets agreements, inflections, and moods, looks up at the teacher and sees only Helen's white eyelashes.

Mr. Burdoff Takes Helen Behind a Statue

Helen succumbs to Mr. Burdoff on their very first date, after an evening spent struggling in the wet grass behind a statue of Leopold Mozart. If it is not hard for Mr. Burdoff to lead Helen to the park in the first place, it is more of a problem to roll her damp girdle up around her waist and then to persuade her, after all the heaving and grunting is over, that she has not been seen by an authority figure or a close friend. Once she is easier on that score, her remaining question to Mr. Burdoff is: Does he still respect her?

Mr. Burdoff During Tannhäuser

Much against his own wishes but out of love for Helen, Mr. Burdoff agrees to attend a Wagner opera at the Cologne opera house. During the first act, Mr. Burdoff, accustomed as he is to the clarity of the eighteenth century, becomes short of breath and is afraid he may faint in his hard seat at the top of the hall. Schooled in the strict progressions of Scarlatti, he cannot detect any advance in this music. At what he considers an arbitrary point, the act ends.

When the lights go up, Mr. Burdoff examines Helen's face. A smile hovers around her lips, her forehead and cheeks are damp, and her eyes glow with satiety, as though she has eaten a large meal. Mr. Burdoff, on the other hand, is overcome by melancholy.

During the rest of the performance, Mr. Burdoff's mind wanders. He tries to calculate the seating capacity of the hall, and then studies the dim frescoes on the underside of the dome. From time to time he glances at Helen's strong hand on the arm of her seat but does not dare disturb her by touching it.

Mr. Burdoff and the Nineteenth Century

Late in their affair, by the time Mr. Burdoff has sat through the entire *Ring* cycle and *The Flying Dutchman*, as well as a symphonic poem by Strauss and what seem to him innumerable violin concertos by Bruch, Mr. Burdoff feels that Helen has taken him deep into the nineteenth century, a century he has always carefully avoided. He is surprised by its lushness, its brilliance, and its female sensibility, and still later, as he travels away from Germany on the train, he thinks of the night—important to the progress of their relationship—when he and Helen made love during her menstruation. The radio was broadcasting Schumann's *Manfred*. As Mr. Burdoff climaxed, sticky with Helen's blood, he confusedly sensed that a profound identification existed between Helen's blood, Helen herself, and the nineteenth century.

Summary

Mr. Burdoff comes to Germany. Lives in a rooming house from which he can see construction. Looks forward to lunch. Eats well every day and gains weight. Goes to class, to museums, and to beer gardens. Likes to listen to a string quartet in the open air, his arms on the metal tabletop and gravel under his feet. Daydreams about women. Falls in love with Helen. A difficult and uncomfortable love. Growing familiarity. Helen reveals her love of Wagnerian opera. Mr. Burdoff unfortunately prefers Scarlatti. The Mystery of Helen's Mind.

Helen's child falls ill and she goes home to Norway to nurse him. She is not sure she won't continue her marriage. Mr. Burdoff writes to her at least once every day. Will she be able to return before he leaves for America? The letters she writes back are very brief. Mr. Burdoff criticizes her letters. She writes less frequently and communicates nothing Mr. Burdoff wants to hear. Mr. Burdoff, finished with his course of study, prepares to leave for America. Alone on his way to Paris, he looks out the train window, feels weak, incapable. Helen sits by her sleeping child, gazes toward the bedroom window, thinks of Mr. Burdoff. Is moved to remember earlier lovers, and their cars.

What She Knew

People did not know what she knew, that she was not really a woman but a man, often a fat man, but more often, probably, an old man. The fact that she was an old man made it hard for her to be a young woman. It was hard for her to talk to a young man, for instance, though the young man was clearly interested in her. She had to ask herself, Why is this young man flirting with this old man?

The Fish

She stands over a fish, thinking about certain irrevocable mistakes she has made today. Now the fish has been cooked, and she is alone with it. The fish is for her—there is no one else in the house. But she has had a troubling day. How can she eat this fish, cooling on a slab of marble? And yet the fish, too, motionless as it is, and dismantled from its bones, and fleeced of its silver skin, has never been so completely alone as it is now: violated in a final manner and regarded with a weary eye by this woman who has made the latest mistake of her day and done this to it.

Mildred and the Oboe

Last night Mildred, my neighbor on the floor below, masturbated with an oboe. The oboe wheezed and squealed in her vagina. Mildred groaned. Later, when I thought she was finished, she started screaming. I lay in bed with a book about India. I could feel her pleasure pass up through the floorboards into my room. Of course there might have been another explanation for what I heard. Perhaps it was not the oboe but the player of the oboe who was penetrating Mildred. Or perhaps Mildred was striking her small nervous dog with something slim and musical, like an oboe.

Mildred who screams lives below me. Three young women from Connecticut live above me. Then there is a lady pianist with two daughters on the parlor floor and some lesbians in the basement. I am a sober person, a mother, and I like to go to bed early—but how can I lead a regular life in this building? It is a circus of vaginas leaping and prancing: thirteen vaginas and only one penis, my little son.

The Mouse

First a poet writes a story about a mouse, in moonlight in the snow, how the mouse tries to hide in his shadow, how the mouse climbs up his sleeve and he shakes it down into the snow before he knows what it is that is clinging to his sleeve. His cat is nearby and her shadow is on the snow, and she is after the mouse. A woman is then reading this story in the bath. Half her hair is dry and half of it is floating in the bathwater. She likes the story.

That night she can't sleep and goes into the kitchen to read another book by the same poet. She sits on a stool by the counter. It is late and the night is quiet, though now and then at some distance a train passes and hoots before a crossing. To her surprise, though she knows it lives there, a mouse comes out of a burner from under a pot and sniffs the air. Its feet are like little thorns, its ears are unexpectedly large, one eye is shut and the other open. It nibbles something off the tray of the burner. She moves and it flashes back in, she is still and in a moment it comes out again, and when she moves again it flashes back into the stove like a snapped elastic. At four in the morning, though she is still wide awake, reading and sometimes watching the mouse, the woman closes her book and goes back to bed.

In the morning a man sits in the kitchen on a stool, the same stool, by the counter, and cradles their young cat in his arms, holding her neck in his broad pink hands and rubbing the crown of her head with his thumbs, and behind him the woman stands leaning against his back, her breasts flattened against his shoulder blades, her hands closed over his chest, and they have laid out crusts of bread on the counter for the mouse to smell and are waiting for the mouse to come out, blindly, and for the young cat to get it.

They stay this way wrapped in nearly complete silence, and they are nearly motionless, only the man's gentle thumbs move over the cat's skull and the woman sometimes lays her cheek down against the man's fragrant soft hair and then lifts it again and the cat's eyes are shifting quickly from point to point. A motor starts up in the kitchen, there is the sudden flare of the gas water heater, the swift passage of some cars on the highway below, and then a single voice in the road. But the mouse knows the company that is there and won't come out. The cat is too hungry to keep still and reaches forth one paw and then another and frees herself from the man's light hold and climbs up on the counter to eat the bread herself.

Often, whenever she can get into the house or is let into the house, the cat crouches sleepily on the counter by the stove, her eyes pointed at the burner where the mouse is likely to appear, but she is not more vigilant than that, half asleep, as though she likes just to place herself in this situation, hunting the mouse but perfectly motionless. Really she is keeping the mouse company, the mouse vigilant or sleeping inside the stove, the cat nearby outside. The mouse has had babies, in the stove, and the cat, too, is carrying kittens in her body, and her nipples are beginning to stand out in the downy fur of her belly.

The woman often looks at the cat and sometimes remembers another story.

The woman and her husband lived in the country in a large empty house. The rooms in this house were so large that the furniture sank into the empty spaces. There were no rugs and the curtains were thin, the windowpanes cold in the winter, and the daylight and the electric lights at night were cold and white, and lit the bare floor and the bare walls but did not change the darkness of the rooms.

On two sides of the house, beyond the yard, were stands of trees. One woods was deep and thick and climbed away up over a hill. At the bottom of the hill was a marshy pond in the trees where the water had been caught by the railroad embankment. The tracks and ties were gone from the embankment, and the mound of it was overgrown with saplings. The other stand of trees was thin and bordered a meadow, and deer crossed through to sleep in the meadow. In the winter the woman could see their tracks in the snow and follow where they leaped in from the road. When the weather grew cold the mice would start coming into the house from the woods and the meadow, and run through the walls and fight and squeak behind the baseboards. The woman and her husband were not troubled by the mice, except for the little black droppings everywhere, but they had heard that mice would sometimes chew through the wires in the walls and start fires, so they decided to try and get rid of them.

The woman bought some traps at the hardware store, made of bright brassy coils of metal and new raw wood printed with red letters. The man at the hardware store showed her how to set them. It was easy to get hurt because the springs were very strong and tight. The woman had to be the one to set them because she was always the one who did things like that. In the evening before they went to bed, she set one carefully, afraid of snapping her fingers, and put it down in a place where she and he would not be likely to walk on it when they came into the kitchen in the morning forgetting it was there.

They went to bed and the woman stayed awake reading. She would read until the man woke up enough to complain about the light. He was often angry about something and when she read at night it was the light. Later in the night she was still awake and heard the sound like a gunshot of the trap springing but did not go downstairs because the house was cold.

In the morning she went into the kitchen and saw that the trap had flipped over and there was a mouse in it and blood smeared around on the pink linoleum. She thought the mouse was dead, but when she moved the trap with her foot she saw that it was not. It started flipping around on the linoleum with the trap closed on its head. Her husband came in then and neither of them knew what to do about this half-dead mouse. They thought that the best thing would be to kill it with a hammer or some other heavy thing but if one of them was going to do it, it would be her and she did not have the stomach for it. Bending over the mouse she felt sick and agitated with the fear of something dead or nearly dead or mutilated. Both of them were excited and kept staring at it and turning away from it and walking around the room. The day was cloudy with more snow coming and the light in the kitchen was white and cast no shadows.

Finally the woman decided just to throw it outside, get it out of there, and it would die in the cold. She took a dustpan and pushed it under the trap and the mouse and walked quickly with it out the wooden door to the porch and through the porch and out the storm door and down the steps, afraid all the time that it would jump again and slip off the dustpan. She walked down the pitted concrete walk and across the driveway to the edge of the woods and threw the trap and the mouse out onto the frozen crust of snow. She tried to believe the mouse didn't feel much pain and was in shock anyway; certainly a mouse did not feel exactly the way a person would lying with his head closed in a trap, bleeding and freezing to death out there on the white crust of snow. She could not be sure. Then she wondered if there was any animal that might come along and be willing to eat a mouse that was already dead but preserved by the frost.

They did not look for the trap later. In midwinter the man left and the woman lived on in the house alone. Then she moved to the city and the house was rented to a schoolteacher and his wife and a year later sold to a lawyer from the city. The last time the woman walked through it the rooms were still empty and dark, and the furniture set against the bare walls, though it was different furniture, had the same look of defeat under the weight of that emptiness.

The Letter

Her lover lies next to her and since she has brought it up he asks her when it ended. She tells him it ended about a year ago and then she can't say any more. He waits and then asks how it ended, and she tells him it ended stormily. He says carefully that he wants to know about it, and everything about her life, but that he doesn't want her to talk about it if she doesn't want to. She turns her face a little away from him so that the lamplight is shining on her closed eyes. She thought she wanted to tell him, but now she can't and she feels tears under her eyelids. She is surprised because this is the second time today that she has cried and she hasn't cried for weeks.

She can't say to herself that it is really over, even though anyone else would say it was over, since he has moved to another city, hasn't been in touch with her in more than a year, and is married to another woman. Now and then she has heard news. Someone gets a letter from him, and the news is that he is nearly out of his financial troubles and is thinking of starting a magazine. Before that, someone else has news that he lives downtown with this woman he later marries. They have no telephone, because they owe the telephone company so much money. The telephone company, in those days, calls her from time to time and asks her politely where he is. A friend tells her he works nights at the docks packing sea urchins and comes home at four in the morning. Then this same friend tells her how he has offered something to a lonely woman in exchange for a large amount of money that makes the woman feel very insulted and unhappy.

Before that, when he still worked nearby, she would drive over to see him and argue with him at the gas station, where he read Faulkner in the office under the fluorescent lights, and he would look up with his eyes full of wariness when he saw her come in. They would argue between customers, and when he was filling a car she would think what she could say next. Later, after she stopped going there, she would walk through the town looking for his car. Once, in the rain, a van turned a corner suddenly at her and she stumbled over her boots into a ditch and then she saw herself clearly: a woman in early middle age wearing rubber boots walking in the dark looking for a white car and now falling into a ditch, prepared to go on walking and to be satisfied with the sight of the man's car in a parking lot even if the man was somewhere else and with another woman. That night she walked around and around the town for a long time, checking the same places over and over again, thinking that during the fifteen minutes it had taken her to walk from one end of the town to the other he might have driven up to the spot she had left fifteen minutes before, but she did not find the car.

The car is an old white Volvo; it has a beautiful soft shape. She sees other old Volvos nearly every day, and some are tan or cream-colored—close to the color of his—and some are his color, white, but undented and unrusted. The license plates never have a *K* in them, and the drivers, always in silhouette, are either women or men with glasses or men with heads that are smaller than his.

That spring she was translating a book because it was the only thing she could do. Every time she stopped typing and picked up the dictionary his face floated up between her and the page and the pain settled into her again, and every time she put the dictionary down and went on typing his face and the pain went away. She did a lot of hard work on the translation just to keep the pain away.

Before that, in late March, in a crowded bar, he told her what she was expecting to hear and what she dreaded hearing. Right away she lost her appetite, but he ate very well and ate her dinner too. He did not have the money to pay for the dinner and so she paid. After dinner he said, Maybe in ten years. She said, Maybe in five, but he didn't answer that.

She stops by the post office to pick up a check. She is already late for where she is going, but she needs the money. She sees his handwriting on an envelope in her mailbox. Though it is very familiar to her, or because it is so familiar to her, she doesn't know right away whose handwriting it is. When she realizes whose it is, she swears aloud over and over again walking back to the car. While she is swearing she is also thinking, and she decides that this envelope will have a check in it for some of the money he owes her. He owes her over $300. If he has been embarrassed about the debt, this would explain the year of silence, and if he now has some money to send her, this would explain the fact that now he is breaking the silence. She gets into the car, puts the key in the ignition, and opens the envelope. There is no check in it, and it is not a letter but a poem in French, carefully copied out in his handwriting. The poem ends *compagnon de silence.* Then his name. She doesn't read all of it because she is late meeting some people she doesn't know very well.

She goes on swearing at him until she gets to the highway. She is angry because he has sent her a letter, and because the letter has immediately made her happy, and then her happiness has brought back the pain. And she is angry because nothing can ever make up for the pain. Though of course it is hard to call it a letter, since it is nothing but a poem, the poem is in French, and the poem was composed by someone else. She is also angry because of the kind of poem it is. And she is also angry because even though later she will try to think of ways to answer this, she has seen right away that there is no possible answer to it. She begins to feel dizzy and sick. She drives slowly in the right-hand lane and pinches the skin of her neck hard until the faintness goes away.

All that day she is with other people and she can't look at the letter again. In the evening, when she is alone, she works on a translation, a difficult prose poem. Her lover calls and she tells him how difficult the translation is but not about the letter. After she is finished working, she cleans the house very carefully. Then she takes the letter out of her purse and goes to bed to see what she can make of it now.

She examines first the postmark. The date and the time of day and the city name are very clear. Then she examines her name above the address. He might have hesitated writing her last name, because there is a small ink blot in a curve of one letter. He has addressed it a little wrong and this is not her zip code. She looks at his name, or rather his first initial, the G. very well formed, and his last name next to it. Then his address, and she wonders why he put a return address on the letter. Does he want an answer to this? It is more likely that he is not sure she is still here and if she is not still here he wants his letter to come back to him so that he will know. His zip code is different from the zip code of the postmark. He must have mailed this somewhere out of his neighborhood. Did he also write it away from home? Where?

She opens the envelope and unfolds the paper, which is clean and fresh. Now she notices more exactly what is on this page. The date, May 10, is in the upper-right-hand corner in a smaller, thicker, more cramped hand than the other writing on the page, as though he wrote it at a different time, either before or after the rest. He writes it first, then stops and thinks, his lips tight shut, or looks for the book he will take the poem from—though that is less likely, because he would have it ready in front of him when he sat down to write. Or he thinks after he is done that he will date it. He reads it over, then dates it. Now she notices that he has put her name at the top, with a comma after it, in line with his name below the poem. The date, her name, comma, then the poem, then his name, period. So the poem is the letter.

Having seen all this, she reads the poem more carefully, several times. There is a word she can't decipher. It comes at the end of a line so she looks at the rhyme scheme and the word it should rhyme with is *pures*, pure (pure thoughts), so that the word she can't read is probably *obscures*, dark (dark flowers). Then she can't read another two words at the beginning of the last line of the octet. She looks at the way he has formed other capital letters and sees that this capital must be *L*, and the words must be *La lune*, the moon, the moon that is generous or kind *aux insensés*—to crazed people.

What she had seen first and the only words she could remember as she drove north on the highway were *compagnon de silence*, companion of silence, and some line about holding hands, another about green meadows, *prairies* in French, the moon, and dying on the moss. She hadn't seen what she sees this time, that although they have died, or these two in the poem have died, they then meet again, *nous nous retrouvions*, we found each other again, up above, in something *immense*, somewhere, which must be heaven. They have found each other crying. And so the poem ends, more or less, we found each other crying, dear companion of silence. She examines the word *retrouvions* slowly, to make sure of the handwriting, that the letters really spell out finding each other again. She hangs on these letters with such concentration that for a moment she can feel everything in her, everything in the room too, and in her life up to now, gather behind her eyes as though it all depends on a line of ink slanted the right way and another line as rounded as she hopes it is. If there can be no doubt about *retrouvions*, and there seems to be no doubt, then she can believe that he is still thinking, eight hundred miles from here, that it will be possible ten years from now, or five years, or, since a year has already passed, nine years or four years from now.

But she worries about the dying part of it: it could mean he does not really expect to see her again, since they are dead, after all; or that the time will be so long it will be a lifetime. Or it could be that this poem was the closest thing he could find to a poem that said something about what he was thinking about companions, silence, crying, and the end of things, and is not exactly what he was thinking; or he happened on the poem as he was reading through a book of French poems, was reminded of her for a moment, was moved to send it, and sent it quickly with no clear intention.

She folds up the letter and puts it back in the envelope, lays it on her chest with her hand on top of it, closes her eyes, and after a while, with the light still on, begins to fall asleep. Half dreaming, she thinks that something of his smell may still be in the paper and she wakes up. She takes the paper out of the envelope and unfolds it and breathes deeply the wide white margin at the bottom of the page. Nothing. Then the poem, and she thinks she can smell something there, though she is probably smelling only the ink.

Extracts from a Life

Childhood

I was brought up in the violin factory, and when I had a fight with my brothers and sisters we even used to hit one another with violins.

If you think of something, do it

Plenty of people often think, "I'd like to do this, or that."

The Japanese poet Issa

As a child I was taught to recite the haiku of the Japanese poet Issa, and I have never forgotten them.

Ah, my old home town,
Dumplings that they used to make,
Snow in springtime, too.

Grown-ups

I cannot live without children. But I love grown-ups too, because I feel a great sympathy for them—"After all, these people too must die."

My meeting with Tolstoy

One day, as usual, I set off for my father's violin factory, where a thousand people were employed. I entered the office, discovered an English typewriter, and started punching the keys.

Just then the chief of the export department came in. "Master Shinichi!"

I lied and said I had merely been touching the keys.

"I see," he replied simply.

Coward, I thought. Why did I dissemble?

I went to a bookstore, filled with severe anger against myself. Fate led me to a copy of Tolstoy's *Diary*. I opened it at random. "To deceive oneself is worse than to deceive others." These harsh words pierced me to the core.

Several years later when, at twenty-three, I went to Germany to study, the book went with me in my pocket.

A little episode

Here follows a little episode of self-praise.

I was then under the strong influence of Tolstoy.

It was in 1919. I received an unexpected letter in early spring inviting me to join an expedition for biological research. The expedition party on board numbered thirty.

At that time I was inseparable from my violin. It had become a part of me.

Our ship circled the islands. While we walked side by side on the beach, we discovered a most unusual patch of moss of reddish-cobalt color growing high up a sheer cliff.

"I very badly wish to have some of that moss," said Professor Emoto, looking up anxiously.

"I will get it for you from here," I boasted, and borrowed a small scoop from a research member.

It turned out to be situated much higher than expected. Heavens! I thought.

I threw the scoop, under the scrutiny of the whole party.

"Oh, wonderful marvelous!" they cried.

As I listened to their applause, I vowed in my heart never again to do such a foolish thing.

I have learned what art really is

Art is not in some far-off place.

Dr. Einstein was my guardian

I took lodgings in the house of a gray-haired widow and her elderly maid. Both the landlady and the maid were hard of hearing so they did not complain no matter how loudly I practiced the violin.

"I shall no longer be able to look after you," said Dr. M., a professor of medicine, "and so I have asked a friend of mine to keep an eye on you." The friend turned out to be Dr. Albert Einstein, who later developed the theory of relativity.

A maestro who performed too well

Eintein's specialties, such as the Bach *Chaconne*, were magnificent. In comparison with his playing, mine, though I tried to play effortlessly and with ease, seemed to me a constant struggle.

"People are all the same, madame"

At a dinner party, an old woman wondered how it was that a Japanese could play the violin in such a way as to convey what was German about Bruch.

After a brief interval, Dr. Einstein said quietly, "People are all the same, madame."

I was tremendously moved.

I now felt as though I were under direct orders from Mozart

The whole program that evening was Mozart. And during the Clarinet Quintet, something happened to me that had never happened before: I lost the use of my arms. After the performance I tried to clap. My blood burned within me.

That night I couldn't sleep at all. Mozart had shown me immortal light, and I now felt as though I were under direct orders from Mozart. He expressed his sadness not only with the minor scale but with the major scale as well. Life and death: the inescapable business of nature. Filled with the joy of love, I gave up sadness.

Well done, young man

I was doing what I wanted to do.

Holding his chopsticks in midair, my father looked at me with a sparkle in his eye. "Well done, Shinichi!"

The House Plans

The land was pointed out to me from the road, which ran along the side of the hill above it, and right away I wanted to buy it. If the agent had spoken to me of disadvantages, I would not have heard him at that moment. I was numbed by the beauty of what I saw: a long valley of blood-red vineyards, half flooded with late summer rain; in the distance, yellow fields choked with weeds and thistles and behind them a forest covering a hillside; in the middle of the valley, higher than the fields, the ruin of a farmhouse: a mulberry tree grew up through the broken stone of its garden wall, and nearby, the shadow of an ancient pear tree lay across the carpet of brown, rotted fruit on the ground.

Leaning against his car, the agent said, "There is one room left intact. Inside, it is filthy. They have had animals there for years." We walked down to the house.

Dung was thick on the tiles of the floor. I felt the wind through the stones and I saw daylight through the lofty roof. None of this discouraged me. I had the papers drawn up that same day.

I had looked forward for so many years to finding a piece of land and building a house on it that I sometimes felt I had not been brought into the world for any other purpose. Once the desire was born in me, all my energies were bent on satisfying it: the job that I got as soon as I could leave school was tiresome and demoralizing, but it brought me more and more money as my responsibilities grew. In order to spend as little as possible I lived a very uneventful life and resisted making friends or enjoying myself. After many years I had enough money to leave my job and begin looking for land. Real estate agents drove me from one property to another. I saw so many pieces of land that I grew confused and no longer knew just what I was looking for. When at last the valley came into sight below me, I felt I had been relieved of a terrible burden.

While the warmth of summer lay over the land, I was content, living in my majestic and soot-blackened room. I cleaned it up, filled it with furniture, and set up a drawing board in one corner, where I worked on plans for rebuilding the house. Looking up from my work, I would see the sunlight on the olive leaves and be lured outdoors. Walking over the grass by the house, I watched, with the tired, expectant eyes of a man who has lived all his life in the city, magpies running through the thyme and lizards vanishing into the wall. In stormy weather, the cypresses by my window bent before the wind.

Then the autumn chill came down and hunters stalked near my house. The explosion of their rifles filled me with dread. Pipes from a sewage-treatment yard in the next field cracked and let a terrible smell into the air. I built fires in my fireplace and was never warm.

One day my window was darkened by the form of a young hunter. The man was wearing leather and carrying a rifle. After looking at me for a moment, he came to my door and opened it without knocking. He stood in the shadow of the door and stared at me. His eyes were milky blue and his reddish beard hardly concealed his skin. I immediately took him for a half-wit and was terrified. He did nothing: after gazing at what was in the room, he shut the door behind him and went away.

I was filled with rage. As though he were strolling around a zoo, this man had come up to my stony little pen and rudely examined me. I fumed and paced around the room. But I was lonely there, out in the country, and he had awakened my curiosity. By the time a few days had gone by, I was anxious to see him.

He came again, and this time he did not hesitate at the door, but walked in, sat down on a chair, and spoke to me. I did not understand his country accent. He repeated one phrase twice and then a third time and still I could only guess at his meaning. When I tried to answer him he had the same trouble understanding my city accent. I gave up and offered him a glass of wine. He refused it. In a diffident sort of way he got up from his chair and ventured to inspect my belongings at closer range. Proceeding from my bookcase around the walls, which were covered with framed prints of houses I particularly liked, some in the Place des Vosges and some in the poor quarters behind Montparnasse, he finally arrived at my drawing board, where he stopped short and stood with his finger in the air, waiting for enlightenment. The fact that I was planning a house, line by line, took him a long while to understand and when he did, he began tracing the walls of each room with his finger, a few inches above the blueprint. When at last he had examined and traced every line, he smiled at me without parting his lips, looking sideways in a rather sly way that I did not understand, and abruptly left me.

Again I was angry, feeling that he had invaded my room and stolen my secrets. Yet when my anger subsided I wanted him to return. He returned the following day, and a few days later he came yet again, though the wind was high. I began to expect him and look forward to his visits. He hunted every morning very early, and several times in the week, after he was finished, he would walk in from the field, where the sun was beginning to color the white clay. His face would gleam and he would be so full of energy that he could hardly contain it: leaping up every few minutes from his chair, he would pace to the door and look out, return to the middle of the room, whistling tunelessly, and sit down again. Slowly this energy would die away, and when it was gone, he would go too. He never accepted anything to eat or drink, and seemed surprised that I would offer it, as though sharing food and drink were an act of great intimacy.

It did not become any easier for us to communicate, but we found more and more things to do together. He helped me prepare for winter by filling the chinks in my walls and stacking wood for the fireplace. After we had worked, we would go out into the fields and the forest. My friend showed me the places he liked to visit—a grove of hawthorns, a rabbit warren, and a cave in the hillside—and though I had only one thing that I could show him, he seemed to find it just as mysterious and absorbing as I did.

Each time he came to see me, we would first go over to my blueprint, where I had added another room or increased the size of my study. There were always changes to show him, because I was never done improving my plan and worked on it almost every hour. Sometimes, now, he would pick up my pencil and awkwardly sketch in something that would not have occurred to me: a smokehouse or a root cellar.

But the excitement of the plan as well as the pleasure of

having a friend were blinding me to a dreadful fact: the longer I lived on my land, letting the time slip by, the more the possibility of building the house faded. My money was trickling away and my dream was going with it. In the village, far from any marketplace, the price of food was double what it had been in the city. Thin as I was, I could not eat any less. Good masons and carpenters, even poor ones, were rare and expensive here: to hire a pair of them for a few months would leave me too little to live on afterwards. I did not give up when I learned this, but I had no answers to the questions that plagued me.

In the beginning, my blueprint had absorbed all my time and attention because I was going to build the house from it. Gradually, the blueprint became more vivid to me than the actual house: in my imagination, I spent more and more time among the penciled lines that shifted at my will. Yet if I had openly admitted that there was no longer any possibility of building this house, the blueprint would have lost its meaning. So I continued to believe in the house, while all the time the possibility of building it eroded steadily from under my belief.

What made the situation all the more frustrating was that on the outskirts of the village new houses were springing up every few months. When I had bought the land, the only structures in the valley were stone field huts—squatting in the middle of each plowed field, they were as black as caves inside, with floors of earth. After signing the deed, I had returned home and stood, well satisfied, looking across the acres of abandoned vineyards and overgrown farmland to the horizon where the village sat piled up on a small hill, like a castle, with its church steeples clustered at the top. Now, here and there on the landscape, there was a wound of raw red earth and in a few weeks a new house would rise like a scab above it. There was no time for the landscape to absorb these changes: hardly had one house been finished before the live oaks were felled right and left for another.

I watched the progress of one house with particular horror and misgiving, because it was within a few minutes' walk of my own. The deliberate speed with which it went up shook me and seemed a mockery of my own situation. It was an ugly house, with pink walls and cheap iron grill-work over the windows. Once it was finished, and the last young tree planted in the dust beside it, the owners drove up from the city and spent All Saints' Day there, sitting on the terrace and looking out over the valley as though they had box seats at the opera. After that, as long as the weather held, they drove up to the house every weekend, filling the countryside with the noise of their radio. I watched them gloomily from my window.

The worst of it was that my friend immediately stopped visiting me on the weekends. I knew he had been drawn away from me by my neighbors. From a distance I saw him standing quietly among them in their yard. I felt utterly miserable. At last I had to admit how bleak my position was. It occurred to me then to sell my land and begin all over again somewhere else.

I thought I might get a good price for the land from other city people. But when I went to see the real estate agent, he told me flatly that because there was a sewage yard in the next field and because my house was uninhabit-able, my property would be almost impossible to sell. He went on to say that the only people who might be inter-ested in buying it were my neighbors, who had in fact resented my presence all this time and would give a very low sum for the land just to be rid of me. They had told the agent in confidence that my house was an eyesore in their front yard and an embarrassment when friends came to spend the day. I was shocked. My strongest feeling, of course, was that I would never sell to my neighbors. I would never give them that triumph. I turned my back on the agent and left without saying a word. As I stood deliberating on the doorstep, I heard him go into another room, say something to his wife, and laugh loudly. This was a very low point in my life.

When, after several weeks, my friend stopped coming altogether, without a word to explain his absence, my bitterness was complete. I sank into a deep depression and decided that I would give up the idea of building a house and return to my job in the city. The directors of my company had not been able to find anyone else willing to put up with the long hours and devote himself to such interminable complications. They had several times written asking me to return and offering me more money. I could easily slip back into my old way of life, I thought; this stay in the country would then have been a protracted holiday. I even managed to convince myself, for a moment, that I missed city life and my few acquaintances in the office, who used to buy me drinks after particularly tedious days. I told the agent to make an offer to my neighbors, and tried to think that I was doing the right thing. But my heart was not in the move, and I felt like a changed man as I packed up my belongings and took a last walk around my narrow boundaries.

The suitcases were out in the early sunlight before the door of the house, the taxi I had hired was bumping over the dirt road toward me, and I was really on the point of leaving, when I thought I might have been too hasty. It would be wrong to go without saying anything to the young man who had been my friend, whose name I did not even know. I paid off the taxi driver and told him to come at the same hour the following day. He gave me a doubtful look and drove back down the road. The dust swirled up behind him and settled. I carried my suitcases inside and sat down. After I had spent some time wondering how to find my friend, I realized that of course I had been foolish, that I had pointlessly committed myself to one more day in these hostile surroundings, that I would not be able to find him. The directors would be annoyed when I did not arrive at the office, they would worry about me and make an attempt to reach me, and would be completely at a loss when they did not succeed. As the morning advanced I became more and more restless and angry with myself, and felt that I had made a terrible mistake. It was small comfort to know that on the following day everything would go forward as planned, and that in the end it would seem as though this day had never passed at all.

During the long, hot afternoon, small birds fluttered in the thorny brush and a sweet smell rose from the earth. The sky was without clouds and the sun cast black shadows over the ground. I sat in my business suit by the wall of the house and was not touched by the beauty of the land. My thoughts were in the city, and my imprisonment in the country chafed me. At suppertime there was nothing to eat, but I was not willing to walk to the village. I lay awake cold and hungry for hours before falling asleep.

I awoke before sunrise. I was so hungry that I felt I had stones in my stomach and I looked forward to eating some breakfast at the train station. Everything outside my window was black. Gusts of wind began moving the leaves as the sky became white behind the black bushes. Color slowly came into the leaves. In the forest and closer to the house bird songs rose and fell on all sides. I listened very intently to them. When the rays of sunlight reached the bushes I went outside and sat by the house. When at last the taxi came, I felt so peaceful that I could not bring myself to leave. After some angry words, the driver went away.

Throughout the morning and into the afternoon, I sat in my business suit beside the house, as I had sat the day before, but I was no longer impatient or eager to be elsewhere. I was absorbed in watching what passed before me—birds disappearing into the bushes, bugs crawling around stones—as though I were invisible, as though I were watching it all in my own absence. Or, being where I should not be, where no one expected me to be, I was a mere shadow of myself, lagging behind for an instant, caught in the light; soon the strap would tighten and I would be gone, flying in pursuit of myself: for the moment, I was at liberty.

When evening came I did not know I was hungry. Light-headed with contentment, I continued to sit still, waiting. Driven inside by the cold and the darkness, I lay down and had savage dreams.

The next morning, I saw a figure at the far edge of the nearest field, walking very slowly across. My eyes felt as if a long emptiness had been filled. Without knowing it, I had been waiting for my friend. But as I watched him, his hesitation began to seem unnatural and then it frightened me: he weaved back and forth over the furrows, put his nose up as though sniffing the air like a spaniel, and did not seem to know where he was going. I started to meet him and as I drew closer I saw that his forehead was wrapped in bandages and that the skin of his face was an awful color of gray. When I came up to him he was bewildered and stared at me as though I were a stranger. I took him by the arm and helped him over the ground. When we reached the house he pushed me aside and lay down on my bed. He was trembling with exhaustion. He had lost so much flesh that his cheeks were like pits and his hands were claws. He had such fever in his eyes that I thought wildly of going to the village for a doctor. But after his breath had returned to him he began speaking quite tranquilly. He explained something at great length while I sat uncomprehending by the bed and listened. He made several motions with his arms and finally I realized he had been in a hunting accident. During all the weeks that I had been reproaching him so bitterly, he had been lying in a hospital somewhere.

He continued to talk on and on, and I found it hard to concentrate on what he said. I became restless and impatient. After a while I could not bear it any longer. I got up and paced stiffly back and forth in the room. At last he stopped speaking and pointed to one corner of the room, under the window. I did not understand, because there was nothing there but the window. Then I saw that he was trying to point to the drawing board, which had been dismantled, and that he wanted to see my blueprint. I unpacked it and gave it to him. Still he was unsatisfied. I found a pencil in my pocket and gave it to him too. He began drawing on the blueprint. After a short time he had covered the entire paper, out to its edges, with complicated forms. Standing over him and staring, at last I recognized a tower and what might have been a doorway among the tangle of lines. When he had filled the page, I gave him more sheets of paper, and he continued to work. His hand hardly paused, and what he drew had the complexity of something conceived and worked over during many solitary days. When he was too tired to move the pencil any longer, he fell asleep. I left him there in the early evening and went to the village for food.

Returning across the fields to my house, I looked at the red landscape and felt that it was deeply familiar to me, as though it had been mine long before I found it. The idea of leaving it seemed to make no sense at all. Within a few days my rage and disappointment had ebbed away, and now, as in the beginning, each thing I looked at seemed only a shell or a husk that would fall away and reveal a perfect fruit. Though I was tired, my mind raced forward: I cleared a patch of land by the house and put up a stable there; I led black-and-white cows into it, and nervous hens ran underfoot; I planted a line of cypress trees on the edge of my property, and it hid my neighbor's house; I pulled down the ruined walls and with the same stones raised my own manor, and when it was finished, I looked upon a spectacle that would excite the envy of everyone who saw it. My dream would be realized as it was first meant to be.

I might have been delirious. It was not likely that things would end that way. But as I stumbled over the field, sinking deep into a furrow with one step and rising to a crest with the next, I was too happy to suspect that at any moment my frustrations and disappointments, like a cloud of locusts, would darken the sky and descend on me again. The evening was serene, the light smooth and soft, the earth paralyzed, and I, far below, the only moving creature.

The Brother-in-Law

He was so quiet, so small and thin, that he was hardly there. The brother-in-law. Whose brother-in-law they did not know. Or where he came from, or if he would leave.

They could not guess where he slept at night, though they searched for a depression on the couch or a disorder among the towels. He left no smell behind him.

He did not bleed, he did not cry, he did not sweat. He was dry. Even his urine divorced itself from his penis and entered the toilet almost before it had left him, like a bullet from a gun.

They hardly saw him: if they entered a room, he was gone like a shadow, sliding around the door frame, slipping over the sill. A breath was all they ever heard from him, and even then they could not be sure it hadn't been a small breeze passing over the gravel outside.

He could not pay them. He left money every week, but by the time they entered the room in their slow, noisy way the money was just a green and silver mist on their grandmother's platter, and by the time they reached out for it, it was no longer there.

But he hardly cost them a penny. They could not even tell if he ate, because he took so little that it was as nothing to them, who were big eaters. He came out from somewhere at night and crept around the kitchen with a sharp razor in his white, fine-boned hand, shaving off slivers of meat, of nuts, of bread, until his plate, paper-thin, felt heavy to him. He filled his cup with milk, but the cup was so small that it held no more than an ounce or two.

He ate without a sound, and cleanly, he let no drop fall from his mouth. Where he wiped his lips on the napkin there was no mark. There was no stain on his plate, there was no crumb on his mat, there was no trace of milk in his cup.

He might have stayed on for years, if one winter had not been too severe for him. But he could not bear the cold, and began to dissipate. For a long time they were not sure if he was still in the house. There was no real way of knowing. But in the first days of spring they cleaned the guest room where, quite rightly, he had slept, and where he was by now no more than a sort of vapor. They shook him out of the mattress, brushed him over the floor, wiped him off the windowpane, and never knew what they had done.

How W. H. Auden Spends the Night in a Friend's House:

The only one awake, the house quiet, the streets darkened, the cold pressing down through his covers, he is unwilling to disturb his hosts and thus, first, his fetal curl, his search for a warm hollow in the mattress . . .

Then his stealthy excursion over the floor for a chair to stand on and his unsteady reach for the curtains, which he lays over the other coverings on his bed . . .

His satisfaction in the new weight pressing down upon him, then his peaceful sleep . . .

On another occasion this wakeful visitor, cold again and finding no curtain in his room, steals out and takes up the hall carpet for the same purpose, bending and straightening in the dim hallway . . .

How its heaviness is a heavy hand on him and the dust choking his nostrils is nothing to how that carpet stifles his uneasiness . . .

Mothers

Everyone has a mother somewhere. There is a mother at dinner with us. She is a small woman with eyeglass lenses so thick they seem black when she turns her head away. Then, the mother of the hostess telephones as we are eating. This causes the hostess to be away from the table longer than one would expect. This mother may possibly be in New York. The mother of a guest is mentioned in conversation: this mother is in Oregon, a state few of us know anything about, though it has happened before that a relative lived there. A choreographer is referred to afterwards, in the car. He is spending the night in town, on his way, in fact, to see his mother, again in another state.

Mothers, when they are guests at dinner, eat well, like children, but seem absent. It is often the case that they cannot follow what we are doing or saying. It is often the case, also, that they enter the conversation only when it turns on our youth; or they accommodate where accommodation is not wanted; smile and are misunderstood. And yet mothers are always seen, always talked to, even if only on holidays. They have suffered for our sakes, and most often in a place where we could not see them.

In a House Besieged

In a house besieged lived a man and a woman. From where they cowered in the kitchen the man and woman heard small explosions. "The wind," said the woman. "Hunters," said the man. "The rain," said the woman. "The army," said the man. The woman wanted to go home, but she was already home, there in the middle of the country in a house besieged.

Visit to Her Husband

She and her husband are so nervous that throughout their conversation they keep going into the bathroom, closing the door, and using the toilet. Then they come out and light a cigarette. He goes in and urinates and leaves the toilet seat up and she goes in and lowers it and urinates. Toward the end of the afternoon, they stop talking about the divorce and start drinking. He drinks whiskey and she drinks beer. When it is time for her to leave to catch her train he has drunk a lot and goes into the bathroom one last time to urinate and doesn't bother to close the door.

As they are getting ready to go out, she begins to tell him the story of how she met her lover. While she is talking, he discovers that he has lost one of his expensive gloves and he is immediately upset and distracted. He leaves her to look for his glove downstairs. Her story is half finished and he does not find his glove. He is less interested in her story when he comes back into the room without having found his glove. Later when they are walking together on the street he tells her happily how he has bought his girlfriend shoes for eighty dollars because he loves her so much.

When she is alone again, she is so preoccupied by what

has taken place during the visit to her husband that she walks through the streets very quickly and bumps into several people in the subway and the train station. She has not even seen them but has come down on them like some natural element so suddenly that they did not have time to avoid her and she was surprised they were there at all. Some of these people look after her and say "Christ!"

In her parents' kitchen later she tries to explain something difficult about the divorce to her father and is angry when he doesn't understand, and then finds at the end of the explanation that she is eating an orange, though she can't remember peeling it or even having decided to eat it.

Cockroaches in Autumn

On the white painted bolt of a door that is never opened, a thick line of tiny black grains—the dung of cockroaches.

They nest in the coffee filters, in the woven wicker shelves, and in the crack at the top of a door, where by flashlight you see the forest of moving legs.

Boats were scattered over the water near Dover Harbor at odd angles, like the cockroaches surprised in the kitchen at night before they move.

The youngest are so bright, so spirited, so willing.

He sees the hand coming down and runs the other way. There is too far to go, or he is not fast enough. At the same time we admire such a will to live.

I am alert to small moving things, and spin around toward a floating dust mote. I am alert to darker spots against a lighter background, but these are only the roses on my pillowcase.

•

A new autumn stillness, in the evening. The windows of the neighborhood are shut. A chill sifts into the room from the panes of glass. Behind a cupboard door, they squat inside a long box eating spaghetti.

The stillness of death. When the small creature does not move away from the lowering hand.

We feel respect for such nimble rascals, such quick movers, such clever thieves.

From inside a white paper bag comes the sound of a creature scratching—one creature, I think. But when I empty the bag, a crowd of them scatter from the heel of rye bread, like rye seeds across the counter, like raisins.

Fat, half grown, with a glossy dark back, he stops short in his headlong rush and tries a few other moves almost simultaneously, a bumper car jolting in place on the white drainboard.

Here in the crack at the top of the door, moving on their legs, they are in such numbers conscious of us behind our flashlight beam.

It is in his moment of hesitation that you sense him as an intelligent creature. Between his pause and his change of direction, you are sure, there is a quick thought.

They eat, but leave no mark of eating, we think. Yet here in the leaf edge, little crescent shapes—their gradual bites.

•

He is like a thickened shadow. See how the shadow at the crack of a window thickens, comes out from the wall, and moves off!

In the cardboard trap, five or six of them are stuck—frozen at odd angles, alive with an uncanny stillness, in this box like a child's miniature theater.

How kindly I feel toward another species of insect in the house! Its gauzy wings! Its confusion! Its blundering walk down the lampshade! It doesn't think to run away!

At the end of the meal, the cheeses were brought. All white except the Roquefort, they lay scattered over the board at odd angles, like cows grazing or ships at sea.

After a week, I take a forgotten piece of bread from the oven where they have visited—now it is dry, a bit of brown lace.

The white autumn light in the afternoon. They sleep behind a child's drawings on the kitchen wall. I tap each piece of paper and they burst out from the edges of pictures that are already filled with shooting stars, missiles, machine guns, land mines . . .

The Bone

Many years ago, my husband and I were living in Paris and translating art books. Whatever money we made we spent on movies and food. We went mostly to old American movies, which were very popular there, and we ate out a lot of the time because restaurant meals were cheap then and neither of us knew how to cook very well.

One night, though, I cooked some fillets of fish for dinner. These fillets were not supposed to contain bones, and yet there must have been a small bone in one of them because my husband swallowed it and it got caught in his throat. This had never happened to either of us before, though we had always worried about it. I gave him bread to eat, and he drank many glasses of water, but the bone was really stuck, and didn't move.

After several hours in which the pain intensified and my husband and I grew more and more uneasy, we left the apartment and walked out into the dark streets of Paris to look for help. We were first directed to the ground-floor apartment of a nurse who lived not far away, and she then directed us to a hospital. We walked on some way and found the hospital in the rue de Vaugirard. It was old and quite dark, as though it didn't do much business anymore.

Inside, I waited on a folding chair in a wide hallway near the front entrance while my husband sat behind a closed door nearby in the company of several nurses who wanted to help him but could not do more than spray his throat and then stand back and laugh, and he would laugh too, as best he could. I didn't know what they were all laughing about.

Finally a young doctor came and took my husband and me down several long, deserted corridors and around two sides of the dark hospital grounds to an empty wing containing another examining room in which he kept his special instruments. Each instrument had a different angle of curvature but they all ended in some sort of a hook. Under a single pool of light, in the darkened room, he inserted one instrument after another down my husband's throat, working with fierce interest and enthusiasm. Every time he inserted another instrument my husband gagged and waved his hands in the air.

At last the doctor drew out the little fishbone and showed it around proudly. The three of us smiled and congratulated one another.

The doctor took us back down the empty corridors and out under the vaulted entryway that had been built to accommodate horse-drawn carriages. We stood there and talked a little, looking around at the empty streets of the neighborhood, and then we shook hands and my husband and I walked home.

More than ten years have passed since then, and my husband and I have gone our separate ways, but every now and then, when we are together, we remember that young doctor. "A great Jewish doctor," says my husband, who is also Jewish.

A Few Things Wrong with Me

He said there were things about me that he hadn't liked from the very beginning. He didn't say this unkindly. He's not an unkind person, at least not intentionally. He said it because I was trying to get him to explain why he changed his mind about me so suddenly.

I may ask his friends what they think about this, because they know him better than I do. They've known him for more than fifteen years, whereas I've known him for only about ten months. I like them, and they seem to like me, though we don't know each other very well. What I want to do is to have a meal or a drink with at least two of them and talk about him until I begin to get a better picture of him.

It's easy to come to the wrong conclusions about people. I see now that all these past months I kept coming to the wrong conclusions about him. For example, when I thought he would be unkind to me, he was kind. Then when I thought he would be effusive he was merely polite. When I thought he would be annoyed to hear my voice on the telephone he was pleased. When I thought he would turn against me because I had treated him rather coldly, he was more anxious than ever to be with me and went to great trouble and expense so that we could spend a little time together. Then when I made up my mind that he was the man for me, he suddenly called the whole thing off.

It seemed sudden to me even though for the last month I could feel him drawing away. For instance, he didn't write as often as he had before, and then when we were together he said more unkind things to me than he ever had before. When he left, I knew he was thinking it over. He took a month to think it over, and I knew it was fifty-fifty he would come to the point of saying what he did.

I suppose it seemed sudden because of the hopes I had for him and me by then, and the dreams I had about us—some of the usual dreams about a nice house and nice babies and the two of us together in the house working in the evening while the babies were asleep, and then some other dreams, about how we would travel together, and about how I would learn to play the banjo or the mandolin so that I could play with him, because he has a lovely tenor voice. Now, when I picture myself playing the banjo or the mandolin, the idea seems silly.

The way it all ended was that he called me up on a day he didn't usually call me and said he had finally come to a decision. Then he said that because he had had trouble figuring all this out, he had made some notes about what he was going to say and he asked me if I would mind if he read them. I said I would mind very much. He said he would at least have to look at them now and then as he talked.

Then he talked in a very reasonable way about how bad the chances were for us to be happy together, and about changing over to a friendship now before it was too late. I said he was talking about me as though I were an old tire that might blow out on the highway. He thought that was funny.

We talked about how he had felt about me at various

times, and how I had felt about him at various times, and it seemed that these feelings hadn't matched very well. Then, when I wanted to know exactly how he had felt about me from the very beginning, trying to find out, really, what was the most he had ever felt, he made this very plain statement about how there were things about me that he hadn't liked from the very beginning. He wasn't trying to be unkind, but just very clear. I told him I wouldn't ask him what these things were but I knew I would have to go and think about it.

I didn't like hearing there were things about me that bothered him. It was shocking to hear that someone I loved had never liked certain things about me. Of course there were a few things I didn't like about him too, for instance an affectation in his manner involving the introduction of foreign phrases into his conversation, but although I had noticed these things, I had never said it to him in quite this way. But if I try to be logical, I have to think that after all there may be a few things wrong with me. Then the problem is to figure out what these things are.

For several days, after we talked, I tried to think about this, and I came up with some possibilities. Maybe I didn't talk enough. He likes to talk a lot and he likes other people to talk a lot. I'm not very talkative, or at least not in the way he probably likes. I have some good ideas from time to time, but not much information. I can talk for a long time only when it's about something boring. Maybe I talked too much about which foods he should be eating. I worry about the way people eat and tell them what they should eat, which is a tiresome thing to do, something my ex-husband never liked either. Maybe I mentioned my ex-husband too often, so that he thought my ex-husband was still on my mind, which wasn't true. He might have been irritated by the fact that he couldn't kiss me in the street for fear of getting poked in the eye by my glasses—or maybe he didn't even like being with a woman who wore glasses, maybe he didn't like always having to look at my eyes through this blue-tinted glass. Or maybe he doesn't like people who write things on index cards, diet plans on little index cards and plot summaries on big index cards. I don't like it much myself, and I don't do it all the time. It's just a way I have of trying to get my life in order. But he might have come across some of those index cards.

I couldn't think of much else that would have bothered him from the very beginning. Then I decided I would never be able to think of the things about me that bothered him. Whatever I thought of would probably not be the same things. And anyway, I wasn't going to go on trying to identify these things, because even if I knew what they were I wouldn't be able to do anything about them.

Late in the conversation, he tried to tell me how excited he was about his new plan for the summer. Now that he wasn't going to be with me, he thought he would travel down to Venezuela, to visit some friends who were doing anthropological work in the jungle. I told him I didn't want to hear about that.

While we talked on the phone, I was drinking some wine left over from a large party I had given. After we hung up I immediately picked up the phone again and made a series of phone calls, and while I talked, I finished one of the leftover bottles of wine and started on another that was sweeter than the first, and then finished that one too. First I called a few people here in the city, then when it got too late for that I called a few people in California, and when it got too late to go on calling California, I called someone in

England who had just woken up and was not in a very good mood.

Between one phone call and the next I would sometimes walk by the window and look up at the moon, which was in its first quarter but remarkably bright, and think of him and then wonder when I would stop thinking of him every time I saw the moon. The reason I thought of him when I saw the moon was that during the five days and four nights he and I were first together, the moon was waxing and then full, the nights were clear, we were in the country, where you notice the sky more, and every night, early or late, we would walk outdoors together, partly to get away from the various members of our families who were in the house and partly just to take pleasure in the meadows and the woods under the moonlight. The dirt road that sloped up away from the house into the woods was full of ruts and rocks, so that we kept stumbling against each other and more tightly into each other's arms. We talked about how nice it would be to bring a bed out into the meadow and lie down on it in the moonlight.

The next time the moon was full, I was back in the city, and I saw it out the window of a new apartment. I thought to myself that a month had passed since he and I were together, and that it had passed very slowly. After that, every time the moon was full, shining on the leafy, tall trees in the backyards here, and on the flat tar roofs, and then on the bare trees and snowy ground in the winter, I would think to myself that another month had passed, sometimes quickly and sometimes slowly. I liked counting the months that way.

He and I always seemed to be counting the time as it passed and waiting for it to pass so that the day would come when we would be together again. That was one reason he said he couldn't go on with it. And maybe he's right, it isn't too late, we will change over to a friendship, and he will talk to me now and then long distance, mostly about his work or my work, and give me good advice or a plan of action when I need one, then call himself something like my "éminence grise."

When I stopped making my phone calls, I was too dizzy to go to sleep, because of the wine, so I turned on the television and watched some police dramas, some old situation comedies, and finally a show about unusual people across the country. I turned the set off at five in the morning when the sky was light, and I fell asleep right away.

It's true that by the time the night was over I wasn't worrying anymore about what was wrong with me. At that hour of the morning I can usually get myself out to the end of something like a long dock with water all around where I'm not touched by such worries. But there will always come a time later that day or a day or two after when I ask myself that difficult question once, or over and over again, a useless question, really, since I'm not the one who can answer it and anyone else who tries will come up with a different answer, though of course all the answers together may add up to the right one, if there is such a thing as a right answer to a question like that.

Sketches for a Life of Wassilly

1

Wassilly was a man of many parts, changeable, fickle, at times ambitious, at times stuporous, at times meditative, at times impatient. Not a man of habits, though he wished to be, tried to cultivate habits, was overjoyed when he found something that truly, for a time, seemed necessary to him and that had possibilities of becoming a habit.

For a while, he sat in his wing chair every evening after supper and found it pleasant. He once thoroughly enjoyed smoking a pipe of fragrant tobacco and thinking over what had happened to him during the day. But the next evening he suffered from wind and could not sit still; the pipe, also, kept going out; the lights for some reason flickered and dimmed constantly, and after a while he gave up the pretense of leisurely contemplation.

Some months later, he decided that a stroll after dinner was also a popular thing to do and might easily become a habit. For many days he went out of his house at a fixed hour and walked through the neighboring streets, successfully evoking in himself a mood of calm speculation, gazing at the swallows as they flew over the river and at the red sun-soaked housefronts and deducing various ill-founded scientific principles from what he saw; or he let his thoughts dwell on the people who walked by him in the street. But this did not become a habit either: he realized with great disappointment that once he had exhausted all the possible routes within an hour's stroll of his house he became frankly bored with walking, and that instead of benefiting his constitution, it upset his stomach enough so that he had to treat himself with some pills upon returning home. The strolls stopped altogether when his sister came unexpectedly to visit him, and did not resume when she left.

Wassilly was ambitious to learn, and yet sometimes for days on end he could not bring himself to study, but would sneak off into a corner, as if to avoid his own anxious gaze, and spend a long time bent over a crossword puzzle. This made him irritable and dull. He tried to throw the puzzles into a more favorable light by including them in his scheme for self-improvement. During three days, he tested himself against his watch: he did most of a puzzle in twenty minutes on one day, all of it in twenty minutes on the next, and then almost none of it in twenty minutes on the third. On that day he changed the rules and decided he would try to finish the puzzle every day, no matter how long it took. He clearly saw the time coming in which he would be master of the game. To this end he started keeping a notebook in which he wrote down all the more obscure words that appeared regularly in the puzzles and that he otherwise forgot as soon as he learned them, such as "*stoa*: Greek porch." In this way he persuaded himself that he was learning something even from the puzzles, and for a few wonderful hours he saw the conjunction of his baser inclinations and his higher ambitions.

His inconsistency. His inability to finish anything. His

sudden terrifying feelings that nothing he did mattered. His realizations that what went on in the outside world had more substance than anything in his life.

Sometimes Wassilly had an inkling that he suffered from a deeper boredom than he could completely picture to himself. At these times, he would brood about the yearly allowance his father gave him: perhaps it was the most unfortunate thing that had ever happened to him; it might ruin what was left of his life. Yet one of the only things Wassilly could be sure of in himself was the recurring hope that things would not turn out as badly as they seemed to be.

His effect on the world was potentially astonishing.

2

Wassilly's few real successes left him unmoved. Or rather, he could not bear to look at an article he had published and would allow his copies of the magazine to become covered with coffee stains and bent at the edges. He could not feel that his printed name was really his, or that the words on the page had really come from his own pen. His sister confirmed this feeling by remaining utterly silent about what he sent to her and also by treating him in exactly the same way she always had—as an agreeable but ineffectual person—when he felt his accomplishments should have made her see him in a new light. As some sort of retaliation, he occasionally wrote her long, deeply serious, and carefully phrased letters criticizing her personal life. These she would mention only months later and in an offhand way.

Not only did his published name and works seem to belong to someone else, but he derived little joy from anything he wrote. Once he had done it, it was out of his hands: it lay in a no-man's-land. It was neutral. It did not speak to him. He wanted to be proud of himself, but felt only guilty—that he had not done more, or better. He envied people who set out to write a book, wrote it, and were pleased with it, and when it was published read it through again with fresh pleasure and turned easily to their next project. He felt only a frightening emptiness ahead of him, a vacancy where there should have been plans, and all his work grew out of impulses.

3

Wassilly was so extremely self-conscious that at times even the soft eyes of his dog made him blush with embarrassment when he tried to attract her attention by some stupid action. Talking to friends on the telephone he would put fantastic interpretations on what they said and respond with clumsy remarks that left them bewildered and nervous.

In strange company he spoke too softly to be heard, afraid that his remarks would be misunderstood. His confidence was further weakened by the fact that people looked puzzled every time he spoke, since they were trying to hear what he was saying, or did not even notice that he had spoken.

Sometimes he was not certain whether or not he should say goodbye to a stranger. He compromised by whispering and looking off to one side.

He did not know exactly when to thank his hostess after attending a dinner or a weekend party. In his uncertainty, he would thank her over and over again. It was as though he did not believe his words carried any weight and hoped to achieve through the effect of accumulation what one speech alone could not accomplish.

Wassily was puzzled by the fact that these social responses did not come naturally to him, as they evidently did to others. He tried to learn them by watching other people closely, and was to some extent successful. But why was it such a difficult game? Sometimes he felt like a wolf-child who had only recently joined humanity.

4

Wassilly kept falling in love. Even with the dullest and plainest women since he was so isolated, out there in the country, that his loneliness soon overcame his initial disgust; when he awoke from his madness he would feel disgusted again and embarrassed.

Wassilly had difficult relations with the girl at the grocery. He felt insulted by her cold manner. At home, he sometimes worked himself into a rage against her and made cutting remarks to her out loud. Then he would become ashamed of himself and try to adopt a more enlightened attitude, realizing that she was only an unattractive girl in a small town working in a grocery, someone with no hopes, no ideals, no future. This would restore his sense of proportion. Then he would remember a certain day the previous spring. At the shooting match on a hill above the town she had flaunted herself in a white hat and had not acknowledged his presence by so much as a nod, though all around him people were in the highest of spirits. As if this was not enough, he had taken a shot at the target on the next hilltop and the gun had recoiled and hurt him badly in the shoulder. Everyone had laughed. But after all, he said to himself, they were experienced hunters and he was only a fat intellectual.

5

There were days when nothing went well, in spite of his good intentions. He would mislay everything he needed for work—pen, notebook, cigarettes—then after settling down would be called away to the telephone or would run out of ink, would resume work and become suddenly hungry, would be delayed by an accident in the kitchen and sit down again too distracted to think.

Even after an hour of good work, the day might be lost: he would feel that a fruitful afternoon was opening up for him, and on the strength of that feeling would take a break, stretching his legs in the garden. He would look up at the sky, his attention would be caught by an unfamiliar bird, and he would take up his bird book and follow the bird over the wild acres outside his garden, plunging through the underbrush, scratching his face, and gathering burrs on his socks. Returning home, he would be too hot and tired to work, and with a sense of guilt would lie down to rest, reading something light.

6

Wassilly sometimes suspected that he worked on his articles only because he enjoyed writing with a fountain pen and black ink. He could not, for example, write anything good with a ballpoint pen. And his work did not go well if he worked with blue ink. When he and his sister played gin rummy together, he enjoyed keeping score—yet if all they had at hand was a pencil, he allowed his sister to keep score.

He liked to use his pen for other things as well: he made lists on scraps of white paper, which he saved in a little pile. One list showed what he must remember to do when he visited the city again (Walk in the poorer neighborhoods,

Take pictures of certain streets), another what he must do before he left the country (Visit the lake, Take a daylong walk). On another scrap of paper he had written out a tentative schedule for the perfect day, with times set aside for physical exercise, work, serious reading, and correspondence. Then there was a scheme he was outlining for a set of camping equipment that would include a writing table and a cookstove and weigh less than forty pounds. And there were more lists—for example, insoluble problems he was encountering in his study of languages, with suggestions for where to find the answers (and on the list of what he must do in the city he would then add: Visit the library).

But far from helping to organize his life, the lists became very confusing to him. Working on a list, he would send himself into a certain room to check a book title or the date and forget why he had gone there, distracted by the sight of another unfinished project. He received from himself a number of unrelated instructions that he could not remember, and spent entire mornings uselessly rushing from room to room. There was a strange gap between volition and action: sitting at his desk, before his work but not working, he dreamt of perfection in many things, and this exhilarated him. But when he took one step toward that perfection, he faltered in the face of its demands. There were mornings when he woke under a weight of discouragement so heavy that he could not get out of bed but lay there all day watching the sunlight move across the floor and up the wall.

7

Wassilly's conception of himself: Wassilly had been an exceptionally healthy, agile, and physically fearless boy—

and so he continued to think of himself. Even when he fell prey to a variety of ailments that followed one after another with hardly a pause for several years, he persisted in regarding each ailment as unusual—even interesting—in a man of his good health. He would not admit that he was becoming frail, until one day his sister dropped in to see him where he lay suffering from a painful sinus attack, and in her blunt way said that she had never known anyone to get sick so often.

He took up yoga for a time after that, and did a shoulder stand every morning, since according to his book this would "drain one's sinuses and at the same time redistribute one's weight." (There his housekeeper would find him, staring up at a fold of his stomach, his chin pressed into his thyroid.)

He resolved to eat more wisely, taking his protein mainly from yogurt.

Vitamin D, said another book he consulted, was the most difficult vitamin to obtain naturally, and was formed on the oil of the skin by the sun's rays in the hours from ten to two in the months from May to September in Western countries (in the Northern Hemisphere). Accordingly, on the morning of May first, Wassilly exposed most of his skin to the feeble sun, lying for half an hour shivering in his backyard before he could not stand it any longer and gave up. Later, in the summer, he decided to combine the shoulder stand and the sunbath. He went out at noon and pointed his toes at the sky, but becoming dizzy he immediately lost all interest and for a time abandoned both yoga and sunbathing.

The key to everything, he decided, was to relax.

8

Wassilly, suddenly enlightened, saw that there was a terrible discrepancy between his conception of himself and the reality. He admired himself and at times felt slightly superior to others, not because of what he really was and what he had really done with himself, but rather because of what he could do, what he would soon do, what he would accomplish in the years ahead, what he would one day become and remain, and for the courage of his spirit. Sometimes he dreamt of obstacles which he would overcome with glory: fatal illness, permanent blindness, a flood or fire where lives could be saved, a long march as a refugee through mountainous country, a dramatic opportunity to defend his principles. But since under these circumstances it would actually be easier—not more difficult—to perform honorably, it followed that the tedium of his present situation was the most difficult obstacle of all.

One important thing was not to forget what he hoped to achieve in life. Another important thing was not to confuse a romantic picture of himself—as a doctor in Africa, for example—with a real possibility. And he tried not to lose sight of the fact that he was an adult in an adult world, with responsibilities. This was not easy: he would find himself sitting in the sun cutting out paper stars for a Christmas tree at the very moment other men were working to support large families or representing their countries in foreign places. When in moments of difficult truth-seeking he saw this incongruity, he felt sick that he should be saddled with himself, as though he were his own unwanted guest.

9

Wassilly's immobility: In midwinter, Wassilly's brother died. His father asked him to go to the apartment and sort through his brother's things. Wassilly's brother had lived alone in the city. Wassilly had never visited him there, because for some years his brother had not wanted to see him.

The door of the apartment had many locks and Wassilly did not know which were closed and which open, so it took him some time to get inside. Once inside, he was taken aback by the squalor and nakedness of the apartment: it looked like the home of a very poor man. There was nothing on the walls or floors. The furniture was shabby, and there was very little of it.

Wassily walked through the rooms. Signs of his brother were everywhere. In the bathroom, a web of black fingermarks surrounded the light switch. There was a ring in the tub, and a crust of dirt in the basin and the toilet. In the kitchen glass bottles and jars were crowded into one corner. Sheaths and roots of garlic buds covered the table like a light snow. It was as though his brother would be coming back at any moment.

Wassilly walked into the living room, where the only furniture was a desk, a cupboard, a few chairs, and the unmade bed from which his brother had been taken to the hospital. On the floor under the window, piles of papers and notebooks collapsed out into the room. Wassilly poked through them and found nothing. He pulled a folding wooden chair out into the middle of the room and sat down. He looked out the window at the brick walls of the apartment buildings that abutted this one, enclosing a courtyard and a spindly locust tree.

Wassilly tried to think about his brother—the stooped, thick figure, the slow speech, the hesitations. But again and again his mind wandered. The room was dark, even though the sun shone on the buildings nearby. A neighbor banged something against the wall behind the kitchen stove and immediately afterwards a door slammed in the hallway. Wassilly began to doze off, his chin on his overcoat lapel.

Startled awake by the silence, he looked around the room, so unfamiliar to him. The sun now shone across one wall. Wassilly and his brother had been far apart in age. Wassilly's earliest memories concerned his brother's leaving, returning, and leaving again. Silently he came home, silently left. And Wassilly always at the window, itching with excitement. It was years before Wassilly's admiration withered. By then his brother had no desire to see him anyway.

Wassilly stood up from the folding chair and unbuttoned his overcoat. He had begun to feel slightly nervous. Was this a responsible way to behave? he asked himself. He had come to sort out his brother's things: by now he should have been nearly finished. Yet for an hour he had been sitting in the same position. What would his brother have done in his place? he wondered. His brother would not have come to the apartment at all. He would not even have gone to the funeral.

Wassilly thought of taking off his overcoat but did not. He went into the bathroom, opened the medicine cabinet, and put all the tubes and bottles into a cardboard box for his own use. He felt like a thief. He pulled the towels off the racks and mats off the floor and stuffed them into a large laundry bag. When it came to throwing away his brother's toothbrush, he felt sick and could not go on.

•

A week later, Wassilly woke up in the right frame of mind, he thought, to do the job. He returned to his brother's apartment. Yet he accomplished no more this time than the last. Something in the very air of the apartment immobilized him. After a few hours he left, carrying away a framed photograph of his grandfather that he had found facedown on the mantelpiece. When he got home he wrote to his sister and asked her to do the job for him.

He lay back on his bed that evening, his dog beside him on the floor, and stared over at the photograph of his grandfather, whose eyes twinkled at him out of a dark corner. He could not move, as though the despair of his family life sat on his chest. Layer upon layer of sadness held him down—that he had not seen his brother more, that he had not liked him, that his brother had died alone, that a member of his family should have lived in such squalor. But if his brother had been a stranger, what did the rest matter? Not for the first time, he puzzled over the curious nature of families—that family bonds tended to keep together people who had little in common.

He would never have chosen the members of his family as friends. He thought it was odd that he should have been obliged to go to the apartment of this dirty stranger and handle his things. He looked over at his grandfather's face, with its suppressed smile and carefully folded cravat. He himself had no desire to start a family. Heavily, he rose from his bed and went down to the kitchen. He returned to bed with several thick sandwiches, which he ate until he was too drowsy to keep his eyes open any longer. As he slept and suffered mild nightmares, his dog crept up beside him and wolfed down what remained of the food.

City Employment

All over the city there are old black women who have been employed to call up people at seven in the morning and ask in a muffled voice to speak to Lisa. This provides work for them that they can do at home. These women are part of a larger corps of city employees engaged to call wrong numbers. The highest earner of all is an Indian from India who is able to insist that he does not have the wrong number.

Others—mainly old people—have been employed to amuse us by wearing strange hats. They wear them as though they were not responsible for what went on above their eyebrows. Two hats bob along side by side—a homburg high up on an old man and a black veiled affair with cherries on a little woman—and under the hats the old people argue. Another old woman, bent and feeble, crosses the street slowly in front of our car, looking angry that she has been made to wear this large cone-shaped red hat that is pressing down so heavily on her forehead. Yet another old woman walks on a difficult sidewalk and is cautious about where she sets her feet. She is not wearing a hat, because she has lost her job.

People of all ages are hired by the city to act as lunatics so that the rest of us will feel sane. Some of the lunatics are beggars too, so that we can feel sane and rich at the same time. There are only a limited number of jobs available as lunatics. These jobs have all been filled. For years the lunatics were locked up together in mental hospitals on islands in New York Harbor. Then the city authorities released them in large numbers to form a reassuring presence on the streets.

Naturally some of the lunatics have no trouble holding down two jobs at once by wearing strange hats as they lope and shuffle along.

Two Sisters

Though everyone wishes it would not happen, and though it would be far better if it did not happen, it does sometimes happen that a second daughter is born and there are two sisters.

Of course any daughter, crying in the hour of her birth, is only a failure, and is greeted with a heavy heart by her father, since the man wanted sons. He tries again: again it is only a daughter. This is worse, for it is a second daughter; then it is a third, and even a fourth. He is miserable among females. He lives, in despair, with his failures.

The man is lucky who has one son and one daughter, though his risk is great in trying for another son. Most fortunate is the man with sons only, for he can go on, son after son, until the daughter is made, and he will have all the sons he could wish for and a little daughter as well, to grace his table. And if the daughter should never come, then he has a woman already, in his wife the mother of his sons. In himself he has not a man. Only his wife has that man. She could wish for a daughter, having no woman, but her wishes are hardly audible. For she is herself a daughter, though she may have no living parents.

The single daughter, the many brothers' only sister, listens to the voice of her family and is pleased with herself and happy. Her softness against her brothers' brutality, her calm against their destruction, is admired. But when there are two sisters, one is uglier and more clumsy than the other, one is less clever, one is more promiscuous. Even when all the better qualities unite in one sister, as most often happens, she will not be happy, because the other, like a shadow, will follow her success with green eyes.

Two sisters grow up at different times and despise each other for being such children. They quarrel and turn red. And though if there is only one daughter she will remain Angela, two will lose their names, and be stouter as a result.

Two sisters often marry. One finds the husband of the other crude. The other uses her husband as a shield against her sister and her sister's husband, whom she fears for his quick wit. Though the two sisters attempt friendship so that their children will have cousins, they are often estranged.

Their husbands disappoint them. Their sons are failures and spend their mothers' love in cheap towns. Strong as iron, only, is now the hatred of the two sisters for each other. This endures, as their husbands wither, as their sons desert.

Caged together, two sisters contain their fury. Their features are the same.

Two sisters, in black, shop for food together, husbands dead, sons dead in some war; their hatred is so familiar that they are unaware of it. They are sometimes tender with each other, because they forget.

But the faces of the two sisters in death are bitter by long habit.

The Mother

The girl wrote a story. "But how much better it would be if you wrote a novel," said her mother. The girl built a dollhouse. "But how much better if it were a real house," her mother said. The girl made a small pillow for her father. "But wouldn't a quilt be more practical," said her mother. The girl dug a small hole in the garden. "But how much better if you dug a large hole," said her mother. The girl dug a large hole and went to sleep in it. "But how much better if you slept forever," said her mother.

Therapy

I moved into the city just before Christmas. I was alone, and this was a new thing for me. Where had my husband gone? He was living in a small room across the river, in a district of warehouses.

I moved here from the country, where the pale, slow people all looked on me as a stranger anyway, and where it was not much use trying to talk.

After Christmas snow covered the sidewalks. Then the snow melted. Even so, I found it hard to walk, then for a few days it was easier. My husband moved into my neighborhood so that he could see our son more often.

Here in the city I had no friends either, for a long time. At first, I would only sit in a chair picking hair and dust off my clothes, and then get up and stretch and sit down again. In the morning I drank coffee and smoked. In the evening I drank tea and smoked and went to the window and back and from one room into the next room.

Sometimes, for a moment, I thought I would be able to do something. Then that moment would pass and I would want to move and not be able to move.

In the country, one day, I had not been able to move. First I had dragged myself around the house and then from the porch to the yard, and then into the garage, where finally my brain spun like a fly. There I stood, over an oil slick. I offered myself reasons for leaving the garage, but no reason was good enough.

Night came, the birds quieted down, the cars stopped going by, everything withdrew into the darkness, and then I moved.

All I retrieved from this day was the decision not to tell certain people what had happened to me. I did tell someone, of course, and right away. But he was not interested. He was not very interested in anything about me by then, and certainly not my troubles.

In the city, I thought I might begin to read again. I was tired of embarrassing myself. Then, when I began to read, it was not just one book but many at once—a life of Mozart, a study of the changing sea, and others I can't remember now.

My husband was encouraged by these signs of activity, and he would sit down and talk to me, breathing into my face until I was exhausted. I wanted to hide from him how difficult my life was.

Because I did not immediately forget what I read, I thought my mind was getting stronger. I wrote down facts that struck me as facts I should not forget. I read for six weeks and then I stopped reading.

In the middle of the summer, I lost my courage again. I began to see a doctor. Right away I was not happy with him and I made an appointment with a different doctor, a woman, though I didn't give up the first doctor.

The woman's office was in an expensive street near Gramercy Park. I rang her doorbell. To my surprise, the door was opened not by her but by a man in a bow tie. The man was very angry because I had rung his doorbell.

Now the woman came out of her office and the two doctors began to argue. The man was angry because the woman's patients were always ringing his doorbell. I stood there between them. After that visit I did not go back.

For weeks I did not tell my doctor that I had tried someone else. I thought this might hurt his feelings. I was wrong. In those days it bothered me that he allowed himself to be endlessly abused and insulted as long as I continued to pay his fee. He protested: "I only allow myself to be insulted up to a certain point."

After every session with him, I thought I would not go back. There were several reasons for this. His office was in an old house hidden from the street by other buildings and set in a garden full of little paths and gates and flower beds. Now and then, as I entered or left the house, I glimpsed a strange figure descending the stairs or disappearing through a doorway. He was a short, stout man with a shock of dark hair on his head, tightly buttoned up to the neck in a white shirt. As he passed me he would look at me, but his face revealed nothing, even though I was certainly there, coming up the stairs. This man disturbed me all the more because I did not understand what his relationship with my doctor might be. Halfway through every session I would hear a male voice call one word down the stairway: "Gordon."

Another reason I did not want to continue seeing my doctor was that he did not take notes. I thought he should take notes and remember the facts about my family: that my brother lived by himself in one room in the city, that my sister was a widow with two daughters, that my father was high-strung, demanding, and easily offended, and that my mother criticized me even more than my father did. I thought my doctor should study his notes after each session. Instead, he came running down the stairs behind me to make a cup of coffee in the kitchen. I thought this behavior showed a lack of seriousness on his part.

He laughed at certain things I told him, and this outraged me. But when I told him other things that I thought were funny, he did not even smile. He said rude things about my mother, and this made me want to cry for her sake and for the sake of some happy times in my childhood. Worst of all, he often slumped down in his armchair, sighed, and seemed distracted.

Remarkably, every time I told him how uneasy and how unhappy he made me feel, I liked him better. After a few months, I did not have to tell him this anymore.

I thought a very long time went by between visits, and then I would see him again. It was only a week, but many things always happened in a week. For instance, I would have a bad fight with my son one day, my landlady would serve me an eviction notice the next morning, and that afternoon my husband and I would have a long talk full of hopelessness and decide that we could never be reconciled.

I had too little time, now, to say what I wanted to, in each session. I wanted to tell my doctor that I thought my life was funny. I told him about how my landlady tricked me, how my husband had two girlfriends and how these women were jealous of each other but not of me, how my in-laws insulted me over the phone, how my husband's friends ignored me, and then how I kept tripping on the street and walking into walls. Everything I said made me want to laugh. But near the end of the hour I was also telling him how face-to-face with another person I couldn't speak. There was always a wall. "Is there a wall between you and me now?" he would ask. No, there was no wall there anymore.

My doctor saw me and looked past me. He heard my words and at the same time he heard other words. He took me apart and put me together in another pattern and showed me this. There was what I did, and there was why he thought I did it. The truth was not clear anymore. Because of him, I did not know what my feelings were. A swarm of reasons flew around my head, buzzing. They deafened me, and I was always confused.

Late in the fall I slowed down and stopped speaking, and early in the new year I lost most of my ability to reason. I slowed down still further, until I hardly moved. My doctor listened to the hollow clatter of my footsteps on the stairs and told me he had wondered if I would have the strength to climb all the way up.

In those days I saw only the dark side of everything. I hated rich people and I was disgusted by the poor. The noise of children playing irritated me and the silence of old people made me uneasy. Hating the world, I longed for the protection of money, but I had no money. All around me women shrieked. I dreamed of some peaceful asylum in the country.

I continued to observe the world. I had a pair of eyes, but no longer much understanding, and no longer any speech. Little by little my capacity to feel was going. There was no more excitement in me, and no more love.

Then spring came. I had become so used to the winter that I was surprised to see leaves on the trees.

Because of my doctor, things began to change for me. I was more unassailable. I did not always feel that certain people were going to humiliate me.

I started laughing at funny things again. I would laugh and then I would stop and think: True, all winter I did not laugh. In fact, for a whole year I did not laugh. For a whole year I spoke so quietly that no one understood what I said. Now people I knew seemed less unhappy to hear my voice on the telephone.

I was still afraid, knowing that one wrong move could expose me. But I began to be excited now. I would spend the afternoon alone. I was reading books again and writing down certain facts. After dark, I would go out on the street and stop to look in shop windows, and then I would turn away from the windows, and in my excitement I would bump into the people standing next to me, always other women looking at clothes. Walking again, I would stumble over the curbstone.

I thought that since I was better, my therapy should end soon. I was impatient, and I wondered: How did therapy come to an end? I had other questions too: for instance, How much longer would I continue to need all my strength just to take myself from one day to the next? There was no answer to that one. There would be no end to therapy, either, or I would not be the one who chose to end it.

French Lesson I:
Le Meurtre

See the *vaches* ambling up the hill, head to rump, head to rump. Learn what a *vache* is. A *vache* is milked in the morning, and milked again in the evening, twitching her dung-soaked tail, her head in a stanchion. Always start learning your foreign language with the names of farm animals. Remember that one animal is an *animal*, but more than one are *animaux*, ending in *a u x*. Do not pronounce the *x*. These *animaux* live on a *ferme*. There is not much difference between that word, *ferme*, and our own word for the place where wisps of straw cover everything, the barnyard is deep in mud, and a hot dunghill steams by the barn door on a winter morning, so it should be easy to learn. *Ferme*.

We can now introduce the definite articles *le*, *la*, and *les*, which we know already from certain phrases we see in our own country, such as *le car, le sandwich, le café, les girls*. Besides *la vache*, there are other *animaux* on *la ferme*, whose buildings are weather-beaten, pocked with rusty nails, and leaning at odd angles, but which has a new tractor. *Les chiens* cringe in the presence of their master, *le fermier*, and bark at *les chats* as *les chats* slink mewing to the back door, and *les poulets* cluck and scratch and are special pets of *le fermier*'s children until they are beheaded by *le fermier* and plucked by *la femme* of *le fermier* with her red-knuckled hands and then cooked and eaten by the entire *famille.* Until further notice do not pronounce the final consonants of any of the words in your new vocabulary unless they are followed by the letter *e*, and sometimes not even then. The rules and their numerous exceptions will be covered in later lessons.

We will now introduce a piece of language history and then, following it, a language concept.

Agriculture is a pursuit in France, as it is in our own country, but the word is pronounced differently, *agriculture.* The spelling is the same because the word is derived from the Latin. In your lessons you will notice that some French words, such as *la ferme*, are spelled the same way or nearly the same way as the equivalent words in our own language, and in these cases the words in both languages are derived from the same Latin word. Other French words are not at all like our words for the same things. In these cases, the French words are usually derived from the Latin but our words for the same things are not, and have come to us from the Anglo-Saxon, the Danish, and so on. This is a piece of information about language history. There will be more language history in later lessons, because language history is really quite fascinating, as we hope you will agree by the end of the course.

We have just said that we have our own words in English for the same things. This is not strictly true. We can't really say there are several words for the same thing. It is in fact just the opposite—there is only one word for many things, and usually even that word, when it is a noun, is too general. Keep this language concept in mind as you listen to the following example:

A French *arbre* is not the elm or maple shading the main street of our New England towns in the infinitely long, hot and listless, vacant summer of our childhoods, which are themselves different from the childhoods of French children, and if you see a Frenchman standing on a street in a small town in America pointing to an elm or a maple and calling it an *arbre*, you will know this is wrong. An *arbre* is a plane tree in an ancient town square with lopped, stubby branches and patchy, leprous bark standing in a row of similar plane trees across from the town hall, in front of which a bicycle ridden by a man with thick, reddish skin and an old cap wavers past and turns into a narrow lane. Or an *arbre* is one of the dense, scrubby live oaks in the blazing dry hills of Provence, through which a similar figure in a blue cloth jacket carrying some sort of a net or trap pushes his way. An *arbre* can also cast a pleasant shade and keep *la maison* cool in the summer, but remember that *la maison* is not wood-framed with a widow's walk and a wide front porch but is laid out on a north-south axis, is built of irregular, sand-colored blocks of stone, and has a red tile roof, small square windows with green shutters, and no windows on the north side, which is also protected from the wind by a closely planted line of cypresses, while a pretty mulberry or olive may shade the south. Not that there are not many different sorts of *maisons* in France, their architecture depending on their climate or on the fact that there may be a foreign country nearby, like Germany, but we cannot really have more than one image behind a word we say, like *maison*. What do you see when you say *house*? Do you see more than one kind of house?

When are we going to return to our *ferme*? As we pointed out earlier, a language student should master *la ferme* before he or she moves on to *la ville*, just as we should all come to the city only in our adolescent years, when nature, or animal life, is no longer as important or interesting to us as it once was.

If you stand in a tilled field at the edge of *la ferme*, you will hear *les vaches* lowing because it is five in the winter evening and their udders are full. A light is on in the barn, but outside it is dark and *la femme* of *le fermier* looks out a little anxiously across the barnyard from the window of her *cuisine*, where she is peeling vegetables. Now the hired man is silhouetted in the doorway of the barn. *La femme* wonders why he is standing still holding a short object in his right hand. The plural article *les*, spelled *l e s*, as in *les vaches*, is invariable, but do not pronounce the *s*. The singular article is either masculine, *le*, or feminine, *la*, depending on the noun it accompanies, and it must always be learned along with any new noun in your vocabulary, because there is very little else to go by, to tell what in the world of French nouns is masculine and what is feminine. You may try to remember that all countries ending in silent *e* are feminine except for *le Mexique*, or that all the states in the United States of America ending in silent *e* are feminine except for Maine—just as in German the four seasons are masculine and all minerals are masculine—but you will soon forget these rules. One day, however, *la maison* will seem inevitably feminine to you, with its welcoming open doors, its shady rooms, its warm kitchen. *La bicyclette*, a word we are introducing now, will also seem feminine, and can be thought of as a young girl, ribbons fluttering in her spokes as she wobbles down the rutted lane away from the farm. *La bicyclette*. But that was earlier in the afternoon. Now *les vaches* stand at the barnyard gate, lowing and chewing their cuds. The word *cud*, and probably also the word *lowing*, are words you will not have to know in

French, since you would almost never have occasion to use them.

Now the hired man swings open *la barrière* and *les vaches* amble across the barnyard, udders swaying, up to their hocks in *la boue*, nodding their heads and switching their tails. Now their hooves clatter across the concrete floor of *la grange* and the hired man swings *la barrière* shut. But where is *le fermier*? And why, in fact, is the chopping block covered with *sang* that is still sticky, even though *le fermier* has not killed *un poulet* in days? You will need to use indefinite articles as well as definite articles with your nouns, and we must repeat that you will make no mistakes with the gender of your nouns if you learn the articles at the same time. *Un* is masculine, *une* is feminine. This being so, what gender is *un poulet*? If you say masculine you are right, though the bird herself may be a young female. After the age of ten months, however, when she should also be stewed rather than broiled, fried, or roasted, she is known as *la poule* and makes a great racket after laying a clutch of eggs in a corner of the poultry yard *la femme* will have trouble finding in the morning, when she will also discover something that does not belong there and that makes her stand still, her apron full of eggs, and gaze off across the fields.

Notice that the words *poule, poulet*, and *poultry*, especially when seen on the page, have some resemblance. This is because all three are derived from the same Latin word. This may help you remember the word *poulet. Poule, poulet*, and *poultry* have no resemblance to the word *chicken*, because *chicken* is derived from the Anglo-Saxon.

In this first lesson we have concentrated on nouns. We can safely, however, introduce a preposition at this point, and before we are through we will also be using one verb, so that by the end of the lesson you will be able to form some simple sentences. Try to learn what this preposition means by the context in which it is used. You will notice that you have been doing this all along with most of the vocabulary introduced. It is a good way to learn a language because it is how children learn their native languages, by associating the sounds they hear with the context in which the sounds are uttered. If the context changed continually, the children would never learn to speak. Also, the so-called meaning of a word is completely determined by the context in which it is spoken, so that in fact we cannot say a meaning is inescapably attached to a word, but that it shifts over time and from context to context. Certainly the so-called meaning of a French word, as I tried to suggest earlier, is not its English equivalent but whatever it refers to in French life. These are modern or contemporary ideas about language, but they are generally accepted. Now the new word we are adding to our vocabulary is the word *dans*, spelled *d a n s*. Remember not to pronounce the last letter, *s*, or, in this case, the next to the last letter, *n*, and speak the word through your nose. *Dans.*

Do you remember *la femme*? Do you remember what she was doing? It is still dark, *les vaches* are gone from her sight and quieter than they were earlier, except for the one bellowing *vache* who is ill and was not let out that morning by *le fermier* for fear that she would infect the others, and *la femme* is still there, peeling vegetables. She is—now listen carefully—*dans la cuisine*. Do you remember what *la cuisine* is? It is the only place, except perhaps for the sunny front courtyard on a cool late summer afternoon, where *une femme* would reasonably peel *les legumes*.

La femme is holding a small knife *dans* her red-knuckled hand and there are bits of potato skin stuck to her wrist, just as there are feathers stuck in *le sang* on the chopping block outside the back door, smaller feathers, however, than would be expected from *un poulet.* The glistening white peeled *pommes de terre* are *dans une bassine* and *la bassine* is *dans* the sink, and *les vaches* are *dans la grange*, where they should have been an hour ago. Above them the bales of hay are stacked neatly *dans* the loft, and near them is a calf *dans* the calves' pen. The rows of bare lightbulbs in the ceiling shine on the clanking stanchions. *Stanchion* is another word you will probably not have to know in French, though it is a nice one to know in English.

Now that you know the words *la femme, dans*, and *la cuisine*, you will have no trouble understanding your first complete sentence in French: *La femme est dans la cuisine.* Say it over until you feel comfortable with it. *La femme est*—spelled *e s t* but don't pronounce the *s* or the *t—dans la cuisine.* Here are a few more simple sentences to practice on: *La vache est dans la grange. La pomme de terre est dans la bassine. La bassine est dans* the sink.

The whereabouts of *le fermier* is more of a problem, but in the next lesson we may be able to follow him into *la ville.* Before going on to *la ville*, however, do study the list of additional vocabulary:

le sac: bag
la grive: thrush
l'alouette: lark
l'aile: wing
la plume: feather
la hachette: hatchet
le manche: handle
l'anxiété: anxiety
le meurtre: murder

Once a Very Stupid Man

She is tired and a little ill and not thinking very clearly and as she tries to get dressed she keeps asking him where her things are and he very patiently tells her where each thing is—first her pants, then her shirt, then her socks, then her glasses. He suggests to her that she should put her glasses on and she does, but this doesn't seem to help very much. There isn't much light coming into the room. Part of the way through this search and this attempt to dress herself she lies down on the bed mostly dressed while he lies under the covers after earlier getting up to feed the cat, opening the can of food with a noise that puzzled her because it sounded like milk squirting from the teat of a cow into a metal bucket. As she lies there nearly dressed beside him he talks to her steadily about various things, and after a while, as she has been listening to him with different reactions according to what he says to her, first resentment, then great interest, then amusement, then distraction, then resentment again, then amusement again, he asks her if she minds him talking so much and if she wants him to stop or go on. She says it is time for her to get ready to go and she gets up off the bed.

She resumes her search for her clothes and he resumes

helping her. She asks him where her ring is and where her shoes are, and where her jacket is and where her purse is. He tells her where each thing is and then gets up and hands her some things even before she asks. By the time she is fully dressed to go, she sees more clearly what is happening, that her situation is very like a Hasidic tale she read on the subway the day before from a book that is still in her purse. She asks him if she can read him a story, he hesitates, and she thinks he probably doesn't like her to read to him, even though he likes to read to her. She says it is only a paragraph, he agrees, and they sit down at the kitchen table. By now he is dressed too, in a white T-shirt and pants that fit him nicely. From the thin brown book she reads the following tale:

" 'There was once a man who was very stupid. When he got up in the morning it was so hard for him to find his clothes that at night he almost hesitated to go to bed for thinking of the trouble he would have on waking. One evening he took paper and pencil and with great effort, as he undressed, noted down exactly where he put everything he had on. The next morning, well pleased with himself, he took the slip of paper in his hand and read: "cap"—there it was, he set it on his head; "pants"—there they lay, he got into them; and so it went until he was fully dressed. But now he was overcome with consternation, and he said to himself: "This is all very well, I have found my clothes and I am dressed, but where am I myself? Where in the world am *I*?" And he looked and looked, but it was a vain search; he could not find himself. And that is how it is with us, said the rabbi.' "

She stops reading. He likes the story, but does not seem to like the ending—"Where am I?"—as much as he likes the beginning, about the man's problem and his solution.

She herself feels she is like the very stupid man, not only because she couldn't find her clothes, not only because sometimes other simple things besides getting dressed are also beyond her, but most of all because she often doesn't know where she is, and particularly concerning this man she doesn't know where she is. She thinks she is probably no place in the life of this man, who is also not only not in his own house, just as she is not in her own house when she visits him and in fact doesn't know where this house is but arrives here as though in a dream, stumbling and falling in the street, but who is not altogether in his own life anymore and might well also ask himself, "Where am I?"

In fact, she wants to call herself a very stupid man. Can't she say, This woman is a very stupid man, just the way a few weeks before she thought she had called herself a bearded man? Because if the very stupid man in the story behaves just the way she herself would behave or is even right now behaving, can't she consider herself to be a very stupid man, just as a few weeks ago she thought anyone writing at the next table in a café might be considered to be a bearded man? She was sitting in a café and a bearded man was writing two tables away from her and two loud women came in to have lunch and disturbed the bearded man and she wrote down in her notebook that they had disturbed the bearded man writing at the next table and then saw that since she herself, as she wrote this, was writing at the next table, she was probably calling herself a bearded man. It was not that she had changed in any way, but that the words *bearded man* could now apply to her. Or perhaps she had changed.

She has read the tale out loud to him because it is so like what has just happened to her, but then she wonders if it is not the other way around and the tale lodged somewhere in her mind the day before and made it possible for her to forget where all her clothes were and have such trouble dressing. Later that morning, or perhaps on another morning, feeling the same stupidity leaving this man who is not quite in his life anymore, as she looks again for herself in his life and can't find herself anywhere, there are other confusions. She cries and may be crying only because it is raining outdoors and she has been staring at the rain coming down the windowpane, and then wonders if she is crying more because it is raining or if the rain made it possible for her to cry in the first place, since she doesn't cry very often, and finally thinks the two, the rain and the tears, are the same. Then, out on the street, there is a sudden great din coming from several places at once—a few cars honking, a truck's loud engine roaring, another truck with loose parts rattling over an uneven road surface, a road mender pounding—and the din seems to be occurring right inside her as if her anger and confusion had emptied her and made a place in the middle of her chest for this great clashing of metal, or as if she herself had left this body and left it open to this noise, and then she wonders, Has the noise really come into me, or has something in me gone out into the street to make such a great noise?

The Housemaid

I know I am not pretty. My dark hair is cut short and is so thin it hardly hides my skull. I have a hasty and lopsided way of walking, as though I were crippled in one leg. When I bought my glasses I thought they were elegant—the frames are black and shaped like butterfly wings—but now I have learned how unbecoming they are and am stuck with them, since I have no money to buy new ones. My skin is the color of a toad's belly and my lips are narrow. But I am not nearly as ugly as my mother, who is much older. Her face is small and wrinkled and black like a prune, and her teeth wobble in her mouth. I can hardly bear to sit across from her at dinner and I can tell by the look on her face that she feels the same way about me.

For years we have lived together in the basement. She is the cook; I am the housemaid. We are not good servants, but no one can dismiss us because we are still better than most. My mother's dream is that someday she will save enough money to leave me and live in the country. My dream is nearly the same, except that when I am feeling angry and unhappy I look across the table at her clawlike hands and hope that she will choke to death on her food. Then no one would be there to stop me from going into her closet and breaking open her money box. I would put on her dresses and her hats, and open the windows of her room and let the smell out.

Whenever I imagine these things, sitting alone in the kitchen late at night, I am always ill the next day. Then it is my mother herself who nurses me, holding water to my lips and fanning my face with a flyswatter, neglecting her duties in the kitchen, and I struggle to persuade myself that she is not silently gloating over my weakness.

Things have not always been like this. When Mr. Martin lived in the rooms above us, we were happier, though we seldom spoke to one another. I was no prettier than I am now, but I never wore my glasses in his presence and took care to stand up straight and to walk gracefully. I stumbled often, and even fell flat on my face because I could not see where I was going; I ached all night from trying to hold in my round stomach as I walked. But none of this stopped me from trying to be someone Mr. Martin could love. I broke many more things then than I do now, because I could not see where my hand was going when I dusted the parlor vases and sponged the dining-room mirrors. But Mr. Martin hardly noticed. He would start from his fireside chair, as the glass shattered, and stare up at the ceiling in a puzzled sort of way. After a moment, as I held my breath by the glittering pieces, he would pass his white-gloved hand over his forehead and sit down again.

He never spoke a word to me, but then I never heard him speak to anyone. I imagined his voice to be warm and slightly hoarse. Perhaps he stammered when he became emotional. I never saw his face, either, because it was hidden behind a mask. The mask was pale and rubbery. It covered every inch of his head and disappeared beneath his shirt collar. In the beginning it upset me; the first time I saw it, in fact, I lost my head and ran out of the room. Everything about it frightened me—the gaping mouth, the tiny ears like dried apricots, the clumsily painted black hair in frozen waves on its crown, and the naked eye sockets. It was enough to fill anyone's dreams with horror and in the beginning it had me tossing and turning in bed until the sheets nearly choked me.

Little by little I became used to it. I began to imagine what Mr. Martin's real expression was. I saw pink blushes spreading over his gray cheek when I caught him daydreaming over his book. I saw his mouth tremble with emotion—pity and admiration—as he watched me work. I would give him a certain little look and toss my head, and his face would break into a smile.

But now and then, when I found his pale gray eyes fixed on me, I had the uneasy feeling that I was quite wrong and that perhaps he never responded to me—a silly, inept housemaid; that if one day a different girl were to walk into the room and begin dusting he would only glance up from his book and continue to read without having noticed the change. Shaken by doubt, I would go on sweeping and scouring with numbed hands as though nothing had happened, and soon the doubt would pass.

I took on more and more work for Mr. Martin's sake. Where at first we used to send out his laundry to be washed, I began to wash it myself, even though I did not do it as well. His linen became dingy and his trousers were badly pressed, but he did not complain. My hands became wrinkled and swollen, but I did not mind. Where before a gardener came once a week to trim the hedges in summertime and cover the rosebushes with burlap during the winter, I now took over those duties, dismissing the gardener myself and working day after day in the worst weather. At first the garden suffered, but after a time it came alive again: the roses were driven out by wildflowers of all colors and the gravel walks were disrupted by thick green grass. I grew strong and hardy and didn't mind that my face erupted in welts and the skin of my fingers dried and cracked open, or that with so much work I grew thin and gaunt and smelled like a horse. My mother complained. But I felt that my body was an insignificant sacrifice.

Sometimes I imagined that I was Mr. Martin's daughter, at other times his wife, at other times even his dog. I forgot that I was nothing more than a housemaid.

My mother never once laid eyes on him, and that made my relationship with him all the more mysterious. During the day she stayed below in the steamy kitchen, preparing his meals and chewing her gums nervously. Only in the evening did she step outside the door and stand hugging herself near the overblown lilac bush, looking up at the clouds. Sometimes I wondered how she could go on working for a man she had never seen, but that was her way. I brought her an envelope of money each month and she took it and hid it with the rest of her money. She never asked me what he was like and I never volunteered anything. I think she didn't ask who he was because she hadn't yet even figured out who I was. Perhaps she thought she was cooking for her husband and family like other women, and that I was her younger sister. Sometimes she spoke of going down the mountain, though we don't live on a mountain, or of digging up the potatoes, though there are no potatoes in our garden. This upset me and I would try to bring her out of it by yelling suddenly or baring my teeth in her face. But nothing made any impression, and I would have to wait until at last she called me by name quite naturally. Since she showed no curiosity about Mr. Martin I was left in peace to take care of him just as I wished, to hover about him as he went out of the house on one of his infrequent walks, to linger behind the swinging door of the dining room and watch him through the crack, to brush his smoking jacket and wipe the dust from the soles of his slippers.

But this happiness didn't last forever. I woke up particularly early one Sunday morning in midsummer to see bright sunlight streaming down the hall where I slept. For a long time I lay in bed listening to the wrens that sit and sing in the bushes outside, and watching the swallows that fly in and out of the broken window at the far end of the hallway. I got up and with great care, as always, I cleaned my face and teeth. It was hot. I slipped a freshly washed summer dress over my head and put my feet into my patent leather pumps. For the last time in my life I drowned my own smell in rosewater. Church bells began wildly to chime ten o'clock. When I went upstairs to put his breakfast on the table, Mr. Martin was not there. I waited by his chair for what felt like hours. I began to search the house. Timidly at first, then in a frantic hurry, as though he were slipping out of each room just as I came to it, I looked everywhere for him. Only after seeing that his wardrobe was stripped of his clothes and his bookcase was empty could I admit that he had gone. Even then, and for days afterwards, I thought he might come back.

A week later an old woman came with three or four shabby trunks and began to line the mantelpiece with her cheap knickknacks. Then I saw that without a word of explanation, without regard for my feelings, without even a present of money, Mr. Martin had packed up and gone for good.

•

This is only a rented house. My mother and I are included in the rent. People come and go, and every few years there is a new tenant. I should have expected that one day Mr. Martin too would leave. But I didn't expect it. I was ill for a long time after that day and my mother, who became more and more loathsome to me, wore herself out bringing me the broth and cold cucumbers that I craved. After my illness I looked like a corpse. My breath stank. My mother would turn away from me in disgust. The tenants shuddered when I came into the room in my clumsy way, tripping over the doorsill even though my glasses again sat like a butterfly on the narrow bridge of my nose.

I was never a good housemaid, but now, though I try hard, I am so careless that some tenants believe I do not clean the rooms at all and others think I am purposely trying to embarrass them in front of their guests. But when they scold me I don't answer. I just look at them indifferently and go on with my work. They have never known such disappointment as I have.

The Cottages

1. On the One Hand, On the Other Hand

She is seventy-nine or so, and on the one hand it's hard to talk to her (she has come for dinner, it's just the two of us; she eats much more than I thought an old lady would and even after several helpings of the main meal and dessert keeps digging into the raisin box with her knotted fingers and spreading raisins on her clean plate and nervously lining them up and tossing them into her mouth as she talks, and when they fall out on her lower lip tipping them back in), it's hard to talk to her because she has only four or five things she wants to talk about and she forgets the name of every person and the name of every thing she wants to talk about and when groping to describe the thing whose name she has forgotten forgets the name of what she needs to describe to identify to me the first thing she has forgotten (she closes her eyes, leans her head back, and taps her twisted fingers on the tablecloth) and in the midst of this description, because she has gone on trying so long, forgets why she began it and stops dead or takes a different direction altogether (she talks with her eyes closed, her wiry white hair is tied back under a thin piece of yarn, and then she opens her eyes and cries out at her lolling dog to lie down and when the dog lies down stamps on his head in further irritation, and he rolls back his eyes in fear); on the other hand, even with only four or five subjects she doesn't exhaust what she has to say because she entirely forgets that she has made a remark or asked a question and had an answer to it already, and so she asks again and I answer again, and she remarks again, and this happens at intervals all through dinner and beyond (I can't convey the truth to her; there is my truth and her memory of it; I do not know a friend of hers but all evening she asks if I know him), but sometimes she tells me something about the Depression and the apartments she owned in the city, and then how her husband wrote his own column for the local paper and she never knew another writer as fine as he was, and then that is part of one long story and she remembers everything that happened and remembers, though she will have forgotten when I see her again, that she has told it to me now, though just barely.

2. Lillian

Lillian in her cap of white hair and her ankle socks and tied brown shoes is a small old woman who works over her sink before sunrise (I hear it through the wall of this cottage standing in the trees above the reedy lake with its black banks of mud and its dock of splintered wood), who washes her white linen by hand and hangs it on lines by the cottage and takes it down in the late morning. Now she sits reading at the picnic table a picture book about Polish Jews, with her white-framed glasses directed at the pictures, and when I walk by and ask, she says she is not really reading but thinking about sour apples and her daughters, she has been waiting all day for her two large daughters and waiting also to cook them the foods of their childhood; but though all day she is clean and ready, her daughters don't come and don't call. I look out from time to time and she is still sitting there alone, and she will not call them for fear of being a nuisance, and because she is disappointed she begins to think as she has thought before that she is too far away, she will not come back to this cottage again though she has come here for so many years, first with her husband, then without her husband, who died between one summer and the next, and she is thinking too how she makes trouble for everyone; well, no one minds! I have told her, but she will never believe that any more than she will uncover her old body to swim in company with the other old people here, and goes down to the lake alone at dawn; and now she puts away her book and her glasses and her shoes untied by the bed, and goes to bed, for it is evening, and she likes to lie and watch the darkness come down into the woods, though tonight, as sometimes before, she does not really watch, or though her eyes rest on the darkening woods, she is not so much watching as waiting, and often, now, feels she is waiting.

Safe Love

She was in love with her son's pediatrician. Alone out in the country—could anyone blame her.

There was an element of grand passion in this love. It was also a safe thing. The man was on the other side of a barrier. Between him and her: the child on the examining table, the office itself, the staff, his wife, her husband, his stethoscope, his beard, her breasts, his glasses, her glasses, etc.

Problem

X is with Y, but living on money from Z. Y himself supports W, who lives with her child by V. V wants to move to Chicago but his child lives with W in New York. W cannot move because she is having a relationship with U, whose child also lives in New York, though with its mother, T. T takes money from U, W takes money from Y for herself and from V for their child, and X takes money from Z. X and Y have no children together. V sees his child rarely but provides for it. U lives with W's child but does not provide for it.

What an Old Woman Will Wear

She looked forward to being an old woman and wearing strange clothes. She would wear a shapeless dark brown or black dress of thin material, perhaps with little flowers on it, certainly frayed at the neck and hem and under the arms, and hanging lopsided from her bony shoulders down past her bony hips and knees. She would wear a straw hat with her brown dress in the summer, and then in the cold weather a turban or a helmet and a warm coat of something black and curly like lamb's wool. Less interesting would be her black shoes with their square heels and her thick stockings gathered around her ankles.

But before she was that old, she would still be a good deal older than she was now, and she also looked forward to being that age, what would be called past the prime of her life and slowing down.

If she had a husband, she would sit out on the lawn with her husband. She hoped she would have a husband by then. Or still have one. She had once had a husband, and she wasn't surprised that she had once had one, didn't have one now, and hoped to have one later in her life. Everything seemed to happen in the right order, generally. She had also had a child; the child was growing, and in a few more years the child would be grown and she would want to slow down and have someone to talk to.

She told her friend Mitchell, as they were sitting together on a park bench, that she was looking forward to her late middle age. That was what she could call it, since she was now past what another friend had called her late youth and well into her early middle age. It will be so much calmer, she said to Mitchell, because of the absence of sexual desire.

Absence? he said, and he seemed angry, although he was no older than she.

The lessening of sexual desire, then, she said. He looked dubious, as far as she could tell, though he was out of sorts that afternoon and had only looked either dubious or angry at everything she had said so far.

Then he answered, as though it was one thing he was sure of, while she was certainly not sure of it, that there would be more wisdom at that age. But think of the pain, he went on, or at best the problems with one's health, and he pointed to a couple in late middle age who were entering the park together, arm in arm. She had already been watching them.

Right now they are probably in pain, he said. It was true that although they were upright, they held on to each other too firmly and the footsteps of the man were tentative. Who knew what pain they might be suffering? She thought of all the people of late middle age and old age in the city whose pain was not always visible on their faces.

Yes, it was in old age that everything would break down. Her hearing would go. It was already going. She had to cup her hands around her ears in certain situations to distinguish words at all. She would have operations for cataracts on both eyes, and before that she would be able to see things only straight ahead in spots like coins, nothing to the sides. She would misplace things. She hoped she would still have the use of her legs.

She would go into the post office wearing a straw hat that sat too high up on her head. She would finish her business and make her way from the counter out past the line of people waiting that would include a little baby flat on its back in its carriage. She would spot the baby, smile a greedy, painful smile with a few teeth showing, say something out loud to the line of people, who would not respond, and go over to look at the baby.

She would be seventy-six, and she would have to lie down for a while because she had been talking and planned to talk again later in the evening. She was going to a party. She was going to the party only to make sure that certain people knew she was still alive. At the party, nearly everyone would avoid talking to her. No one would admire it when she drank too much.

She would have trouble sleeping, waking often in the night and staying awake early in the morning when it was still dark, feeling as alone in the world as she would ever feel. She would go out early and sometimes dig up a small plant from a neighbor's garden, looking first to see that her neighbor's blinds were down. When she sat in a train or a bus with her eyes fixed on the scenery outside the window, she would hum without stopping for an hour at a time in a high-pitched, quavering voice that sounded a little like a mosquito, so that people around her would become irritated. When she stopped humming, she would be asleep with her head tipped back and her mouth open.

But first there would be the slowing down, a little past the prime, when there would not be as much going on, not as much as there was now, when she wouldn't expect as much, not as much as she did now, when she either would or would not have achieved a certain position that was not likely to change, and best of all when she would have developed some fixed habits, so she would know they were going to sit out on the lawn after supper, for example, she and her husband, and read their books, in the long evenings of summer, her husband in shorts and she in a clean skirt and blouse with her bare feet up on the edge of his chair, and maybe even her mother or his mother there too, reading a book, and the mother would be twenty years older than she was, and therefore well into her old age, though still able to dig in the garden, and they would all dig in the garden together, and pick up leaves, or plan the garden together; they would stand under the sky on this little piece of ground here in the city, planning it out together, the way it should be, surrounding them as they sit in the evening on three folding chairs close together, reading and rarely saying a word.

But she was not looking forward only to that age, she said to Mitchell, when things would slow down and when she would have a husband who had slowed down too, she was also looking forward to a time about twenty years after that when she could wear any hat she wanted to and not care if she looked foolish, and wouldn't even have a husband to tell her she looked foolish.

Her friend Mitchell did not appear to understand her at all.

Though of course she knew it might be true that when the time came, a hat and that freedom would not make up for everything else she had lost with the coming of old age. And now that she had said this out loud, she thought maybe there was no joy, after all, in even thinking about such freedom.

The Sock

My husband is married to a different woman now, shorter than I am, about five feet tall, solidly built, and of course he looks taller than he used to and narrower, and his head looks smaller. Next to her I feel bony and awkward and she is too short for me to look her in the eye, though I try to stand or sit at the right angle to do that. I once had a clear idea of the sort of woman he should marry when he married again, but none of his girlfriends was quite what I had in mind and this one least of all.

They came out here last summer for a few weeks to see my son, who is his and mine. There were some touchy moments, but there were also some good times, though of course even the good times were a little uneasy. The two of them seemed to expect a lot of accommodation from me, maybe because she was sick—she was in pain and sulky, with circles under her eyes. They used my phone and other things in my house. They would walk up slowly from the beach to my house and shower there, and later walk away clean in the evening, with my son between them, hand in hand. I gave a party and they came and danced with each other, impressed my friends, and stayed till the end. I went out of my way for them, mostly because of our boy. I thought we should all get along for his sake. By the end of their visit I was tired.

The night before they went, we had a plan to eat out in a Vietnamese restaurant with his mother. His mother was flying in from another city, and then the three of them were going off together the next day, to the Midwest. His wife's parents were giving them a big wedding party so that all the people she had grown up with, the stout farmers and their families, could meet him.

When I went into the city that night to where they were staying, I took what they had left in my house that I had found so far: a book, next to the closet door, and somewhere else a sock of his. I drove up to the building and I saw my husband out on the sidewalk flagging me down. He wanted to talk to me before I went inside. He told me his mother was in bad shape and couldn't stay with them, and he asked me if I would please take her home with me later. Without thinking I said I would. I was forgetting the way she would look at the inside of my house and how I would clean the worst of it while she watched.

In the lobby, they were sitting across from each other in two armchairs, these two small women, both beautiful in different ways, both wearing heavy lipstick, different shades, both frail, I thought later, in different ways. The reason they were sitting here was that his mother was afraid to go upstairs. It didn't bother her to fly in an airplane, but she couldn't go up more than one story in an apartment building. It was worse now than it had been. In the old days she could be on the eighth floor if she had to, as long as the windows were tightly shut.

Before we went out to dinner my husband took the book up to the apartment, but he had stuck the sock in his back pocket without thinking when I gave it to him out on the street and it stayed there during the meal in the restaurant, where his mother sat in her black clothes at the end of the table opposite an empty chair, sometimes playing with my son, with his cars, and sometimes asking my husband and then me and then his wife questions about the peppercorns and other strong spices that might be in her food. Then after we all left the restaurant and were standing in the parking lot, he pulled the sock out of his pocket and looked at it, wondering how it had got there.

It was a small thing, but later I couldn't forget the sock, because there was this one sock in his back pocket in a strange neighborhood way out in the eastern part of the city in a Vietnamese ghetto, by the massage parlors, and none of us really knew this city but we were all here together and it was odd, because I still felt as though he and I were partners; we had been partners a long time, and I couldn't help thinking of all the other socks of his I had picked up, stiff with his sweat and threadbare on the sole, in all our life together from place to place, and then of his feet in those socks, how the skin shone through at the ball of the foot and the heel where the weave was worn down; how he would lie reading on his back on the bed with his feet crossed at the ankles so that his toes pointed at different corners of the room; how he would then turn on his side with his feet together like two halves of a fruit; how, still reading, he would reach down and pull off his socks and drop them in little balls on the floor and reach down again and pick at his toes while he read; sometimes he shared with me what he was reading and thinking, and sometimes he didn't know whether I was there in the room or somewhere else.

I couldn't forget it later, even though after they were gone I found a few other things they had left, or rather his wife had left them in the pocket of a jacket of mine—a red comb, a red lipstick, and a bottle of pills. For a while these things sat around in a little group of three on one counter of the kitchen and then another, while I thought I'd send them to her, because I thought maybe the medicine was important, but I kept forgetting to ask, until finally I put them away in a drawer to give her when they came out again, because by then it wasn't going to be long, and it made me tired all over again just to think of it.

Five Signs of Disturbance

Back in the city, she is alone most of the time. It is a large apartment that is not hers, though it is not unfamiliar either.

She spends the days by herself trying to work and sometimes looking up from her work to worry about how she will find a place to live, because she can't stay in this apartment beyond the end of the summer. Then, in the late afternoon, she begins to think she should call someone.

She is watching everything very closely: herself, this apartment, what is outside the windows, and the weather.

There is a day of thunderstorms, with dark yellow and green light in the street, and black light in the alley. She looks into the alley and sees foam running over the concrete, washed out from the gutters by the rain. Then there is a day of high wind.

Now she stands by the door watching the doorknob. The brass doorknob is moving by itself, very slightly, turning back and forth, then jiggling. She is startled, then she hears a foot shuffle on the other side of the doorsill, and a cloth brush against the panel, and other soft noises, and realizes after a moment that this is the doorman who has come to clean the outside of the door. But she does not go away until the doorknob stops moving.

She looks at the clock often and is aware of exactly what time it is now, and then ten minutes from now, even though she has no need to know what time it is. She also knows exactly how she is feeling, uneasy now, angry ten minutes from now. She is sick to death of knowing what she is feeling, but she can't stop, as though if she stops watching for longer than a moment, she will disappear (wander off).

There is a bright light coming from the kitchen. She did not turn a light on there. The light is coming from the open window (it is late summer). It is morning.

On another day, the early, low sun shines on the park across the street, on the near edge of it, so that one bare trunk, and the outer leaves of the trees on this side of the grove, are whitened with sunlight as though someone has thrown a handful of gray dust over them. Behind them, darkness.

Before her as she stands at the front window looking out at the park, the plants on the windowsill have dropped some of their leaves.

She knows that if she speaks on the telephone, her voice will communicate something no one will want to listen to. And she will have trouble making herself heard.

In the midst of the random noises from the courtyard (she catalogs them in the evening: the clatter of dishes, an electric guitar, a woman's laughter, a toilet flushing, a television, running water), suddenly a quarrel begins, between a man and his mother (he shouts in his deep voice, "Mother!").

She thinks, having come back after some years, that this is a place full of difficulty.

She watches a great deal of television, even though there is very little that she likes and she also has trouble focusing the picture. She watches anything that comes in clearly, even though she may find it offensive. One evening she watches one face in a movie for two hours and feels that her own face has changed. Then, the next night at the same hour, she is not watching television and she thinks: The hour may be the same but the night is not the same.

Later, when she lists and counts the signs of disturbance, at least two are associated with the television.

Now she can't put it off any longer. She has to go out and look for a place to live. She doesn't want to do this, because she doesn't want to say to herself that she really has no place of her own. She would rather do nothing about the problem and stay inside this apartment all day.

Several times she goes out to look at apartments. She can't afford to pay much, and so she looks at the very cheapest apartments. She looks at one above a candy store and one above an Italian men's social club. The third one she looks at is nothing but a shell with a large hole in the floor of the back room, and the garden is overgrown with brambles. The real-estate agent apologizes to her.

She is glad when it grows too late in the afternoon to look at anything more and she can go back to the apartment and watch television and eat and drink.

She often cries over what she sees on television. Usually it is something on the evening news, a death or many deaths somewhere, or an act of heroism, or a film of a newborn baby with a disease. But sometimes an ad, if it involves old people or children, will also make her cry. The younger the child is, the more easily she cries, but even a film of an adolescent will sometimes make her cry, though she does not like adolescents. Often, after the news is over, she is still catching her breath as she walks out to the kitchen.

She eats dinner in front of the television. After another hour or two she begins drinking. She drinks until she is drunk enough so that she drops things and her handwriting becomes hard to read and she leaves out some of the letters from certain words and has to read all the words over again carefully, adding the missing letters and after that printing some words a second time above the illegible script.

She is forgetting the idea she had about moderation.

She does the dishes so wildly that soap flies everywhere and water splashes on the floor and the front of her clothes. During the day she washes her hands often, rubbing them together briskly, almost violently, because she feels that everything she touches is coated with grease.

She stands by the door and hears someone whistling in the marble lobby.

One day she sees an apartment she is willing to take. It is not very pretty, but she is ready to take it because she wants to have a home again, she wants to be bound to this city by a lease, she doesn't want to go on feeling the way she does, loose in the world, the only one without any place. She imagines that when she moves in, she will have a party. She signs some papers. The agent will call her later and tell her whether the deal has gone through or not. She walks home and shops for food with a sort of forced tranquillity, as though if she moves too quickly something will break. She continues to move this way, gently, with deliberation, the rest of the day. Then, later in the evening, the agent calls and tells her she has lost the apartment. The owner has decided suddenly not to rent it. She can hardly believe this explanation.

Now she is sure she will never find a place to live.

She lies in bed with a bottle of beer. She finishes the

beer and wants to put it down. She can't put it on the bare wood of the bedside table because it will leave a mark, and the table is not hers. She puts it on a book, but the book is not hers either. She moves it to another book, which is hers, a songbook.

Then she gets up because she sees that the clothes she took off earlier are heaped on a chair. She wants to lay them out straight in case she decides to wear them the next day, and she lays them out, but since she is quite drunk they are not straight, as she can see. She is drunk because she has had two bottles of beer, a glass of Drambuie, and then a third bottle of beer.

In spite of being drunk, she can still hold on to some things in her mind, though with an effort. She sees how well she is holding on to things and thinks that she is still smart. She thinks about how her smartness doesn't seem to count for much anymore, the way it used to. Her smartness has counted for less and less as she has grown older. She lies there in the dark trying to pull herself together. She can feel this is a cliff edge, this return. Now it is after two in the morning, but she can't let herself fall asleep.

On the white side of a truck, a dark blue eagle with its wings raised. Watching for it, she sees, outside the window, the mail truck pull up by the hydrant. She sees the mailbag tossed out of the truck onto the sidewalk and the handyman of the building drag it across the sidewalk and then stand holding it by the neck while he talks to another handyman and she grows angry as she watches because there may be a letter for her in the bag.

She is told about an apartment in a nice small street, but she won't look at it because she is also told that on the floor below lives a retarded man and his father and they argue and shout and she would have to listen to that.

The day is dark again with the threat of rain. In the yellow light she sweeps up the dead leaves of the houseplants and waters the pots. On this day there is more order.

In the dining room she pushes upright the heavy books that have been leaning far over to one side on the shelves and sprawling open for so long now that their covers are warped out of shape. There is another bookcase in the living room, with glass doors, and on top of it a clock that hisses every time the second hand passes a certain point. Now she walks down the hall, straightening more books as she comes to them. The hall is long and dark, with many angles, so that around every bend more hallway opens out and this hallway seems to her, sometimes, infinitely long.

In the bedroom, where she watches television, she can often hear the sound of a string quartet or some other classical music. It is a small sound, but perfectly clear. When she first heard it, she wondered if there was a radio somewhere in the room, turned very low. She walked slowly around the room, listening. The walls of the room are dark, the windows are shaded, and there is a large low bureau of scratched green wood with a mirror above it into which she looks again and again, as she also looks into the three long mirrors on the three doors of the closet. The music was coming from the radiator, which stands below a framed photograph of a bearded man; he is the classicist whose books were falling over in the other room. She put her ear down near the radiator and found that the music was coming from the knob. Now she sometimes lies on the bed listening to the music. It is just low enough so that it doesn't stop her from thinking.

One day a fly walks over her hand and she feels that the fly is a friendly presence. The same day, she wants to stop a policeman in the street and talk to him. Then that impulse passes.

She decides to call several people. She tells herself she has to talk to some people. She is worried, and then she is angry at herself for worrying, for always thinking about herself and for always looking at the world so darkly. But she doesn't know how to stop.

She reads a book about Zen and she writes down on a piece of paper the eight parts of Buddha's eightfold path and thinks she might follow it. She sees that it mainly involves doing everything right.

Even though it is late enough to go to sleep she has something more to eat. Cereal, then, after the cereal, bread and butter, then marshmallows and other foods. She turns over onto her stomach and looks at the covers of some books. She can go on reading now without eating. Her stomach is so full that she can't lie on it comfortably, and she feels as though she were lying on a rock or a bundle of sticks. She has filled her stomach as though she were filling a knapsack or a boat for a long journey. It will be slow and hot, and she will wake and sleep again several times and have uncomfortable dreams, or there will be no sleep but hard questions. No tears, though.

The rain continues to fall steadily just beyond the sound of an air conditioner. It is a soft drumming with an occasional louder splat into the courtyard.

She can't fall asleep. She lies with her ear on the mattress and listens to her loud heartbeat, first the rush of blood from her heart, which she can feel, then a split second later the thump in her ear. The sound is *shethump, shethump*. Then she starts to fall asleep and wakes again when she begins dreaming that her heart is a police station.

Another night it is her lungs; she shuts her eyes and her lungs seem as large as the room, and as dark, and enclosed in a fragile shell of bone, and in one dark lung she is crouching and the wind whistles around her, in and out.

Some things in her behavior now strike her as odd. Then something happens that should frighten her, but she is not frightened.

The way it happens: at the end of the day she turns on the news and immediately she is addressed eye to eye, with almost unbearable intensity, by a male newscaster. He is the first person who has spoken to her all day. Shaken by these few minutes of direct address, she goes out to the kitchen to make an omelet. She mixes the eggs and pours them into the pan, where the butter is beginning to burn. As the omelet forms, it bubbles and chatters, making its own violent kind of noise, and she suddenly thinks it is going to speak to her. Bright yellow, glistening, spotted with oil, it is heaving gently and subsiding in the pan.

Or rather, she doesn't expect the omelet to speak, but when it doesn't articulate something she is surprised. But when she later thinks of what happened, she sees that really she suffered something like a physical assault. The muteness of the omelet emanated from it in a large balloon and pressed against her eardrums.

But it is not this incident, but the very latest sign of disturbance, on the highway, that frightens her enough to make her list and count up the signs of disturbance, though even then she cannot always decide whether what seems to her a sign of disturbance should be counted as such, since it is fairly normal for her, such as talking aloud to herself or eating too much, or whether it should be counted because to someone else it might seem at least somewhat abnormal, and so, after thinking of ten or eleven signs, she wavers between counting five and seven signs as real signs of disturbance and finally settles on five, partly because she cannot accept the idea that there could be as many as seven.

She hopes this is all just the effect of exhaustion. She thinks it will end when she finds a place to live. She will not care very much what sort of place it is, not at first, anyway. Now there are two choices: a light and roomy apartment in a neighborhood she thinks is dangerous, or a cramped and noisy railroad flat in a part of town she likes.

What happened was that coming up to a line of tollbooths on the highway, she had three quarters in her hand. The toll was fifty cents so she had to keep two quarters in her hand and put one back. The problem was that she couldn't decide which one to put back. She kept looking down at the quarters and then up again, trying to drive at the same time, coming closer and closer to the tollbooths, veering left toward the center as though she knew that she might have to stop. Each time she looked down at them, the three quarters separated into groups of one quarter and two quarters, but each time she was prepared to put one back it appeared to her as one of a pair, so that she couldn't put it back. This happened over and over again as she rolled closer to the booths, until finally, against her will, she put one quarter back. She told herself the choice was arbitrary, but she felt strongly that it was not. She felt that it was in fact governed by an important rule, though she did not know what the rule was.

She was frightened, not only because she had violated something but because this was not the first time she had for some minutes lost the capacity to act. And because although she had managed, in the end, to put one quarter back, drive up to the tollbooth, pay the toll, and go on where she was going, she might just as well not have been able to make any move and might have stopped the car in the center of the highway and remained there indefinitely.

And further, if she had not been able to make a decision

about this one small thing, as she might not have, then she might not be able to make a decision about anything else either, because all day long there were such decisions to make, as whether to go into this room or that room, to walk down the street in this direction or the other, to leave the subway by this exit or that one. There were many ways of reasoning through every decision, and often she could not even decide which way to reason, let alone make the decision itself. And so, in this way, she might become entirely paralyzed and unable to go on with her life.

But later that day, as she stands waist high in the water, she thinks that she is right: all this is probably nothing but exhaustion. She is standing without her glasses waist high in the water on a rocky beach. She is waiting for some sort of revelation, because she feels a revelation coming, but although various other thoughts have come, not one of them seems much like a revelation to her.

She stands looking full into the gray waves that come at her crossed by a strong breeze so that they have hard facets like rocks, and she feels her eyes washed by the grayness of the water. She knows it is the greater disruption of her life that is disturbing her, not just the homelessness, but finding a home will help. She thinks that all this will probably come out all right, that it won't end badly. Then she looks out at the smokestacks far away and nearly invisible across the sound and thinks, though, that this was not the revelation she was waiting for either.

ALMOST NO MEMORY

(1997)

Meat, My Husband

My husband's favorite food, in childhood, was corned beef. I found this out yesterday when friends came over and we started talking about food. At some point they asked what our favorite childhood foods had been. I couldn't think of any, but my husband didn't have to think before answering.

"Corned beef," he said.

"Corned beef with an egg on it!" one of our friends added.

My husband often ate in diners before we met. He had two he liked, but he preferred the one where they did a particularly good hot roast beef sandwich. He still likes a good piece of roast beef, or steak, or hamburger mixed with sauce and spices and grilled outdoors with brochettes of onions and peppers.

But I'm the one who cooks most of his meals now. Often I make him meals with no meat in them at all because I don't think meat is good for us. Often there is no seafood in them either, because most seafood isn't good for us either, and there is almost never any fish in them, partly because I can't remember which sorts of fish may be safe to eat and which are almost certainly not, but mainly because he likes fish only when it's served in a restaurant or cooked in such a way that he can't tell it's fish. Often there is no cheese in our meals either, because of the problem with fat. I'll make him a brown-rice casserole, for example, or winter vegetables with parsley sauce, or turnip soup with turnip greens, or white bean and eggplant gratin, or polenta with spicy vegetables.

"Why don't you make the foods I like?" he asks sometimes.

"Why don't you like the foods I make?" I answer.

Once I marinated slabs of tofu in tamari sauce, champagne vinegar, red wine, toasted marjoram, and dried Chinese mushrooms simmered in water. I marinated them for four or five days and then served them to him, sliced thin, in a sandwich with horseradish and mayonnaise, slices of red onion, lettuce and tomato. First he said the tofu was still very bland, which is what he always says about tofu, then he said that on the other hand, if he hadn't known it was there, he wouldn't have been able to taste the tofu anyway because there were so many other things in the sandwich. He said it was all right, and then he said he knew tofu was good for him.

Sometimes he likes what I make, and if he's in a good mood he says so. Once I made him a cucumber salad with feta cheese and red onion and he liked it, saying it tasted Greek. Another time I made him a lentil salad with peppers and mint and he liked that, too, though he said it tasted like dirt.

But generally he doesn't like what I cook as much as what he used to eat in diners and certainly not as much as what he used to make for himself before he met me.

For instance, he used to make a roulade of beef cooked in a Marsala sauce. He would take thin slices of top round or sirloin, dust them with flour, coat one side with crushed dill seeds, roll them around cooked Italian sausage meat, and pierce them with a toothpick. Then he would sauté them in butter and simmer them in a brown Marsala sauce with mushrooms. He would also make roulades of veal stuffed with prosciutto and Gruyère. Another favorite was a meat loaf of veal, pork, and sirloin. It would contain garlic, rosemary, two eggs, and whole-wheat bread crumbs. He would lay smoked bacon underneath it and on top of it.

Now the loaf I make for him is of ground turkey. It, too, has mushrooms, fresh whole-wheat bread crumbs and garlic in it, but in other ways it is not the same. I make it with one egg, celery, leeks, sweet red peppers, salt and pepper, and a dash of nutmeg.

Outdoors on the deck, he eats it and says nothing, gazing over the water past the willow tree. He is calm and contemplative. I don't think he's calm because I'm feeding him so much less meat, but because he is teaching himself to accept what I do. He doesn't like it but knows that I believe I'm doing it for his own good.

When he says nothing about the turkey loaf, I question him, and when I press him to answer, he says that it's all right but he's not excited about it. He excuses himself by saying that in general he's not very excited about food. I disagree, because I have seen him excited about food, though almost never about what I serve him. In fact, I can remember only one occasion on which he was excited by what I served him.

It was the night I made polenta and spicy vegetables for our dinner, though that was not what excited him. The polenta, spreading in a thick ocher circle under the heap of reddish-brown vegetables, looked strange and reminded us both of a cow patty. When he had eaten some of it, though, my husband said it tasted better than it looked, something he has said before about other meals of mine. The cookbook had suggested a certain dessert to follow: a ripe pear, chilled, with walnuts. As we sat down to our meal, I told my husband what I was planning for dessert, though I was not going to bother chilling the pear.

That's one of my problems as a cook—that I don't bother to do each thing the way it should be done. I don't seem to understand the importance of detail, in cooking. My husband does, and when I told him my plan for dessert, he got right up from the table and put the pear in the freezer to chill.

When we came to eat the pear and the walnuts, the contrast between the cool, juicy sweetness of the fruit and the warmer, oily fragrance of the nuts certainly excited my husband, enough for him to imagine other desserts of fruit—poached figs with ginger, apricot fritters, and sliced blood oranges with pecans. Certainly he was more excited about this dessert than he had been about anything else I had served him. But then he was the one who had put the pear in the freezer, and I've learned by now that when he's involved in preparing a meal, or anything else for that matter, he's more apt to like it.

Jack in the Country

Henry encounters Jack on the street and asks how his weekend with Laura was. Jack says he hasn't spoken to Laura in at least a month. Henry is angry. He thinks Ellen has been lying to him about Laura. Ellen says she has been telling the truth: Laura told her over the phone that Jack was coming for the weekend to her house up there in the country. Henry is still angry, but now he is angry because he thinks Laura was lying to Ellen when she told her Jack was coming up for the weekend. At this point, with embarrassment, Ellen realizes her mistake: more than one Jack is involved here. Laura said only that Jack was coming to visit her for the weekend, and it was not the Jack that Ellen and Henry know but the Jack that only Ellen knows, and only slightly, who was about to arrive at Laura's house in the country. With some misgiving, she explains this to Henry. Now Henry is even angrier than before, but he is angry because Laura has been seeing a Jack he does not know instead of the Jack he knows. He is angry because the Jack he knows is an old friend of Laura's, whereas the Jack he does not know must be a new lover. Henry declares he will not speak to Laura again except to ask her to send back his keys. He will take her name out of his address book and refuse to hear any further mention of her from Ellen of the Jack he knows. Henry cannot know, since he will not speak to Laura, that in fact a third Jack has become involved in this story, to the distress of the second Jack, for Laura's affections have already strayed from the Jack that Ellen knows only slightly and that Henry does not know, and fastened on a Jack in the country unknown to them all.

Foucault and Pencil

Sat down to read Foucault with pencil in hand. Knocked over glass of water onto waiting-room floor. Put down Foucault and pencil, mopped up water, refilled glass. Sat down to read Foucault with pencil in hand. Stopped to write note in notebook. Took up Foucault with pencil in hand. Counselor beckoned from doorway. Put away Foucault and pencil as well as notebook and pen. Sat with counselor discussing situation fraught with conflict taking form of many heated arguments. Counselor pointed to danger, raised red flag. Left counselor, went to subway. Sat in subway car, took out Foucault and pencil but did not read, thought instead about situation fraught with conflict, red flag, recent argument concerning travel: argument itself became form of travel, each sentence carrying arguers on to next sentence, next sentence on to next, and in the end, arguers were not where they had started, were also tired from traveling and spending so long face-to-face in each other's company. After several stations on subway thinking about argument, stopped thinking and opened Foucault. Found Foucault, in French, hard to understand. Short sentences easier to understand than long ones. Certain long ones understandable part by part, but so long, forgot beginning before reaching end. Went back to beginning, understood beginning, read on, and again forgot beginning before reaching end. Read on without going back and without understanding, without remembering, and without learning, pencil idle in hand. Came to sentence that was clear, made pencil mark in margin. Mark indicated understanding, indicated forward progress in book. Lifted eyes from Foucault, looked at other passengers. Took out notebook and pen to make note about passengers, made accidental mark with pencil in margin of Foucault, put down notebook, erased mark. Returned thoughts to argument. Argument not only like vehicle, carried arguers forward, but also like plant, grew like hedge, surrounding arguers at first thinly, some light coming through, then more thickly, keeping light out, or darkening light. By argument's end, arguers could not leave hedge, could not leave each other, and light was dim. Thought of question to ask about argument, took out notebook and pen and wrote down. Put away notebook and returned to Foucault. Understood more clearly at which points Foucault harder to understand and at which points easier: harder to understand when sentence was long and noun identifying subject of sentence was left back at beginning, replaced by male or female pronoun, when forgot what noun pronoun replaced and had only pronoun for company traveling through sentence. Sometimes pronoun then giving way in midsentence to new noun, new noun in turn replaced by new pronoun which then continued on to end of sentence. Also harder to understand when subject of sentence was noun like *thought*, *absence*, *law*; easier to understand when subject was noun like *beach*, *wave*, *sand*, *santorium*, *pension*, *door*, *hallway*, or *civil servant*. Before and after sentence about sand, civil servant, or pension, however, came sentence about attraction, neglect, emptiness, absence, or law, so parts of book understood were separated by parts not understood. Put down Foucault and pencil, took out notebook and made note of what was now at least understood about lack of understanding reading Foucault, looked up at other passengers, thought again about argument, made note of same question about argument as before though with stress on different word.

The Mice

Mice live in our walls but do not trouble our kitchen. We are pleased but cannot understand why they do not come into our kitchen, where we have traps set, as they come into the kitchens of our neighbors. Although we are pleased, we are also upset, because the mice behave as though there were something wrong with our kitchen. What makes this even more puzzling is that our house is much less tidy than the houses of our neighbors. There is more food lying about in our kitchen, more crumbs on the counters and filthy scraps of onion kicked against the base of the cabinets. In fact, there is so much loose food in the kitchen I can only think the mice themselves are defeated by it. In a tidy kitchen, it is a challenge for them to find enough food night after night to survive until spring. They patiently hunt and nibble hour after hour until they are satisfied. In our kitchen, however, they are faced with something so out of proportion to their experience that they cannot deal with it. They might venture out a few steps, but soon the overwhelming sights and smells drive them back into their holes, uncomfortable and embarrassed at not being able to scavenge as they should.

The Thirteenth Woman

In a town of twelve women there was a thirteenth. No one admitted she lived there, no mail came for her, no one spoke of her, no one asked after her, no one sold bread to her, no one bought anything from her, no one returned her glance, no one knocked on her door; the rain did not fall on her, the sun never shone on her, the day never dawned on her, the night never fell for her; for her the weeks did not pass, the years did not roll by; her house was unnumbered, her garden untended, her path not trod upon, her bed not slept in, her food not eaten, her clothes not worn; and yet in spite of all this she continued to live in the town without resenting what it did to her.

The Professor

A few years ago, I used to tell myself I wanted to marry a cowboy. Why shouldn't I say this to myself—living alone, excited by the brown landscape, sometimes noticing a cowboy in a pickup truck in my rearview mirror, as I drove on the broad highways of the West Coast? In fact, I realize I would still like to marry a cowboy, though by now I'm living in the East and married already to someone who is not a cowboy.

But what would a cowboy want with a woman like me—an English professor, the daughter of another English professor, not very easygoing? If I have a drink or two, I'm more easygoing, but I still speak correctly and don't know how to joke with people unless I know them well, and often these are university people or the people they live with, who also speak correctly. Although I don't mind them, I feel cut off from all the other people in this country—to mention only this country.

I told myself I liked the way cowboys dressed, starting with the hat, and how comfortable they were in their clothes, so practical, having to do with their work. Many professors seem to dress the way they think a professor should dress, without any real interest or love. Their clothes are too tight or else a few years out of style and just add to the awkwardness of their bodies.

After I was hired to teach for the first time, I bought a briefcase, and then after I started teaching I carried it through the halls like the other professors. I could see that the older professors, mostly men but also some women, were no longer aware of the importance of their briefcases, and that the younger women pretended they weren't aware of it, but the younger men carried their briefcases like trophies.

At that same time, my father began sending me thick envelopes containing material he thought would help me in my classes, including exercises to assign and quotes to use. I didn't read more than a few pages sometimes when I was feeling strong. How could an old professor try to teach a young professor? Didn't he know I wouldn't be able to carry my briefcase through the halls and say hello to my colleagues and students and then go home and read the instructions of the old professor?

In fact, I liked teaching because I liked telling other people what to do. In those days it seemed clearer to me than it does now that if I did something a certain way, it had to be right for other people, too. I was so convinced of it that my students were convinced, too. Still, though I was a teacher outside, I was something else inside. Some of the old professors were also old professors inside, but inside, I wasn't even a young professor. I looked like a woman in glasses, but I had dreams of leading a very different kind of life, the life of a woman who would not wear glasses, the kind of woman I saw from a distance now and then in a bar.

More important than the clothes a cowboy wore, and the way he wore them, was the fact that a cowboy probably wouldn't know much more than he had to. He would think about his work, and about his family, if he had one, and about having a good time, and not much else. I was tired of so much thinking, which was what I did most in those days. I did other things, but I went on thinking while I did them. I might feel something, but I would think about what I was feeling at the same time. I even had to think about what I was thinking and wonder why I was thinking it. When I had the idea of marrying a cowboy I imagined that maybe a cowboy would help me stop thinking so much.

I also imagined, though I was probably wrong about this, too, that a cowboy wouldn't be like anyone I knew—like an old Communist, or a member of a steering committee, a writer of letters to the newspaper, a faculty wife serving tea at a student tea, a professor reading proofs with a sharp pencil and asking everyone to be quiet. I thought that when my mind, always so busy, always going around in circles, always having an idea and then an idea about an idea, reached out to his mind, it would meet something quieter, that there would be more blanks, more open spaces, that some of what he had in his mind might be the sky, clouds, hilltops, and then other concrete things like ropes, saddles, horsehair, the smell of horses and cattle, motor oil, calluses, grease, fences, gullies, dry streambeds, lame cows, stillborn calves, freak calves, veterinarians' visits, treatments, inoculations. I imagined this even though I knew that some of the things I liked that might be in his mind, like the saddles, the saddle sores, the horsehair, and the horses themselves, weren't often a part of the life of a cowboy anymore. As for what I would do in my life with this cowboy, I sometimes imagined myself reading quietly in clean clothes in a nice study, but at other times I imagined myself oiling tack or cooking large quantities of plain food or helping out in the barn in the early morning while the cowboy had both arms inside a cow to turn a calf so it would present properly. Problems and chores like these would be clear and I would be able to handle them in a clear way. I wouldn't stop reading and thinking, but I wouldn't know very many people who did a lot of that, so I would have more privacy in it, because the cowboy, though so close to me all the time, wouldn't try to understand but would leave me alone with it. It would not be an embarrassment anymore.

I thought if I married a cowboy, I wouldn't have to leave the West. I liked the West for its difficulties. First I liked the difficulty of telling when one season was over and another had begun, and then I liked the difficulty of finding any beauty in the landscape where I was. To begin with, I had gotten used to its own kind of ugliness, all those broad highways laid down in the valleys and the new constructions placed up on the bare hillsides. Then I began to find beauty in it, and liked the bareness and the plain brown of the hills in the dry season, and the way the folds in the hills where some dampness tended to linger would fill up with grasses and shrubs and other flowering plants. I liked the plainness of the ocean and the emptiness when I looked out over it. And then, especially since it had been so hard for me to find this beauty, I didn't want to leave it.

I might have gotten the idea of marrying a cowboy from a movie I saw one night in the springtime with a friend of mine who was also a professor—a handsome and intelligent man kinder than I am, but even more awkward around people, forgetting even the names of old friends in his sudden attacks of shyness. He seemed to enjoy the movie, though I have no idea what was going through his mind. Maybe he was imagining a life with the woman in the movie, who was so different from his thin, nervous, and beautiful wife. As we drove away from the movie theater, on one of those broad highways with nothing ahead or behind but taillights and headlights and nothing on either side but darkness, all I wanted to do was go out into the middle of the desert, as far away as possible from everything I had known all my life, and from the university where I was teaching and the towns and the city near it with all the intelligent people who lived and worked in them, writing down their ideas in notebooks and on computers in their offices and their studies at home and taking notes from difficult books. I wanted to leave all this and go out into the middle of the desert and run a motel by myself with a little boy, and have a worn-out cowboy come along, a worn-out middle-aged cowboy, alcoholic if necessary, and marry him. I thought I knew of a little boy I could take with me. Then all I would need would be the aging cowboy and the motel. I would make it a good motel, I would look after it and I would solve any problems sensibly and right away as they came along. I thought I could be a good, tough businesswoman just because I had seen this movie showing this good, tough businesswoman. This woman also had a loving heart and a capacity to understand another fallible human being. The fact is that if an alcoholic cowboy came into my life in any important way I would probably criticize him to death for his drinking until he walked out on me. But at the time I had that strange confidence, born of watching a good movie, that I could be something different from what I was, and I started listening to country-western music on the car radio, though I knew it wasn't written for me.

At that point I met a man in one of my classes who

seemed reasonably close to my idea of a cowboy, though now I can't tell exactly why I thought so. He wasn't really like a cowboy, or what I thought a cowboy might be like, so what I wanted must have been something else, and the idea of a cowboy just came up in my mind for the sake of convenience. The facts weren't right. He didn't work as a cowboy but at some kind of job where he glued the bones of chimpanzees together. He played jazz trombone, and on the days when he had a lesson he wore a dark suit to class and carried a black case. He just missed being good-looking, with his square, fleshy, pale face, his dark hair, mustache, dark eyes; just missed being good-looking, not because of his rough cheeks, which were scarred from shrapnel, but because of a loose or wild look about him, his eyes wide open all the time, even when he smiled, and his body very still, only his eyes moving, watching everything, missing nothing. Wary, he was ready to defend himself as though every conversation might also be something of a fight.

One day when a group of us were having a beer together after class, he was quiet, seemed very low, and finally said to us, without raising his eyes, that he thought he might be going to move in with his father and send his little girl back to her mother. He said he didn't think it was fair to keep her because sometimes he would just sit in a chair without speaking—she would try to talk to him and he wouldn't be able to open his mouth, she would keep on trying and he would sit there knowing he had to answer her but unable to.

His rudeness and wildness were comfortable to me at that point, and because he would tease me now and then, I thought he liked me enough so that I could ask him to go out to dinner with me, and finally I did, just to see what would happen. He seemed startled, then pleased to accept, sobered and flattered at this attention from his professor.

The date didn't turn out to be something that would change the direction of my life, though that's not what I was expecting then, only what I thought about afterwards. He was very late coming to pick me up at the graduate-student housing compound where I was staying. Just when I had decided he wasn't coming, after I had spent an hour pacing more and more hopelessly out onto my tiny tree-shaded balcony, which overlooked a playground and the parking lot, and back into my tiny living room, which was crowded with the things of some young couple I didn't know, he came in wearing an old work shirt with the sleeves rolled up and brown corduroys with the cord worn off on the thighs. He stopped and looked around as though he were about to get to work on something, then spotted the piano and bent over it for a moment and played a fast, pretty tune just long enough to make me happy again, then broke it off in the middle.

I was very curious about him, as though everything that added itself to what I knew already would be a revelation. When we got into the car he reached across me and unlocked the glove compartment and when we prepared to get out he reached across me and locked it again. I asked him why he did that, and he lifted up a bundle of papers in the glove compartment and showed me the wooden butt of a gun. He told me a couple of men were after him, and that it had something to do with his little girl.

We parked near the restaurant, he took a gray jacket off a hanger in the car and put it over his arm, and as we walked along he tucked in his shirt and then put on the jacket. I thought to myself this was how a cowboy might do it—carry his gray suit in the car on a hanger, and when he neatened up to go into some place with a woman he would also touch his hair gently.

He drank milk with his Chinese dinner. He talked about his job, offering me pieces of scientific information, and then told some bad jokes. We didn't either of us eat very much, embarrassed, I think, to be alone together like this. He told me that he had married his wife right after he got back from the war. She was half Chinese and half Mexican. He told me his hearing had been damaged in the war and I noticed that he watched my lips as I talked. He told me his balance had been affected, too, and outside the restaurant I noticed how he would veer toward the curb when he walked. He drank milk in the restaurant but beer in the bar where we went to play pool. He put his arm around me outside the bar, but back in the car he said he had to get home to his babysitter. Then he changed his mind and took me to a spot on a cliff that looked out over the ocean and kissed me. Other cars were parked around us, and a pickup truck.

He kissed me a number of times there in his old maroon Ford with the radio on, so that I could have imagined I was a teenager again except that when I was a teenager I had never done anything like that. Then we got out of the car and went to the edge of the cliff to look down at the ocean, the black water of the bay, and the strings of lights that reached out into the water from the town where we had been playing pool. We sat down on the sand not far from the edge of the cliff and he told me a little more about how hard it had been with his wife, how he had tried to get back together with her, how he had done his best to charm her and she wouldn't be charmed. He told me he had been alone with his little girl for six months now, and his wife was coming home in a few days to try living with him again, even though nothing he did had ever worked. He said he wouldn't be able to see me again. I told him I wasn't expecting that anyway, because I was leaving the West soon. It wasn't quite true that I hadn't expected to see him again, but it was true that I was leaving soon. Finally he took me home and kissed me good night.

As far as I could tell, I didn't mind the way the date turned out, though I started crying the next day in my car on my way to the drive-in bank. I thought I was crying for him, his fears, his difficulties, the mysterious men he thought were after him and his daughter, but I was probably crying for myself, out of disappointment, though exactly what I wanted I'm not sure. Months later, after I was living in the East again, I called him long-distance one night after having a couple of beers by myself in my apartment, and when he answered there was noise in the background of people talking and laughing, either his family or a party, I can't remember which, and he sounded just as pleased to hear from me, and flattered, as he had sounded when I asked him out on the date.

I still imagine marrying a cowboy, though less often, and the dream has changed a little. I'm so used to the companionship of my husband by now that if I were to marry a cowboy I would want to take him with me, though he would object strongly to any move in the direction of the West, which he dislikes. So if we went, it would not be as it was in my daydream a few years ago, with me cooking plain food or helping the cowboy with a difficult calf. It would end, or begin, with my husband and me standing awkwardly there in front of the ranch house, waiting while the cowboy prepared our rooms.

The Cedar Trees

When our women had all turned into cedar trees they would group together in a corner of the graveyard and moan in the high wind. At first, with our wives gone, our spirits rose and we all thought the sound was beautiful. But then we ceased to be aware of it, grew uneasy, and quarreled more often among ourselves.

That was during the year of high winds. Never before had such tumult raged in our village. Sparrows could not fly, but swerved and dropped into calm corners; clay tiles tumbled from the roofs and shattered on the pavement. Shrubbery whipped our low windows. Night after night we drank insanely and fell asleep in one another's arms.

When spring came, the winds died down and the sun was bright. At evening, long shadows fell across our floors, and only the glint of a knife blade could survive the darkness. And the darkness fell across our spirits, too. We no longer had a kind word for anyone. We went to our fields grudgingly. Silently we stared at the strangers who came to see our fountain and our church: we leaned against the lip of the fountain, our boots crossed, our maimed dogs shying away from us.

Then the road fell into disrepair. No strangers came.

Even the traveling priest no longer dared enter the village, though the sun blazed in the water of the fountain, the valley far below was white with flowering fruit and nut trees, and the heat seeped into the pink stones of the church at noon and ebbed out at dusk. Cats paced silently over the beaten dirt, from doorway to doorway. Birds sang in the woods behind us. We waited in vain for visitors, hunger gnawing at our stomachs.

At last, somewhere deep in the heart of the cedar trees, our wives stirred and thought of us. And lazily, it seemed to us, carelessly, returned home. We looked on their mean lips, their hard eyes, and our hearts melted. We drank in the sound of their harsh voices like men coming out of the desert.

The Cats in the Prison Recreation Hall

The problem was the cats in the prison recreation hall. There were feces everywhere. The feces of a cat try to hide in a corner and when discovered look angry and ashamed like a monkey.

The cats stayed in the prison recreation hall when it rained, and since it rained often, the hall smelled bad and the prisoners grumbled. The smell did not come from the feces but from the animals themselves. It was a strong smell, a dizzying smell.

The cats could not be driven away. When shooed, they did not flee out the door but scattered in all directions, running low, their bellies hanging. Many went upward, leaping from beam to beam and resting somewhere high above, so that the prisoners playing Ping-Pong were aware that although the dome was silent, it was not empty.

The cats could not be driven away because they entered and left the hall through holes that could not be discovered. Their steps were silent; they could wait for a person longer than a person would wait for them.

A person has other concerns, but at each moment in its life, a cat has only one concern. This is what gives it such perfect balance, and this is why the spectacle of a confused or frightened cat upsets us: we feel both pity and the desire to laugh. It faces the source of danger or confusion and its only recourse is to spit a foul breath out between its mottled gums.

The prisoners were all small men that year. They had committed crimes that could not be taken very seriously and they were treated with leniency. Now, although small men are often inclined to take pride in their good health, these prisoners began to develop rashes and eczemas. The backs of their knees and the insides of their elbows stung and their skin flaked all over. They wrote angry letters to the governor of their state, who also happened to be a small man that year. The cats, they said, were causing reactions.

The governor took pity on the prisoners and asked the warden to take care of the problem.

The warden had not been inside the hall in years. He entered it and wandered around, sickened by the curious smell.

In the dead end of a corridor, he cornered an ugly tomcat. The warden was carrying a stick and the cat was armed only with its teeth and claws, besides its angry face. The warden and the cat dodged back and forth for a time, the warden struck out at the cat, and the cat streaked around him and away, making no false moves.

Now the warden saw cats everywhere.

After the evening activities, when the prisoners had been shut up in their cell blocks, the warden returned carrying a rifle. All night long, that night, the prisoners heard the sound of shots coming from the hall. The shots were muffled and seemed to come from a great distance, as though from across the river. The warden was a good shot and killed many cats—cats rained down on him from the dome, cats flipped over and over in the hallways—and yet he still saw shadows flitting by the basement windows as he left the building.

There was a difference now, however. The prisoners' skin condition cleared. Though the bad smell still hung about the building, it was not warm and fresh as it had been. A few cats still lived there, but they had been disoriented by the odors of gunpowder and blood and by the sudden disappearance of their mates and kittens. They stopped breeding and skulked in corners, hissing even when no one was anywhere near them, attacking without provocation any moving thing.

These cats did not eat well and did not clean themselves carefully, and one by one, each in its own way and in its own time died, leaving behind it a different strong smell that hung in the air for a week or two and then dissipated. After some months, there were no cats left in the prison recreation hall. By then, the small prisoners had been succeeded by larger prisoners, and the warden had been replaced by another, more ambitious; only the governor remained in office.

Wife One in Country

Wife one calls to speak to son. Wife two answers with impatience, gives phone to son of wife one. Son has heard impatience in voice of wife two and tells mother he thought caller was father's sister: raging aunt, constant caller, troublesome woman. Wife one wonders: is she herself perhaps another raging woman, constant caller? No, raging woman but not constant caller. Though, for wife two, also troublesome woman.

After speaking to son, much disturbance in wife one. Wife one misses son, thinks how some years ago she, too, answered phone and talked to husband's raging sister, constant caller, protecting husband from troublesome woman. Now wife two protects husband from troublesome sister, constant caller, and also from wife one, raging woman. Wife one sees this and imagines future wife three protecting husband not only from raging wife one but also from troublesome wife two, as well as constantly calling sister.

After speaking to son, wife one, often raging though now quiet woman, eats dinner alone though in company of large television. Wife one swallows food, swallows pain, swallows food again. Watches intently ad about easy-to-clean stove: mother who is not real mother flips fried egg onto hot burner, then fries second egg and gives cheerful young son who is not real son loving kiss as spaniel who is not real family dog steals second fried egg off plate of son who is not real son. Pain increases in wife one, wife one swallows food, swallows pain, swallows food again, swallows pain again, swallows food again.

The Fish Tank

I stare at four fish in a tank in the supermarket. They are swimming in parallel formation against a small current created by a jet of water, and they are opening and closing their mouths and staring off into the distance with the one eye, each, that I can see. As I watch them through the glass, thinking how fresh they would be to eat, still alive now, and calculating whether I might buy one to cook for dinner, I also see, as though behind or through them, a larger, shadowy form darkening their tank, what there is of me on the glass, their predator.

The Center of the Story

A woman has written a story that has a hurricane in it, and a hurricane usually promises to be interesting. But in this story the hurricane threatens the city without actually striking it. The story is flat and even, just as the earth seems flat and even when a hurricane is advancing over it, and if she were to show it to a friend, the friend would probably say that, unlike a hurricane, this story has no center.

It was not an easy story to write, because it was about religion, and religion was not something she really wanted to write about. Something, though, made her want to write this story. Now that it is finished, it puzzles her, and there is a peculiar yellow pall over it, either because of the religion or because of the light in the sky before the hurricane.

She can't think where the center of the story might be.

She was reading the Bible in a time of hurricane, not because she was afraid of a major disaster, though she was afraid, or because these days also happened to be the High Holy Days, but because she needed to know exactly what was in it. She read slowly and took many notes. Outside her apartment, the weather was changing: the wind rose, the branches swayed on the young trees, and the leaves fluttered. She read about Noah and the Ark and tried to picture very exactly what she read, the better to understand it: a man hundreds of years old trying to walk and give directions to his family, the mud covering the earth after the flood receded, the stink of rot, and then the sacrifice of animals and the stink of burning hair, fur, and horn.

She did little else but read the Bible for several days, and she looked out the window often and listened to the news. Certainly the Bible and the hurricane belong in the story, though whether at the center or not she does not know. She had started the story with her landlady. Her landlady, an old woman from Trinidad, was alone in the downstairs hall talking quietly about the mayor, while she was upstairs, thinking of writing a letter to the president. Her landlady said the red carpet remnant on the hall floor was given to her by her friend the mayor. She will probably take out the president and the landlady, but leave in the Bible and the hurricane. Perhaps if she takes out things that are not interesting, or do not belong in the story for other reasons, this will give it more of a center, since as soon as there is less in a story, more of it must be in the center.

In another part of the story, a man is very ill and thinks he is dying. He was not dying, he had eaten something that poisoned him and drunk too much on top of it, but he thought he was dying, and telephoned her to come help him. This was at the very moment the hurricane was supposed to strike the city, and some of the windows in the neighborhoods between her house and his were covered with tape in the shape of asterisks. In his room, the blinds were drawn, the light was yellow, and the windows rattled. He lay on his back in bed with a hand on his bare chest. His face was gray.

It is unclear what his place is, in the story. Certainly his illness has little connection with the rest of the story except that it overcame him at the height of the hurricane. But then he also told her something on the phone about blasphemy. He had recently blasphemed in a dreadful way, he said, by committing a certain forbidden act on a Holy Day. What he realized as he did it, he said, was that for complicated reasons he was trying to hurt God, and if he was trying to hurt God he must believe in Him. He had experienced the truth of what he had been taught long ago, that blasphemy proved one's belief in God.

This man, his illness, his fear for his life, and the blasphemy that had caused his illness, as he probably thought, and also something else he said about God that she remembered later, riding a train out of the city, could be at the center of the story, with the Bible and the hurricane at the edge of it, but there may not be enough to tell about him for him to be the center, or this may be the wrong time to tell it.

So there is the hurricane that did not strike the city but cast a yellow light over it, and there is this man, and there is the Bible, but no landlady, no president, and no newscasters, though she watched the news several times a day, every day, to see what the hurricane was going to do. The newscasters would tell her to look out the window and she would look. They would tell her that at that very moment, because the sun had just set, rams' horns were being blown all over the city, and she would be excited, even though she could not hear any rams' horns in her neighborhood. But though the newscasters serve to hold the story together from one day to the next, they are not in themselves very interesting and certainly not central to a story that has trouble finding its center.

In those days she also visited churches and synagogues.

The last church she visited was a Baptist congregation in the north of the city. There, large black women in white uniforms asked her to sit down but she was too nervous to sit. Then, standing at the back of the crowded hall, she began to feel faint when a procession of women in red robes came toward her at a stately pace, singing. She left, found the ladies' room, and sat in a stall watching a fly, not sure she would be able to stand up again.

In fact, close to the center of the story may be the moment when she realizes that, even though she is not a believer, she has an unusual, religious sort of peace in her, perhaps because she has been visiting churches and synagogues and studying the Bible, and that this peace has allowed her to accept the possibility of the worst sort of disaster, one even worse than a hurricane.

She rides the train up along the river away from the city. The danger of the hurricane is past. The water in the river has not risen to cover the tracks, though it is close to them. As she looks out at the water, she suddenly remembers the devil. She has not made a place for him in what she might believe, or even in the questions she is asking about what she believes. She has asked several friends whether they thought there was a God, but she has not mentioned the devil to anyone. After she remembers this, she realizes something else: the very fact that she has forgotten the devil must mean he has, at this point, no place in her beliefs, though she thinks she believes in the power of evil.

This comes close to the end of the story as it is now, but she can't really end with the devil and a train ride. So the end is a problem, too, though less of a problem than the center. There may be no center. There may be no center because she is afraid to put any one of these elements in the center—the man, the religion, or the hurricane. Or—

which is or is not the same thing—there is a center but the center is empty, either because she has not yet found what belongs there or because it is meant to be empty: there, but empty, in the same way that the man was sick but not dying, the hurricane approached but did not strike, and she had a religious calm but no faith.

Love

A woman fell in love with a man who had been dead a number of years. It was not enough for her to brush his coats, wipe his inkwell, finger his ivory comb: she had to build her house over his grave and sit with him night after night in the damp cellar.

Our Kindness

We have ideals of being very kind to everyone in the world. But then we are very unkind to our own husband, the person who is closest at hand to us. But then we think he is preventing us from being kind to everyone else in the world. Because he does not want us to know those other people, we think! He would prefer us to stay here in our own house. He says the car is old. We know that really he would prefer us to be acquainted with only a small number of people in the world, as he is. But what he says is that the car would not take us very far. We know he would prefer us to look after our own house and our own family. Our house is not clean, not completely clean. Our family is not completely clean. We think the car would serve us well enough. But he thinks we may want to go out and be kind to other people only because we would prefer not to be at home, because we would prefer not to have to try to be kind only to these three people, of all the people in the world the hardest three for us, though we can easily be kind to so many other people, such as those we meet at the stores, where we go because there our car, he says, may safely take us.

A Natural Disaster

In our home here by the rising sea we will not last much longer. The cold and the damp will certainly get us in the end, because it is no longer possible to leave: the cold has cracked open the only road away from here, the sea has risen and filled the cracks down by the marsh where it is low, has sunk and left salt crystals lining the cracks, has risen again higher and made the road impassable.

The sea washes up through the pipes into our basins, and our drinking water is brackish. Mollusks have appeared in our front yard and our garden and we can't walk without crushing their shells at every step. At every high tide the sea covers our land, leaving pools, when it ebbs, among our rosebushes and in the furrows of our rye field. Our seeds have been washed away; the crows have eaten what few were left.

Now we have moved into the upper rooms of the house and stand at the window watching the fish flash through the branches of our peach tree. An eel looks out from below our wheelbarrow.

What we wash and hang out the upstairs window to dry freezes: our shirts and pants make strange writhing shapes on the line. What we wear is always damp now, and the salt rubs against our skin until we are red and sore. Much of the day, now, we stay in bed under heavy, sour blankets; the wooden walls are wet through; the sea enters the cracks at the windowsills and trickles down to the floor. Three of us have died of pneumonia and bronchitis at different hours of the morning before daybreak. There are three left, and we are all weak, can't sleep but lightly, can't think but with confusion, don't speak, and hardly see light and dark anymore, only dimness and shadow.

Odd Behavior

You see how circumstances are to blame. I am not really an odd person if I put more and more small pieces of shredded Kleenex in my ears and tie a scarf around my head: when I lived alone I had all the silence I needed.

St. Martin

We were caretakers for most of that year, from early fall until summer. There was a house and grounds to look after, two dogs, and two cats. We fed the cats, one white and one calico, who lived outside and ate their meals on the kitchen windowsill, sparring in the sunlight as they waited for their food, but we did not keep the house very clean, or the weeds cut in the yard, and our employers, kind people though they were, probably never quite forgave us for what happened to one of the dogs.

We hardly knew what a clean house should look like. We would begin to think we were quite tidy, and then we would see the dust and clutter of the rooms, and the two hearths covered with ash. Sometimes we argued about it, sometimes we cleaned it. The oil stove became badly blocked and we did nothing for days because the telephone was out of order. When we needed help, we went to see the former caretakers, an old couple who lived with their cages of breeding canaries in the nearest village. The old man came by sometimes, and when he saw how the grass had grown so tall around the house, he scythed it without comment.

What our employers needed most from us was simply

that we stay in the house. We were not supposed to leave it for more than a few hours, because it had been robbed so often. We left it overnight only once, to celebrate New Year's Eve with a friend many miles away. We took the dogs with us on a mattress in the back of the car. We stopped at village fountains along the way and sprinkled water on their backs. We had too little money, anyway, to go anywhere. Our employers sent us a small amount each month, most of which we spent immediately on postage, cigarettes, and groceries. We brought home whole mackerels, which we cleaned, and whole chickens, which we beheaded and cleaned and prepared to roast, tying their legs together. The kitchen often smelled of garlic. We were told many times that year that garlic would give us strength. Sometimes we wrote letters home asking for money, and sometimes a check was sent for a small sum, but the bank took weeks to cash it.

We could not go much farther than the closest town to shop for food and to a village half an hour away over a small mountain covered with scrub oaks. There we left our sheets, towels, table linen, and other laundry to be washed, as our employers had instructed us to do, and when we picked it up a week later, we sometimes stayed to see a movie. Our mail was delivered to the house by a woman on a motorcycle.

But even if we had had the money, we would not have gone far, since we had chosen to live there in that house, in that isolation, in order to do work of our own, and we often sat inside the house trying to work, not always succeeding. We spent a great deal of time sitting inside one room or another looking down at our work and then up and out the window, though there was not much to see, one bit of landscape or another depending on which room we were in—trees, fields, clouds in the sky, a distant road, distant cars on the road, a village that lay on the horizon to the west of us, piled around its square church tower like a mirage, another village on a hilltop to the north of us across the valley, a person walking or working in a field, a bird or a pair of birds walking or flying, the ruined outbuilding not far from the house.

The dogs stayed near us almost all the time, sleeping in tight curls. If we spoke to them, they looked up with the worried eyes of old people. They were purebred yellow Labradors, brother and sister. The male was large, muscular, perfectly formed, of a blond color so light he was nearly white, with a fine head and a lovely broad face. His nature was simple and good. He ran, sniffed, came when we called, ate, and slept. Strong, adept, and willing, he retrieved as long as we asked him to, running down a cliff of sand no matter how steep or how long, plunging into a body of water in pursuit of a stick. Only in villages and towns did he turn shy and fearful, trembling and diving toward the shelter of a café table or a car.

His sister was very different, and as we admired her brother for his simple goodness and beauty, we admired her for her peculiar sense of humor, her reluctance, her cunning, her bad moods, her deviousness. She was calm in villages and cities and would not retrieve at all. She was small, with a rusty-brown coat, and not well formed, a barrel of a body on thin legs and a face like a weasel.

Because of the dogs, we went outside the house often in the course of the day. Sometimes one of us would have to leave the warm bed at five in the morning and hurry down the cold stone steps to let them out, and they were so eager that they leaked and left a pattern of drops on the red tiles of the kitchen and the patio. As we waited for them, we would look up at the stars, bright and distinct, the whole sky having shifted from where it was when we last saw it.

In the early fall, as grape pickers came into the neighboring fields to harvest, snails crept up the outside of the windowpanes, their undersides greenish-gold. Flies infested the rooms. We swatted them in the wide bands of sunlight that came through the glass doors of the music room. They tormented us while alive, then died in piles on the windowsills, covering our notebooks and papers. They were one of our seven plagues, the others being the fighter jets that thundered suddenly over our roof, the army helicopters that batted their more leisurely way over the treetops, the hunters who roamed close to the house, the thunderstorms, the two thieving cats, and, after a time, the cold.

The guns of the hunters boomed from beyond the hills or under our windows, waking us early in the morning. Men walked alone or in pairs, sometimes a woman trailed by a small child, spaniels loping out of sight and smoke rising from the mouths of the rifles. When we were in the woods, we would find a hunter's mess by the ruins of a stone house where he had settled for lunch—a plastic wine bottle, a glass wine bottle, scraps of paper, a crumpled paper bag, and an empty cartridge box. Or we would come upon a hunter squatting so motionless in the bushes, his gun resting in his arms, that we did not see him until we were on top of him, and even then he did not move, his eyes fixed on us.

In the village café, at the end of the day, the owner's young son, in olive-green pants, would slip around the counter and up the stairs with his two aged, slinking, tangerine-colored dogs, at the same time that women would come in with the mushrooms they had gathered just before dusk. Cartridge cases peppered the ground across a flat field near the house, one of the odd waste patches that lay in this valley of cultivated fields. Its dry autumn grass was strewn with boulders, among them two abandoned cars. Here from one direction came the smell of wild thyme, from the other the smell of sewage from a sewage bed.

We visited almost no one, only a farmer, a butcher, and a rather pompous retired businessman from the city. The farmer lived alone with his dog and his two cats in a large stone house a field or two away. The businessman, whose hyphenated name in fact contained the word *pomp*, lived in a new house in the closest village, to the west of us across the fields. The young butcher lived with his childless wife in town, and we would sometimes encounter him there moving meat across the street from his van to his shop. Cradling a beef carcass or a lamb in his arms, he would stop to talk to us in the sunlight, a wary smile on his face. When he was finished working for the day, he often went out to take photographs. He had studied photography through a correspondence course and received a degree. He photographed town festivals and processions, fairs and shooting matches. Sometimes he took us with him. Now and then a stranger came to the house by mistake. Once it was a young girl who entered the kitchen suddenly in a gust of wind, pale, thin, and strange, like a stray thought.

Because we had so little money, our amusements were simple. We would go out into the sun that beat down on the white gravel and shone off the leaves of the olive tree and toss pebbles one by one, overhand, from a distance of ten feet or so into a large clay urn that stood among the rosemary plants. We did this as a contest with each other, but also alone when we were finished working or couldn't work. One would be working and hear the dull click, over and over, of a pebble striking the urn and falling back onto the gravel, and the more resonant pock of the pebble landing inside the urn, and would know the other was outside.

When the weather grew too cold, we stayed inside and played gin rummy. By the middle of winter, when only a few rooms in the house were heated, we were playing so much, day and night, that we organized our games into tournaments. Then, for a few weeks, we stopped playing and studied German in the evenings by the fire. In the spring, we went back to our pebble game.

Nearly every afternoon, we took the dogs for a walk. On the coldest days of winter, we went out only long enough to gather kindling wood and pinecones for the fire. On warmer days, we went out for an hour or more at a time, most often into the government forest that spread for miles on a plateau above and behind the house, sometimes into the fields of vines or lavender in the valley, or into the meadows, or across to the far side of the valley, into old groves of olive trees. We were surrounded for so long by scrub brush, rocks, pine trees, oaks, red earth, fields, that we felt enclosed by them even once we were back inside the house.

We would walk, and return with burrs in our socks and scratches on our legs and arms where we had pushed through the brambles to get up into the forest, and go out again the next day and walk, and the dogs always trusted that we were setting out in a certain direction for a reason, and then returning home for a reason, but in the forest, which seemed so endless, there was hardly a distinguishing feature that could be taken as a destination for a walk, and we were simply walking, watching the sameness pass on both sides, the thorny, scrubby oaks growing densely together along the dusty track that ran quite straight until it came to a gentle bend and perhaps a slight rise and then ran straight again.

If we came home by an unfamiliar route, skirting the forest, avoiding a deeply furrowed, overgrown field and then stepping into the edge of a reedy marsh, veering close to a farmyard, where a farmer in blue and his wife in red were doing chores trailed by their dog, we felt so changed ourselves that we were surprised nothing about home had changed: for a moment the placidity of the house and yard nearly persuaded us we had not even left.

Between the forest and the fields, in the thickets of underbrush, we would sometimes come upon a farmhouse in ruins, with a curving flight of deep stone steps, worn at the edges, leading to an upper story that was now empty air, brambles and nettles and mint growing up inside and around it, and sometimes, nearby, an ancient, awkward and shaggy fruit tree, half its branches dead. In the form of this farmhouse, we recognized our own house. We went up the same curving flight of stone steps to bed at night. The animals had lived downstairs in our house, too—our vaulted dining room had once been a sheepfold.

Sometimes, in our walks, we came upon inexplicable things, once, in the cinders of an abandoned fire, two dead jackrabbits. Sometimes we lost our way, and were still lost after the sun had set, when we would start to run, and run without tiring, afraid of the dark, until we saw where we were again.

We had visitors who came from far away to stay with us for several days and sometimes several weeks, sometimes welcome, sometimes less so, as they stayed on and on. One was a young photographer who had worked with our employer and was in the habit of stopping at the house. He would travel through the region on assignments for his magazine, always taking his pictures at dawn or at sunset when the shadows were long. For every night he stayed with us, he paid us the amount he would have paid for a room at a good hotel, since he traveled on a company expense account. He was a small, neat man with a quick, toothy smile. He came alone, or he came with his girlfriend.

He played with the dogs, fondling them, wrestling with them overhead as we sat in the room below trying to work, while we spoke against him angrily, to ourselves. Or he and his girlfriend ironed their clothes above us, with noises we did not at first understand, the stiff cord knocking and sliding against the floorboards. It was hard enough for us to work, sometimes.

They were curiously disorganized, and when they went out on an errand left water coming to a boil on the stove or the sink full of warm soapy water as though they were still at home. Or when they returned from an errand, they left the doors wide open so that the cold air and the cats came in. They were still at breakfast close to noon, and left crumbs on the table. Late in the evening, sometimes, we would find the girlfriend asleep on the sofa.

But we were lonely, and the photographer and his girlfriend were friendly, and they would sometimes cook dinner for us, or take us out to a restaurant. A visit from them meant money in our pockets again.

At the beginning of December, when we began to have the oil stove going full blast in the kitchen all day, the dogs slept next to it while we worked at the dining-room table. We watched through the window as two men returned to work in a cultivated field, one on a tractor and one behind a plow that had been sitting for weeks growing rusty, after opening perhaps ten furrows. Violent high winds sometimes rose during the night and then continued blowing all day so that the birds had trouble flying and dust sifted down through the floorboards. Sometimes one of us would get up in the night, hearing a shutter bang, and go out in pajamas onto the tiles of the garage roof to tie it back again or remove it from its hinge.

A rainstorm would last hours, soaking the ruined outbuilding nearby, darkening its stones. The air in the morning would be soft and limp. After the constant dripping of the rain or wuthering of the wind, there was sometimes complete silence, minute after minute, and then abruptly the rocky echoes of a plane far away in the sky. The light on the wet gravel outside the house was so white, after a storm, it looked like snow.

By the middle of the month, the trees and bushes had begun to lose their leaves and in a nearby field a stone shed, its black doorway overgrown by brambles, gradually came into view.

A flock of sheep gathered around the ruined outbuilding, fat, long-tailed, a dirty brown color, with pale scrawny lambs. Jostling one another, they poured up out of the ruin, climbing the tumbledown walls, the little ones crying in high human voices over the dull clamor of the bells. The shepherd, dressed all in brown with a cap pulled low over his eyes, sat eating on the grass by the woodpile, his face glowing and his chin unshaven. When the sheep became too active, he grunted and his small black dog raced once around the side of the flock and the sheep cantered away in a forest of sticklike legs. When they came near again, streaming out between the walls, the dog sent them flying again. When they disappeared into the next field, the shepherd continued to sit for a while, then moved off slowly, in his baggy brown pants, a leather pouch hanging on long straps down his back, a light stick in one hand, his coat flung over his shoulder, the little black dog charging and veering when he whistled.

One afternoon we had almost no money left, and almost no food. Our spirits were low. Hoping to be invited to dinner, we dropped in on the businessman and his wife. They had been upstairs reading, and came down one after the other holding their reading glasses in their hands, looking tired and old. We saw that when they were not expecting company, they had in their living room a blanket and a sleeping bag arranged over the two armchairs in front of the television. They invited us to have dinner with them the next night.

When we went to their house the next night, we were offered rum cocktails by Monsieur Assiez-de-Pompignan before dinner and afterwards we watched a movie with them. When it ended, we left, hurrying to our car against the wind, through the narrow, shuttered streets, dust flying in our teeth.

The following day, for dinner, we had one sausage. The only money left now was a pile of coins on the living-room table collected from saucers around the house and amounting to 2.97 francs, less than fifty cents, but enough to buy something for dinner the next day.

Then we had no money at all anywhere in the house, and almost nothing left to eat. What we found, when we searched the kitchen carefully, was some onions, an old but unopened box of pastry crust mix, a little fat, and a little dried milk. Out of this, we realized, we could make an onion pie. We made it, baked it, cut ourselves two pieces, and put the rest back in the hot oven to cook a little more while we ate. It was surprisingly good. Our spirits lifting, we talked as we ate and forgot all about the pie as it went on baking. By the time we smelled it, it had burned too badly to be saved.

In the afternoon of that day, we went out onto the gravel, not knowing what to do now. We tossed pebbles for a while, there in the boiling sun and the cool air, saying very little because we had no answer to our problem. Then we heard the sound of an approaching car. Along the bumpy dirt road that led to our house from the main road, past the house of the weekend people, of pink stucco with black ironwork, and then past a vineyard on one side and a field on the other, came the photographer in his neat rented car. By pure chance, or like an angel, he was arriving to rescue us at the very moment we had used up our last resource.

We were not embarrassed to say we had no money, and no food either, and he was pleased to invite us out to dinner. He took us into town to a very good restaurant on the main square where the rows of plantain trees stood. A television crew were also dining there, twelve at the table, including a hunchback. By the large, bright fire on one wall, three old women sat knitting: one with liver spots covering her face and hands, the second pinched and bony, the third younger and merrier but slow-witted. The photographer fed us well on his expense account. He stayed with us that night and a few nights after, leaving us with several fifty-franc notes, so we were all right for a while, since a bottle of local wine, for instance, cost no more than one franc fifty.

When winter set in, we closed one by one the other rooms in the house and confined ourselves to the kitchen with its fat oil-burning stove, the vaulted dining room with its massive oak table where we played cards in the thick heat from the kitchen, the music room with its expensive electric heater burning our legs, and at the top of the stone stairway the unheated bedroom with its floor of red tiles so vast there was ample time for it to dip down in the center and rise again on its way to the single small casement window that looked out onto the almond tree and the olive tree below. The house had a different feeling to it when the wind was blowing and parts of it were darkened because we had closed the shutters.

Larks fluttered over the fields in the afternoons, showing silver. The long, straight, deeply rutted road to the village turned to soft mud. In certain lights, the inner walls of the ruined outbuilding were as rosy as a seashell. The dogs sighed heavily as they lay down on the cold tiles, closing their almond-shaped eyes. When they were let out into the sunlight, they fought, panting and scattering gravel. The shadow of the olive tree in the bright, hard sunlight flowed over the gravel like a dark river and lapped up against the wall of the house.

One night, during a heavy rainstorm, we went to the farmer's house for dinner. Nothing grew around his house, not even grass; there was only the massive stone house in a yard of deep mud. The front door was heavy to push open. The entryway was filled with a damp, musty smell from the truffles hanging in a leather pouch from a peg. Sacks full of seed and grain lined the wall.

With the farmer, we went out to the side of the house to collect eggs for dinner. Under the house, in the pens where he had once kept sheep, hens roosted now, their faces sharp in the beam of his flashlight. He gathered the eggs, holding the flashlight in one hand, and gave them to us to carry. The umbrella, as we started back around to the front of the house, turned inside out in the wind.

The kitchen was warm from the heat of a large oil stove. The oven door was open and a cat sat inside looking out. When he was in the house, the farmer spent most of his time in the kitchen. When he had something to throw away, he threw it out the window, burying it later. The table was crowded with bottles—vinegar, oil, his own wine in whiskey bottles which he had brought up from the cellar—and among them cloth napkins and large lumps of sea salt. Behind the table was a couch piled with coats. Two rifles hung in racks against the wall. Taped to the refrigerator was a photograph of the farmer and the truck he used to drive from Paris to Marseille.

For dinner he gave us leeks with oil and vinegar, bits of hard sausage and bread, black olives like cardboard, and scrambled eggs with truffles. He dried lettuce leaves by shaking them in a dishtowel and gave us a salad full of garlic, and then some Roquefort. He told us that his first breakfast, before he went out to work in the fields, was a piece of bread and garlic. He called himself a Communist and talked about the Resistance, telling us that the people of the area knew just who the collaborators were. The collaborators stayed at home out of sight, did not go to the cafés much, and in fact would be killed immediately if there was trouble, though he did not say what he meant by trouble. He had opinions about many things, even the Koran, in which, he said, lying and stealing were not considered sins, and he had questions for us: he wondered if it was the same year over there, in our country.

To get to his new, clean bathroom, we took the flashlight and lit our way past the head of the stairs and through an empty, high-ceilinged room of which we could see nothing but a great stone fireplace. After dinner, we listened in silence to a record of revolutionary songs that he took from a pile on the floor, while he grew sleepy, yawning and twiddling his thumbs.

When we returned home, we let the dogs out, as we always did, to run around before they were shut in for the night. The hunting season had begun again. We should not have let the dogs out loose, but we did not know that. More than an hour passed and the female came back but her brother did not. We were afraid right away, because he never stayed out more than an hour or so. We called and called, near the house, and then the next morning, when he had still not returned, we walked through the woods in all directions, calling and searching among the trees.

We knew he would not have stayed away so long unless he had somehow been stopped from coming back. He could have wandered into the nearest village, lured by the scent of a female in heat. He could have been spotted near the road and taken by a passing motorist. He could have been stolen by a hunter, someone avid for a good-natured, handsome hunting dog, proud to show it off in a smoke-filled café. But we believed first, and longest, that he lay in the underbrush poisoned, or caught in a trap, or wounded by a bullet.

Day after day passed and he did not come home and we had no news of him. We drove from village to village asking questions, and put up notices with his photograph attached, but we also knew that the people we talked to might lie to us, and that such a beautiful dog would probably not be returned.

People called us who had a yellow dog, or had found a stray, but each time we went to see it, it was not much like our dog. Because we did not know what had happened to him, because it was always possible that he might return, it was hard for us to accept the fact that he was gone. That he was not our dog only made it worse.

After a month, we still hoped the dog would return, though signs of spring began to appear and other things came along to distract us. The almond tree blossomed with flowers so white that against the soft plowed field beyond them they were almost blue. A pair of magpies came to the scrub oak beside the woodpile, fluttering, squawking, diving obliquely down.

The weekend people returned, and every Sunday they called out to each other as they worked the long strip of earth in the field below us. The dog went to the border of our land and barked at them, tense on her stiff legs.

Once we stopped to talk to a woman at the edge of the village and she showed us her hand covered with dirt from digging in the ground. Behind her we could see a man leading another man back into his garden to give him some herbs.

Drifts of daffodils and narcissus bloomed in the fields. We gathered a vase full of them and slept with them in the room, waking up drugged and sluggish. Irises bloomed and then the first roses opened, yellow. The flies became numerous again, and noisy.

We took long walks again, with one dog now. There were bugs in the wiry, stiff grass near the house, small cracks in the dirt, ants. In the field, purple clover grew around our ankles, and large white and yellow daisies at our knees. Bloodred bumblebees landed on buttercups as high as our hands. The long, lush grass in the field rose and fell in waves before the wind, and near us in a thick grove of trees dead branches clacked together. Whenever the wind died, we could hear the trickle of a swollen stream as though it were falling into a stone basin.

In May, we heard the first nightingale. Just as the night fully darkened, it began to sing. Its song was not really unlike the song of a mockingbird, with warbles, and twitters, and trills, warbles, chirps, and warbles again, but it issued in the midst of the silence of the night, in the dark, or in the moonlight, from a spot mysteriously hidden among the black branches.

Agreement

First she walked out, and then while she was out he walked out. No, before she walked out, he walked out on her, not long after he came home, because of something she said. He did not say how long he would be gone or where he was going, because he was angry. He did not say anything except "That's it." Then, while he was out, she walked out on him and went down the road with the children. Then, while she was out, he came back, and when she did not return and it grew dark, he went out looking for her. She returned without seeing him, and after she had been back some time, she walked out again with the children to find him. Later, he said she had walked out on him, and she agreed that she had walked out on him, but said she had walked out on him only after he walked out on her. Then he agreed that he had walked out on her, but only after she said something she should not have said. He said she should agree that she should not have said what she said and that she had caused the evening's harm. She agreed that she should not have said what she said, but then went on to say that the trouble between them had started before, and if she agreed she had caused the evening's harm, he should agree he had caused what started the trouble before. But he would not agree to that, not yet anyway.

In the Garment District

A man has been making deliveries in the garment district for years now: every morning he takes the same garments on a moving rack through the streets to a shop and every evening takes them back again to the warehouse. This happens because there is a dispute between the shop and the warehouse that cannot be settled: the shop denies it ever ordered the clothes, which are badly made and of cheap material and by now years out of style; while the warehouse will not take responsibility because the clothes cannot be returned to the wholesalers, who have no use for them. To the man all this is nothing. They are not his clothes, he is paid for this work, and he intends to leave the company soon, though the right moment has not yet come.

Disagreement

He said she was disagreeing with him. She said no, that was not true, he was disagreeing with her. This was about the screen door. That it should not be left open was her idea, because of the flies; his was that it could be left open first thing in the morning, when there were no flies on the deck. Anyway, he said, most of the flies came from other parts of the building: in fact, he was probably letting more of them out than in.

The Actors

In our town there is an actor, H.—a tall, bold, feverish sort of man—who easily fills the theater when he plays Othello, and about whom the women here become very excited. He is handsome enough compared to the other men, though his nose is somewhat thick and his torso rather short for his height. His acting is stiff and inflexible, his gestures obviously memorized and mechanical, and yet his voice is strong enough to make one forget all that. On the nights when he is unable to leave his bed because of illness or intoxication—and this happens more often than one would imagine—the part is taken by J., his understudy. Now, J. is pale and small, completely unsuitable for the part of a Moor; his legs tremble as he comes onstage and faces the many empty seats. His voice hardly carries beyond the first few rows, and his small hands flutter uselessly in the smoky air. We feel only pity and irritation as we watch him, and yet by the end of the play we find ourselves unaccountably moved, as though something timid and sad in Othello's character had been conveyed to us in spite of ourselves. But the mannerisms and skill of H. and J.—which we analyze minutely when we visit together in the afternoons and contemplate even when we are alone, after dinner—suddenly seem insignificant when the great Sparr comes down from the city and gives us a real performance of Othello. Then we are so carried away, so exhausted with emotion, that it is impossible to speak of what we feel. We are almost grateful when he is gone and we are left with H. and J., imperfect as they are, for they are familiar to us and comfortable, like our own people.

What Was Interesting

It is hard for her to write this story, too, or rather she should say it is hard for her to write it well. She has shown it to a friend, and he has said it needs to be more interesting. She is disappointed, even though she knew that only one part of it was interesting. She tries to think why the rest is not.

Maybe there is no way to make it interesting, because it is so simple: a woman, slightly drunk but not too drunk to discuss a plan for the summer, was put into a cab and told to go home by her lover, the man with whom she thought she was going to discuss this plan.

She asks her friend if this, at least, was something that would hurt a woman, or if this was nothing. He thinks it would hurt, and she is right about that much, but it is not very interesting.

He had put her into a cab with two men who were not pleased to be riding with her, as she was not pleased to be riding with them, because of some complicated events that had occurred years before. She was talking politely to them but feeling angry at the man who had done this to her.

It is not entirely clear, in the story, why being put in a cab by this man should cause so much anger in her. Or rather, it is perfectly clear to her, but hard to explain to anyone else, though she knows that anyone else, put in the same cab with the same two men, would be angry.

As soon as she arrived home she telephoned him. She raged at him and he laughed, she raged more and he gave her a slight apology and laughed more and said he was sleepy and wanted to go to bed. She hung up. She went on crying and then began drinking. She was so angry she would have been happy to take her fists to him, but he was not there, he was sleeping and probably smiling in his sleep. As she drank she thought hard, and angrily.

What was he trying to do to her this time? she wondered. She and he did not have many chances to be together, and there they were sitting across from each other at dinner, and they had recently started talking about a plan to go away together in the summer, which they had never done before, or even talked about doing before, and he had even sent her a photograph of the house. They had said that after dinner they would talk about it more, and she was very happy about all this, and felt that at last their love was becoming something solid, something she could count on. And then, when she was prepared to walk off with him down the street, her head pleasantly light, her stomach comfortably full, he had suddenly, without warning, taken her arm and led her up to a taxi just as these two men were getting into it, and because there were other people there they both knew, she couldn't say anything but had to pretend this was something she did not mind. And what did he mean by it? What was she supposed to think now, and what was she supposed to do?

At a certain point in her angry thinking she decided she had to give up the idea of a summer plan with him. If he had done this now, what would he do to her during the summer, and, even worse, when the summer was over? And now she drank more to give vent to her disappointment.

The fact that they were involved in a love affair ought to have been interesting, because any kind of affair is usually more interesting than no affair, as two people in a story should be more interesting than one, and a difficult love affair should be more interesting than an easy one. As, for example, a happy woman walking arm in arm with her lover after a noisy restaurant dinner with friends, enjoying the fact that he is so tall and the feel of his smooth hair under her palm when she reaches up, walking with him and discussing summer plans, as she had been sure they were going to do, may be less interesting than being put into a cab with embarrassing haste and awkwardness, or finding a pair of keys that have been lost, as she did later, and then certainly the idea of a key is more interesting than the idea of a cab, and the idea of something lost and then found is more interesting than the idea of already knowing where she was, that is, in the cab and then at home, though it was true that in a more general way she certainly did not know where she was with him, what he expected from her and what he expected would happen to them.

The love affair as they conducted it was irregular, intermittent, and painful to her, painful because in the arrangements they made at long intervals, after months had gone by, he always did something she had not known he was going to do and it was often in contradiction to a plan they had made. She would borrow an apartment especially so that they could have a comfortable place to meet, and he would agree to come there late in the evening, and then he would not come, and after calling him where he was, and hearing his sleepy voice, she would pace from room to room in the borrowed apartment wringing her hands. On another occasion he would say firmly that he would not be coming to the borrowed apartment, and then come to her there without warning. Or they would meet for lunch and nothing more, and then he would suddenly propose that they go to a motel. In the motel, to her surprise, he would say he wanted to keep the room and meet there that night, and she would be happy, and all evening, at home, would wait for him to call and say when he could meet her, and then finally she would call him and hear him say he had not kept the room and could not see her.

But if he always did what she did not expect him to do, and if she knew this, why didn't she think ahead and see that whatever he said he was going to do, he would not do? Though she was not a stupid woman, she did not do this. And what he did that was unexpected was also unkind, almost every time, but perhaps that was more interesting than if he had been kind and reliable, as she wanted him to be, as well as charming and open to her, as he often was: how happy he had looked the last time she had seen him, sitting by her in a bar where they had just met, purely happy in his face, until she said he looked happy and asked why, and he said a few other things and then the truth, that he was happy to see her, after which he looked just slightly less happy.

She was not yet quite finished with crying and raging, but unable to stay there in her apartment, in a place that seemed to contain only her and what had happened and the disappointment of it. She was on her knees on her living-room rug, trying to think where she had put some keys, the keys to a friend's apartment. She wanted to go to this apartment even though she knew the friend was not home and would not be coming home. She could not have gone to him with her trouble, and she supposed, even through the fog of her drunkenness, that she should not go to his apartment with her trouble either. But she would not be stopped from something she wanted so badly. She needed to let the walls of a different place that belonged to a different time relieve her, a little, of herself and what had just happened.

She took a large, heavy drawer out of her bureau and emptied it on the rug. It was awkward to carry and awkward to turn over. She went through everything in it, not seeing very well, but couldn't find the keys, and put everything back, and put the drawer back in the bureau. Then she took a shoe box down from a shelf, lighter and easier to carry. She emptied it on the rug, but the keys weren't there either, so she was still on her knees, crying, and then lying facedown on the rug, because she couldn't find the keys. If she couldn't find them, she didn't know what she would do with herself.

She stopped crying, washed and dried her face, and tried to remember where she had last seen them. Then she remembered that they weren't loose, but sealed in a white envelope, and once she remembered that, she knew where she had seen that crumpled envelope recently, and found it in a wooden tray on her desk. She put the keys in her pocket, called a taxi, left the apartment, rode through the silent streets of several different neighborhoods, past two darkened hospitals, to her friend's apartment, and once inside fell asleep on his living-room rug, a thicker and more comfortable rug than her own.

She woke up when the clean light of dawn was coming through his tall windows, and left the apartment soon after, to avoid meeting him. By now she could return to her own apartment, as though she had climbed up to some high, difficult place during the night and climbed down again by morning.

She would never tell her friend she had slept in his apartment. It had been a long time since she had used his keys. His reaction, if he knew, would be interesting. In fact, this friend would possibly have been the most interesting person in the story, if she had put him instead of his apartment into it.

She was sick that day from all she had drunk. It would be more interesting to be well after drinking so much than to be sick, but she preferred being sick to being well that day, as though it were a celebration of the change that had happened, that she would not be sitting out in the Mediterranean sunshine with her lover that summer. After this, she would have almost nothing more to do with him. She would not answer his letters, and would barely speak to him if she chanced to meet him, but this anger of hers, lasting so long, was certainly more interesting to her, because in the end she found it harder to explain than the fact that she had loved him so long.

In the Everglades

Today I am riding in a canopied car on rubber wheels through Jungle Larry's African Safari. We pass a strangler fig tree and some caged cougars. A female leopard hides from us behind a rock. High up on the trunk of a palm in the Orchid Cathedral, one flower blooms beside a rusty faucet. Afterward we throw our trash into the mouth of a yawning plaster lion and leave for the Seminole Indian Village.

The Village is closed, and though the Village Shop is open we do not buy anything, perhaps because the Indians who wait on us and watch us pick through the beaded goods are so very sullen.

Later I sit in a short row of people at the front of an air-boat, and with an unpleasant racket we skim the saw grass, moving fast suddenly. Animals everywhere in the mangrove swamp are disturbed, and one by one, with difficulty, herons and egrets rise up before us for miles around into the white sky.

All day I have been looking at a landscape charged with the sun, and when as instructed by the captain of the air-boat I watched the water for alligators, the broken light of the reflected sun sparkled painfully. Now it is evening and my eyes ache as I sit in the lamplight incapable of thinking.

I look at what is around me: the papered walls, the gold-leafed decorations, the table in lamplight, my hands on the table, and in particular the back of my right hand on which today a woman has stamped the figure of a huddled monkey that is now becoming indistinct and ugly, and though I try again and again I can't remember exactly where or why this happened.

The Family

In the playground near the river, toward evening, in the lowering sun, on the green grass, only one family. Swings creak and cry out going back and forth. Shadows of swinging children foreshorten, fly over the grass into the weeds. (1) Fat young white woman pulls white baby by one arm onto quilt spread on grass. (2) Little black boy struggles with older black girl over swing, (3) is ordered to sit down on grass, (4) stands sullen while (5) fat white woman heaves to her feet, walks to him, and smacks him. (6) Little black boy whimpers, lies on his back on grass while (7) fat white woman plays with baby and (8) young black man orders black girl off swing. (9) Young black man begins wrestling in play with long-haired white girl who (10) protests while (11) tall, bony, wrinkled, mustachioed white man in baseball cap stands with arms crossed, back hunched, walkie-talkie attached to right hip and (12) black girl lies down with face in baby's face. (13) Baby peers up and around black girl when (14) white girl protests more loudly as (15) young black man slaps her buttocks and (16) older white man watches with arms crossed. (17) White girl breaks free of young black man and runs toward river crying as (18) young black man runs easily after her and (19) older white man in baseball cap runs awkwardly after her, one hand on walkie-talkie at his hip. (20) Young black man picks up white girl and carries her back to fat young white woman who (21) takes her onto her lap as (22) little black boy sits up in grass and watches. (23) White girl squirms in arms of young white woman, breaks free and runs again, crying, toward river. (24) Black girl, taller, follows, overtakes her, lifts and carries her back. (25) Young white woman holds white girl who struggles, hair covering her face, while (26) black girl swings on swing holding white baby and (27) white man stands still, back hunched, hips forward, eyes invisible under visor of baseball cap. (28) Young black man goes off toward concrete hut in setting sun and (29) returns to call out to white woman, who (30) leaves white girl and follows after him with baby to concrete hut while (31) black girl continues to swing alone and (32) black boy sits on grass alone and (33) white man stands still with arms crossed looking out from under visor. (34) White woman returns with black man and bends to gather quilt and bag from grass. (35) White man in baseball cap holds small sleeping bag open while (36) young white woman puts baby in. (37) Young white woman orders black boy up off ground. (38) Black boy shakes head and stays on ground. (39) White woman slaps black boy, who (40) begins crying. (41) White woman carrying baby walks away with young black man and two girls while (42) older white man follows, holding crying black boy by hand. (43) Family leaves playground and enters dusty road. (44) Family stops to wait for white man in baseball cap, who (45) returns slowly to park, picks up pair of child's thongs from grass, and (46) rejoins family. (47) Family walks on, heading toward marsh, short bridge, and red sky.

Trying to Learn

I am trying to learn that this playful man who teases me is the same as that serious man talking money to me so seriously he does not even see me anymore and that patient man offering me advice in times of trouble and that angry man slamming the door as he leaves the house. I have often wanted the playful man to be more serious, and the serious man to be less serious, and the patient man to be more playful. As for the angry man, he is a stranger to me and I do not feel it is wrong to hate him. Now I am learning that if I say bitter words to the angry man as he leaves the house, I am at the same time wounding the others, the ones I do not want to wound, the playful man teasing, the serious man talking money, and the patient man offering advice. Yet I look at the patient man, for instance, whom I would want above all to protect from such bitter words as mine, and though I tell myself he is the same man as the others, I can only believe I said those words not to him, but to another, my enemy, who deserved all my anger.

To Reiterate

Michel Butor says that to travel is to write, because to travel is to read. This can be developed further: To write is to travel, to write is to read, to read is to write, and to read is to travel. But George Steiner says that to translate is also to read, and to translate is to write, as to write is to translate and to read is to translate. So that we may say: To translate is to travel and to travel is to translate. To translate a travel writing, for example, is to read a travel writing, to write a travel writing, to read a writing, to write a writing, and to travel. But if because you are translating you read, and because writing translate, because traveling write, because traveling read, and because translating travel; that is, if to read is to translate, and to translate is to write, to write to travel, to read to travel, to write to read, to read to write, and to travel to translate; then to write is also to write, and to read is also to read, and even more, because when you read you read, but also travel, and because traveling read, therefore read and read; and when reading also write, therefore read; and reading also translate, therefore read; therefore read, read, read, and read. The same argument may be made for translating, traveling, and writing.

Lord Royston's Tour

Gotheberg: Greatly Daring Dined

He was a good deal tossed and beaten about off the Skaw, before sailing up the river this morning. On board also were the Consul, Mr. Smith, and an iron merchant, Mr. Damm. Neither he nor his two servants have any common language with any inhabitant of the inn. Considerable parts of the town of Gotheberg were burned down, it being built almost entirely of wood, and they are rebuilding it with white brick.

He has completely satisfied his curiosity about the town.

On an excursion to Trolhatte, the harness breaks three or four times between every post. Here the traveler drives, and the peasant runs by the side of the carriage or gets up behind. He views with great interest the falls of Trolhatte. In an album at a small inn at Trolhatte, he inscribes some Greek anapests evoking his impressions of them.

He inspects the canal and the cataracts under the guidance of a fine old soldier. He sees several vessels loaded with iron and timber pass through the sluices. He receives great civilities from the English merchants, particularly from Mr. Smith, the Consul. He eats cheese and corn brandy, raw herrings and caviar, a joint, a roast, fish and soup, and can't help thinking of Pope's line, "greatly daring dined."

To Copenhagen: The Water, Merely Brackish

Leaving Gotheborg, he passes through country uncommonly dreary, destitute of wood, covered with sand or rock, then country that is well wooded and watered, bearing crops chiefly of rye or barley, with a few fields of wheat and occasional hop grounds. Many of the wood bridges are quite rotten and scarcely bear the weight of a carriage. Crossing the Sound after reaching Helsinborg, he sees with great surprise a flock of geese swimming in the sea, tastes the water, and finds it merely brackish.

His knowledge of Copenhagen is so far limited to the streets he has driven through and the walls of the room he is sitting in, but there is no appearance of poverty, none of the wooden houses of Sweden, and the people are well dressed. He has reason to be satisfied with his servants, particularly Poole, who is active and intelligent.

The Danish nobility have mostly retired to their country houses.

The Barren Province of Smolang

Leaving Helsinborg, he has traveled through extensive forests of fir and birch: this is the barren Province of Smolang, so thinly inhabited that in two days he met only one solitary traveler.

Poole has contrived to get on by composing a language of English, Dutch, German, Swedish, and Danish in which euphony is not the most predominant feature.

For some time he has got nothing to eat but some rye bread—much too hard, black, and sour, he thinks, for any human being to eat. He might have had plenty of some raw salt goose if he had liked.

Stockholm is not so regular as Copenhagen, but more magnificent.

He has been to the Arsenal and seen the skin of the horse that carried Gustavus Adolphus at the battle of Lutzen, and the clothes in which Charles XII was shot.

He has sent his father two pieces of Swedish money, which is so heavy that when it was used as current coin, a public officer receiving a quarter's allowance had to bring a cart to carry it away.

To Westeras

In Upsala he visited the Cathedral and found there a man who could speak Latin very fluently. The Rector Magnificus was not at home. He was detained some time in a forest of fir and birch by the axletree breaking. In general, he is annoyed by having to find separate lodgings for himself and his horses in each town.

His Swedish has made the most terrible havoc with the little German he knows.

In Abo

He understands there is a gloom over the Russian court.

St. Petersburg: Rubbers of Whist

The immense forests of fir strike the imagination at first but then become tedious from their excessive uniformity. He has eaten partridges and a cock of the woods. As he advances in Russian Finland he finds everything getting more and more Russian: the churches begin to be ornamented with gilt domes and the number of persons wearing beards continues to increase. A postmaster addresses him in Latin but in spite of that is not very civil. The roads are so bad that eight horses will not draw him along and he is helped up the mountain by some peasants. He sees two wolves. He crosses the Neva over a wooden bridge. He is amused at finding his old friends the Irish jaunting cars.

The most striking objects here are certainly the common people.

He has a poor opinion of the honesty of the country when he finds in the Russian language a single word to express "the perversion of Justice by a Judge," as in Arabic there is a word to express "a bribe offered to a Judge."

In the Russian language they have only one word to express the ideas of *red* and *beautiful*, as the Romans used the word *purple* without any reference to color, as for instance "purple snow."

He is bored by the society of the people of St. Petersburg, where he plays rubbers of whist without any amusing conversation. He considers card games even more dull and unentertaining than spitting over a bridge or tapping a tune with a walking stick on a pair of boots.

The general appearance of the city is magnificent, and he sees this as proof of what may be done with brick and plaster—though the surrounding country is very flat, dull, and marshy. The weather begins to be cold, and a stove within and a pelisse without doors are necessary.

He wishes to see the ice-hills and sledges, and the frozen markets.

He goes to a Russian tragedy in five acts by mistake,

thinking it is a French opera. Yet he expects in course of time to be able to converse with his friends the Sclavonians. He sees the Tauride, now lapsed to the crown, behind which is a winter garden laid out in parterres and gravel walks, filled with orange trees and other exotics, and evenly heated by a great number of stoves. The Neva is now blocked by large pieces of ice floating down from the Ladoga. Though the temperature has been down to twenty degrees Fahrenheit below freezing, that is not considered to be much at all here.

The Empress gives birth to an Archduchess. When the Court assembles to pay their respects the person who most attracts attention is Prince Hypsilantes, the Hospodar of Wallachia, and the Greeks of his train.

There is not much variety in his mode of life. He studies Russian in the morning.

He begins to be very tired of this place and its inhabitants: their hospitality; the voracious gluttony on every side of him; their barefaced cheating; their conversation, with its miserable lack of information and ideas; their constant fear of Siberia; their coldness, dullness, and lack of energy. The Poles are infinitely the most gentlemanlike, and seem a superior order of men to their Russian masters.

He won't remain here as long as he had intended, but will purchase two sledge kibitkas, and other supplies, and depart, not for Moscow but for Archangel.

He imagines there must be something curious in driving reindeer on the ice of the White Sea.

To Archangel: The Mayor Makes a Speech

He buys two sledges covered with a tilt, furnishes them with a mattress, and lays in frozen beefsteaks, Madeira, brandy, and a large saucepan. For the trip he dresses in flannel, over that his ordinary clothes, over his boots fur shoes, over the fur shoes a pair of fur boots, covers his head with a cap of blue Astrachan wool, wraps himself in a sable pelisse, and over it all throws a bear skin.

On the road there are no accommodations, so he sees inside the houses of the peasantry. The whole family lives in one room in suffocating heat and smell and with a number of cockroaches, which swarm in the wooden huts. The dirt is excessive. But the people are civil, hospitable, cheerful, and intelligent, though addicted to spirits, quarrelsome among themselves, and inclined to cheat. They are more like the common Irish than anyone else he has seen. Peter the Great has by no means succeeded in forcing them to abandon their beards.

In the cottage, people come to see him dine. Twenty or thirty women crowd around him, examining him and asking him questions.

He passes through Ladoga and Vitigra. Approaching Kargossol, he counts from a distance nineteen churches, most of which have five balloon-like domes, gilt, copper, or painted in the most gaudy colors, and thinks it must be a magnificent town, but the number of churches here almost equals the number of houses.

In Archangel the Archbishop speaks Latin very fluently, but does not know whether the Samoyeds of his diocese are Pagans or Christians.

His hostess is anxious to show that they, too, have fruit, and brings in some specimens preserved. Here they have in the woods a berry with a strong taste of turpentine.

The mayor comes in during the evening and makes a speech to him in Russian three-quarters of an hour long.

The temperature in Archangel is fifty-one degrees

below freezing, both his hands are frozen, and Pauwells has a foot frozen. He goes northeast of Archangel, procures three sledges and twelve reindeer, and sets out over the unbeaten snow in search of a horde of Samoyeds. He finds them exactly on the Arctic Circle in an immense plain of snow surrounded by several hundred reindeer. They are Pagans.

Back in Archangel, the cold has increased, and he is forced to bake his Madeira in an oven to get at it, and to carve his meat with an axe. It is nearly seventy degrees below freezing, barely three points above the point of congelation of mercury.

Moscow Is Immense and Extraordinary

Moscow is immense and extraordinary, after a journey over the worst road he has ever traveled in his life through a forest which scarcely ever suffered any interruption but continued with dreary uniformity from one capital to another.

He begins to be able to read Russian fairly easily, and speak it sufficiently. Poole has also picked up enough.

He sends his younger brother a Samoyed sledge and three reindeer cut out of the teeth of a seahorse by a peasant at Archangel.

The extent of Moscow is prodigious despite its small population because in no quarter of the city do the houses stand contiguous. The Kremlin is certainly the most striking quarter, and nearly thirty gilt domes give it a most peculiar appearance.

He is much interested by the passage of regiments composed of some of the wandering nations. One day there passed two thousand Bashkirs from the Oremburg frontiers on their lean desert horses, armed with lances and bows, some clothed in complete armor, some with the twisted coat of mail or hauberk, some with grotesque caps, others with iron helmets. These people are Mohammedans. Their chief is dressed in a scarlet caftan, their music is a species of flute which they place in the corner of their mouths, singing at the same time. They are almost always at war with the Kirghese.

A regiment of Calmucs passes through. Their features are scarcely human. They worship the Dalai Lama. He also sees a number of Kirghese of the lesser and middle hordes.

He continues his study of Russian, finds the language sonorous, but thinks it hardly repays anyone the trouble of learning it, because there are so few original authors—upon the introduction of literature it was found much easier to translate. The national epic poem, however, about the conquest of the Tartars of Casan, would be good if it weren't for the insufferable monotony of the meter.

Another Trip to Petersburg

Proceeding along the frozen river, the postilions missed their road, came to a soft place on the ice, and the horses broke through. The kibitka in which he lay could not be opened from the inside and the postilions paid no attention to him, being concerned only with trying to save their horses. One of them woke Poole in his sledge to request an axe. Poole saw the vehicle half-floating in the water and had just time to open the leather covering. He jumped out upon the ice with his writing desk and the carriage went down to the bottom. One horse drowned.

In Petersburg, the Carnival was taking place: theaters erected on the river, ice-hills, long processions of sledges, multitudes of people, and public masquerades given morning and evening.

In Moscow Again, He Plans the Continuation of His Tour

Now Moscow is very dull during the fast.

He plans to get a large boat, embark at Casan, and float down the Volga to Astracan sitting on a sofa. He will reach the banks of the Caspian.

The carriages he will use have not a particle of iron in their whole composition.

There is a sect of Eunuchs who do this to themselves for the kingdom of heaven. They had at one time propagated their doctrines to such an extent that the government was forced to interfere, afraid of depopulation. It seized a number of them and sent them to the mines of Siberia.

He is preparing for his journey, and he will be accompanied as far as Astracan by an American of South Carolina, Mr. Poinsett, one of the few liberal and literary and gentlemanlike men he has seen emerge from the forests of the New World.

He has hired a Tartar interpreter, whom his valet de chambre is somewhat afraid of and calls "Monsieur le Tartare."

He is waiting for letters from Casan about the condition of the roads, but because it is spring and travel by both sledge and carriage is precarious, there is almost no communication between towns.

An edict has appeared forbidding conversation on political subjects.

In the Russian Empire, where perhaps of three men whom you meet, one comes from China, another from Persia, and the third from Lapland, you lose your ideas of distance.

Foreign newspapers are prohibited.

He has gone up to the top of a high tower at one in the morning to see the spectacle of Moscow with its hundreds of churches illuminated on Easter Eve.

Then he has been very surprised to see all the females of the family run up to him and cry out, "Christ is risen from the dead!"

When he sets out he and Mr. Poinsett will each be armed with a double-barreled gun, a brace of pistols, a dagger, and a Persian saber; each of the four servants also will have his pistols and cutlass. He will be sorry to leave Moscow.

Casan: No Man Could Suppose Himself to Be in Europe

The accommodations along the way are as they have been all over Muscovy: one room, in which you sleep with the whole family in the midst of a suffocating heat and smell; no furniture to be found but a bench and table; and an absolute dearth of provisions.

As he proceeds he finds the Tartars in the villages increasing in numbers, and the Russian fur cap giving way to the Mohammedan turban or the small embroidered coif of the Chinese.

He sleeps in the cottage of a Tcheremisse, with neither chimney nor window. The women have their petticoats only to the knee and braid their hair in long tresses, to which are tied a number of brass cylinders.

No man could suppose himself to be in Europe—though by courtesy Casan is in Europe—when he contemplates the Tartar fortifications, the singular architecture of the churches and shops, and the groups of Tartars, Tcheremesses, Tchouasses, Bashkirs, and Armenians.

An Armenian merchant promises to have a boat ready in two or three days.

To the Quarantine Grounds Near the Astracan

The beauty of the scenery on the Volga is gratifying, the right bank mountainous and well wooded. After passing Tsauritzin, where both banks were in Asia, there is nothing on either side but vast deserts of sand.

He sees great numbers of pelicans. Islands are white with them. He sees prodigious quantities of eagles, too. He and the others eat well on sterlet and its caviar. The number of fish in the Volga is astounding. The Russian peasants won't eat some of them for reasons of superstition. For example, he had too much of a sort of fish like the chad, and offered them to the boat's crew, but they refused them, saying that the fish swam round and round, and were insane, and if they ate them they, too, would become insane.

There is some reason for refusing pigeons, too, and also hares.

Samara is the winter home of a number of Calmouks. Only during the summer do they wander with their flocks in the vast steppes on the Asiatic side and encamp in their circular tents of felt. The heat of the Steppe is suffocating. The blasts of wind during the summer immediately destroy the flocks exposed to them, which instantly rot. The Tartars and Calmouks make every species of laitage known in Europe and also ardent spirits they distill from cow's and mare's milk.

He comes upon a village as distinguished for the excessive cleanliness of the houses and the neatness of the gardens as the Russian habitations are for their dirt and filth.

The town of Astracan is inhabited by thirteen or fourteen different nations, each description of merchants in a separate caravanserai.

His next excursion before he proceeds to the northern provinces of Persia will be a short distance into the desert to the habitation of a Calmouk Prince. He wants to go hawking with his daughter the Princess, who with her pipe at her mouth hunts on the unbroken horses of the desert.

Solianka: Banners in the Wind

He is staying in a village inhabited exclusively by Tartars. He visits a Calmouk camp and enters the tent of the chief Lama. It is very neat and covered with white felt, the floor matted and strewn with rose leaves. The priest shows the idols and sacred books. He brings out the banner of silk painted with the twelve signs of the zodiac. Some banners are inscribed with prayers. These are placed at the door of the tent, in the wind: letting them flutter about is supposed to be equivalent to saying the prayers. The Lama orders tea: the leaves and stalks are pressed into a large square cake and this is boiled up with butter and salt in the Mongol manner. It forms a nauseous mixture, but he drinks it and then takes his leave, all the village coming out of their tents and going down with him to the waterside. At least a third of the men in the village are priests.

To the Tartar Prince: An Enormous Sturgeon

He proceeds through the desert, which extends to the foot of Mount Caucasus. How different it is from Archangel: terrible heat instead of terrible cold, a plain of sand instead of a plain of snow, herds of camels belonging to the Calmouks instead of flocks of reindeer.

The ground is so flat they have no trouble getting along in their kibitkas. But they are often fooled by the appearance of extensive ranges of hills on the horizons, which are actually merely small inequalities magnified by intervening vapors.

The careless servants lose most of the water they have brought along with them, and then they suffer from extreme thirst, for the pools are as salt as sea water: their bottoms and sides are covered with beautiful crystals exhaling a strong smell of violets.

The plants all taste of salt, the dews are salt, and even some milk he gets from a Tartar is brackish.

Then there are swarms of mosquitoes, and he can't even talk or eat without having a mouthful of them. Sleeping is out of the question.

They cross a river where the water comes up to the windows of the carriage, which floats. They cross a marsh four miles broad and three or four feet deep.

In Kizliar he sells his kibitka and sends his carriage back to Moscow. He will cross the rest of the desert on horseback.

They spend the night in an encampment of Tartars, who bring them sour mare's milk. Early in the morning they arrive at the residence of the Tartar Prince. The people of the village bring him an enormous sturgeon that is still alive and lay it at his feet.

In the courtyard he observes a man with long hair, contrary to custom.

Derbend: His Apparent Magnitude Is Directly as His Distance

He sets out for Derbend with an escort. The caravan is very oddly composed: he and his American companion, a Swiss, a Dutchman, a Mulatto, a Tartar of Rezan, a body of Lesgees for escort, two Jews, an envoy from one of the native Princes returning from Petersburg, and three Circassian girls whom one of the guides has bought in the mountains and is taking to sell at Baku.

In Derbend he has lodgings in the home of an absent Persian. He is sent carpets and cushions and inundated with fruits and pilaus. His apparent magnitude is directly as his distance: if he was a great man at Kizliar with one orderly man to wait on him, here he is twice as great, since he has two.

In the evening he rides out with Persian friends on a white horse with its tail dyed scarlet. The Persians amuse themselves trying to unhorse each other, while he himself admires the view of the Caspian Sea, the steep rock on which the town is situated, the gardens surrounding it, and part of the chain of Caucasus rising behind it.

Garden of the World

The Russian commandant has given him an escort of Cossacks and Persians as far as the River Samoor to point out the most fordable parts and help them over.

The merchant of women is still part of the group. Now, because his girls attracted some attention in the earlier part of the journey, he encloses them in great sacks of felt, though the sun is burning hot.

It would be worthwhile for a traveler to enquire into

the traditions of a colony of Jews who live in the Dagestan near the Samoor. The groundwork of their language is Hebrew, though apparently not intelligible to the Jews of other countries.

The country from the River Samoor to Baku is fit to be the garden of the world. The crops cultivated seem to be rice, maize, cotton, millet, and a kind of bearded wheat. From the woods come apples, pears, plums, pomegranates, quinces, and white mulberries often covered with pods of silk. Almost every bush and forest tree has a vine creeping up it covered with clusters of very tolerable grapes. The main draft animal is the buffalo, the antelope is the main wild animal, and the howls of the jackals in the mountains would have disturbed their rest if they hadn't been so tired.

A Large Party of Persians

They are met by a large party of Persians headed by two brothers, who beg them to turn back to visit the Khan of Cuba. They refuse, and one brother declares they will not go farther and must fight their passage through, which they prepare to do. Since they are better armed, they would have been able to go on unmolested, but the merchant of women begs them not to desert him or he will be ruined: they have stolen his horses and say they will put him to death if he does not sell his women at their price. The party of travelers threatens to complain to the Khan at Cuba and the Persians restore the horses.

They rest in the evening at a rock called Beshbarmak, or "the five fingers," which is a great sea mark on the Caspian. From there to Baku is almost a desert with now and then a ruined caravanserai.

The day after he arrives, he receives a visit from Cassim Elfina Beg, the principal Persian of the place.

All the innumerable arches he has seen have been pointed.

The Famous Sources of Naphtha

General Gurieff, the commandant, has made a party for them to see the famous sources of naphtha, and with him and Beg and several other Persians they ride out to the principal wells. The strong smell is perceptible at a great distance and the ground about appears of the consistency of hardened pitch. One of the wells yields white naphtha; in all the others it is black, but very liquid.

The Everlasting Fire and the Fruits Thereabouts

He rides five miles farther to see the everlasting fire and the adoration of the Magi. For about two miles square, if the earth is turned up and fire applied, the vapor that escapes inflames and burns until extinguished by a violent storm. In this way the peasants calcine their lime.

In the center of this spot of ground is a square building enclosing a court. The building contains a number of cells with separate entrances. The arches of the doors are pointed, and over each is a tablet with an inscription, in characters unknown to him. In one of the cells is a small platform of clay with two pipes conveying the vapor, one of which is kept constantly burning. The inhabitant of the cell says he is a Parsee from Hindostan, the building was paid for by his countrymen, and a certain number of persons were sent from India and remained until relieved. When asked why they were sent, he answered: To venerate and adore that flame. In the center of the quadrangle is a tumulus, from an opening in which blazes out the eternal fire, surrounded by smaller spiracles of flame.

The fruits thereabout come spontaneously to perfection.

Across the Desert: A Large Panther

From Baku he sets off across the desert to Shamachee. After seventy versts they stop at a stream of water and scare up a large panther that escapes into the mountains. Early the next morning they come to old Baku, now in ruins, and in the evening to Shamachee. Here he sleeps in one of the cells of a ruined caravanserai. The poor peasants who live in the ruins have been ordered by Mustapha Khan to give the travelers provisions.

The Town of Fettag

The next day he travels over hills covered with fruit trees, down into a valley, and up a very steep mountain near the summit of which he enters the town of Fettag, residence of Mustapha the Khan of Shirvaun. The Khan lives entirely in tents and appears to be the most unpolished, ignorant, and stupid of any of the native Princes so far.

The Khan gives them a feast where the precepts of Mohammed are totally disregarded; at the conclusion, singing and dancing girls are introduced according to the Persian custom. The Khan makes them a present of horses, carpets, etc.

Fettag to Teflis: The Secretary Falls Ill

In the evening of the next day they come to a camp occupied by Azai Sultan, who is gleeful because he has won a fight over stolen cattle with some mountain people belonging to the next Sultan. The following day they are received by Giafar Kouli Khan, who gives him a long account of the way he beat the Shach's troops with an inferior number. There are puzzling things about his story but they ask no questions because it is dangerous to puzzle a potentate.

Two nights later he sleeps on the banks of the River Koor, the Cyrus of the ancients. On the road from Ganja to Teflis, his secretary Pauwells falls ill with a putrid fever. There is no cart to be procured and they are given false information that causes them to lie out for three nights exposed to the unwholesome dews of the Koor. They then reach a Cossack station, where they leave the secretary. They ride on to Teflis and send back a cart for him, but though he has medical attention he dies within four or five days.

In Teflis: One of the Best Cities

He is glad to be at Teflis, one of the best cities in this part of Asia. The baths are supplied by a fine natural warm spring. The women deserve their reputation for beauty. Those that are sold for slaves to the Mohammedans are those that are called Circassians, for the Circassians or Tcherkesses who are themselves Mohammedans seldom sell their children.

He has a letter of introduction to the Queen of Imiretia in her capital on the banks of the Phasis. She is in fact merely a nominal sovereign. She does not live in a cave, as he had been told, but receives them in her house, in a room fitted with sofas, ornamented with looking glasses, and hung round with pictures of the imperial family.

The climate here, however, is unwholesome, singularly prejudicial to strangers, and he and his companion Poinsett go to bed with violent attacks of fever. The other three servants are ill, too.

He decides that Ispahan can't any longer be considered the capital of Persia.

He learns that Count Gudovitch has obtained a victory near Cars over Yussuff Pacha.

He hears that there are rumors of peace between France and Russia; nobody knows if England is included.

With the Help of Some Bark: Over the Caucasus

As soon as he can sit a horse he takes leave of his Georgian friends, and rides out of the town. The snow and ice on Mount Caucasus, along with the help of some bark he gets from a Roman Catholic missionary, restore him to perfect health and strength as soon as he begins ascending the mountain.

The Caucasus is inhabited by about twenty nations, most of them speaking distinct languages, so that the inhabitants of one valley, insulated from the rest of the world, often can't make themselves understood if they cross the mountain.

They have purchased a tent and thus avoid stopping in towns where there is plague. On this side of the Russian frontier, it almost threatens to wipe out some of the Mohammedan nations. In some of the villages he passes, all the people have died, other villages are completely deserted, they scarcely see one man in the whole country and the few they see they carefully avoid.

Some people of the tribe of the Caftouras intend to attack them but by mistake attack some Cossacks instead. One Cossack is left dead and one mortally wounded.

They make thirty-six versts to Kobia, pass by Kazbek, the highest part of the Caucasus, make twenty-eight versts in the rocky valley of Dagran, then leave the mountain and advance to the fortress of Vladi Caveass. They cross the little Cabarda entirely depopulated by the plague. On the road he sees the dead bodies of Cossacks and fragments of their lances strewn about.

Here in Mozdok, they are in quarantine.

Mozdok to Taman: Fevers

The ground has recently been overflowed by the Terek, his tent is not waterproof and the country is famous for fevers. He lies several days on the earth with a violent fever, surrounded by basins to catch the rain, which does not stop him from being drenched by it.

A change of situation and a thorough tanning of bark make him well again, but he is detained at Georgievsk by the illness of his fellow traveler.

They will go along the Cuban to Taman, the site of the Greek colony Phanagoria, and so over the Cimmerian Bosphorus to Kerch, the ancient Panticapaeum.

Taman: In the European Manner

At Stauropol he has a third fever that reduces him so low he cannot stand without fainting away. His optic nerves become so relaxed as to make him blind; with his right eye he can scarcely distinguish at night the flame of a candle. As he regains strength, his vision returns.

He recovers from the fever by using James's Powder in very large doses, but remains some time very deaf, subject to alarming palpitations of the heart, and so weak that he cannot stand long.

At Taman, they are detained some time by their interpreter falling ill. They are determined to wait there for his recovery, but he grows weaker rather than stronger, being housed in a damp lodging. Fellow traveler Poinsett suffers so severely from a bilious fever and becomes so weak they are very apprehensive for him, but then all rapidly regain strength, due to some light frost, to living in the European manner, and to the great attention of General Fanshaw, the Governor of the Crimea, who is an Englishman.

Back to Moscow: A Scotch Physician

They stop off in Kiev, the third city in Russia. Here the language is more Polish than Russian.

He loses another servant. The man is lethargic, refuses to exercise, secretly throws away his medicine, grows worse, is brought along lying on a bed in a kibitka toward the house of an English merchant, halfway there gets out, with the help of another servant gets in again, falls into a lethargic sleep, and on their arrival at the inn in Moscow is found dead.

Thus, of four servants who left this city with them, only one has returned, a stout Negro of Poinsett's, who has borne the climate better than any of them.

Of his wardrobe, all he has left now is one coat and a pair of pantaloons.

He hopes to sail directly from Petersburg to Harwich.

In the meantime, here in Moscow, he has put himself under the direction of a Scotch physician, Dr. Keir, who prescribes absolute repose for the next four months and has ordered a course of bark and vitriolic acid, beef, mutton, and claret.

Improved Health: A Gentlemanlike Slimness

His health has improved quickly, he has lost every bad symptom: his dropsical legs have reduced to a gentleman-like slimness, a fair round belly swelled and as hard as a board has shrunk to its former insignificance, and he is no longer annoyed by palpitations of the heart and pulsations of the head.

Within the past three days he has recovered his voice, which he had lost for two months. He is leading the life of a monk.

Poinsett leaves soon. Then he will set about writing a journal of the tour, though the mode of traveling during the first part of the journey, and the scarcity of chairs and tables, as well as the illness of the second part, have been very unfavorable to journalizing. In addition, the few notes he had taken were rendered illegible by crossing a torrent.

The End of the Tour: Shipwreck

He goes to Petersburg and finds his friends Colonel and Mrs. Pollen. Together they will go to Liebau in the Dutchy of Courland and try to sail to England by way of Sweden. He is suffering from the shock his constitution received in the south of Russia. He has frequent attacks of fever and ague and is nursed by the Colonel and his wife.

After three weeks in Liebau they engage a passage to

Carlscrona on the ship *Agatha*, embarking on April 2. They sail, the weather is fine, the ice lies close about a mile from shore, they get through it at the rate of two miles an hour and are in clear water by 3 p.m. All that day and the next they have light breezes from the southeast. On the fourth, at about 2 p.m., they sight the Island of Oeland at a distance of eight or nine miles. It is blowing very hard: in an hour they get close in and see the ice about a mile from the shore.

Colonel Pollen wonders if they can anchor under Oeland, and another passenger, an English seaman by the name of Mr. Smith, thinks not, as the ice would drift off and cut the cables. The captain says he will stand on to the southward till eight o'clock, then return to the island, but at eight and at twelve he will not go back: now it blows a gale of wind from the westward with a very heavy sea. The vessel makes much water and the pumps are choked with ballast. The crew will bail very little; the water gains fast.

On the fifth they run the whole day before the wind. At noon on the sixth, Colonel Pollen wonders if the vessel can keep the sea. The English seaman says that unless the sailors make more efforts to bail she can't live long, since they already have three feet of water in the hold and it is gaining on them. The best way to save themselves is to steer for some port in Prussia. The Colonel agrees and tells the captain. The captain agrees and recommends Liebau, but the Colonel objects on account of the English seaman and a certain Mr. Renny, who have both escaped from Russia without passports. The captain agrees to go to Memel, but says he has never been there in his life: if the English seaman will take the ship in, he will give it over into his charge when they come to the bar. The seaman agrees because he knows the harbor perfectly well.

At two o'clock in the morning on the seventh they sight land to the southward about fifteen miles from Memel. They are close in to a lee shore because of the captain's ignorance and carelessness in running so far in the dark. They haul the ship to by the wind on the larboard tack, and at four o'clock get sight of Memel, which the captain takes for Liebau until he is told otherwise, when he is very surprised. Colonel Pollen and the other gentlemen come on deck and tell the captain to give the charge to the English seaman, which he does.

At six they come to the bar, the tide running very high, with two men at the helm. The passengers are pressing around the helm in a way that is dangerous to themselves and prevents the helmsmen from seeing ahead very well, so the English seaman asks them to go below. But now, unfortunately, the captain sees the sea breaking over the bar and becomes so frightened that he runs immediately to the helm and with the help of his people puts it hard-a-port. Though the English seaman strives against this, in ten minutes they are on the Southlands.

The third time the ship strikes, she grounds and fills with water. They are about a mile and a half from shore.

There is a small roundhouse on deck and Mrs. Pollen, Mrs. Barnes, her three children, two gentlemen, a man- and a maidservant get into this to save themselves from the sea. Colonel Pollen and the English seaman begin to clear the boats out; the sailors will not help. They get the small one out and three sailors get into it with the captain. Lord Royston, who is in a very weak state of health, tries to follow them but the English seaman prevents him, telling him it is not safe. When the captain hears this, he gets out. When the boat leaves the ship's side it turns over and the three men drown.

They begin to clear the large boat. It is lashed to the deck by strong tackling to the ring-bolts. A sea comes and forces away part of the tackling. The English seaman calls to Colonel Pollen to jump out or the next sea will carry her and them all away. They are scarcely out of her when she is washed overboard. Now they have no hope but in the mercy of Providence. At nine o'clock they cut away the mast to ease the vessel, but can see nothing of the lifeboat, which makes them very uneasy, for the sea is tremendous, breaking right over their heads, and it is so very cold that it is impossible to hold fast by anything.

Colonel Pollen wonders if the roundhouse will stand and is told it will, as long as the bottom of the vessel.

Colonel Pollen goes to the door of the roundhouse and begs Mrs. Pollen not to stir from the roundhouse, for the lifeboat will soon come. It is now about half past nine but no boat is to be seen. The vessel is entirely full of water except near the roundhouse. Mr. Renny is soon washed overboard and after him, at about ten o'clock, all within a few seas of each other, Colonel Pollen, Mr. Baillie, and Mr. Becker, one sailor, Lord Royston's servant, Mrs. Barnes's servant, and Lord Royston himself.

An account of the catastrophe is published three years later in the *Gentleman's Magazine* by the English seaman, Mr. Smith.

The Other

She changes this thing in the house to annoy the other, and the other is annoyed and changes it back, and she changes this other thing in the house to annoy the other, and the other is annoyed and changes it back, and then she tells all this the way it happens to some others and they think it is funny, but the other hears it and does not think it is funny, but can't change it back.

A Friend of Mine

I am thinking about a friend of mine, how she is not only what she believes she is, she is also what friends believe her to be, and what her family believes her to be, and even what she is in the eyes of chance acquaintances and total strangers. About certain things, her friends have one opinion and she has another. She thinks, for instance, that she is overweight and not as well educated as she should be, but her friends know she is perfectly thin and better educated than most of us. About other things she agrees, for instance that she is amusing in company, likes to be on time, likes other people to be on time, and is not orderly in her housekeeping. Perhaps it must be true that the things about which we all agree are part of what she really is, or what she really would be if there were such a thing as what she really is, because when I look for what she really is, I find only contradictions everywhere: even when she and her friends all agree about something, this thing may not seem correct to a chance acquaintance, who may find her sullen in company or her rooms very neat, for instance, and will not be entirely wrong, since there are times when she is dull, and times when she keeps a neat house, though they are not the same times, for she will not be neat when she is feeling dull.

All this being true of my friend, it occurs to me that I must not know altogether what I am, either, and that others know certain things about me better than I do, though I think I ought to know all there is to know and I proceed as if I do. Even once I see this, however, I have no choice but to continue to proceed as if I know altogether what I am, though I may also try to guess, from time to time, just what it is that others know that I do not know.

This Condition

In this condition: stirred not only by men but by women, fat and thin, naked and clothed; by teenagers and children in latency; by animals such as horses and dogs; by certain vegetables such as carrots, zucchinis, eggplants, and cucumbers; by fruits such as melons, grapefruits, and kiwis; by certain plant parts such as petals, sepals, stamens, and pistils; by the bare arm of a wooden chair, a round vase holding flowers, a little hot sunlight, a plate of pudding, a person entering a tunnel in the distance, a puddle of water, a hand alighting on a smooth stone, a hand alighting on a bare shoulder, a naked tree limb; by anything curved, bare, and shining, as the limb or bole of a tree; by any touch, as the touch of a stranger handling money; by anything round and freely hanging, as tassels on a curtain, chestnut burrs on a twig in spring, a wet tea bag on its string; by anything glowing, as a hot coal; anything soft or slow, as a cat rising from a chair; anything smooth and dry, as a stone, or warm and glistening; anything sliding, anything sliding back and forth; anything sliding in and out with an oiled surface, as certain machine parts; anything of a certain shape, like the state of Florida; anything pounding, anything stroking; anything bolt upright, anything horizontal and gaping, as a certain sea anemone; anything warm, anything wet, anything wet and red, anything turning red, as the sun at evening; anything wet and pink; anything long and straight with a blunt end, as a pestle; anything coming out of anything else, as a snail from its shell, as a snail's horns from its head; anything opening; any stream of water running, any stream running, any stream spurting, any stream spouting; any cry, any soft cry, any grunt; anything going into anything else, as a hand searching in a purse; anything clutching, anything grasping; anything rising, anything tightening or filling, as a sail; anything dripping, anything hardening, anything softening.

Go Away

When he says, “Go away and don’t come back,” you are hurt by the words even though you know he does not mean what the words say, or rather you think he probably means “Go away” because he is so angry at you he does not want you anywhere near him right now, but you are quite sure he does not want you to stay away, he must want you to come back, either soon or later, depending on how quickly he may grow less angry during the time you are away, how he may remember other less angry feelings he often has for you that may soften his anger now. But though he does mean “Go away,” he does not mean it as much as he means the anger that the words have in them, as he also means the anger in the words “don’t come back.” He means all the anger meant by someone who says such words and means what the words say, that you should not come back, ever, or rather he means most of the anger meant by such a person, for if he meant all the anger he would also mean what the words themselves say, that you should not come back, ever. But, being angry, if he were merely to say, “I’m very angry at you,” you would not be as hurt as you are, or you would not be hurt at all, even though the degree of anger, if it could be measured, might be exactly the same. Or perhaps the degree of anger could not be the same. Or perhaps it could be the same but the anger would have to be of a different kind, a kind that could be shared as a problem, whereas this kind can be told only in these words he does not mean. So it is not the anger in these words that hurts you, but the fact that he chooses to say words to you that mean you should never come back, even though he does not mean what the words say, even though only the words themselves mean what they say.

Pastor Elaine's Newsletter

We went to church a year ago on Easter Sunday because we had just moved to this town and wanted to feel part of the community. At that time we put our name on the church mailing list and now we receive its newsletter.

Every day, almost, we walk to the post office in the late afternoon and then around by the park and on to the hardware store or the library.

On our way from the playground to the library, we sometimes see Pastor Elaine in her yard, in her shorts, weeding around the phlox near the back door, which has a sign on it that reads "Pastor's Study." Now we learn from what she writes in the church newsletter that she has lost most of her newly planted tomatoes and eggplants to a "night creature" and is angry.

"I was furious!" she says. She is furious not only at the night creature but also at herself for her carelessness or forgetfulness, because the same thing happened to her last year. "Why had I forgotten it?" she asks.

There is a point to her story, a lesson she wants to teach us, which is that "it is our human condition that brings us back again and again to doing the things we would rather not be doing. We are far from perfection. I forget this at times and get so annoyed with myself."

We are often angry at ourselves, too, for such things as carelessness and forgetfulness, and things we feel are much worse.

Pastor Elaine uses the Bible to illustrate her lesson. "Paul put it so well," she says, before going on to quote from Romans: "I do not understand what I do; for I don't do what I would like to do, but instead I do what I hate. What an unhappy man I am. Who will rescue me from this body that is taking me to death?"

This seems too strong a reaction for the mistake Pastor Elaine has made in her garden, since she is not doing what she "hates" by setting plants in the ground without proper fencing, but we read closely what she has to say because it does describe exactly what we often do. We often do what we hate. We often tell ourselves what we would like to do, most importantly that we would like to be kind to our children, and gentle with them, and patient, and then we do not do what we would like to do, but what we hate; that is, we lose our patience suddenly and shout at them, or squeeze them, or shake them, or pound our fist on the table and frighten them. And we, too, do not understand why. Is it that we do not want to do what we so much believe we want to do?

We are sometimes aware that the ugly sounds coming from us may be overheard by the good family next door, whose younger son is an altar boy at what they call the BVM or the Perpetual. But this does not have the power to stop us.

We are not Christian but we have a Bible belonging to a churchgoing mother of ours, and although we are not believers, we think that if we read the same words believers read, we might also be comforted or learn something. The passage quoted by Pastor Elaine is a little different in our Bible. It begins: "For that which I do I know not: for what

I would, that do I not; but what I hate, that do I. For to will is present with me; but how to perform that which is good I find not. For the good that I would I do not: but the evil which I would not, that I do."

This sounds quite like our situation, though what we do, we would not call evil but wrong. We will, we will with great determination, up in the privacy of our study, up in the bathroom, anywhere we are alone. But when it comes to performing what is good, sitting over lunch between our two children, who are not bad children, if the older one, bored, is teasing us and the younger one, tired, is fussing, our will is weak, in fact it is powerless. Then what does it mean to will, at all, if we can't perform? All that willing, upstairs, is for nothing. It seems that we are able to will only from a very shallow place and when we draw upon all the will in us it is quickly used up and there is nothing left. Or something else, if not that, is wrong with the way we will.

When we lose our patience so suddenly, we feel possessed, as by some outside force, almost as it is described in the next lines we read: "Now if I do that I would not, it is no more I that do it, but sin that dwelleth in me. For I know that in me (that is, in my flesh), dwelleth no good thing." It is as though it were not we who were doing what we do, but some being we do not recognize. Certainly we do not recognize ourselves, in our fury, as what we have so lately been, gentle, for we can be gentle. Only, this other being does not seem like sin to us, but a living demon, and does not seem to dwell in us, but only to come into us sometimes and then leave again. Unless it is in us all the time, but quiet, and is then roused by some aggravation.

"I see another law in my members, warring against the law of my mind," says our Bible. But if there is another law in us, it does not seem to be in our members, in our body, but elsewhere, in our passions, raging like a storm, possessing us, and warring against the law of our mind. Unless, arising in our passions, it then spreads to our members, for we can sometimes feel that into our flesh no good thing comes: our blood becomes hot and our nerves sing, when we are angry.

A small italic *c* next to "in me (that is, in my flesh) dwelleth no good thing" refers us to two sentences in Genesis and we look through the book for those sentences. The first one we find reads: "The imagination of man's heart is evil from his youth." The second uses many of the same words but does not mean exactly the same thing: "Every imagination of the thoughts of his heart was only evil continually." We will not say that we are filled with evil continually, because if no good thing comes into our flesh, it comes only sometimes. If we know it is not in us all the time, though, we may be able to say it is not just wrong but evil, this thing, this demon or poison that comes into us and pinches and wrinkles our features so that we are told, "You should see your face!"

"Who shall deliver me from the body of this death?" the passage continues. But in our case, we often become so ashamed that we wish we might be rescued right now, in the midst of life, from this body that is sometimes so filled with no good thing and so obedient to a law that wars against the law of our mind—our sharp mind, but our weak mind. Or our sharp mind, but our weak will. Or our strong will, but our disobedient will. Is that it—that our mind is sharp and has a law, but our will is strong and disobedient?

Toward the end of the newsletter we read that Pastor Elaine will be away for some weeks over the summer and that if we should need spiritual assistance during this time we may call any elder or the vice president, whose telephone number she gives. But in this town we would not be able to go to any elder or the vice president with our troubles.

If we were to go to Pastor Elaine herself for spiritual assistance, she might point to another passage, one we have seen by chance in Galatians: "But the fruit of the Spirit is love, joy, peace, long-suffering, gentleness, goodness, faith." How we would like to have in us this thing, the fruit of the Spirit. We read the list again and this time read it against the list of what is sometimes in us: love, joy, peace, gentleness, and goodness. We do not seem to have faith. As for long-suffering, we do not know if it is something one can have in small amounts. And now we see that it may be in the absence of long-suffering that no good thing comes into our flesh and we become vicious, as though possessed, and in the same moment lose, for a time, all love, joy, peace, gentleness, and goodness. Yet we do not know how to gain more long-suffering. It is not enough to want it, or to will it, or to will it from such a shallow place, anyway, as we do.

We take our usual walk to the post office and then by Pastor Elaine's house and on to the hardware store to look for a fluorescent lightbulb. We see that Pastor Elaine has hung her wash on the line in back, above her phlox. We see through the window that the light is on in her study, although here, outside, the sun is bright. We think how we have been with our children this day or the day before, how we have stood holding the little one, so heavy, and put out our hand to push the arm of the older one to get him out of our way or to make him move faster, or driven in the car with them in the heat, damp, with a knot of rage in us, and yearned to reach inside, or outside, somewhere, and find more long-suffering, and have not known how to do it. And we wonder: What stores of anger have we laid down in the older one already? What hardness are we putting in the heart of the little one, where there was no hardness?

A Man in Our Town

A man in our town is both a dog and its master. The master is impossibly unjust to the dog and makes its life a misery. One minute he wants to romp with it and the next minute he slaps it down for being so unruly. He beats it severely over its nose and hindquarters because it has slept on his bed and left its hairs on his pillow, and yet there are evenings when he is lonely and pulls the dog up to lie beside him, though the dog trembles with fear.

But the fault is not all on one side. No one else would tolerate a dog like this one. The smell of this dog is so sour and pungent that it is far more frightening and aggressive than the dog itself, who is shy and pees uncontrollably when taken by surprise. It is a foul and sopping creature.

Yet the master should hardly notice this, since he often drinks himself sick and spends the night curled against an alley wall.

At sundown we see him loping easily along the edge of the park, his nose to the breeze; he slows to a trot and circles to find a scent, scratches the stubble on his head and takes out a cigarette, lights it with trembling hands, and then sits down on a bench after wiping it with his handkerchief. He smokes quietly until his cigarette has burned down to a stub. Then he explodes into wild anger and begins punching his head and kicking himself in the legs. When he is exhausted, he turns his face up to the sky and howls in frustration. Only sometimes, then, he will pet himself on the head until he is comforted.

A Second Chance

If only I had a chance to learn from my mistakes, I would, but there are too many things you don't do twice; in fact, the most important things are things you don't do twice, so you can't do them better the second time. You do something wrong, and see what the right thing would have been, and are ready to do it, should you have the chance again, but the next experience is quite different, and your judgment is wrong again, and though you are now prepared for this experience should it repeat itself, you are not prepared for the next experience. If only, for instance, you could get married at eighteen twice, then the second time you could make sure you were not too young to do this, because you would have the perspective of being older, and would know that the person advising you to marry this man was giving you the wrong advice because his reasons were the same ones he gave you the last time he advised you to get married at eighteen. If you could bring a child from a first marriage into a second marriage a second time, you would know that generosity could turn to resentment if you did not do the right things and resentment back to kindness if you did, unless the man you married when you married a second time for the second time was quite different in temperament from the man you married when you married a second time for the first time, in which case you would have to marry that one twice also in order to learn just what the wisest course would be to take with a man of his temperament. If you could have your mother die a second time you might be prepared to fight for a private room that had no other person in it watching television while she died, but if you were prepared to fight for that, and did, you might have to lose your mother again in order to know enough to ask them to put her teeth in the right way and not the wrong way before you went into her room and saw her for the last time grinning so strangely, and then yet one more time to make sure her ashes were not buried again in that plain sort of airmail container in which she was sent north to the cemetery.

Fear

Nearly every morning, a certain woman in our community comes running out of her house with her face white and her overcoat flapping wildly. She cries out, "Emergency, emergency," and one of us runs to her and holds her until her fears are calmed. We know she is making it up; nothing has really happened to her. But we understand, because there is hardly one of us who has not been moved at some time to do just what she has done, and every time, it has taken all our strength, and even the strength of our friends and families, too, to quiet us.

Almost No Memory

A certain woman had a very sharp consciousness but almost no memory. She remembered enough to get by from day to day. She remembered enough to work, and she worked hard. She did good work, and was paid for it, and earned enough to get by, but she did not remember her work, so that she could not answer questions about it when people asked, as they did ask, since the work she did was interesting.

She remembered enough to get by, and to do her work, but she did not learn from what she did, or heard, or read. For she did read, she loved to read, and she took good notes on what she read, on the ideas that came to her from what she read, since she did have some ideas of her own, and even on her ideas about these ideas. Some of her ideas were even very good ideas, since she had a very sharp consciousness. And so she kept good notebooks and added to them year by year, and because many years passed this way, she had a long shelf of these notebooks, in which her handwriting became smaller and smaller.

Sometimes, when she was tired of reading a book, or when she was moved by a sudden curiosity she did not altogether understand, she would take an earlier notebook from the shelf and read a little of it, and she would be interested in what she read. She would be interested in the notes she had once taken on a book she was reading or on her own ideas. It would seem all new to her, and indeed most of it would be new to her. Sometimes she would only read and think, and sometimes she would make a note in her current notebook of what she was reading in a notebook from an earlier time, or she would make a note of an idea that came to her from what she was reading. Other times she would want to make a note but choose not to, since she did not think it quite right to make a note of what was already a note, though she did not fully understand what was not right about it. She wanted to make a note of a note she was reading, because this was her way of understanding what she read, though she was not assimilating what she read into her mind, or not for long, but only into another notebook. Or she wanted to make a note because to make a note was her way of thinking this thought.

Although most of what she read was new to her, sometimes she immediately recognized what she read and had no doubt that she herself had written it, and thought it. It seemed perfectly familiar to her, as though she had just thought it that very day, though in fact she had not thought it for some years, unless reading it again was the same as thinking it again, or the same as thinking it for the first time, and though she might never have thought it again, if she had not happened to read it in her notebook. And so she knew by this that these notebooks truly had a great deal to do with her, though it was hard for her to understand, and troubled her to try to understand, just how they had to do with her, how much they were of her and how much they were outside her and not of her, as they sat there on the shelf, being what she knew but did not know, being what she had read but did not remember reading, being what she had thought but did not now think, or remember thinking, or if she remembered, then did not know whether she was thinking it now or whether she had only once thought it, or understand why she had had a thought once and then years later the same thought, or a thought once and then never that same thought again.

Mr. Knockly

Last fall my aunt burned to death when the boardinghouse where she lived went up in flames. There was nothing left of her but a small pile of half-destroyed objects in one corner of her room, where I think she must have been sitting when the fire broke out: her false teeth, the frames of her glasses, her pearls, the eyelets of her leather boots, and her two long knitting needles coiled like snakes in the ash.

It was a gray day. Friends of the dead picked their way through the rubble like lonely ants, wheeling and backtracking. Every now and then a woman cried out in horror and was taken away. The chimneys were still intact: everything else had crumbled. Rain began to fall slowly on the crowd. Two firemen, pale from sleeplessness, kicked the rubble with their boots and stopped several people from going near the house.

My aunt was dead. Or worse than dead, since there was nothing left of her to call dead. I wondered, with some fear, what would become of her old lover Mr. Knockly, a small man, who stood in the thickest cluster of men and women, his face like a white pimple among their overcoats, staring at the ruin as though his heart had been burned out of him. When I went near him he ran away from me in his tiny boots. The collar of his jacket was turned up and his gray crew cut sparkled with rain. He moved as though he had been wounded in the legs and arms, the chest, the neck, as though he had been shot full of holes.

I saw him again on the following Sunday, at the funeral. In front of the church there were seven coffins. It occurred to me later that the coffins must have been empty. The church was full: only one of the dead had been a complete stranger—the police were still sending photographs of his teeth to cities as far away as Chicago. Near me sat an old man with glassy eyes who was drawn like a magnet to any gathering of people: I had once seen him throwing confetti onto a parade from the window of a deserted house. In the first pew was a pious woman who spent a great deal of time in church praying. Mr. Knockly was at the back, his head bowed so far over that it was barely visible.

He rode in the car with me behind the hearse, but looked out the window at the scrap-iron conversion plants and did not answer when I spoke to him. In the cemetery he stood by my aunt's coffin until it was lowered into the grave. His face was so palsied with grief, he seemed so nearly out of control, that I thought he would jump into the grave with her. But instead he turned away abruptly after the "dust to dust," and walked alone through the gate. There was no sign of him on the road when I returned in the car.

It was early October. The days were long and cool. I went out every evening and walked. I would leave home before the sun set and stay out until night had fallen and the sky was completely dark. I went a different way each time, through back alleys, along dirt paths by the river, away from the river, over the hill on the outskirts of town, down through the main streets. I looked into doorways, into living rooms, into store windows; I watched through the glass as people ate dinner by themselves in coffee shops; I walked behind restaurants through clouds of steam from the kitchens and through the noise of clattering dishes.

I think I might have been searching for Mr. Knockly, though often I went where I was unlikely to find him. I didn't even know if he was still in town: with my aunt gone, there was no reason for him to stay here. But when I saw him again, I felt as though I had wanted, all this time, to see him again.

I was walking in the muddy lane behind a seafood restaurant, after a heavy rainstorm. The clouds had broken up and the sky was light in places, but the sun had set. I thought there was no one with me in the lane, but I heard a noise at the other end, and saw him. He was wearing a white work shirt and white apron with a red anchor on it, and he was emptying a small garbage pail into one of the large ones that stood in a row by the back door of the restaurant. As I went up to him, he was jerking the pail up and down to free the clotted garbage. His head was bowed. I spoke to him and he looked up quickly. Garbage spilled onto the ground. He stood still for a moment; the emotion that had been in his face at the funeral had died away: his eyes, his mouth, were blunt and dogged. I said something to him, and for a moment I thought he would answer: his face moved, his lips unstuck. But when I put out my hand to take hold of him, he shied away and went indoors. There was a break in the noise from the kitchen. I stood there sinking into the mud and looking at the spilled garbage: crab's claws, sauce. The door opened a crack, and a black face blocked the light, then the door shut again. I felt uncomfortable. I felt suddenly that it was very strange for me to be there. I left.

But I went back the next evening, and the evening after. The rest of the town had little meaning for me. I would stop on the sidewalk in front of the restaurant, pushed back and forth by the people passing behind me, and stare at the red neon anchor in the window, the tables inside, the cashier's desk, the waitresses, the manager, and the assistant manager, with whom I had once had some unpleasant dealings. I would catch glimpses of Mr. Knockly through the swinging door at the back. When someone noticed me, I would leave. Or I would walk quickly through the lane behind, almost afraid of being discovered there. I did this so often that, even in the deepest silence, the noise of the restaurant was in my ears, the sharp noise by the lane, the softer noise fronting the street.

I stayed out later and later in the evenings. I walked after the sky was completely dark, after I had seen people go home or into restaurants for dinner or into the movie house; sometimes I went on walking until the streets were deserted, the movie house darkened, and no one left in the restaurant but the owner sitting at one of the tables and writing something; and then I would not go home until the only waking life was in the bars along the riverfront. I explored every corner of the town: I thought there was not much in it that I liked, but there were things—a flight of steps, an arched doorway, the front of a factory—that drew me, and I would return to them again and again, look at them under different lights and in the dark, as if trying to discover something about them. The people of the town, though, remained strangers: I could not realize that I must be seeing some of them over and over again, it was as though each passed through only once, as though there were always new strangers coming here. And I felt so much a stranger myself that when, as rarely happened, I crossed the path of someone who knew me, and who spoke to me, I was startled and could hardly answer.

I expected to see Mr. Knockly again, but it did not occur to me to wait for him outside the restaurant. When I followed him, it was almost involuntary.

I was pushing my way through the crowd of people leaving work early in the evening when I saw his bowed shoulders and small head in front of me, moving more slowly than the people around him. I stopped, in order not to stumble over him. I watched him: he walked with his legs wide apart as if otherwise he might lose his balance, and he rocked slightly from side to side. I walked after him to the end of the main street. I dropped farther behind, and followed him in and out of the side streets. He circled back to the main street, more empty now, and then headed down to the river. There was no logic to the path he took. I was puzzled and tired. After an hour, night had fallen. We were not five minutes from where I had first seen him. Then he stopped short on the sidewalk. He stood still for a little while, then moved, then nearly ran, toward the river. I lost him.

The next night I waited for him outside the restaurant. I followed him again, and the same thing happened as had happened the night before, and for several nights after, the same. Always his brown coat ahead of me like a smudge in the gloom, always his pause and his sudden running, and always emptiness when I went after him. Then one night I did not lose him, but, running myself, followed him across the bridge and up to the door of a bar. I stopped there.

For a long while, I walked up and down the river trying to decide whether or not to go in and talk to Mr. Knockly. I knew I had no business bothering him, and I was embarrassed. I leaned against a wall above the water, watching the wharf lights speckled on the surface: there was almost no current, but sometimes a slight breeze moved the water, and then the lights jumped. Below me, on the narrow and sodden strip of land, a woman, bulky in her coat, blacker than the black water, rummaged in a bag that stood at her feet, pulled things out of it that I couldn't identify in the dark, and threw them into the water. The soft splashes were the only noises, except for an occasional passing car up on the main street across the river, and an occasional shouting voice from over on the left somewhere beyond the warehouses.

At last I walked back to the bar. I don't know why I was so sure he would still be there. I went in and looked around the room. There were a few men standing over their drinks, watching me. Mr. Knockly was not one of them. I looked back into a smoky corner and saw two prostitutes sitting silently together. Their legs were crossed, their bare arms rested on the table in front of them. I went closer and saw that Mr. Knockly was there. He lay asleep with his head in the lap of one of them, his arms and legs tightly folded against his body, the tail of his overcoat in the sawdust on the floor. Then, as I stood there, the woman picked up her glass and emptied a little beer into his eyes, and into his ear. He hardly moved, only kicked the back of the bench with his foot. The women smiled slightly at him, looked away, looked up at me, and stared with hostility. I didn't know what to do, thought of buying a drink, but wasn't thirsty. I went out.

Weeks passed before I dared go to the back door of the seafood restaurant and ask for Mr. Knockly. A thin man of about forty, dressed in the same white shirt and apron that Mr. Knockly had worn, with pale arms, a dish towel over one shoulder and a stack of clean plates with red anchors on them in his hands, looked me up and down curiously. Other men in the kitchen also paused in their work. The man said that for weeks Mr. Knockly had not worked there. In a skeptical tone of voice he added that Mr. Knockly had found work somewhere else. He didn't know where.

For days after that, it rained. When the rain stopped, the wind sprang up, and when the wind abated, the rain came down again. I lost the sense of what clear daylight was. I had nearly given up hope of speaking to Mr. Knockly: I had thrown away the one reasonable chance. Then I saw him again late in the evening on the main street, in the rain. He was weaving back and forth over the sidewalk and jabbing the air with his fists. His hair had grown longer and was plastered to his forehead and cheeks. He plunged toward a woman who drew back against the wall in fright, he veered into the entrance of the movie house and out again, a tall man in a business suit caught him by the arms and pushed him aside, he stumbled over the curbstone and fell. As I went toward him, he picked himself up and rushed headlong into the alley beside the movie house. I went after him under the fire escapes. Though I had nearly caught up with him at the next corner, when I turned it the street was empty.

After that night, which was in late December, I was completely worn out. I did not walk as often, and when I walked did not see what was around me: though I looked up at the housefronts, at the sky, again and again I found myself watching the pavement that rolled out under my feet.

The days lengthened. In town, there was little sign of the changing season. I walked out into the country now and then, but though I tried to look, I saw nothing, or remembered nothing, of the spring. At the day's end I only felt, in the soles of my feet, the blanket of grass beyond the factories, the rutted road that skirted the woods, and the vibrating iron of the bridge over the narrow part of the river.

When Mr. Knockly died, I was there. Summer had come. I had walked in the morning, to the town dump. On the other side of the wire fence, among the hillocks of broken glass and old shoes, I saw a cluster of men bending over and flailing something with sticks and bottles. When I came up to the wire fence, they ran off over the rubble. I went through to Mr. Knockly. One arm was twisted under him. One temple was dented. His face was hidden in the ashes. I saw no blood.

On the far side of the dump, fires were blazing. The flames were barely visible in the sunlight. The meadows beyond trembled in the heat.

I telephoned the police and reported his murder. I hung up when they asked my name.

How He Is Often Right

Often I think that his idea of what we should do is wrong, and my idea is right. Yet I know that he has often been right before, when I was wrong. And so I let him make his wrong decision, telling myself, though I can't believe it, that his wrong decision may actually be right. And then later it turns out, as it often has before, that his decision was the right one, after all. Or, rather, his decision was still wrong, but wrong for circumstances different from the circumstances as they actually were, while it was right for circumstances I clearly did not understand.

The Rape of the Tanuk Women

One day when the Tanuk men were away from their village hunting, an entire village of Tunit men came to their igloos and raped their women to satisfy an old grudge. When the Tanuk men returned and saw the traces of blood and tears, they vowed to take revenge for this insult and immediately left for the village of the Tunit, several days' journey away over the thick coastal ice. They knew they would find the Tunit men sleeping as only men can sleep who have raped and traveled several days through the bitter winds of mid-winter. Yet when they arrived in the Tunit village and crept through the passageways into the Tunit igloos, they found them cold and empty. They hacked off pieces of frozen meat from Tunit seal carcasses and chewed them as they deliberated upon their next move.

But in the absence of the Tanuk men, as the Tanuk women slowly recovered their calm, the Tunit men came creeping into their camp again and down the passageways into their igloos. Again the Tunit men lay with the Tanuk women and vanished into the vast stretches of sunless, ice-bound land that lay beyond the circle of igloos. While this was happening, however, the Tunit women returned to their camp and found the Tanuk men dozing there in frustration. Too disheartened to rape the Tunit women in revenge, as they might have done, the Tanuk men left them in order to search for the Tunit men elsewhere.

As they started toward home, Nigerk, the south wind, filled the air with snow and made it difficult for them to walk. They struggled on through the wall of dancing flakes, and suddenly before them they saw the shapes of men. They sprang with blood lust, thinking vengeance was within reach. Yet the shapes of men melted away at their touch and re-formed at a distance. Though the Tanuk men attacked them again and again, they could not harm them, for these were not the Tunit, as the Tanuk thought, but merely polar spirits.

Several days later, the Tanuk men reached their village and the igloos of their crazed wives and sisters. As their men had remained away, the women had been visited a third time by the Tunit and then, as though that were not injury enough, by the polar spirits as well, and they no longer recognized their own husbands and brothers. Their fear did not leave them until the sun rose in the spring. Only then, as the ice began to loosen its hold and the waters to reappear, did their eyes rest once again gently on their husbands and brothers.

What I Feel

These days I try to tell myself that what I feel is not very important. I've read this in several books now: what I feel is important but not the center of everything. Maybe I do see this, but I do not believe it deeply enough to act on it. I would like to believe it more deeply.

What a relief that would be. I wouldn't have to think about what I felt all the time, and try to control it, with all its complications and all its consequences. I wouldn't have to try to feel better all the time. In fact, if I didn't believe what I felt was so important, I probably wouldn't even feel so bad, and it wouldn't be so hard to feel better. I wouldn't have to say, Oh, I feel so awful, this is like the end for me here, in this dark living room late at night, with the dark street outside under the streetlights, I am so very alone, everyone else in the house asleep, there is no comfort anywhere, just me alone down here, I will never calm myself enough to sleep, never sleep, never be able to go on to the next day, I can't possibly go on, I can't live, even through the next minute.

If I believed that what I felt was not the center of everything, then it wouldn't be, but just one of many things, off to the side, and I would be able to see and pay attention to other things that were equally important, and in this way I would have some relief.

But it is curious how you can see that an idea is absolutely true and correct and yet not believe it deeply enough to act on it. So I still act as though my feelings were the center of everything, and they still cause me to end up alone by the living-room window late at night. What is different, now, is that I have this idea: I have the idea that soon I will no longer believe my feelings are the center of everything. This is a real comfort to me, because if you despair of going on, but at the same time tell yourself that your despair may not be very important, then either you stop despairing or you still despair but at the same time begin to see how your despair, too, might move off to the side, one of many things.

Lost Things

They are lost, but also not lost but somewhere in the world. Most of them are small, though two are larger, one a coat and one a dog. Of the small things, one is a valuable ring, one a valuable button. They are lost from me and where I am, but they are also not gone. They are somewhere else, and they are there to someone else, it may be. But if not there to someone else, the ring is, still, not lost to itself, but there, only not where I am, and the button, too, there, still, only not where I am.

Glenn Gould

I happened to write to my friend Mitch telling him what my life here was like and what I did all day. I told him that among other things I watched the *Mary Tyler Moore Show* every afternoon. I knew that he, unlike some people, would understand this. I have just gotten a letter back from him saying that I am not the only person he knows who watches it.

Mitch has a lot of odd pieces of information about people, both famous people and ordinary people. He is always reading books and newspapers, he has a very good memory and a lot of curiosity, and he is always talking to people, both friends and strangers. If he talks to a stranger, he likes to know where that person went to high school. If he talks to a friend, he often asks what that person had for lunch or dinner. He once told me that he tried to remember everything he learned from a conversation with a stranger in order to use it to begin or develop a conversation with another stranger. How suddenly talkative a stranger would become when he found that Mitch already knew a good deal about the politics of Buffalo, New York, for instance. He told me this as we were standing in front of an expensive boutique with a sidewalk display of purses on a busy avenue in the city. We were surrounded by strangers and he had just had a conversation with the man selling the purses.

At this time, which was a few years ago, before he and I both moved out of the city, he used to call me on the phone regularly and talk to me for as long as an hour if I was able to talk that long. I usually told him at some point in the conversation that I couldn't go on talking because I had to get back to work, and for that he would become annoyed with me. He wasn't working himself and spent a lot of time in his apartment reading, thinking, playing with his dog, and calling the few friends he stayed in touch with. I never saw his apartment. He told me it was filled with old paperback mysteries. He also borrowed books on a variety of subjects from the public library. He was the only person I knew, at that time, who used the public library. When he asked me what I had had for lunch or dinner, I was always surprised, but also pleased to tell him, probably because no one else was interested in what I had had for lunch or dinner.

In his letter Mitch says that he himself likes the show, and that Glenn Gould also liked it. I am terribly surprised by this. I see two of my worlds coming together that I had thought were as far apart as they could be.

This pianist was a model for me all the time I was a child growing up and learning to play the piano. I listened to certain of his records over and over and studied the jacket photographs of his handsome young face and thin shoulders and chest. Once out of my adolescence, I stopped studying his photographs with such attention but continued to imitate as best I could the clarity of his fingering, his peculiar ornamentation, and his interpretations of Bach in particular. I practiced the piano for as long as four hours at a time, sometimes six, beginning with scales and arpeggios and five-finger exercises, then working on one or two pieces, and then playing through whatever I liked from the books I had. I did not intend to make a career of music, but I could happily have spent my days working as hard at the piano as any professional, partly to avoid doing other things that were harder, but partly for the pleasure of it.

Now that my initial surprise has passed, I am pleased in several ways by the fact that he liked this show. For one thing, I now feel I have a companion watching the show with me, even though Glenn Gould is no longer alive. During his lifetime, he said several times that he would not play the piano after the age of fifty, and ten days after he turned fifty, he died of a stroke. This was a few years ago.

For another, the fact that this companion was so intelligent gives me a new respect for the show. Glenn Gould's standards were very high, at least concerning the composition and performance of music, and concerning his own writing. He was also articulate and opinionated, and wrote well about music and other subjects. He wrote about Schoenberg, Stokowski, Menuhin, Boulez, and he also wrote about musicians like Petula Clark. He said that when he was a student it had dismayed and puzzled him that any sane adult would include Mozart's pieces among the great musical treasures of the West, although he enjoyed playing them—he said he had instinctively disapproved of Alberti basses. He wrote about Toronto, television, and the idea of the North. He said that very few people who went into the North emerged unscathed: excited by the creative possibilities of the North, they tended to become philosophers of their own work. Rubinstein loved hotels, but Glenn Gould called himself a "motel man." He said that twice a year or so he would go along the north shore of Lake Superior where there were lumber and mining towns every fifty miles or so. He would stay in a motel and write for a few days. He said these towns had an extraordinary identity because they had grown up around one industry or one plant. He said that if he could arrange it, that would really be the sort of place in which he would like to spend his life.

Of course, it is also true, as I gradually discovered over the years, that he had many strange notions and habits. Schoenberg was one of his favorite composers, but Strauss was another. He was known to be a hypochondriac and excessively careful of his hands. He dressed warmly no matter what the season, and took his own folding chair with him to concerts, when he still gave concerts, sitting very low in relation to the keyboard. He sometimes practiced with the vacuum cleaner on because that way, he said, he could hear the skeleton of the music. Now Mitch tells me he was fond of a certain rather ugly female pop singer whom he taped, as he also taped this show I like so much. He called the singer's voice a "natural wonder," and was amazed by what she could do with it. Mitch does not explain what it was he liked about the television show, and I am still puzzling over this. His sense of humor must have had something to do with it—in his own writings he is quite funny.

Now that we live in a town where so many channels come in clearly, and I'm home alone with the baby so much, I watch the show almost every day. My husband has come to realize that I will always watch it when I can, and sometimes over dinner when we have nothing else to say to each other, he will ask about it. I will tell him something one of the characters said and I can see he is ready to laugh even before I tell it, though so often, in the case of other subjects, he is not terribly interested in what I say to him, especially when he sees that I am becoming enthusiastic.

He knows the characters because he used to watch the show when he lived alone in the city. When I lived alone in the city I watched it, too. It was on late at night, and there was a certain intimacy and intensity to watching it alone that way, with the darkness and quiet outside the windows. I watched with such concentration that I forgot everything else and entered the lives of those characters in that other city.

The intensity is gone now. In the late afternoon, the sun comes in the window almost horizontally across the living-room floor, there are wooden blocks everywhere on the rug, the baby is often playing beside me, I play with him to keep him busy, and I look up at the screen as often as I can. The baby is happy, and his noise, at the top of his voice, is often too loud for me to hear what the characters are saying, especially, it always seems, when they say something funny: there will be a remark that sets up the joke, the baby will yell over the next remark, and then there will be the laughter of the audience, so I know I've missed something that would probably have amused me, too, because the show is funny most of the time—it is well written and well acted and even on a bad day it has one or two truly funny moments. So I certainly can't forget where I am, or my own life.

Glenn Gould did not have children. He was not married. I don't know what he felt about women, even if I now know he liked the ugly singer and this show in which one woman is the central character and other women play important parts. I don't know whether he taped the show so that he wouldn't miss any of the episodes when he was away from the house performing, or, when that ended, recording, or for other reasons, or whether he taped it while he watched it, in order to build up a library of the series.

My routine with the baby is that I leave the house at about four o'clock, stop by the post office to pick up the mail, go on to the park, let the baby play for a while, go around by the hardware store or the library, and head home in time for the show, which starts at five thirty. The streets are broad and peaceful, which is one reason we moved here, and the trees are in full leaf now. In fact, the main reason we moved here was so that I could do just what I'm doing, walk with the baby around the backstreets and to the stores and the park.

When I walked in the city there was always a great deal to look at, and I could walk a mile or two without noticing how far I had gone. Every building was different, every person was different. Every building had some kind of interesting detail on its cornice or above its windows and doorways, and the streets were so crowded that I passed another person every few seconds no matter what the time of day. Even the sky was more interesting there than it is here, because it spread out so softly behind and above the towers and the sharp upper edges of the buildings.

There is not much to look at in this town of bare and plain houses and yards, so I look hard at what there is, lawns, ornamental trees and foundation plantings, sometimes a very modest and carefully limited flower bed lining a front walk for a few yards or forming a small island in a lawn. I look at the shapes of the houses, the rooflines, the garages, trying to find something to think about. For instance, I will realize that a certain garage set back behind a house must once have been a small barn, with a horse and carriage in it and hay in the hayloft above.

Many of the houses are old, and must have had a henhouse out back, a fruit tree or two, a vegetable garden, and grapevines. Then little by little properties were neatened, shade trees and hedges were cut down, vines uprooted, trim removed from porches, porches removed from houses, and outbuildings dismantled. There are just a few interesting things to see: on a dead-end street, three disused greenhouses side by side with a For Sale sign in the grass in front of them; one slightly wild yard with a picket fence, overgrown shrubs and trees, and a fish pond; and a few old barns, though the oldest, once a livery stable, was set on fire by teenagers around Christmas and burned to the ground.

The only livestock in town is kept by a former prisoner of war and his wife, who have a small house and yard near the grocery store, a tall hedge in front tangled in vines and decorated with windblown trash from the street, a driveway deep in pine needles instead of asphalt. They keep ducks and geese in back, surrounded by several layers of high fencing that conceals them from the eyes of customers in the adjacent bank parking lot. Only on certain days in the warm weather do I remember the birds are there because the smell of manure hangs over the sidewalk, and then again on certain days in winter because the geese honk when it begins to snow.

If I go directly from the post office to the hardware store or the library without going to the park, I pass the Reformed Church and Pastor Elaine's house. It is a large house, though she lives alone. Stout tree roots have buckled the sidewalk next to it and the baby carriage jolts over that spot. At the hardware store, the two women in charge always speak kindly to the baby. They are both mothers, though their children are older and come into the store after school to do their homework and help out at the cash register. To reach the library I cross the street by the butcher shop, at the only traffic light in town. On the way back, I sometimes stop in at the grocery store to buy milk and bananas. I get home in time for the show, put the carriage on the back porch by the trumpet vine, take the baby into the living room, and settle on the floor with him.

He has changed in the months since I started watching the show here. Now he can stand up and is tall enough to reach over the edge of the table and touch the controls. The show does not change the same way, going forward chronologically, but jumps around in time. One day it jumped all the way back to the beginning of the series, to what appeared to be the first episode. I told my husband about it, but, maybe because I was excited and pleased, he was not very interested, and only shrugged.

Because the show jumps around in time, hairstyles are different every day, sometimes longer and flatter, sometimes shorter and more buoyant, sometimes so dated they look silly. Sometimes the fashions of the clothes are silly too, sometimes merely prim. When the clothes and hairstyles look silly, I feel sillier watching the show, and when they are closer to what I would wear myself, I feel less silly, though now, after what Mitch told me, I no longer feel embarrassed to be watching it.

At the end of the half hour I am sorry the show is over. I hunger for more. If I could, I would watch another half hour, and another, and another. I wish the baby would go to sleep and my husband would not come home for dinner. I want to stay in that other place, that other city that is a real city but one I have never visited. I want to go on looking through a window into someone else's life, someone else's office, someone else's apartment, a friend coming in the door, a friend staying for supper, usually salad, a woman tossing salad, always neatly dressed. There is order in that other world. Mary says that order is possible and, since she is gentle and kind if somewhat brittle, that kindness is possible, too. The friend who comes down from upstairs and stays for supper is not so tidy, and is not always kind, but sometimes selfish, so there is also room for human failing, and for a kind of recklessness or passion.

Another comedy follows this one, and now and then I try to watch it just in order to stay somewhere else for a while, but it is not well acted or well written, it is not funny, even the audience laughter sounds forced, and I can't believe it. Instead, I go into the kitchen and begin to prepare dinner, if the baby will not stop me by holding on to my legs.

I am still trying to understand just how Glenn Gould identified with the orderly woman and the passionate woman, just what sort of companionship he found with these two women and the other characters, if that's what it was. He was something of a recluse, by choice. He arranged his life as he wanted it, scheduled his outside appointments as it suited him, watched television when he needed to, and was able to be selfish without hurting anyone. He was a generous and considerate friend, but he didn't meet his friends in person very often because he believed that personal encounters were distracting and unnecessary. He said he could comprehend a person's essence better over the phone. He had long conversations with his friends over the phone, always with a cup of tea in front of him. These conversations usually started at midnight, just before he went to work, since he slept through the day and worked through the night.

Smoke

Hummingbirds make explosions in the dying white flowers—not only the white flowers are dying but old women are falling from branches everywhere—in smoking pits outside the city, other dead things, too, are burning—and what can be done? Few people know. Dogs have been lost in more than one place, and their owners do not love the countryside anymore. No—old women have fallen and lie with their cancerous cheeks among the roots of oak trees. Everywhere, everywhere. And the earth is sprouting things we do not dare look at. And the smoking pits have consumed other unnamable things, things we are glad to see go. The smoke, tall and thick as mountains, makes our landscape. There are no more mountains. Long ago they were gone, not even in the memory of our grandfathers. The cloud, low over our heads, is our sky. It has been a long age since anyone saw a sky, saw anything blue. The fog is our velvet, our armchair, our bed. The trees are purple in it. The candles of flowers are out now. The fog is soft, it has no claws, not yet. Our grandmothers' purple teeth crave. They crave things we would not even recognize anymore, though our grandmothers remember—they cry out at a bridge. Too many things to name are gone and we are left with this clowning earth, these cynical trees—shadows, all, of themselves. And we, too, are beyond help. Some only are less cancerous than others, that is all, some have more left, of their bones, of their hair, of their organs. Who can find a way around the smoking pits, the greedy oaks? Who can find a path to take among the lost and dying dogs back to where the hummingbirds, though mad, still explode the flowers, flowers still though dying?

From Below, as a Neighbor

If I were not me and overheard me from below, as a neighbor, talking to him, I would say to myself how glad I was not to be her, not to be sounding the way she is sounding, with a voice like her voice and an opinion like her opinion. But I cannot hear myself from below, as a neighbor, I cannot hear how I ought not to sound, I cannot be glad I am not her, as I would be if I could hear her. Then again, since I am her, I am not sorry to be here, up above, where I cannot hear her as a neighbor, where I cannot say to myself, as I would have to from below, how glad I am not to be her.

The Great-Grandmothers

At the family gathering, the great-grandmothers were put out on the sun porch. But because of some problem with the children, at the same time as the brother-in-law had fallen into a drunken stupor, the great-grandmothers were forgotten by everyone for a very long time. When we opened the glass door, made our way through the rubber trees, and approached the sunlit old women, it was too late: their gnarled hands had grown into the wood of their cane handles, their lips had cleaved together into one membrane, their eyeballs had hardened and were immovably focused out on the chestnut grove where the children were flashing to and fro. Only old Agnes had a little life left in her, we could hear her breath sucking through her mouth, we could see her heart laboring beneath her silk dress, but even as we went to her she shuddered and was still.

Ethics

"Do unto others as you would have others do unto you." I heard, on an interview program about ethics, that this concept underlies all systems of ethics. If you really do unto your neighbor as you would have him do unto you, you will be living according to a good system of ethics. At the time, I was pleased to learn of a simple rule that made such sense. But now, when I try to apply it literally to one person I know, it doesn't seem to work. One of his problems is that he has a lot of hostility toward certain other people and when I imagine how he would have them do unto him I can only think he would in fact want them to be hostile toward him, as he imagines they are, because he is already so very hostile toward them. He would also want them to be suspicious of him to the same degree that he is suspicious of them, and bitter about him as he is bitter about them, because his feelings against them are so strong that he needs the full strength of what he imagines to be their feelings against him in order to continue feeling what he wants to feel against them. So, really, he is already doing unto those certain others as he would have them do unto him, though in fact it occurs to me that at this point he is only having certain feelings about them and not doing anything to them, so he may still be quite within some system of ethics, unless to feel something toward someone is in fact to do something to that person.

The House Behind

We live in the house behind and can't see the street: our back windows face the gray stone of the city wall and our front windows look across the courtyard into the kitchens and bathrooms of the front house. The apartments inside the front house are lofty and comfortable, while ours are cramped and graceless. In the front house, maids live in the neat little rooms on the top floor and look out upon the spires of St-Étienne, but under the eaves of our house, tiny cubicles open in darkness onto a dusty corridor and the students and poor bachelors who sleep in them share one toilet by the back stairwell. Many tenants in the front house are high civil servants, while the house behind is filled with shopkeepers, salesmen, retired post-office employees, and unmarried schoolteachers. Naturally, we can't really blame the people in the front house for their wealth, but we are oppressed by it: we feel the difference. Yet this is not enough to explain the ill will that has always existed between the two houses.

I often sit by my front window at dusk, staring up at the sky and listening to the sounds of the people across from me. As the hour passes, the pigeons settle over the dormers, the traffic choking the narrow street beyond thins out, and the televisions in various apartments fill the air with voices and the sounds of violence. Now and again, I hear the lid of a metal trash can clang below me in the courtyard, and I see a shadowy figure carry away an empty plastic pail into one of the houses.

The trash cans were always a source of embarrassment, but now the atmosphere has sharpened: the tenants from the house in front are afraid to empty their trash. They will not enter the courtyard if another tenant is already there. I see them silhouetted in the doorway of the front hall as they wait. When there is no one in the courtyard, they empty their pails and walk quickly back across the cobblestones, anxious not to be caught there alone. Some of the old women from the house in front go down together, in pairs.

The murder took place nearly a year ago. It was curiously gratuitous. The murderer was a respected married man from our building and the murdered woman was one of the few kind people in the front house; in fact, one of the few who would associate with the people of the house behind. M. Martin had no real reason to kill her. I can only think that he was maddened by frustration: for years he had wanted to live in the house in front, and it was becoming clear to him that he never would.

It was dusk. Shutters were closing. I was sitting by my window. I saw the two of them meet in the courtyard by the trash cans. It was probably something she said to him, something perfectly innocent and friendly yet that made him realize once again just how different he was from her and from everyone else in the front house. She never should have spoken to him—most of them don't speak to us.

He had just emptied his pail when she came out. There

was something so graceful about her that although she was carrying a garbage pail, she looked regal. I suppose he noticed how even her pail—of the same ordinary yellow plastic as his—was brighter, and how the garbage inside was more vivid than his. He must have noticed, too, how fresh and clean her dress was, how it wafted gently around her strong and healthy legs, how sweet the smell was that rose from it, and how luminous her skin was in the fading daylight, how her eyes glimmered with the constant slightly frenetic look of happiness that she wore, and how her light hair glinted with silver and swelled under its pins. He had stooped over his pail and was scraping the inside of it with a blunt hunting knife when she came out, gliding over the cobblestones toward him.

It was so dark by then that only the whiteness of her dress would have been clearly visible to him at first. He remained silent—for, scrupulously polite, he was never the first to speak to a person from the front house—and quickly turned his eyes away from her. But not quickly enough, for she answered his look and spoke.

She probably said something casual about how soft the evening was. If she hadn't spoken, his fury might not have been unleashed by the gentle sound of her voice. But in that instant he must have realized that for him the evening could never be as soft as it was for her. Or else something in her tone—something too kind, something just condescending enough to make him see that he was doomed to remain where he was—pushed him out of control. He straightened like a shot, as though something in him had snapped, and in one motion drove his knife into her throat.

I saw it all from above. It happened very quickly and quietly. I did not do anything. For a while I did not even realize what I had seen: life is so uneventful back here that

I have almost lost the ability to react. But there was also something arresting in the sight of it: he was a strong and well-made man, an experienced hunter, and she was as slight and graceful as a doe. His gesture was a classically beautiful one; and she slumped down onto the cobblestones as quietly as a mist melting away from the surface of a pond. Even when I was able to think, I did not do anything.

As I watched; several people came to the back door of the house in front and the front door of our own house and stopped short with their garbage pails when they saw her lying there and him standing motionless above her. His pail stood empty at his feet, scraped clean, the handle of her pail was still clenched in her hand, and her garbage had spilled over the stones beside her, which was, strangely, almost as shocking to us as the murder itself. More and more tenants gathered and watched from the doorways. Their lips were moving, but I could not hear them over the noise of the televisions on all sides of me.

I think the reason no one did anything right away was that the murder had taken place in a sort of no-man's-land. If it had happened in our house or in theirs, action would have been taken—slowly in our house, briskly in theirs. But, as it was, people were in doubt: those from the house in front hesitated to lower themselves so far as to get involved in this, and those from our house hesitated to presume so far. In the end it was the concierge who dealt with it. The body was removed by the coroner and M. Martin left with the police. After the crowd had dispersed, the concierge swept up the spilled garbage, washed down the cobblestones, and returned each pail to the apartment where it belonged.

For a day or two, the people of both houses were visibly

shaken. Talk was heard in the halls: in our house, voices rose like wind in the trees before a storm; in theirs, rich confident syllables rapped out like machine-gun fire. Encounters between the tenants of the two houses were more violent: people from our house jerked away from the others, if we met them in the street, and something in our faces cut short their conversations when we came within earshot.

But then the halls grew quiet again, and for a while it seemed as though little had changed. Perhaps this incident had been so far beyond our understanding that it could not affect us, I thought. The only difference seemed to be a certain blank look on the faces of the people in my building, as though they had gone into shock. But gradually I began to realize that the incident had left a deeper impression. Mistrust filled the air, and uneasiness. The people of the house in front were afraid of us here behind, now, and there was no communication between us at all. By killing the woman from the house in front, M. Martin had killed something more: we lost the last traces of our self-respect before the people from the house in front, because we all assumed responsibility for the crime. Now there was no point in pretending any longer. Some, it is true, were unaffected and continued to wear the rags of their dignity proudly. But most of the people in the house behind changed.

A night nurse lived across the landing from me. Every morning when she came home from work, I would wake to hear her heavy iron key ring clatter against the wooden door of her apartment, her keys rattle in the keyholes. Late in the afternoon she would come out again and shuffle around the landing on little cloth pads, dusting the banisters. Now she sat behind her door listening to the radio and coughing gently. The older Lamartine sister, who used to keep her door open a crack and listen to conversations going on in the hallway—occasionally becoming so excited that she stuck her sharp nose in the crack and threw out a comment or two—was now no longer seen at all except on Sundays, when she went out to early-morning Mass with a blue veil thrown over her head. My neighbor on the second floor, Mme Bac, left her laundry out for days, in all weathers, until the sour smell of it rose to me where I sat. Many tenants no longer cleaned doormats. People were ashamed of their clothes, and wore raincoats when they went out. A musty odor filled the hallways: delivery boys and insurance salesmen groped their way up and down the stairs looking uncomfortable. Worst of all, everyone became surly and mean: we stopped speaking to one another, told tales to outsiders, and left mud on each other's landings.

Curiously enough, many pairs of houses in the city suffer from bad relations like ours: there is usually an uneasy truce between the two houses until some incident explodes the situation and it begins deteriorating. The people in the front houses become locked in their cold dignity and the people in the back houses lose confidence, their faces gray with shame.

Recently I caught myself on the point of throwing an apple core down into the courtyard, and I realized how much I had already fallen under the influence of the house behind. My windowpanes are dim and fine curlicues of dust line the edges of the baseboards. If I don't leave now, I will soon be incapable of making the effort. I must lease an apartment in another section of the city and pack up my things.

I know that when I go to say goodbye to my neighbors,

with whom I once got along quite well, some will not open their doors and others will look at me as though they do not know me. But there will be a few who manage to summon up enough of their old spirit of defiance and aggressive pride to shake my hand and wish me luck.

The hopeless look in their eyes will make me feel ashamed of leaving. But there is no way I can help them. In any case, I suspect that after some years things will return to normal. Habit will cause the people here behind to resume their shabby tidiness, their caustic morning gossip against the people from the house in front, their thrift in small purchases, their decency where no risk is involved—and as the people in both houses move away and are replaced by strangers, the whole affair will slowly be absorbed and forgotten. The only victims, in the end, will be M. Martin's wife, M. Martin himself, and the gentle woman M. Martin killed.

The Outing

An outburst of anger near the road, a refusal to speak on the path, a silence in the pine woods, a silence across the old railroad bridge, an attempt to be friendly in the water, a refusal to end the argument on the flat stones, a cry of anger on the steep bank of dirt, a weeping among the bushes.

A Position at the University

I think I know what sort of person I am. But then I think, But this stranger will imagine me quite otherwise when he or she hears this or that to my credit, for instance that I have a position at the university: the fact that I have a position at the university will appear to mean that I must be the sort of person who has a position at the university. But then I have to admit, with surprise, that, after all, it is true that I have a position at the university. And if it is true, then perhaps I really am the sort of person you imagine when you hear that a person has a position at the university. But, on the other hand, I know I am not the sort of person I imagine when I hear that a person has a position at the university. Then I see what the problem is: when others describe me this way, they appear to describe me completely, whereas in fact they do not describe me completely, and a complete description of me would include truths that seem quite incompatible with the fact that I have a position at the university.

Examples of Confusion

1

On my way home, late at night, I look in at a coffee shop through its plate-glass front. It is all orange, with many signs about, the countertops and stools bare because the shop is closed, and far back, in the mirror that lines the back wall, back the depth of the shop and the depth of the reflected shop, in the darkness of that mirror, which is or is not the darkness of the night behind me, of the street I'm walking in, where the darkened Borough Hall building with its cupola stands at my back, though invisible in the mirror, I see my white jacket fluttering past disembodied, moving quickly since it is late. I think how remote I am, if that is me. Then think how remote, at least, that fluttering white thing is, for being me.

2

I sit on the floor of the bathroom adjoining my hotel room. It is nearly dawn and I have had too much to drink, so that certain simple things surprise me deeply. Or they are not simple. The hotel is very quiet. I look at my bare feet on the tiles in front of me and think: Those are her feet. I stand up and look in the mirror and think: There she is. She's looking at you.

Then I understand and say to myself: You have to say *she* if it's outside you. If your foot is over there, it's there away from you, it's *her* foot. In the mirror, you see something like your face. It's *her* face.

3

I am filled that day with vile or evil feelings—ill will toward one I think I should love, ill will toward myself, and discouragement over the work I think I should be doing. I look out the window of my borrowed house, out the narrow window of the smallest room. Suddenly there it is, my own spirit: an old white dog with bowed legs and swaying head staring around the corner of the porch with one mad, cataract-filled eye.

4

In the brief power outage, I feel my own electricity has been cut off and I will not be able to think. I fear that the power outage may have erased not only the work I have done but also a part of my own memory.

5

Driving in the rain, I see a crumpled brown thing ahead in the middle of the road. I think it is an animal. I feel sadness for it and for all the animals I have been seeing in the road and by the edge of the road. When I come closer, I find that it is not an animal but a paper bag. Then there is a moment when my sadness from before is still there along with the paper bag, so that I appear to feel sadness for the paper bag.

6

I am cleaning the kitchen floor. I am afraid of making a certain phone call. Now it is nine o'clock and I am done cleaning the floor. If I hang up this dustpan, if I put away this bucket, then there will be nothing left between me and the phone call, just as in W.'s dream he was not afraid of his execution until they came to shave him, when there was nothing left between him and his execution.

I began hesitating at nine o'clock. I think it must be nearly nine thirty. But when I look at the clock, I see that only five minutes have gone by: the length of time I feel passing is really only the immensity of my hesitation.

7

I am reading a sentence by a certain poet as I eat my carrot. Then, although I know I have read it, although I know my eyes have passed along it and I have heard the words in my ears, I am sure I haven't really *read* it. I may mean *understood* it. But I may mean *consumed* it: I haven't consumed it because I was already eating the carrot. The carrot was a line, too.

8

Late in the evening, I am confused by drink and by all the turns in the streets he has led me through, and now he has his arm around me and asks me if I know where I am, in the city. I do not know exactly. He takes me up a few flights of stairs and into a small apartment. It looks familiar to me. Any room can seem like a room remembered from a dream, as can any doorway into a second room, but I look at it longer and I know I have been here before. It was another month, another year, he was not here, someone else was here, I did not know him, and this was an apartment belonging to a stranger.

9

As I sit waiting at a restaurant table I see out of the corner of my eye again and again a little cat come up onto the white marble doorstep of the restaurant entryway and then, every time I look over, it is not a little cat I see but the shadow, cast by the streetlamp, of a branch of large midsummer leaves moving in the wind from the river.

10

I am expecting a phone call at ten o'clock. The phone rings at nine forty. I am upstairs. Because I was not expecting it, the ring is sharper and louder. I answer: it is not the person I was expecting, and so the voice is also sharper and louder.

Now it is ten o'clock. I go out onto the front porch. I think the phone may ring while I am out here. I come in, and the phone rings just after I come in. But again it is someone else, and later I will think it was not that person but the other, the one who was supposed to call.

11

There is his right leg over my right leg, my left leg over his right leg, his left arm under my back, my right arm around his head, his right arm across my chest, my left arm across his right arm, and my right hand stroking his right temple.

Now it becomes difficult to tell what part of what body is actually mine and what part his.

I rub his head as it lies pressed against mine, and I hear the strands of his hair chafing against his skull as though it is my own hair chafing against my own skull, as though I now hear with his ears, and from inside his head.

12

I have decided to take a certain book with me when I go. I am tired and can't think how I will carry it, though it is a small book. I am reading it before I go, and I read: *The antique bracelet she gave me with dozens of flowers etched into the tarnished brass.* Now I think that when I go out I will be able to wear the book around my wrist.

13

Looking out through the window of the coffee shop, I watch for a friend to appear. She is late. I am afraid she will not find this place. Now, if the many people passing in the street are quite unlike my friend, I feel she is still far away, or truly lost. But if a woman passes who is like her, I think she is close and will appear at any moment; and the more women pass who resemble her, or the more they resemble her, the closer I think she is, and the more likely to appear.

14

I was an unlikely person to invite to this party, and no one is talking to me. I believe the invitation was for someone else.

All day the clock answers my questions about the time

very well, and so, wondering what the title of that book was, I look at the face of the clock for an answer.

I so nearly missed the bus, I still believe I am not on it now.

Because it is almost the end of the day, I think it is almost the end of the week.

That was such a peculiar thing to say to me, I do not believe it was said to me.

Because that expert gave me helpful information about his subject, which is horticulture, I think I can ask his advice about another subject, which is family relations.

I had such trouble finding this place, I believe I did not find it. I am talking to the person I came here to meet, but I believe he is still alone, waiting for me.

15

The ceiling is so high the light fades up under the peak of the roof. It takes a long time to walk through. Dust is everywhere, an even coating of blond dust; around every corner, a rolling table with a drawing board on it, a paper pinned to the board. Around the next corner, and the next, a painting on a wall, half finished, and before it, on the floor, cans of paint, brushes across the cans, and pails of soapy water colored red or blue. Not all the cans of paint are dusty. Not all parts of the floor are dusty.

At first it seems clear that this place is not part of a dream, but a place one moves through in waking life. But rounding the last corner into the remotest part, where the dust lies thickest over the boxes of charcoal sticks from Paris, and a yellowed sheet of muslin over the window is torn symmetrically in two spots, showing a white sky through two small panes of dusty glass, a part of this place that seems to have been forgotten or abandoned, or at least lain undisturbed longer than the rest, one is not sure that this place is not a place in a dream, though whether it lies entirely in that dream or not is hard to say, and if only partly, how it lies at once in that dream and in this waking—whether one stands in this waking and looks through a doorway into that more dusty part, into that dream, or whether one walks from this waking around a corner into the part more thickly covered with dust, into the more filtered light of the dream, the light that comes in through the yellowed sheet.

The Race of the Patient Motorcyclists

In this race, it is not the swiftest who wins, but the slowest. At first it would seem easy to be the slowest of the motorcyclists, but it is not easy, because it is not in the temperament of a motorcyclist to be slow or patient.

The machines line up at the start, each more impressively outfitted and costly than the next, with white leather seats and armrests, with mahogany inlays, with pairs of antlers on their prows. All these accessories make them so exciting that it is hard not to drive them very fast.

After the starting gun sounds, the racers fire their engines and move off with a great noise, yet gain only inches over the hot, dusty track, their great black boots waddling alongside to steady them. Novices open cans of beer and begin drinking, but seasoned riders know that if they drink they will become too impatient to continue the race. Instead, they listen to radios, watch small portable televisions, and read magazines and light books as they keep an even step going, neither fast enough to lose the race nor slow enough to come to a stop, for, according to the rules, the motorcycles must keep moving forward at all times.

On either side of the track are men called checkers,

watching to see that no one violates this rule. Almost always, especially in the case of a very skillful driver, the motion of the machine can be perceived only by watching the lowering forward edges of the tires settle into the dust and the back edges lift out of it. The checkers sit in directors' chairs, getting up every few minutes to move them along the track.

Though the finish line is only a hundred yards away, by the time the afternoon is half over, the great machines are still clustered together midway down the track. Now, one by one the novices grow impatient, gun their engines with a happy racket, and let their machines wrest them from the still dust of their companions with a whiplike motion that leaves their heads crooked back and their locks of magnificently greasy hair flying straight out behind. In a moment they have flown across the finish line and are out of the race, and in the grayer dust beyond, away from the spectators, and away from the dark, glinting, plodding group of more patient motorcyclists, they assume an air of superiority, though in fact, now that no one is looking at them anymore, they feel ashamed that they have not been able to last the race out.

The finish is always a photo finish. The winner is often a veteran, not only of races for the slow but also of races for the swift. It seems simple to him, now, to build a powerful motor, gauge the condition and lie of the track, size up his competitors, and harden himself to win a race for the swift. Far more difficult to train himself to patience, steel his nerves to the pace of the slug, the snail, so slow that by comparison the crab moves as a galloping horse and the butterfly a bolt of lightning. To inure himself to look about at the visible world with a wonderful potential for speed between his legs, and yet to advance so slowly that any change in position is almost imperceptible, and the world, too, is unchanging but for the light cast by the traveling sun, which itself seems, by the end of the slow day, to have been shot from a swift bow.

Affinity

We feel an affinity with a certain thinker because we agree with him; or because he shows us what we were already thinking; or because he shows us in a more articulate form what we were already thinking; or because he shows us what we were on the point of thinking; or what we would sooner or later have thought; or what we would have thought much later if we hadn't read it now; or what we would have been likely to think but never would have thought if we hadn't read it now; or what we would have liked to think but never would have thought if we hadn't read it now.

SAMUEL JOHNSON IS INDIGNANT

(2001)

Boring Friends

We know only four boring people. The rest of our friends we find very interesting. However, most of the friends we find interesting find us boring: the most interesting find us the most boring. The few who are somewhere in the middle, with whom there is reciprocal interest, we distrust: at any moment, we feel, they may become too interesting for us, or we too interesting for them.

A Mown Lawn

She hated a *mown lawn*. Maybe that was because *mow* was the reverse of *wom*, the beginning of the name of what she was—a *woman*. A *mown lawn* had a sad sound to it, like a *long moan*. From her, a *mown lawn* made a *long moan*. *Lawn* had some of the letters of *man*, though the reverse of *man* would be *Nam*, a bad war. A *raw war. Lawn* also contained the letters of *law*. In fact, *lawn* was a contraction of *lawman*. Certainly a *lawman* could and did *mow* a *lawn*. *Law and order* could be seen as starting from *lawn order*, valued by so many Americans. *More lawn* could be made using a *lawn mower*. A *lawn mower* did make *more lawn*. *More lawn* was a contraction of *more lawmen*. Did *more lawn* in America make *more lawmen* in America? Did *more lawn* make *more Nam? More mown lawn* made *more long moan*, from her. Or a *lawn mourn*. So often, she said, Americans wanted *more mown lawn*. All of America might be one *long mown lawn*. A *lawn* not *mown* grows *long*, she said: better a *long lawn*. Better a *long lawn* and a *mole*. Let the *lawman* have the *mown lawn*, she said. Or the *moron*, the *lawn moron*.

City People

They have moved to the country. The country is nice enough: there are quail sitting in the bushes and frogs peeping in the swamps. But they are uneasy. They quarrel more often. They cry, or she cries and he bows his head. He is pale all the time now. She wakes in a panic at night, hearing him sniffle. She wakes in a panic again, hearing a car go up the driveway. In the morning there is sunlight on their faces but mice are chattering in the walls. He hates the mice. The pump breaks. They replace the pump. They poison the mice. Their neighbor's dog barks. It barks and barks. She could poison the dog.

"We're city people," he says, "and there aren't any nice cities to live in."

Betrayal

In her fantasies about other men, as she grew older, about men other than her husband, she no longer dreamed of sexual intimacy, as she once had, perhaps for revenge, when she was angry, perhaps out of loneliness, when he was angry, but only of an affection and a profound sort of understanding, a holding of hands and a gazing into eyes, often in a public place like a café. She did not know if this change came out of respect for her husband, for she did truly respect him, or out of plain weariness, at the end of the day, or out of a sense of what activity she could expect from herself, even in a fantasy, now that she was a certain age. And when she was particularly tired, she couldn't manage even the affection and the profound understanding, but only the mildest sort of companionship, such as being in the same room alone together, sitting in chairs. And it happened that as she grew older still, and more tired, and then still older, and still more tired, another change occurred and she found that even the mildest sort of companionship, alone together, was now too vigorous to sustain, and her fantasies were limited to a calm sort of friendliness among other friends, the sort she really could have had with any man, with a clear conscience, and did in fact have with many, who were friends of her husband's too, or not, a friendliness that gave her comfort and strength, at night, when the friendships in her waking life were not enough, or had not been enough by the end of the day. And so these fantasies came to be indistinguishable from the reality of her waking life, and should not have been any sort of betrayal at all. Yet because they were fantasies she had alone, at night, they continued to feel like some sort of betrayal, and perhaps, because approached in this spirit of betrayal, as perhaps they had to be, to be any comfort and strength, continued to be, in fact, a sort of betrayal.

The White Tribe

We live near a tribe of bloodless white people. Day and night they come to steal things from us. We have put up tall wire fences but they spring over them like gazelles and grin fiendishly up at us where we stand looking out of our windows. They rub the tops of their heads until their thin flaxen hair stands up in tufts, and they strut back and forth over our gravel terrace. While we are watching this performance, others among them have crept into our garden and are furtively taking our roses, stuffing them into bags that hang from their naked shoulders. They are pitifully thin, and as we watch them we become ashamed of our fence. Yet when they go, slipping away like white shadows in the gloom, we grow angry at the devastation they have left among our Heidelbergs and Lady Belpers, and resolve to take more extreme measures against them. It is not always the roses they come for, but sometimes—though the countryside for miles is covered with boulders and shards of stone—they carry away the very rocks from our woods, and walking out in the morning we find the ground pitted with hollows where pale bugs squirm blindly down into the earth.

Our Trip

My mother asks on the phone how our drive home was, and I say "Fine," which is not the truth but a fiction. You can't tell everyone the truth all the time, and you certainly can't tell anyone the whole truth, ever, because it would take too long.

The word *fine* is the greatest abbreviation and obviously wrong. Even a long drive with two people can be difficult, and with three it can be much worse. We almost always start a trip with some cross words anyway, because I can't seem to leave on time and Mac can't stand leaving a minute late, and then there's Junior. Mac generally cheers up once we're on our way, but this time he went on snapping at me because I didn't tell him where to turn far enough ahead of time or I gave him too many instructions at once. On top of that I kept telling him to shift up. The car is old and the transmission is noisy, so it's hard for me to tell if Mac's in the right gear.

Then we began to smell burning oil. There was another van in front of us, packed full of some religious group, so we knew it could be them, and when we came to a garage they pulled in and that was the end of the burning smell, so Mac's mood improved a little.

But we were still in mountain country, and Junior started saying which mountains he was planning to climb next year—I'm going to climb that one, he said, pointing, and that one, what's the name of that one? Whiteface? I'm going to climb Whiteface, and then that one. I'm going to climb that one over there, what's the name of that one? Charles? What about that one over there? What's the name? Mungus? Fungus? Mangoes? Mongoose? Hey, look at that one—that's gotta be the biggest one. What's the name of that one?

I was turning the map this way and that, trying to figure out what the names of these mountains were, and even though Junior was talking so fast, and acting more like six years old than nine, I didn't see any big harm in this conversation. But Mac said he felt as if he was on a tour bus and would we be quiet. Anything a little out of control makes him nervous.

Eventually we got onto the highway and then of course I had to go to the bathroom. I always have to go to the bathroom when we get onto a major highway. Luckily we came to a rest stop pretty soon, and since we were there anyway we sat down at a picnic table to eat our sandwiches. The picnic table wasn't all that clean—it had a few sticky spills and some bird lime on it—but the sun was warm and I was just beginning to relax and enjoy watching the people walk past us to the restrooms when Junior came back from the restrooms and asked me for money for a soda. He always asks for a soda if he sees a soda machine, and I usually say no, which is what I said this time.

Now he decided to make an issue of it, and said he wouldn't get back in the car if we didn't get him a soda, and he went off over the grass toward the Dog Walk Area and sat down to sulk on some kind of large bent pipe sticking up out of the grass. So then Mac, who is more likely to give in than I am, said to let him have his soda, and I called Junior back and gave him the money and he went off and came back with the soda. I made the mistake of reading the ingredients, though, and when I saw how much caffeine there was in it, I began going on about that and I wouldn't stop, even back in the car, until I saw that now Junior was getting upset again and the whole thing was pointless. So I shut up and started cleaning my hands with some pre-moistened towelettes called Wet Ones, which have a sickly sweet smell to them, and the smell filled the car so badly that now the two of them turned on me.

After that, Junior was pretty cheerful because the soda made him feel a few years older, I could see it by the way he slouched with his knees apart and his hands dangling, and the atmosphere in the car improved even more when a crowd of men and women on motorcycles passed us going about ninety miles per hour. Mac said he hoped they would get stopped for speeding, and the thought of that cheered him up so much he started a conversation with me. He asked me what kind of car we should get when we bought a new car. He pointed out a Dodge Caravan, and Junior woke up from his daydream and said he wanted a Corvette. Mac asked where he was going to get the $30,000. Junior didn't have an answer, then he thought to ask how much Mac had paid for our Voyager. $7,000, Mac said, which stumped Junior but didn't seem fair to me, because he didn't tell Junior he had gotten it secondhand, so I threw in that information just to make it fair, and of course Junior said he would get his Corvette secondhand too. Cars aren't my favorite subject, though, so pretty soon we had run it into the ground and I went back to doing what I had been doing, which was looking out the window.

We passed a spot where the Highway Department had cleared the forest by the side of the road and planted some trees. The trees were covered with shriveled reddish foliage and obviously dying. This started me thinking about deforestation, and then about the disappearance of family farms, which somehow took me back to caffeine levels again. At that point, I started trying to identify the new trees I had learned on our vacation, and when I gave up on that I just watched the fat on my arm ripple in the wind from the open window.

Things went on pretty much like that. At some point I began to think I had spider bites on my legs; later Mac asked me if I had put something strange in the sandwiches; Junior rolled up the toll ticket to make a telescope, and Mac yelled at him; but then we all quieted down to watch the remains of a pretty dramatic accident by the side of the road.

At the rest stop I had been thinking that about 50 percent of the people I saw looked as though they'd had a better vacation than we had. But then 50 percent of them looked as though they'd had a worse one, so I felt all right about it.

When we were twenty minutes from home, Junior wanted to stop at a Holiday Inn and spend the night and couldn't understand why we said no. But I realized about then that as a family we have a certain kind of loyalty to one another, and the way it works is that no two of us will get mad at the third one at the same time, except occasionally, as in the case of the Wet Ones.

Special Chair

He and I are both teachers in the university system and we will be teachers until we are too old to teach, and we would certainly like to be given a special chair at our universities, but what we have gotten so far is the wrong kind of special chair, a special chair belonging to a friend, a chair that swivels and has splayed feet and is special to her for reasons we can't remember. We who teach in the university system would like a special chair so that we would be paid more and not have to teach as much and not have to sit on so many committees—we would sit instead on our special chair. But we have not been given any special chairs by our universities, only this strange heavy chair belonging to our friend, who moved away many years ago and had to leave it behind, and who does not want to give it up for reasons we have forgotten or never knew. All this time we have been employed by our universities only to teach from year to year without even the security of tenure. But now one of us has had some good luck and has been given a job with tenure, though not by his own university, and in leaving his present job, the job without tenure, he must also leave behind the chair special to our friend, because he is moving far away and there will not be room for it where he is going. Even though there is a great deal of large empty space in the state where he is going, more empty space than practically any other state but Wyoming, he will be living there in a very small house, too small for an extra chair, especially such a heavy one made out of a wine barrel. And so I will be the one to keep our friend's chair for her now; it has passed from him to me, though not without effort, since it is so heavy. And perhaps, I am thinking, her special chair with its strange red vinyl upholstery, with its bunghole in the back, and its genuine cork, will now bring me good luck of a professional kind too.

Certain Knowledge from Herodotus

These are the facts about the fish in the Nile:

Priority

It should be so simple. You do what you can while he is awake, and then once he is asleep, you do what you can do only when he is asleep, beginning with the most important thing. But it is not so simple.

You ask yourself what is the most important thing. It should be easy to say which thing has priority and go and do it. But not just one thing has priority, and not just two or three. When several things have priority, which of the several things having priority is given priority?

In the time in which you can do something, the time when he is asleep, you can write a letter that has to be written immediately because many things depend on it. And yet if you write the letter, your plants will not get watered and it is a very hot day. You have already put them out on the balcony hoping the rain will water them, but this summer it almost never rains. You have already taken them in from the balcony hoping that if they are out of the wind they will not have to be watered as often, but they will still have to be watered.

And yet if you water the plants, you will not write the letter, on which so much depends. You will also not tidy the kitchen and living room, and later you will become confused and cross because of the disorder. One counter is covered with shopping lists and pieces of glassware your husband bought at a liquidation sale. It should be simple enough to put the glassware away, but you can't put it away until you wash it, you can't wash it until the sink is clear of dirty dishes, and you can't wash the dishes until you empty the drainboard. If you begin by emptying the drainboard, you may not get any farther, while he is asleep, than washing the dishes.

You may decide that the plants have priority, in the end, because they are alive. Then you may decide, since you must find a way of organizing your priorities, that all the living things in the house will have priority, starting with the youngest and smallest human being. That should be clear enough. But then, though you know exactly how to care for the mouse, the cat, and the plants, you are not sure how to give priority to the baby, the older boy, yourself, and your husband. It is certainly true that the larger and older the living thing is, the harder it is to know how to care for it.

The Meeting

I tried so hard, the clothes I wore, new look I had, I thought. Competent, I thought, casual. New raincoat. Brown. Things seemed all right at first, promising, in the waiting room. Top secretary offered me the comfortable chair, a cup of tea—top secretary or second secretary. Declined the tea—how could I swallow it, how could I even hold the cup? Opened my little book. Thought once I got in there he might even ask me what I was reading—Wait, he might say, is that Addison? Kept my head down, eyes on the page. Listened to the secretaries, thought I was learning the inside dope. Feeling smart. Thought I was all buttoned up. Yes, and now here we were alone for the first time, at last, and I thought we might have a special rapport, he might become a friend, at least. I thought he might say to himself: Here is this woman, this attractive woman, I've talked to her before, never at length, unfortunately, now she's here across my desk from me in an attractive raincoat with some jewelry on. I thought he might say: She's quiet but I know from what I've heard and from the way she sits there so composed, holding that small book bound in green leather—could it be Addison?—that she's intelligent, though obviously shy, it will be interesting to talk to her . . . Here he is, the boss, and there are no distractions, there's no one coming into the room, no one offering something from a tray, no one walking past, no one drinking next to him, no one asking him a sudden question that left me out, rudely, no one standing in a circle with him, here we are alone, my face floating over that piled desk. But he!—he rails against the whole project, he uses bad language, though it isn't my fault, it really isn't my fault, what he doesn't like, the change of title, and in fact he's wrong about that, things have to change, even titles have to change. How he jumps on me, how he strafes me, how he slangs me. I'm rocked. Of course—anyone can make an appointment to see the president, that's the easy part. I try again, surface and take another breath, say something, he stops railing and listens, he says something back, asks me a decent question, but I can't remember that name, I just can't remember it, me with my shaky voice, now what can I say, don't have a single million-dollar word, say something dumb, now he's doing his best, he's trying to remember his manners. But after all that yelling he says he isn't the one who can help me, no, even though they said I should go talk to him myself, they both said that. And they know him, I thought I could trust them, just plant the idea in his head at least, they said. I guess maybe they sold me a pup. What a blunder. And I wore all this jewelry, every piece I had that was decent. He never noticed, I'm sure. No, he just said to himself: Not my concern, sorry. Wait, I thought, give me time, another five minutes. But it's no use, now he stands up and sticks his hand across the desk at an angle and flat as a piece of cardboard, he's offering to shake, it's his signal, I'm supposed to leave. Well, lost opportunity, Mr. President! Old bean! We're not all so clever, you know—not on the spot like that. Beanpole! Someday you'll make me an offer, I'll say I can't help you. Such a mistake, even to go in there. So wrong. Some other frequency. Can't do anything right. Not worth shucks. Strange hat, brown coat, drooping hem, bare neck, yellow skin, wrong jewelry, too much jewelry. So many mistakes. Electric hair. So many mistakes. Too much, too little, wrong time, wrong place, can't do it right. Do it anyway. Spoil it. Do it again. Spoil it again. A slime, a weed. I wanted respect. Did he even see me? Did he even see my head poking up above those piles? He was seeing another appointment! This was my appointment! Maybe the raincoat gave a bad impression. Maybe I was wrong to wear brown. Maybe he thought: Uh-oh, there's something depressing out there in the waiting room. Brown woman with a proposal, sitting in a chair with her book. And then I wasn't prepared. Didn't know the name. I nodded. Anyone can nod. I didn't know what was coming! I was so dumb. I'm aching. What shame—ready to kill. Wish I'd had my mother with me. She would have said something. A gasbag. He would have said she was a gabby old woman, an ulcer—What's she doing in here? Who let her in? Get her out of here! In her pastel suit. But there she'd be. She'd account for him. She'd give it to him—right in the clock! He'd say: Get the old bag off my dark wood paneling! That's my mother! What a barney, hoo-ha! She'd give him a mouse, all right! He'd say: Get the old bag in her pink suit away from in front of my dark wood paneling! Get him, Mother! Sic him! Old Iowa bag. Come in here with her replaced hip, her replaced knee, one leg shorter than the other, built-up shoe. Determined. She'd lam him in his little Mary, quick and smart, she'd have the edge on him. What's this? he would have said. Kick this old lady out of here! In her spring suit. He might have used bad language about her too: Kick this old fart out of here! Maybe I should have taken my whole family in there with me. Brother watching, father watching, sister getting up to help. But Mother's the one who would floor him. Mother would thrash him, she'd baste his jacket. She's high-rent. She would have said, Be nice to her! He wasn't nice to me. That's *my daughter*! He wasn't nice. She would have given him a piece of her fist. See this?—shaking it right in his pan. Names for him. She doesn't come as a water carrier for anyone. Annihilate him, Mother! Crush him! No more—Bam!—president of this place. New president, please! Better one, please. Oh boy! Sock! You'll see, Mr. President! Summer complaint! Dog's breakfast!

Companion

We are sitting here together, my digestion and I. I am reading a book and it is working away at the lunch I ate a little while ago.

Blind Date

"There isn't really much to tell," she said, but she would tell it if I liked. We were sitting in a midtown luncheonette. "I've only had one blind date in my life. And I didn't really have it. I can think of more interesting situations that are like a blind date—say, when someone gives you a book as a present, when they fix you up with that book. I was once given a book of essays about reading, writing, book collecting. I felt it was a perfect match. I started reading it right away, in the backseat of the car. I stopped listening to the conversation in the front. I like to read about how other people read and collect books, even how they shelve their books. But by the time I was done with the book, I had taken a strong dislike to the author's personality. I won't have another date with *her*!" She laughed. Here we were interrupted by the waiter, and then a series of incidents followed that kept us from resuming our conversation that day.

The next time the subject came up, we were sitting in two Adirondack chairs looking out over a lake in, in fact, the Adirondacks. We were content to sit in silence at first. We were tired. We had been to the Adirondack Museum that day and seen many things of interest, including old guide boats and good examples of the original Adirondack chair. Now we watched the water and the edge of the woods, each thinking, I was sure, about James Fenimore Cooper. After some parties of canoers had gone by, older people in canvas boating hats, their quiet voices carrying far over the water to us, we went on talking. These were precious days of holiday together, and we were finishing many unfinished conversations.

"I was fifteen or sixteen, I guess," she said. "I was home from boarding school. Maybe it was summer. I don't know where my parents were. They were often away. They often left me alone there, sometimes for the evening, sometimes for weeks at a time. The phone rang. It was a boy I didn't know. He said he was a friend of a boy from school—I can't remember who. We talked a little and then he asked me if I wanted to have dinner with him. He sounded nice enough so I said I would, and we agreed on a day and a time and I told him where I lived.

"But after I got off the phone, I began thinking, worrying. What had this other boy said about me? What had the two of them said about me? Maybe I had some kind of a reputation. Even now I can't imagine that what they said was completely pure or innocent—for instance, that I was pretty and fun to be with. There had to be something nasty about it, two boys talking privately about a girl. The awful word that began to occur to me was *fast*. She's *fast*. I wasn't actually very fast. I was faster than some but not as fast as others. The more I imagined the two boys talking about me the worse I felt.

"I liked boys. I liked the boys I knew in a way that was much more innocent than they probably thought. I trusted them more than girls. Girls hurt my feelings, girls ganged up on me. I always had boys who were my friends, starting back when I was nine and ten and eleven. I didn't like this feeling that two boys were talking about me.

"Well, when the day came, I didn't want to go out to dinner with this boy. I just didn't want the difficulty of this date. It scared me—not because there was anything scary about the boy but because he was a stranger, I didn't know him. I didn't want to sit there face-to-face in some restaurant and start from the very beginning, knowing nothing. It didn't feel right. And there was the burden of that recommendation—'Give her a try.'

"Then again, maybe there were other reasons. Maybe I had been alone in that apartment so much by then that I had retreated into some kind of inner, unsociable space that was hard to come out of. Maybe I felt I had disappeared and I was comfortable that way and did not want to be forced back into existence. I don't know.

"At six o'clock, the buzzer rang. The boy was there, downstairs. I didn't answer it. It rang again. Still I did not answer it. I don't know how many times it rang or how long he leaned on it. I let it ring. At some point, I walked the length of the living room to the balcony. The apartment was four stories up. Across the street and down a flight of stone steps was a park. From the balcony on a clear day you could look out over the park and see all the way across town, maybe a mile, to the other river. At this point I think I ducked down or got down on my hands and knees and inched my way to the edge of the balcony. I think I looked over far enough to see him down there on the sidewalk below—looking up, as I remember it. Or he had gone across the street and was looking up. He didn't see me.

"I know that as I crouched there on the balcony or just back from it I had some impression of him being puzzled, disconcerted, disappointed, at a loss what to do now, not prepared for this—prepared for all sorts of other ways the date might go, other difficulties, but not for no date at all. Maybe he also felt angry or insulted, if it occurred to him then or later that maybe he hadn't made a mistake but that I had deliberately stood him up, and not the way I did it—alone up there in the apartment, uncomfortable and embarrassed, chickening out, hiding out—but, he would imagine, in collusion with someone else, a girlfriend or boyfriend, confiding in them, snickering over him.

"I don't know if he called me, or if I answered the phone if it rang. I could have given some excuse—I could have said I had gotten sick or had to go out suddenly. Or maybe I hung up when I heard his voice. In those days I did a lot of avoiding that I don't do now—avoiding confrontations, avoiding difficult encounters. And I did a fair amount of lying that I also don't do now.

"What was strange was how awful this felt. I was treating a person like a thing. And I was betraying not just him but something larger, some social contract. When you knew a decent person was waiting downstairs, someone you had made an appointment with, you did not just not answer the buzzer. What was even more surprising to me was what I felt about myself in that instant. I was behaving as though I had no responsibility to anyone or anything, and that made me feel as though I existed outside society, some kind of criminal, or didn't exist at all. I was annihilating myself even more than him. It was an awful violation."

She paused, thoughtful. We were sitting inside now, because it was raining. We had come inside to sit in a sort of lounge or recreation room provided for guests of that lakeside camp. The rain fell every afternoon there, sometimes for minutes, sometimes for hours. Across the water, the white pines and spruces were very still against the gray sky. The water was silver. We did not see any of the water-birds we sometimes saw paddling around the edges of the lake—teals and loons. Inside, a fire burned in the fireplace. Over our heads hung a chandelier made of antlers. Between us stood a table constructed of a rough slab of wood resting on the legs of a deer, complete with hooves. On the table stood a lamp made from an old gun. She looked away from the lake and around the room. "In that book about the Adirondacks I was reading last night," she remarked, "he says this was what the Adirondacks was all about, I mean the Adirondacks style: things made from things."

A month or so later, when I was home again and she was back in the city, we were talking on the telephone and she said she had been hunting through one of the old diaries she had on her shelf there, which might say exactly what had happened—though of course, she said, she would just be filling in the details of something that did not actually happen. But she couldn't find this incident written down anywhere, which of course made her wonder if she had gotten the dates really wrong and she wasn't even in boarding school anymore by then. Maybe she was in college by then. But she decided to believe what she had told me. "But I'd forgotten how much I wrote about boys," she added. "Boys and books. What I wanted more than anything else at the age of sixteen was a great library."

Examples of Remember

Remember that thou art but dust.
I shall try to *bear it in mind.*

Old Mother and the Grouch

"Meet the sourpuss," says the Grouch to their friends.

"Oh, shut up," says Old Mother.

The Grouch and Old Mother are playing Scrabble. The Grouch makes a play.

"Ten points," he says. He is disgusted.

He is angry because Old Mother is winning early in the game and because she has drawn all the *s*'s and blanks. He says it is easy to win if you get all the *s*'s and blanks. "I think you marked the backs," he says. She says a blank tile doesn't have a back.

Now he is angry because she has made the word *qua*. He says *qua* is not English. He says they should both make good, familiar words like the words he has made—*bonnet*, *realm*, and *weave*—but instead she sits in her nasty corner making *aw*, *eh*, *fa*, *ess*, and *ax*. She says these are words, too. He says even if they are, there is something mean and petty about using them.

Now the Grouch is angry because Old Mother keeps freezing all the food he likes. He brings home a nice smoked ham and wants a couple of slices for lunch but it is too late—she has already frozen it.

"It's hard as a rock," he says. "And you don't have to freeze it anyway. It's already smoked."

Then, since everything else he wants to eat is also frozen, he thinks he will at least have some of the chocolate ice cream he bought for her the day before. But it's gone. She has eaten it all.

"Is that what you did last night?" he asks. "You stayed up late eating ice cream?"

He is close to the truth, but not entirely correct.

Old Mother cooks dinner for friends of theirs. After the friends have gone home, she tells the Grouch the meal was a failure: the salad dressing had too much salt in it, the chicken was overdone and tasteless, the cherries hard, etc.

She expects him to contradict her, but instead he listens carefully and adds that the noodles, also, were "somehow wrong."

She says, "I'm not a very good cook."

She expects him to assure her that she is, but instead he says. "You should be. Anybody can be a good cook."

Old Mother sits dejected on a stool in the kitchen.

"I just want to teach you something about the rice pot," says the Grouch, by way of introduction, as he stands at the sink with his back to her.

But she does not like this. She does not wish to be his student.

One night Old Mother cooks him a dish of polenta. He remarks that it has spread on the plate like a cow patty. He tastes it and says that it tastes better than it looks. On another night she makes him a brown rice casserole. The Grouch says this does not look very good either. He covers it in salt and pepper, then eats some of it and says it also tastes better than it looks. Not much better, though.

"Since I met you," says the Grouch, "I have eaten more beans than I ever ate in my life. Potatoes and beans. Every night there is nothing but beans, potatoes, and rice."

Old Mother knows this is not strictly true.

"What did you eat before you knew me?" she asks.

"Nothing," says the Grouch. "I ate nothing."

Old Mother likes all chicken parts, including the liver and heart, and the Grouch likes the breasts only. Old Mother likes the skin on and the Grouch likes it off. Old Mother prefers vegetables and bland food. The Grouch prefers meat and strong spices. Old Mother prefers to eat her food slowly and brings it hot to the table. The Grouch prefers to eat quickly and burns his mouth.

"You don't cook the foods I like," the Grouch tells her sometimes.

"You ought to like the foods I cook," she answers.

"Spoil me. Give me what I want, not what you think I should have," he tells her.

That's an idea, thinks Old Mother.

Old Mother wants direct answers from the Grouch. But when she asks, "Are you hungry?" he answers, "It's seven o'clock." And when she asks, "Are you tired?" he answers, "It's ten o'clock." And when she insists, and asks again, "But are you tired?" he says, "I've had a long day."

Old Mother likes two blankets at night, on a cold night, and the Grouch is more comfortable with three. Old

Mother thinks the Grouch should be comfortable with two. The Grouch, on the other hand, says, "I think you like to be cold."

Old Mother does not mind running out of supplies and often forgets to shop. The Grouch likes to have more than they need of everything, especially toilet paper and coffee.

On a stormy night the Grouch worries about his cat, shut outdoors by Old Mother.

"Worry about me," says Old Mother.

Old Mother will not have the Grouch's cat in the house at night because it wakes her up scratching at the bedroom door or yowling outside it. If they let it into the bedroom, it rakes up the carpet. If she complains about the cat, he takes offense: he feels she is really complaining about him.

Friends say they will come to visit, and then they do not come. Out of disappointment, the Grouch and Old Mother lose their tempers and quarrel.

On another day, friends say they will come to visit, and this time the Grouch tells Old Mother he will not be home when they come: they are not friends of his.

A phone call comes from a friend of hers he does not like.

"It's for you, *angel*," he says, leaving the receiver on the kitchen counter.

Old Mother and the Grouch have quarreled over friends, the West Coast, the telephone, dinner, what time to go to bed, what time to get up, travel plans, her parents, his work, her work, and his cat, among other subjects. They have not quarreled, so far, over special sale items, acquisitions for the house, natural landscapes, wild animals, the town governing board, and the local library.

A woman dressed all in red is jumping up and down in a tantrum. It is Old Mother, who cannot handle frustration.

If Old Mother talks to a friend out of his earshot, the Grouch thinks she must be saying unkind things about him. He is sometimes right, though by the time he appears glowering in the doorway, she has gone on to other topics.

One day in June, the Grouch and Old Mother take all their potted plants out onto the deck for the summer. The next week, the Grouch brings them all back in and sets them on the living-room floor. Old Mother does not understand what he is doing and is prepared to object, but they have quarreled and are not speaking to each other, so she can only watch him in silence.

The Grouch is more interested in money than Old Mother and more careful about how he spends it. He reads sale ads and will not buy anything unless it is marked down. "You're not very good with money," he says. She would like to deny it but she can't. She buys a book, secondhand, called *How to Live Within Your Income.*

They spend a good deal of time one day drawing up a list of what each of them will do in their household. For instance, she will make their dinner but he will make his own lunch. By the time they are finished, it is time for lunch and Old Mother is hungry. The Grouch has taken some care over a tuna fish salad for himself. Old Mother says it looks good and asks him if she can share it. Annoyed, he points out that now, contrary to the agreement, he has made *their* lunch.

Old Mother could only have wanted a man of the highest ideals but now she finds she can't live up to them; the Grouch could only have wanted the best sort of woman, but she is not the best sort of woman.

Old Mother thinks her temper may improve if she drinks more water. When her temper remains bad, she begins taking a daily walk and eating more fresh fruit.

Old Mother reads an article that says: If one of you is in a bad mood the other should stay out of her way and be as kind as possible until the bad mood passes.

But when she proposes this to the Grouch, he refuses to consider it. He does not trust her: she will claim to be in a bad mood when she is not, and then require him to be kind to her.

Old Mother decides she will dress up as a witch on Halloween, since she is often described as a witch by the Grouch. She owns a pointed black hat, and now she buys more items to make up her costume. She thinks the Grouch will be amused, but he asks her please to remove the rubber nose from the living room.

The Grouch is exasperated. Old Mother has been criticizing him again. He says to her, "If I changed that, you'd only find something else to criticize. And if I changed that, then something else would be wrong."

The Grouch is exasperated again. Again, Old Mother has been criticizing him. This time he says, "You should have married a man who didn't drink or smoke. And who also had no hands or feet. Or arms or legs."

Old Mother tells the Grouch she feels ill. She thinks she may soon have to go into the bathroom and be sick. They have been quarreling, and so the Grouch says nothing. He goes into the bathroom, however, and washes the toilet bowl, then brings a small red towel and lays it on the foot of the bed where she is resting.

Weeks later, Old Mother tells the Grouch that one of the kindest things he ever did for her was to wash the toilet bowl before she was sick. She thinks he will be touched, but instead, he is insulted.

"Can't you agree with me about anything?" asks the Grouch.

Old Mother has to admit it: she almost always disagrees with him. Even if she agrees with most of what he is saying, there will be some small part of it she disagrees with.

When she does agree with him, she suspects her own motives: she may agree with him only so that at some future time she will be able to remind him that she does sometimes agree with him.

Old Mother has her favorite armchair, and the Grouch has his. Sometimes, when the Grouch is not at home, Old Mother sits in his chair, and then she also picks up what he has been reading and reads it herself.

Old Mother is dissatisfied with the way they spend their evenings together and imagines other activities such as taking walks, writing letters, and seeing friends. She proposes these activities to the Grouch, but the Grouch becomes angry. He does not like her to organize anything in his life.

Now the way they spend this particular evening is quarreling over what she has said.

Both the Grouch and Old Mother want to make love, but he wants to make love before the movie, whereas she wants to make love either during it or after. She agrees to before, but then if before, wants the radio on. He prefers the television and asks her to take her glasses off. She agrees to the television, but prefers to lie with her back to it. Now he can't see it over her shoulder because she is lying on her side. She can't see it because she is facing him and her glasses are off. He asks her to move her shoulder.

Old Mother hears the footsteps of the Grouch in the lower hall as he leaves the living room on his way to bed. She looks around the bedroom to see what will bother him. She removes her feet from his pillow, stands up from his side of the bed, turns off a few lights, takes her slippers out of his way into the room, and shuts a dresser drawer. But she knows she has forgotten something. What he complains about first is the wrinkled sheets, and then the noise of the white mice running in their cage in the next room.

"Maybe I could help with that," says Old Mother sincerely as they are driving in the car, but after what she did the night before she knows he will not want to think of her as a helpful person. The Grouch only snorts.

Old Mother shares a small triumph with the Grouch, hoping he will congratulate her. He remarks that someday she will not bother to feel proud of that sort of thing.

•

"I slept like a log," he says in the morning. "What about you?"

Well, most of the night was fine, she explains, but toward morning she slept lightly trying to keep still in a position that did not hurt her neck. She was trying to keep still so as not to bother him, she adds. Now he is angry.

"How did you sleep?" she asks him as he comes downstairs late.

"Not very well," he answers. "I was awake around one thirty. You were still up."

"No, I wasn't still up at one thirty," she says.

"Twelve thirty, then."

"You were very restless," says the Grouch in the morning. "You kept tossing and turning."

"Don't accuse me," says Old Mother.

"I'm not accusing you, I'm just stating the facts. You were very restless."

"All right: the reason I was restless was that you were snoring."

Now the Grouch is angry. "I don't snore."

Old Mother is lying on the bathroom floor reading, her head on a small stack of towels and a pillow, a bath towel covering her, because she has not been able to sleep and doesn't want to disturb the Grouch. She falls asleep there on the bathroom floor, goes back to bed, wakes again, returns to the bathroom, and continues to read. Finally the Grouch, having woken up because she was gone, comes to the door and offers her some earplugs.

•

The Grouch wants to listen to Fischer-Dieskau singing, accompanied by Brendel at the piano, but to his annoyance he finds that Fischer-Dieskau accompanied by Brendel is also accompanied by Old Mother humming, and he asks her to stop.

Old Mother makes an unpleasant remark about one of their lamps.

The Grouch is sure Old Mother is insulting him. He tries to figure out what she is saying about him, but can't, and so remains silent.

The Grouch is on his way out with heavy boxes in his arms when Old Mother thinks of something else she wants to say.

"Hurry up, I'm holding these," says the Grouch.

Old Mother does not like to hurry when she has something to say. "Put them down for a minute," she tells him.

The Grouch does not like to be delayed or told what to do. "Just hurry up," he says.

In the middle of an argument, the Grouch often looks at Old Mother in disbelief that is either real or feigned: "What a minute," he says. "Wait just a minute."

Well into an argument, Old Mother often begins to cry in frustration. Though her frustration and her tears are genuine she also hopes the Grouch will be moved to pity. The Grouch is never moved to pity, only further exasperated, saying, "Now you start sniveling."

The Grouch often arrives home asking such questions as:

"What is this thing? Are you throwing coffee grounds

under this bush? Did you mean to leave the car doors unlocked? Do you know why the garage door is open? What is all that water doing on the lawn? Is there a reason all the lights in the house are on? Why was the hose unscrewed?"

Or he comes downstairs and asks:

"Who broke this? Where are all the bath mats? Is your sewing machine working? When did this happen? Did you see the stain on the kitchen ceiling? Why is there a sponge on the piano?"

Old Mother says, "Don't always criticize me."

The Grouch says, "I'm not criticizing you. I just want certain information."

They often disagree about who is to blame: if he is hurt by her, it is possible that she was harsh in what she said; but it is also possible that her intentions were good and he was too sensitive in his reaction.

For instance, the Grouch may be unusually sensitive to the possibility that a woman is ordering him around. But this is hard to decide, because Old Mother is a woman who tends to order people around.

Old Mother is excited because she has a plan to improve her German. She tells the Grouch she is going to listen to Advanced German tapes while she is out driving in the car.

"That sounds depressing," says the Grouch.

The Grouch is cross about his own work when he comes home and therefore cross with her. He snaps at her: "I can't do everything at once."

She is offended and becomes angry. She demands an apology, wanting him to be sincere and affectionate.

He apologizes, but because he is still cross, he is not sincere and affectionate.

She becomes angrier.

Now he complains: "When I'm upset, you get even more upset."

"I'm going to put on some music," says the Grouch.

Old Mother is immediately nervous.

"Put on something easy," she says.

"I know that whatever I put on, you won't like it," he says.

"Just don't put on Messiaen," she says. "I'm too tired for Messiaen."

The Grouch comes into the living room to apologize for what he has said. Then he feels he must explain why he said it, though Old Mother already knows. But as he explains at some length, what he says makes him angry all over again, and he says one or two more things that provoke her, and they begin arguing again.

Now and then Old Mother wonders just why she and the Grouch have such trouble getting along. Perhaps, given her failures of tact, she needed a man with more confidence. Certainly, at the same time, given his extreme sensitivity, he needed a gentler woman.

They receive many Chinese fortunes. The Grouch finds it correct that her mentality is "alert, practical, and analytical," especially concerning his faults. He finds it correct that "The great fault in women is to desire to be like men," but it has not been true, so far, most of the time anyway, that "Someone you care about seeks reconciliation" or that

"She always gets what she wants through her charm and personality."

Certainly the Grouch wanted a strong-willed woman, but not one quite as strong-willed as Old Mother.

The Grouch puts on some music. Old Mother starts crying. It is a Haydn piano sonata. He thought she would like it. But when he put it on and smiled at her, she started crying.

Now they are having an argument about Charpentier and Lully: he says he no longer plays Charpentier motets when she is at home because he knows she does not like them.

She says he still plays Lully.

He says it's the Charpentier motets she doesn't like.

She says it's the whole period she doesn't like.

Now she has put her stamps in his stamp box, thinking to be helpful. But the stamps are of many different denominations and have stuck together in the damp weather. They argue about the stamps, and then go on to argue about the argument. She wants to prove he was unfair to her, since her intentions were good. He wants to prove she was not really thinking of him. But because they cannot agree on the sequence in which certain remarks were made, neither one can convince the other.

The Grouch needs attention, but Old Mother pays attention mainly to herself. She needs attention too, of course, and the Grouch would be happy to pay attention to her if the circumstances were different. He will not pay her much attention if she pays him almost none at all.

•

Old Mother is in the bathroom for an inordinately long time. When she comes out, the Grouch asks her if she is upset with him. This time, however, she was only picking raspberry seeds out of her teeth.

Samuel Johnson Is Indignant:

that Scotland has so few trees.

New Year's Resolution

I ask my friend Bob what his New Year's resolutions are and he says, with a shrug (indicating that this is obvious or not surprising): to drink less, to lose weight . . . He asks me the same, but I am not ready to answer him yet. I have been studying my Zen again, in a mild way, out of desperation over the holidays, though mild desperation. A medal or a rotten tomato, it's all the same, says the book I have been reading. After a few days of consideration, I think the most truthful answer to my friend Bob would be: My New Year's resolution is to learn to see myself as nothing. Is this competitive? He wants to lose some weight, I want to learn to see myself as nothing. Of course, to be competitive is not in keeping with any Buddhist philosophy. A true nothing is not competitive. But I don't think I'm being competitive when I say it. I am feeling truly humble, at that moment. Or I think I am—in fact, can anyone be truly humble at the moment they say they want to learn to be nothing? But there is another problem, which I have been wanting to describe to Bob for a few weeks now: at last, halfway through your life, you are smart enough to see that it all amounts to nothing, even success amounts to nothing. But how does a person learn to see herself as nothing when she has already had so much trouble learning to see herself as something in the first place? It's so confusing. You spend the first half of your life learning that you are something after all, now you have to spend the second half learning to see yourself as nothing. You have been a negative nothing, now you want to be a positive nothing. I have begun trying, in these first days of the new year, but so far it's pretty difficult. I'm pretty close to nothing all morning, but by late afternoon what is in me that is something starts throwing its weight around. This happens many days. By evening, I'm full of something and it's often something nasty and pushy. So what I think at this point is that I'm aiming too high, that maybe nothing is too much, to begin with. Maybe for now I should just try, each day, to be a little less than I usually am.

First Grade: Handwriting Practice

Were you there when
they crucified my Lord?
Were you there when
they crucified my Lord?
Oh! Sometimes it causes me
to tremble, tremble, tremble.
Were you there when

(turn over)

they crucified my Lord?

Interesting

My friend is interesting but he is not in his apartment.

Their conversation appears interesting but they are speaking a language I do not understand.

They are both reputed to be interesting people and so I'm sure their conversation is interesting, but they are speaking a language I understand only a little, so I catch only fragments such as "I see" and "on Sunday" and "unfortunately."

This man has a good understanding of his subject and says many things about it that are probably interesting in themselves, but I am not interested because the subject does not interest me.

Here is a woman I know coming up to me. She is very excited, but she is not an interesting woman. What excites her will not be interesting, it will simply not be interesting.

At a party, a highly nervous man talking fast says many smart things about subjects that do not particularly interest me, such as the restoration of historic houses and in particular the age of wallpaper. Yet, because he is so smart and because he gives me so much information per minute, I do not get tired of listening to him.

Here is a very handsome English traffic engineer. The fact that he is so handsome, and so animated, and has such a fine English accent makes it appear, each time he begins to speak, that he is about to say something interesting, but he is never interesting, and he is saying something, yet again, about traffic patterns.

Happiest Moment

If you ask her what is a favorite story she has written, she will hesitate for a long time and then say it may be this story that she read in a book once: an English-language teacher in China asked his Chinese student to say what was the happiest moment in his life. The student hesitated for a long time. At last he smiled with embarrassment and said that his wife had once gone to Beijing and eaten duck there, and she often told him about it, and he would have to say the happiest moment of his life was her trip, and the eating of the duck.

Jury Duty

Q.
A. Jury duty.
Q.
A. The night before, we had been quarreling.
Q.
A. The family.
Q.
A. Four of us. Well, one doesn't live at home anymore. But he was home that night. He was leaving the next morning—the same morning I had to go in to the courtroom.
Q.
A. We were all four of us quarreling. Every which way. I was just now trying to figure it out. There are so many different combinations in which four people can quarrel: one on one, two against one, three against one, two against two, etc. I'm sure we were quarreling in just about every combination.
Q.
A. I don't remember now. Funny. Considering how heated it was.
Q.
A. Well, I put the older boy on the bus, and went on to the

courthouse. No, that's not true. He stayed home alone, I trusted him home alone for a couple of hours. He was supposed to catch the bus in front of the house. That worked out all right, he was gone when I came home later. He hadn't taken anything, as far as I could see.

Q.

A. That's a long story.

Q.

A. The younger one was at school and my husband was at work. I had to be at the courthouse at nine. It was a Monday.

Q.

A. I was a little late—I had trouble parking. But of course the parking lot was full because I was already late. Most of the others were there. A couple of people came in after me.

Q.

A. A big old building uptown, very old. It was the same courthouse where Sojourner Truth testified when . . .

Q.

A. Sojourner Truth.

Q.

A. Sojourner.

Q.

A. She was a former slave who fought for women's rights back in the 1850s. I read that on the historic plaque they have out front. They also said she was illiterate.

Q.

A. Sojourner Truth testified there in that same building, probably in the very same courtroom we were sitting in. Although they didn't say that, come to think of it, and you'd think they would have, since they told us how the room had just been completely restored. In fact they asked us to admire it. That was strange, under the circumstances.

Q.

A. Strange that they would begin talking about the building, the architecture, in the midst of all the instructions they were giving us. As if we were there for a tour, instead of because we had to be there.

Q.

A. It was like a big old library reading room. Or one of those large waiting rooms with high ceilings in an old train station—there's one in New Haven, and there's Grand Central, of course.

Q.

A. Wooden pews, actually. Like a church or an old train station. But comfortable. Surprisingly.

Q.

A. About 175.

Q.

A. They were very quiet. Some of them were reading, some were talking to each other very quietly, just a few. I think they had found someone they knew or they were just being sociable with the person next to them.

Q.

A. No, I didn't talk to any of them, really. There was one older Italian man sitting near me. He couldn't understand anything they said, so I told him what we were supposed to do. He said he used to work in the garment district down in the city. He was a tailor.

Q.

A. Most were just sitting there looking around or staring straight ahead. They were very calm. They were also very alert. I'm sure they felt the same thing I did, that at any moment something might happen, we might be asked to do something, go somewhere. All very expectant, all these people, under that very high ceiling.

Q.

A. Well, first they called the roll—all our names. Most of us were there. Then they told us some of what would be happening. Then we waited.

Q.

A. I don't know—an hour, maybe.

Q.

A. I forget what we were waiting for. Something to do with the judges, or the case. There was a lot of waiting.

Q.

A. Then, after an hour, there was another instruction. I think we were told we could go out for twenty minutes if we wanted a cigarette or to go to the bathroom. I told the Italian man to be sure to come back in twenty minutes.

Q.

A. Someone employed by the court, some officer of the court. I forget if they told us. First it was a man, telling us what the day would be like, roughly, and the week. Then a woman. Still, we didn't really know what to expect. It's funny to think about, but we were all prepared to do whatever they told us. They could have told us to go to another room and sit there and we would have. Then they could have told us to come back and sit. They could have told half of us to go to another room, and we would have done that. We were very trusting of them.

Q.

A. Very gently. Very calmly, gently. They would say something and then leave, go out some door, come back in, say something else. They would look up from some papers and say something to us almost intimately, as though we weren't a whole crowd. And very respectfully. It was very soothing. As though they were treating us as kindly as possible because they were about to give us some bad news.

And we couldn't answer them. We weren't invited to, but we also didn't dare.

Q.

A. No, it wasn't. I thought about that: first I thought of church, then an AA meeting, then something like going to an opera, or a concert. I thought of a large town meeting. But it was different. It was much more peaceful. For one thing, we weren't talking, none of us were talking, really. We weren't supposed to. And also, it was peaceful because we weren't looking for anything, we hadn't come there looking for some kind of spiritual uplift, or rehabilitation. Also, we weren't doing anything, we weren't even waiting for a train, or for an appointment. Actually, we were waiting, but we didn't know what we were waiting for, we didn't know what to expect. So there was this sort of blank wall ahead of us.

Q.

A. A blank wall ahead of us where the rest of the day would normally be, where you could normally see more or less what was coming next.

Q.

A. Yes, but they didn't explain much, and no one dared to ask.

Q.

A. It wasn't emotional. Going to church would be emotional. Going to an AA meeting or even a concert would be emotional. This was the most unemotional thing you could imagine. Maybe that's why it was such a relief.

Q.

A. After all that awful quarreling the night before. It was like some sort of therapy, some sort of treatment. A prescription. As though after such quarreling I was required by law to report to a place where I had to sit very still with other people who were sitting very still, and we would all be treated very kindly and gently until we were completely well again.

Q.

A. Not the way we do. Not like our family. It scares me. It scares the pets. God knows what it's doing to my younger boy.

Q.

A. Yes, we had no choice. We couldn't avoid it. By law, we had to be there. So there was no possibility of conflict—should I be here, should I not be here? And they didn't want us in particular—it wasn't in the least personal, it was random, we had been called randomly. And we weren't here because we had done anything wrong. We were innocent. In fact we were more than innocent. We were good. We were good citizens, good enough to be asked to judge other citizens. The law was saying that we were good. Maybe that's another reason it felt so deeply soothing. It was not emotional, it was not personal, and yet there was this feeling of approval. The law thinks you're a good person, or at least good enough.

Q.

A. Yes, they checked us for weapons down at the side entrance where we came in. They didn't use the old front entrance anymore. We went in through some modern, ugly side doors and down some steps below street level, then we went up to the second floor in an elevator.

Q.

A. There was a metal detector and a guard who looked into our bags and purses. He was very kind and gentle, too. He smiled in a kind way. The sign said something like, "No weapons beyond this point." So it was as though symbolically, too, we were supposed to leave behind anything we could fight with. We were not going in there to fight. Anyone who entered through the metal detector and went beyond it was not dangerous, almost by definition.

Q.

A. Yes, as though we were in suspension, everything in our lives suspended, waiting. We were waiting.

Q.

A. Yes, I thought of the word *patient.* But it wasn't that. Patience is something you need in a strained situation, a situation in which you have to put up with something uncomfortable or difficult. This wasn't difficult. That's what I'm trying to say: we had to be there, and so it relieved us of all personal responsibility. I don't think there is anything else quite like it. Then you have to add on to that the spaciousness of the room. Imagine if it had been a small, crowded room with a low ceiling. Or if people had been noisy, talkative. Or if the people in charge had been confused, or rude.

Q.

A. Finally. The woman had a drum with all our names in it. She turned the drum and then picked names out of the drum one at a time to go up and sit in the jury box and be interviewed. This was going to be the interesting part—that's what I was thinking.

Q.

A. No, we all had to stay there. All the rest of us had to stay there in case the ones being questioned were disqualified or excused. Since it was random, any one of us might be called up to replace them, so we all had to stay.

Q.

A. Again, very gently, very respectfully. And calling them by their first names, gently, like a doctor or a nurse.

Q.

A. There was an unexpected sort of excitement to it. Something ceremonious. The suspense before she called out the name—everyone thinking it might be their name next, of course. Then when the names were called, they had to go up there in front of all these people, and then they had to answer these personal questions with everyone listening and watching them. There were so many of us. We had no idea who all these people were. Then the lives of some of us were gradually revealed, all the rest of us sitting there and listening. We would hear about these people, we would hear their stories. Now we knew the names of some of them. It was like some Indian ritual, some Navajo ceremony.

Q.

A. Oh, some questions you'd expect, some general questions, like, Are you employed? What do you do for a living? Do you have a family? Then more specific questions. Do you drive? Have you ever been in an accident? Do you have any relatives on the police force? Do you have any relatives in the insurance business? Are you familiar with the Palisades Parkway?

Q.

A. The part just north of Exit 11.

Q.

A. It took a long time. I couldn't hear very well.

Q.

A. Very calmly. They called them by their first names. And there were all these pauses. Question. Pause. One lawyer would consult another lawyer while everyone waited, so quiet, so obedient. These quiet voices, and then long silences, and this expectant atmosphere.

Q.

A. Well, so first they were special, the Chosen. Up in front of everyone. I heard enough of their answers to decide I liked them, or I didn't like them. One woman was a real estate dealer, divorced, a cold, tense sort of woman. Grim. I didn't like her. Then there was a tall, strong man, an artist, a family man, obviously a nice guy. I liked him right away. There was a college student who was afraid he'd miss too many days of classes, but then they pointed out to him that this was going to be a short trial and he might miss even more if he didn't go ahead and sit on this jury. So he decided to stay on the jury. And once he was on the jury you had to see him as rather special because he was so young—he was like the child on the jury, the child prodigy, young but wise enough to stand in judgment, who would be taken care of by the older people. And then after a while you even began to dislike him and resent him for being so young, for presuming, for saying in front of everyone that he might not do this thing that he had been asked to do, then for being the child prodigy, so young and bright and being taken care of by the others.

So these ones, who stayed on the jury, they were the Chosen. And the ones who were excused, after all that questioning, when they were excused, when they had to walk back to their seats in front of everybody, they became the Unchosen, they lost all that special prestige, they were ordinary again, they were not special anymore. Or rather, the ones who were rejected for obvious or technical reasons were simply ordinary. But the ones who were rejected for mysterious reasons, for reasons that probably said something not so good about their lives and who they were, they were not just ordinary anymore, now, they had somehow been declared unfit. The others were still sitting up there.

Q.

A. No, not many. Three or four, maybe. One, I think, because he was unemployed and hadn't driven for eleven years—no, longer than that, not since 1979. He used a bicycle to get around. It also came out that he had been in an accident in 1979, or caused one. He had been sued, but he had won. You get only part of the story.

Q.

A. He was dressed more formally than most of the others, in a dark suit and a tie. But his hair was long, in a ponytail, and he was wearing tinted glasses. They asked him about his glasses.

Q.

A. I wasn't surprised that they excused him. He was unemployed. And it also turned out that he wasn't married and had no children. But they don't have to say why they're excusing them. I wondered what he was feeling when he went back to his seat, and after that, for the rest of the day. He was so carefully dressed I thought he might have felt proud that he had been called for jury duty in the first place. Then he might have been embarrassed or humiliated that they didn't want him after all.

Q.

A. Yes, another one was excused because he had a nephew on the police force.

Q.

A. Well, they were all selected by lunchtime, and we were allowed to leave for an hour. They pinned special badges on the ones who had been selected for the jury and instructed them not to talk to anyone, and told us not to talk to them.

Q.

A. Yes. I happened to go to the same café as one of the jurors, and I smiled at her, and she smiled back at me, she knew why I was smiling, she seemed nice, but I didn't dare even say hi.

Q.

A. Yes, we did see some. I think they were brought in from next door. I think the jail was next door and maybe there was an underground passage. Anyway, as far as I can remember, when I first went in, in the morning, I was waiting for the elevator when a line of them came out of another door in the hallway there, in the basement, and went up the stairs next to the elevator. There was one policeman in front of them and one policeman behind them. Then, when we all went out at lunchtime, going back down in the elevator and back out those side doors, they were also being taken back downstairs again and back through that door in the basement hallway. Then, when we came back in from lunch, they were being taken up again. I didn't see them when we left in the afternoon. I guess they were in a courtroom.

Q.

A. There were four or five of them, all men, in orange suits. They were wearing handcuffs and each one was carrying a manila folder, holding it in front of him. They weren't talking, and they looked pretty subdued. They were walking in a line, single file. They all had to keep their arms and hands, and those manila folders, in the same position because of the handcuffs. So they were a little like a show on stage, coordinated.

Q.

A. Yes, it made me feel even more that I was good, or that I was not bad. That it was all very simple, some people were good and some people were not so good. There were people who were proceeding correctly with their lives, and this could be proved by asking them a few questions. And there were people who were not proceeding correctly with their lives.

Q.
A. Though you sensed a bond with the others, when you were all standing around outside during a break. The feeling that you were all in this together, thrown together by chance.
Q.
A. Yes, at lunchtime, when we all went out at once, it reminded me of something and I wasn't sure what. Then I realized it was ladybugs. You can order a package of ladybugs and you get a few hundred in the package. You keep them in the refrigerator until the warm weather comes, and then you release them to feed in your yard. Some of them stay nearby and feed, and some fly away. That's how it was. We were released all at the same time into the neighborhood, nearly two hundred of us, most of us not knowing the neighborhood, and we went out and looked for a place to eat. Most of us stayed and ate near the courthouse.
Q.
A. It was two o'clock when we finally went home. They had us waiting there after lunch in case there was going to be a selection for another trial, but there wasn't another selection, so they let us go. They told us to call that night after six, and to call each night after that for the rest of the week, to see if we had to come in the next day. I called every night for the rest of the week, but I didn't have to go in again. In a way, that felt like therapy too, or some kind of discipline. As though I had to be prepared to do the job again, and if I was prepared, and did the right thing, I might be excused from doing the job. So I did the right thing, each night, and each night I was excused and allowed to stay home the next day.
Q.
A. No, not really. I would have liked to be on a jury. I

would have been very interested. But at the same time I had a lot of work I was supposed to be doing at home.

Q.

A. Yes, that was all. I didn't have to do anything more. And I won't be eligible again for two years.

Q.

A. Yes!

A Double Negative

At a certain point in her life, she realizes it is not so much that she wants to have a child as that she does not want not to have a child, or not to have had a child.

The Old Dictionary

I have an old dictionary, about one hundred and twenty years old, that I need to use for a particular piece of work I'm doing this year. Its pages are brownish in the margins and brittle, and very large. I risk tearing them when I turn them. When I open the dictionary I also risk tearing the spine, which is already split more than halfway up. I have to decide, each time I think of consulting it, whether it is worth damaging the book further in order to look up a particular word. Since I need to use it for this work, I know I will damage it, if not today, then tomorrow, and that by the time I am done with this work it will be in poorer condition than it was when I started, if not completely ruined. When I took it off the shelf today, though, I realized that I treat it with a good deal more care than I treat my young son. Each time I handle it, I take the greatest care not to harm it: my primary concern is not to harm it. What struck me today was that even though my son should be more important to me than my old dictionary, I can't say that each time I deal with my son, my primary concern is not to harm him. My primary concern is almost always something else, for instance to find out what his homework is, or to get supper on the table, or to finish a phone conversation.

If he gets harmed in the process, that doesn't seem to matter to me as much as getting the thing done, whatever it is. Why don't I treat my son at least as well as the old dictionary? Maybe it is because the dictionary is so obviously fragile. When a corner of a page snaps off, it is unmistakable. My son does not look fragile, bending over a game or manhandling the dog. Certainly his body is strong and flexible, and is not easily harmed by me. I have bruised his body and then it has healed. Sometimes it is obvious to me when I have hurt his feelings, but it is harder to see how badly they have been hurt, and they seem to mend. It is hard to see if they mend completely or are forever slightly damaged. When the dictionary is hurt, it can't be mended. Maybe I treat the dictionary better because it makes no demands on me, and doesn't fight back. Maybe I am kinder to things that don't seem to react to me. But in fact my houseplants do not seem to react much and yet I don't treat them very well. The plants make one or two demands. Their demand for light has already been satisfied by where I put them. Their second demand is for water. I water them but not regularly. Some of them don't grow very well because of that and some of them die. Most of them are strange-looking rather than nice-looking. Some of them were nice looking when I bought them but are strange-looking now because I haven't taken very good care of them. Most of them are in pots that are the same ugly plastic pots they came in. I don't actually like them very much. Is there any other reason to like a houseplant, if it is not nice-looking? Am I kinder to something that is nice-looking? But I could treat a plant well even if I didn't like its looks. I should be able to treat my son well when he is not looking good and even when he is not acting very nice. I treat the dog better than the plants, even though he is more active and more demanding. It is simple to give him food and water. I take him for walks, though not often enough. I have also sometimes slapped his nose, though the vet told me never to hit him anywhere near the head, or maybe he said anywhere at all. I am only sure I am not neglecting the dog when he is asleep. Maybe I am kinder to things that are not alive. Or rather if they are not alive there is no question of kindness. It does not hurt them if I don't pay attention to them, and that is a great relief. It is such a relief it is even a pleasure. The only change they show is that they gather dust. The dust won't really hurt them. I can even get someone else to dust them. My son gets dirty, and I can't clean him, and I can't pay someone to clean him. It is hard to keep him clean, and even complicated trying to feed him. He doesn't sleep enough, partly because I try so hard to get him to sleep. The plants need two things, or maybe three. The dog needs five or six things. It is very clear how many things I am giving him and how many I am not, therefore how well I'm taking care of him. My son needs many other things besides what he needs for his physical care, and these things multiply or change constantly. They can change right in the middle of a sentence. Though I often know, I do not always know just what he needs. Even when I know, I am not always able to give it to him. Many times each day I do not give him what he needs. Some of what I do for the old dictionary, though not all, I could do for my son. For instance, I handle it slowly, deliberately, and gently. I consider its age. I treat it with respect. I stop and think before I use it. I know its limitations. I do not encourage it to go farther than it can go (for instance to lie open flat on the table). I leave it alone a good deal of the time.

Honoring the Subjunctive

It invariably precedes, even if it do not altogether supersede, the determination of what is absolutely desirable and just.

How Difficult

For years my mother said I was selfish, careless, irresponsible, etc. She was often annoyed. If I argued, she held her hands over her ears. She did what she could to change me but for years I did not change, or if I changed, I could not be sure I had, because a moment never came when my mother said, "You are no longer selfish, careless, irresponsible, etc." Now I'm the one who says to myself, "Why can't you think of others first, why don't you pay attention to what you're doing, why don't you remember what has to be done?" I am annoyed. I sympathize with my mother. How difficult I am! But I can't say this to her, because at the same time that I want to say it, I am also here on the phone coming between us, listening and prepared to defend myself.

Losing Memory

You ask me about Edith Wharton.
Well, the name is very familiar.

Letter to a Funeral Parlor

Dear Sir,

I am writing to you to object to the word *cremains*, which was used by your representative when he met with my mother and me two days after my father's death.

We had no objection to your representative, personally, who was respectful and friendly and dealt with us in a sensitive way. He did not try to sell us an expensive urn, for instance.

What startled and disturbed us was the word *cremains*. You in the business must have invented this word and you are used to it. We the public do not hear it very often. We don't lose a close friend or a family member very many times in our life, and years pass in between, if we are lucky. Even less often do we have to discuss what is to be done with a family member or close friend after their death.

We noticed that before the death of my father you and your representative used the words *loved one* to refer to him. That was comfortable for us, even if the ways in which we loved him were complicated.

Then we were sitting there in our chairs in the living room trying not to weep in front of your representative, who was opposite us on the sofa, and we were very tired first from sitting up with my father, and then from worrying about whether he was comfortable as he was dying, and then from worrying about where he might be now that he was dead, and your representative referred to him as "the cremains."

At first we did not even know what he meant. Then, when we realized, we were frankly upset. *Cremains* sounds like something invented as a milk substitute in coffee, like Cremora, or Coffee-mate. Or it sounds like some kind of a chipped beef dish.

As one who works with words for a living, I must say that any invented word, like *Porta Potti* or *pooper-scooper*, has a cheerful or even jovial ring to it that I don't think you really intended when you invented the word *cremains.* In fact, my father himself, who was a professor of English and is now being called *the cremains*, would have pointed out to you the alliteration in *Porta Potti* and the rhyme in *pooper-scooper.* Then he would have told you that *cremains* falls into the same category as *brunch* and is known as a portmanteau word.

There is nothing wrong with inventing words, especially in a business. But a grieving family is not prepared for this one. We are not even used to our loved one being gone. You could very well continue to employ the term *ashes.* We are used to it from the Bible, and are even comforted by it. We would not misunderstand. We would know that these ashes are not like the ashes in a fireplace.

Yours sincerely.

Thyroid Diary

Tonight we are going to a party to celebrate my dentist's wife's graduation from college. All these years, while the dentist has been working on my teeth, his wife has been earning credits at the college, just a few at a time. Every semester, along with her other courses, she has been studying painting with my husband, who teaches painting and drawing at the college. She has been studying with him in a tutorial situation. She is an enthusiastic flower gardener and paints mostly flowers. She has written texts about her flower gardens, to go with her paintings. My husband told me that a flower painting of hers that was hanging in the Art Building at commencement time was stolen—by a student, he thought, or a student's parents.

I didn't know she was actually earning a degree until we received the invitation to this party to be given by her friend, who is a faculty secretary at the college. A few days after the invitation arrived, we received another one from the same woman, but for a different date. I was sure there had been a mistake. But in fact she is simply giving two parties, and we are invited to both.

Now I have to wonder why my serious and extensive dental work ended—which it did—just a couple of months before the dentist's wife's graduation. When the dentist said I didn't need any further work, I thought I still had at least two more crowns to go. I can't remember a time when I haven't had more work to be done on my teeth.

I have always been puzzled, anyway, by the economics of the thing, because I would pay the dentist, and he would presumably give his wife the money for her courses at the college, she would pay the college, the college would pay my husband a separate fee for her tutorials, and then my husband would give me money for the dentist, I would pay the dentist, the dentist would give money to his wife, and so it would continue. I thought that if no one paid anyone, it would work out just the same, but that didn't seem quite right, either.

This spring the dentist, who is a gardener like his wife, but grows vegetables and grapes, and has a small apple orchard, made the transactions a little more complicated by proposing to my husband that they share certain shipments of bedding plants that could be bought more economically in large quantities. He said they might share two varieties of tomatoes as well as some onions and peppers. My husband thought it over and then agreed. In general he is wary of the obligations of any sort of partnership, but he is also interested in saving money, and in this case he appreciated the gesture of goodwill and trust.

The party we are going to tonight will be at the home of the faculty secretary in a small town on the other side of the river. But as soon as I say that, I realize I have made a mistake. This is not the party in honor of the dentist's wife, but the other one. This one is for the faculty secretary's nephew, who is going off on a long sea voyage. After many years of living sometimes on land and sometimes on the water, he has sold his house and will be living on his sailboat, though he still has a girlfriend here on land. I should have remembered this, because my husband and I were just discussing at lunch what to give him as a going-away present. We were considering three choices: a copy of Richard Henry Dana's *Two Years Before the Mast*, or a book that my husband saw about tying knots, or a bottle of wine. My husband also suggested a bottle of good brandy, but I thought that would only encourage our friend to drink alone on his boat.

If I'm confused about all this, it may be because of my underactive thyroid. Slow thinking is one symptom of an underactive thyroid, but I can't tell if I'm thinking more slowly than I used to. Since my brain is the only thing I have for observing how I am thinking, I can't be truly objective. If it is slow, it will not necessarily know that it's slow, since it will be moving at a rate that seems appropriate to it.

And then, there have always been days when my mind does not make connections very fast. There are always days when my mind is cloudy, or I forget things, or I feel as if I am in a different town or a different house—that something around me or about me is not normal.

When the doctor was explaining my condition to me, I took notes. I had to stop her once or twice and ask her to repeat something so that I could write it down. I told her it helped me to remember. She said I would not have to take notes if my thyroid were more active. That made me a little angry, but I did not try to defend myself. I did not answer her that for one thing, the self-help medical books always tell you to take notes during a meeting with a doctor, and for another I have a habit of taking notes anyway, especially when I am on the telephone, and even during conversations when it is not at all necessary, when the information I am hearing is something that does not have to be remembered. I take notes on things I have just said to someone else. I write down words I have just used myself, like *nice guy* or *responsible.* I write down names of people in my family, and my own telephone number.

I did notice, one evening when I was playing a board game with my family, that over and over again I could not remember whose turn it was or see where my piece was on the board. This could have been due to my underactive thyroid.

I thought I wasn't worried about my thyroid, because I believed I could correct whatever problem there was with a strategy involving diet. But maybe I am worried after all, because for the past week, ever since my doctor called me, I haven't been sleeping well. My trouble sleeping, though, may be due to the underactive thyroid.

My doctor is not actually a doctor, as my husband is quick to say: she's only a physician's assistant. He says this as though she may not know what she's talking about. He says this in my defense, as though to protect me from her or from my condition. But I think she's careful and competent, and I believe her. Now I'm eating only vegetables for dinner, preparing to begin my dietary strategy. I truly believe the body can cure itself of whatever is wrong with it, given the right diet and other treatments. I am only waiting for some more tests, which I will have this week, before I make a plan for my care. I'm sure that whatever diet I choose, I should not drink any alcohol, but I have already planned to make an exception for the party tonight.

My physician's assistant told me the thyroid gland controls every part of the body—not only the brain but also the heart, the digestion, the metabolism, the circulation, and other things I may be forgetting. In the case of a significantly underactive thyroid, everything slows down. I have a slow heartbeat, slow digestion, possibly slow thinking, a low temperature, cold hands and feet. Sometimes my heart rate goes down to fifty or below. I never knew what a thyroid gland did. Now I find out it is so important that if it were allowed to continue functioning poorly like this, I would eventually die—die early, I mean. I have never associated myself with such an unexpected part of the body as the thyroid, so it feels as though my body is suddenly strange to me, or I am strange to myself.

Now I have learned more about what is wrong with me, and I do not think the body can always cure itself of whatever is wrong with it. Or rather, I still believe this as a general principle, but I don't think my body can cure itself in this case, because no one seems to know enough about this particular disease, which is an autoimmune disease. It is called Hashimoto's disease, though my husband keeps calling it Kurosawa's, or Nagasaki's.

By now I have also been to the first party, given for our sailor friend, as well as the second party, given for our dentist's wife. The parties were very different even though they were at the same house. In the perennial beds, different flowers were in bloom. The first party was informal, as was appropriate for a going-away party for a sailor. Neighbors wearing casual clothes came out onto the lawn from shortcuts through the woods. At the second, there were trays of catered hors d'oeuvres and a uniformed serving woman. At that party I learned that not one, but two, of the dentist's wife's paintings had been stolen at commencement time. I learned that the paintings were much smaller than I had thought. One from the same series was hanging on the wall in the faculty secretary's house. It was small enough to put in your pocket or your purse. The dentist was sitting in a wicker chair on the screened porch. I did not find it strange to see him there instead of in his office, but I also couldn't smile at him socially in quite the same way I would at anyone else, since he knows my teeth so well, particularly my upper left incisor.

A corkscrew willow grows by a tiny stream in the front yard of the faculty secretary's house. At the first party, she cut a shoot of the corkscrew willow for me to take home and plant. I forgot to take it. From the second, I took several more shoots, but at home I put them in a bucket of water in the garage and forgot them for a few days. I then offered them to a friend, but forgot to give them to her, and the water in the bucket evaporated and they withered.

I have also been up to see a specialist in Albany several times, more often than was necessary, my husband believes. My husband thinks the specialist could simply read the numbers and look at the results of the blood tests, and that like other doctors he schedules extra office visits to make more money. But a friend of mine said, "With gland problems, they like to look at you." I do not remember which friend it was.

And yet this specialist seemed to avoid looking at me. At least he avoided it when he first walked into the room—he looked down at my file instead. He did eventually look at me, with his head cocked a little to one side and a slight smile on his face that seemed to express a private amusement that was not completely unfriendly. But he looked at me only when he was ready to deliver his opinion, which he had already formed by reading the numbers in my file.

Meanwhile, my husband has been having trouble with his tomato plants. The dentist gave him four or five healthy, well-grown plants, neatly potted in peat pots, and they are doing well. In return, my husband is supposed to give him four or five of another variety. But most of these arrived in the mail half dead. Some died, two are doing fairly well, and the rest are not dead, but are not growing, either, at least not visibly. My husband does not want to give away the only two that are thriving. He also does not want to give the dentist spindly and sickly plants. He is waiting, time is passing, but the plants that were not growing well are not growing any better.

I have been trying to see if I am thinking more slowly than before. In my translation work, for instance, I see that I sometimes try to find an equivalent in English before I really understand the French. Then I realize that I don't understand the French, even after trying several times, and I cast my eye rather listlessly here and there within the paragraph hoping the meaning of it will fall into place by itself, which it sometimes does. But today it does not, and then my mind wanders. I go back to work on it, look in the dictionary again, reading every word of a very long entry, but there's nothing in the dictionary that helps me. I want to put something down, anything at all, just to mark the place so that I can go on translating and come back to the problem later. I need to put down something noticeably wrong, so that later I will see that the spot needs work, but everything I think of is so poor that it is embarrassing. I don't know why I should be embarrassed, if there is no one to see it, but I am embarrassed and will not go on until I put down something decent, though wrong. At least, this morning, as I was studying the dictionary carefully in order to see if I really wanted to use the word, I learned more about *embarrassment* and its earlier, concrete meaning of "encumbrance" or "obstruction."

But then, even though I had been awake since six o'clock and had been working for an hour already, someone who didn't know me, in fact someone from the doctor's office, said to me on the phone, "Sounds like you're not up yet. Can you call me back when you are?" I was not insulted, but I was a little worried. I apparently sounded very slow on the phone, even if I did not think I was very slow. Now, if I do this whole translation, which is an important job, with my mind not working very clearly, but not knowing that my mind isn't working very clearly, then the translation may not be very good—though I may not know that. And if it isn't very good, that would really be unfortunate, since some of my future income may depend on it.

Actually, what the receptionist or nurse took to be slowness may be something else, an attitude I now have that is more casual toward health-care professionals. I used to be very respectful of them and slightly intimidated. Now I have noticed that I want to make fun of the men and joke with the women, or I should say, joke with both men and women, but rather more aggressively with the men.

I first noticed this a few years ago with my oral surgeon. I liked him and respected him, but I noticed after a while that I would not deal in a straightforward, courteous way with him, but had to make some kind of a joke. That shocked me, because all my life I have been so respectful of health-care professionals, or have at least behaved with respect, whatever I thought of them privately. The jokes just popped out as though someone else had taken over for a moment. Once, for instance, I saw a skull in his office and made what was no doubt the obvious joke—that it must be a former patient. He was startled, but did not seem to mind. Another time, when he had just hurt me badly by giving me a long injection in my gum, I bit down hard on his index finger. That was not a joke, and I did not do it on purpose. His two female assistants were amazed but also delighted. Although he frowned in pain and shook his finger in the air, the doctor took it very well and said it happened from time to time, that it was actually a reflex. I slightly antagonized my present doctor, or physician's assistant, by saying that I did not like taking medicine because I did not like being dependent on any drug. What if I were lost in a jungle without my thyroid medicine? I asked her, and it is true that I always believe that someday I may be lost in a jungle, even though we do not call them jungles anymore, and we are losing them anyway, so that the word *jungle* is becoming just an idea. She said I would get along well enough without it until I could find my way out of the jungle.

There was a small emergency situation quite recently, though, in which I was not tempted to make fun of the doctor. He was a young doctor, I admired his decisiveness and his technical skill, and I was also quiet because of my pain. I had bruised my finger badly, and what he had to do was to release some of the pressure under the nail. He did this in what he said was the best way, but also the old-fashioned way, using nothing but a candle and a large paper clip.

The receptionist or nurse this morning thought I wasn't "up" yet because I didn't know the exact dose or the full name of my thyroid medicine. But I was careless about that information because of my skeptical attitude toward the health-care profession and because I do not try to conceal that attitude. I did not mean to be disrespectful to her in particular. But after she said this, I noticed two other possible signs of poor functioning: a real estate dealer I called on the phone later in the morning thought at first that I was another real estate dealer. I asked her why she thought this. She had trouble answering, but I guessed that it might have been my lack of enthusiasm, or a coldness in my tone of voice. Then, still later, when I was talking to my husband on the telephone, I was so confusing, contradictory, and long-winded that he compared me to a legal brief he was reading. This document is fifty pages long and concerns a possible class action against an insurance company for misrepresentation.

After wondering for some weeks what to do about the tomato plants, my husband told me he was going to explain to the dentist that none of the plants was good enough to give him, though that is not strictly true. Then, just hours later, he told me that he had changed his mind. He was going to patch the soaker hose and give the plants a little more time.

But on the other hand, it occurs to me that maybe my brain is working well enough but simply more slowly than usual. Maybe the quality of my work will be good but I will take longer than usual to make it good. Or maybe the dose of thyroid supplement I'm taking, which has been increased once without much effect, will be increased to the proper level soon enough so that by the time I reach the final draft of this translation I will be thinking sharply and quickly again. Then I wonder if I will think even better than before this whole condition began, because my brain will have been trying so hard in the meantime, without adequate support from my thyroid, that maybe it will have developed new cells. But I don't know enough about the brain's anatomy to know if that is possible.

Or maybe some of the time I go ahead quickly enough but without producing very high-quality work, while some of the time I go ahead slowly and produce better-quality work, so that it is a choice: either go slowly and do good work, or go quickly and do poor work. But then, those have always been the two options in translation, I see, so I should say that now the choice is: go even more slowly than before and do adequately good work, or go more quickly and do really poor work.

But with any luck, the dosage will gradually be raised high enough so that in a couple of months I will be able to do work that is both quick and adequately good or quite good. The dosage can't be raised too abruptly or my heart will suffer.

I had thought at first, If my brain is working this well with inadequate amounts of thyroid hormone, how well my brain will work with the proper amounts of thyroid hormone! But then I began to distrust the thought, because what seemed like good working of the brain seemed good to that very same brain that was lacking the proper dose of hormone, and that brain could be quite mistaken.

Another question I had recently was this: Is the rather pessimistic turn that my thoughts have taken these days due to the state of the world, which is bad and which gets worse more quickly than one can hope to save it, so that I become quite scared? Or is it due simply to the low level of my thyroid hormone, which would mean that maybe the world is not really in such a frightening state and seems that way only to me? So that I could say to myself: Remember your low thyroid hormone level and have faith that the world will be all right?

What an insult to the mind, I think then, that the chemicals of the body and nothing else are causing my thoughts, which I take so seriously, to move in a certain direction. What an insult to the amazing brain that such a simple thing as a level of chemicals should point it in a certain direction. Then I think, No, it's not an insult, I can think of it not as an insult, but as part of another fascinating system. I can say, I would prefer to see it as part of a single, interesting system. Then I think, And, after all, it is this amazing brain that, in thinking this, is being so magnanimous to the dumb body. Though of course maybe it is the chemicals of the dumb body that are permitting the amazing brain to be magnanimous.

Now I have been to the dentist again for a cleaning and checkup, and he has found a large cracked filling in a tooth that he said should really have a crown or a cap. He said he had predicted this years ago. But when I objected to more major work, and asked for a postponement, he consented to treat it with a bonded filling that might or might not last for a long time. I was a little surprised that he agreed to this. I wondered if he was losing his enthusiasm, or losing the conviction—which all my dentists seem to have had—that all work on my teeth should be as extreme and as complete as possible. I also noticed that he was curiously silent about tomatoes, saying nothing, either, about the other vegetables in his garden, or about his harvests. We talked instead about crowded holiday spots and the westward expansion of the United States during the nineteenth century. His grandfather had actually lived in the days of the westward expansion and used to talk to him about it. He said it was surprising how recent that time was.

Our talk extended out into the reception area while I paid my bill and took a pencil from the box of gift pencils. Considering the rapid population growth, he said, he did not want to come back after he died. I agreed that I would not want to come back either, at least not as a person, adding the qualification, which I believe, that if we have to come back we may be safer coming back as cockroaches.

The receptionist and dental hygienist, who were listening, looked surprised at this.

Now that the fall semester has begun, the woman who gave both parties is back at work at the college. Nearly every day, I read notices that she sends out to all the faculty. She has a very sharp and funny mind, a good education, and an interesting background, but her notices are deliberately neutral in tone and strictly practical. Some are about empty cardboard boxes free for the taking, some about stray cats on the campus, and a great many about misuse of the Xerox machines. Only now and then can I detect from something she says about a page of sonnets left in her office, or from her rhetorically balanced sentences, or from her use of the word *criterion*, how sharp she is.

Since the dentist's wife now has her degree, she is no longer studying with my husband, but I do not remember what she is doing, though I was told, probably by my husband.

We have been eating the tomatoes from our garden, though the harvest is not as good as it has been in other years. A woodchuck has dug a hole down under the fence and up among the tomato plants and has been eating the tomatoes as they ripen. My husband puts heavy stones in the hole, but during the night the woodchuck moves them.

I thought this was the end of it, that I would hear no more about the dentist and the results of the season's planting. I thought there was a slight embarrassment all around. But last week my husband came home from his three-month cleaning with a bag of onions and told me that the issue had been tacitly resolved, that he and the dentist had talked about the long dry spells coming at the wrong times and how the summer had been a poor one for tomatoes. Even the dentist's plants had not done well. And yesterday, during the insertion of my bonded filling, the dentist told me how he makes grape jelly. I am relieved that there are apparently no hard feelings. The dentist's onions are pretty, small and fresh. I will want to think of some way of preparing them so that they will be particularly noticeable as we eat them.

My heart seems to be beating a little faster now. If it is true that I have been thinking more slowly, I have still been able to learn new things and remember them, in the past few months. I forget what we actually gave to our sailor friend, and there are other things I know I have forgotten, and still others that I must have forgotten, but I have learned the history of the word *embarrassment* and many other word histories, I have been introduced to the corkscrew willow, I have learned the term *bonded filling*, and many other new definitions from the dictionaries, for instance that the verb *flense* means "to cut up a whale," and that the adjective *next* is the superlative of *nigh*. I have learned two new terms for familiar things: in music, the *Alberti bass*, and in grammar, the *Oxford comma*. I have had new thoughts about the westward expansion of the United States. I have heard the expression *dead soldiers* twice in two days and learned that it means empty bottles. Maybe it also means anything that is no more use to anyone, since I first heard it from a woman at a plant nursery who was looking through a bin of gourds and tossing out the rotten ones. I learned from the dentist that if I make grape jelly I should heat the sugar in the oven before adding it to the grape juice. I have learned more about the Kennedy family and particularly Edward Kennedy from a magazine in the dentist's office. I had no trouble, after a few minutes, recognizing Dvořák's *New World Symphony* on the radio while I was having my bonded filling put in.

After reading the introduction again, having read it years ago and forgotten what I learned from it, I have learned yet again how Richard Henry Dana's *Two Years Before the Mast* came to be written, that when Dana was a student at Harvard he fell ill and could not continue his studies, went to sea to recover his health, and subsequently wrote about his experiences, so that it is the book of a young man, whereas I had thought of it as the book of an older man just because it has been a classic for so many decades. What I don't know yet is why I see it so often in secondhand bookstores and at library sales.

Information from the North Concerning the Ice:

Each seal uses many blowholes and each blowhole is used by many seals.

Murder in Bohemia

In the city of Frydlant in Bohemia where all the people are anyway pale as ghosts and dressed in dark winter clothes, an old woman was unable any longer to bear the inevitable falling of her life into destitution and disgrace, and went mad and murdered out of pity her husband, her two sons, and her daughter, out of anger her neighbors on one side and her neighbors across the street, who had scorned her family, out of revenge the grocer from whom she had had to beg for credit, and the pawnbroker, and two money-lenders, then a streetcar conductor whom she did not know, and finally—rushing with her long knife into the Town Hall—the young mayor and one of his councilmen as they sat puzzling over an amendment.

Happy Memories

I imagine that when I am old, I will be alone, and in pain, and my eyes will be too weak to read. I am afraid of those long days. I like my days to be happy. I try to think what would be a happy way to spend those difficult days. It may be that the radio will be enough to fill those days. An old person has her radio, I have heard it said. And I have heard it said that in addition to her radio, she has her happy memories. When her pain is not too bad, she can go over her happy memories and be comforted. But you must have happy memories. What bothers me is that I'm not sure how many happy memories I will have. I am not even sure just what makes a happy memory, the kind that will both comfort me and give me pleasure when I can't do anything else. Just because I enjoy something now does not mean that it will make a happy memory. In fact, I know that many of the things I enjoy now will not make good happy memories later. I am happy doing the work I do, alone at a desk. That work is a great part of every day. But when I am old and alone all the time, will it be enough to think about the work I used to do? Another thing I enjoy is eating candy by myself while I read a book in the evening, but I don't think that will make a good happy memory either.

I like to play the piano, I like to look at the plants that come up in the yard beginning in March, I enjoy walking with my dog, and looking down into his face at his good eye and his bad eye, I like to see the sky in the late afternoon, especially in November, I like petting my cats, hearing their cries, and holding them. But I suspect that the memory of my pets will not be enough, either, even if I love them. There are things that make me laugh, but often they are grim things, and they will not make a good happy memory either, unless I share them with someone else. Then it is not the amusement but the sharing of it that makes the happy memory. It seems as though a happy memory has to involve other people. I think of all the different people. I think of the good encounters with people. Most of the people I talk to on the telephone are friendly, even when I have called a wrong number. I have a happy memory of stopping my car by the side of the road to talk to a woman about her garden. I talk to the people who work in the post office and the drugstore, and I used to talk to the people at the bank before they put an automated teller machine in the lobby. When a man came to fix the dehumidifier in the basement, we talked about the history of this town. I enjoy my conversations with the librarian down the street. I enjoy the friendly messages I receive from bookstores selling secondhand books. But I don't think any of these encounters will make a memory that will comfort me when I am old. Maybe a happy memory can't involve people who were only strangers or casual friends. You can't be left alone, in your old age and pain, with memories that include only people who have forgotten you. The people in your happy memories have to be the same people who want to have you in their own happy memories. A lively dinner party does not make a good happy memory if no one there cared very much for any of the others. I think of some of the good or meaningful times I have had with the people close to me, to see if they would make good happy memories. Meeting a friend at a railway station on a sunny day seems to have made a good happy memory, even though later we talked about some difficult things, like starvation and dehydration. There were walks in the woods with friends looking for mushrooms that may make happy memories. There have been a few times of gardening together as a family that may make a good happy memory. Working together at some arduous cooking one evening is a happy memory so far. There was a good trip out to a department store. Sitting by the bedside of someone who was dying may actually make a good happy memory. My mother and I once carried a piece of coal on a train to Newcastle together. My mother and I once played cards with some longshoremen on a snowy morning waiting for a ship to come in. There was a time when I lived in a foreign city and returned again and again to a certain botanical garden to look at a certain cedar of Lebanon, and that is a happy memory, even though I was alone. My neighbor across the street once brought a plate of cake to the back door during a time of mourning. But I can see that if someday she and I were to become estranged, that would spoil the happy memory. I see that happy memories can be erased. A happy memory can be erased if you do the same thing on another day and you are not happy, for instance if on another day you garden or cook together with bad feeling. I can see that an experience does not make a happy memory if it started out well but ended badly. There is no happy memory if there was something nice about an experience but also some problem, if two of you enjoyed an outing but the third was sitting at home angry because you were so late returning. You have to make sure, somehow, that nothing spoils the thing while it is happening, and then that no later experience erases it. I could have happy memories. I can see that the things I do with another person, and with a feeling of warmth toward that person, and with a person who will want to have me in his or her happy memory may make a good happy memory, while the things I do alone and especially with a feeling of ambition, or pride, or power, even if they are good in themselves, will not make a good happy memory. It is all right to have candy and enjoy it, but I should remember that the memory of candy will not be a happy one. If I am playing a board game with people close to me and we are happy, I must be sure we don't quarrel before the end of it. I must be sure that at some later time we don't play another board game that is unhappy. I should check now and then to make sure I am not alone too much, or unhappy with other people too often. I should add them up, now and then: what are my happy memories so far?

They Take Turns Using a Word They Like

"It's *extraordinary*," says one woman.
"It *is* extraordinary," says the other.

Marie Curie, So Honorable Woman

Preface

Woman of pride, passion, and labor, who was actress of her time because she had the ambition of her means and the means of her ambition, actress of ours, finally, since between Marie and atomic force, the filiation is direct.

Besides, she died of it.

Character

From birth, Marie possesses the three dispositions that make brilliant subjects, cherished by professors: memory, power of concentration, and appetite for learning.

"My heart breaks when I think of my spoiled aptitudes which, all the same, had to be worth something . . ."

Then what? The "ordinary destiny of women"? She never imagined making it her own.

In the Chalet of Zakopane

But in the chalet of Zakopane where she lingers, alone, in September 1891, walking her melancholy under the great black pines of the Carpathians, dragging a grippe that does not finish, one man, Casimir, could take her away. And a part of herself hopes.

In two months she will be twenty-four years.

She is poor. She is not yet beautiful. For all diploma she has the Polish baccalaureate. Why would she become "someone"? Besides, she loves Casimir, and waits for him.

Four years have not cooled the sentiments of the young man, probably exalted on the contrary by the obstacle . . . And he has lost nothing of his charm . . .

What he does not know, when he mentions their shared future, is that he now has a rival. And what a rival! A laboratory.

Where does she come from, this nervous young woman, who curiously combines timidity and assurance? It is a daughter of the earth, who has need of air, space, trees. She entertains with nature a relationship that is almost carnal. The plants know it and under her fingers blossom.

What she denies, on the other hand, is her animal part. Her brief angers, for example, which betray like a bolt of lightning what she is controlling in the way of concealed storms.

Poverty

Now, however, her father is deprived of his attributions, loses the lodging that accompanies them and half of his appointments.

How to join the two ends?

He gnaws at himself. Ah!

What afflicts her is not that she has only one dress, which must be made over by a seamstress, but that she does not see any way out of the tunnel in which she is engaged.

Then she is rescued by her sister.

Studies in Paris

French science, whose milk Marie Sklodowska has come to Paris to suck, happily has one great man, Pasteur, who is reaching the end of his life.

In Paris, she will spend her leisure time with her sister Bronia and Bronia's own Casimir. Though they work hard they know how to amuse themselves, with Slavic hospitality. There are infinite discussions around the samovar and the piano in which they remake the world.

They organize parties, put on amateur spectacles, tableaux vivants: a young woman draped in a garnet tunic, her blond hair falling over her shoulders, incarnates Poland breaking its bonds while Paderewski plays Chopin in the wings: it's Marie, proud of having been chosen.

But chatting pleasantly will never be her specialty.

Austerity

Her austerity sometimes borders on masochism. One night she is so cold in her fireless little room that she piles on her bed everything contained in her trunk along with a chair, while the water freezes in her basin.

She sometimes faints from having fed herself exclusively on radishes and tea. Bronia and Casimir rescue her and a cure of beefsteak puts her to rights.

Language

A summer passes. She perfects her French. When classes resume, she has driven out all the "Polishisms" from her vocabulary. Only the gently rolled *r*'s will bear witness until her last day to her Slavic origins, adding a certain charm to her voice that does not lack it already. And, like all the world, she will always calculate in her mother tongue.

License

Not only does she pass her exam, but when the results are announced before all the candidates in order of merit, her name is spoken first. Marie Sklodowska is licensed in physical sciences by the University of Paris. And it is admirable.

Courtship

Did she even notice, on the eve of her exam, that Sadi Carnot, the president of the Republic, was stabbed in his carriage by an Italian militant anarchist?

Perhaps she did not speak of it, even for an instant, with the physicist she has been seeing for several weeks, and who, as others offer chocolates, has brought her, when he has come to chat with her in her room, the offprint of an article titled "On symmetry in physical phenomena, the symmetry of an electric field and of a magnetic field." The brochure is dedicated "To Mlle Sklodowska with the respect and the friendship of the author P. Curie."

Together they speak enormously, but about physics or themselves.

And, everyone knows, to tolerate a person telling you about his childhood it is necessary to be in love with him.

Previous Loves

Marie has not attained twenty-six years, soon twenty-seven, she has not lived three years in Paris without having met at Bronia's, at the Faculty, at the laboratory, representatives of the male species sensitive to her attractions. An enamored Polish student had once thought to swallow laudanum to make himself interesting in her eyes. Marie's reaction: "That young man has no sense of priorities."

In any case, they did not have the same.

Pierre

Pierre Curie has come on stage in Marie's life at the precise moment at which it was suitable that he should appear.

The year 1894 has begun. Marie is assured of obtaining her license in July. She is beginning to look beyond, she is more available, and the spring is beautiful. Pierre is already captive to this singular little blond person.

It is clear that, making his way at once through the realms of the sublime and of theoretical physics, Pierre still finds himself alone at thirty-five years. And Marie Sklodowska very quickly appears to him as the Unique, capable of accompanying him there.

But lofty thinking is ill compensated. At thirty-six years, Pierre Curie earns thirty-six hundred francs per year at the School of Physics.

Bolt of Lightning

Marie Curie is over fifty years when she writes lines that describe their first meeting and she is never a woman to express herself, publicly at least, like the Portuguese Nun. But under the convention of the style and the eternal constraint certainly appears a little of what was, it seems, a reciprocal bolt of lightning.

Marie will be perceptibly longer in being convinced that she must alienate her independence, even to this physicist with limpid eyes.

Pierre Curie has said it to her: "Science, is your destiny." Science, that is to say research pursued for practical ends.

Marie tells, in the stilted book she devotes to him: "Pierre Curie wrote me during the summer of 1894 letters which I think admirable taken as a whole."

To one, Pierre adds a postscript: "I have shown your photograph to my brother. Was I wrong? He finds you very good. He says: 'She has a look that is very decided and even stubborn.' "

Stubborn, oh how much!

She, always dressed in gray, gentle yet stern, childlike yet mature, sweet yet uncompromising . . . the woman from Poland.

He . . .

And then they . . .

Domestic Life

The only competition that Pierre has ever accepted and that he has just won is against Poland.

And thus it is in July 1894 that Marie takes, on the sly, lessons of a new kind with Bronia: How does one make a roast chicken? Fries? How does one feed a husband?

We know, on the other hand, that a cousin has the good idea of sending a check as a wedding present. That the check is exchanged for two bicycles. And that the "little queen," the entirely new invention that became the darling of the French, will be the honeymoon vehicle of M. and Mme Pierre Curie.

The bicycle, is freedom.

Research

To extract uranium from pitchblende, there are at that time factories. To extract radium from it, there is a woman in a hangar.

She is sure of her method. But her means are derisory.

Working with Radium

Marie gives birth to a daughter, yet does not take time off from work. Why are they so tired, the Curies, when they arrive, with Irene who is cutting her seventh tooth, at Auroux where they have rented a house for the summer?

They struggle to swim in the river and they struggle on their bicycles. And Marie has the tips of her fingers chapped, painful. She does not know, nor Pierre either, that they are beginning to suffer from the irradiation of the radioactive substances they are manipulating.

It is in the following December, on a page of the black notebook not precisely dated and bearing Pierre's writing, that appears for the first time the word *radium*.

What remains is to prove the existence of the new element. "I would like it to have a beautiful color," says Pierre.

Pure salts of radium are colorless, quite simply. But their own radiations color with a blue-mauve tint the glass tubes that contain them. In sufficient quantity, their radiations provoke a visible glow in the darkness.

When that glow begins to irradiate in the darkness of the laboratory, Pierre is happy.

Children

Marie makes jams and the clothes of her daughters out of a spirit of thrift. Not from zeal.

Relationship

When it comes to mathematics, he judges her stronger than he and says it good and loud. She, for her part, admires in her companion "the sureness and the rigor of his reasonings, the surprising suppleness with which he can change the object of his research . . ."

Each of them has a very high idea of the value of the other.

Fellow Workers

An aura has been created that attracts and impresses at the same time. The echo of their works, the radiance of Pierre, the intensity of Marie, that force which is all the more moving because the young blond woman appears more and more slender under her black smock, the couple they form, the almost religious spirit of their scientific engagement, their asceticism, all this has attracted young researchers in their wake.

A disheveled chemist, André Debierne, will enter the life of the Curies never to leave it again.

Marie Curie is neither a saint nor a martyr. She is young at a time when most women oscillate between remorse and hysteria, either guilty or "out of their bodies."

Genius: Radioactivity

In fact, two German researchers announce that radioactive substances have physiological effects. Pierre immediately exposes his arm deliberately to a source of radium. With happiness, he sees a lesion form.

To be recognized by their peers—the Curies certainly appreciate that satisfaction. Besides, it is "fair."

Now, it happens that at night she gets up and starts to wander through the sleeping house. Little crises of somnambulism that alarm Pierre. Or it is he who is ravaged by pains that alter his sleep. Marie watches over him, worried, powerless.

And her appearance? Marie is sitting next to Lord Kelvin, in her "formal dress." She has only one, still the same after ten years, black, with a discreet neckline. In truth, it is better that she has no love of toilette, because she has no taste at all and never will have. Black—which distinguishes her, because it is not customary to wear it—and gray to which she has subscribed out of convenience, settle matters well and make a good setting for her ash-blond hair.

Fame

There exists a threshold beyond which disdain for honors borders on affectation, and one would be tempted to think that Marie Curie has crossed it when she complains, in sum, at having received, with Pierre, the Nobel Prize.

Wrested from their bowl, our two goldfish suffocate and thrash about. No, they wish no banquet; no, they wish no tour of America; no, they do not wish to visit the Automobile Show.

However, they are both unconditional admirers of Wagner.

The Death of Pierre

He takes the train back from the country Monday evening, carrying a bouquet of ranunculus.

Marie returns Wednesday evening. The rain has resumed in Paris.

The next day, Thursday, Pierre is on his way from his publisher, Gauthier-Villars, to the Institute. The rain has started again. He opens his umbrella. The rue Dauphine is narrow, congested, he crosses behind a fiacre . . .

As always, he is absentminded . . . Approaching the fiacre in the opposite direction, the driver of a wagon with two horses, coming from the quays and going up the rue Dauphine, sees appear before his left horse a man in black, an umbrella . . . The man totters, he tries to seize the horse's harness . . . Hampered by his umbrella, he has slipped between the two horses which their driver has attempted with all his strength to hold back. But the weight of the heavy wagon, five meters long and loaded with military equipment, drags him forward. It is the back left wheel that crushes Pierre's skull. And now that famous brain, that beloved brain, seeps out on the wet cobblestones . . .

At the Police Station

The body is removed to a police station. An officer picks up his telephone. But Pierre Curie no longer has ears to be annoyed that he belongs, in death as in life, to the number of those for whom one disturbs the minister of the interior.

Marie

Marie remains frozen; then she says: "Pierre is dead? Completely dead?"

Yes, Pierre was completely dead.

Reaction

Telegrams flow in, from all corners of the world, letters pile up, the condolences are royal, republican, scientific, formal, or simply emotional and sincere. Fame and love have been brutally mown down by death . . .

A new title, a sinister one, is added to those with which Marie has up to then been dubbed. Henceforth she will be called only "the illustrious widow."

Eleven years—that is long. Long enough so that the roots of love, if the tree is robust, plunge so deep that they will subsist always, even dried up.

Letters to Pierre

She begins to write to Pierre, a sort of laboratory notebook of grief.

"My Pierre, I arise after having slept fairly well, relatively calm. There is scarcely a quarter of an hour of that and here I again want to howl like a wild beast."

Summer is here and the sun, so wounding when in oneself everything is black . . .

"I spend all my days in the laboratory. I can no longer conceive of anything that can give me personal joy, except perhaps scientific work—but no, because if I were successful, I could not tolerate that you should not know it."

She will be successful. And she will tolerate. Because that is the law of life.

Teaching at the Sorbonne

As she gives her first lecture, continuing where Pierre left off, something is happening that clouds the eyes, tightens the throats, holds the audience from top to bottom of the tiers of seats frozen with emotion before that little black silhouette.

It was fifteen years ago, to the day, that, arriving from Warsaw, a little Polish student crossed for the first time the courtyard of the Sorbonne. The second life of Marie Curie has begun.

And the chronicler of the *Journal*: "A great victory for feminism . . . For if woman is admitted to give higher instruction to students of both sexes, where henceforth will be the so-called superiority of the male man? In truth, I tell you: the time is close when women will become human beings."

Proving that Radium Is an Element by Extracting the Metal Itself

Marie is the only one to be able to do it. All haloed with that melancholy fame that she bears so soberly, she has touched one heart in particular by the simplicity of her bearing and the precision of the objectives she has fixed for herself: that of Andrew Carnegie.

He decides to finance her research, which he knows how to do with elegance.

In the eyes of the international scientific community, she has become an implacable person, without rival in the domain in which she is an authority, a unique star, because she is a woman, in the constellation that then shines in the sky of science.

Yet "her nerves are ill," as she has been told by some of

the doctors participating in the congress. Nerves are never ill. They say only that in some part one is ill.

But in 1910, no one knows that a certain Doctor Freud has already analyzed Dora.

A trip to the Engadine will succeed in restoring her.

Sorrow and Her Children

Many years will pass before her daughters are old enough so that she can speak with them about what is occupying her days. If she never speaks to them of their father, whose name she has forbidden one to pronounce in her presence, it is that fresh wounds are so prompt to bleed, and since when does one bleed in front of one's children?

To say nothing in order to be sure of controlling herself is her rule, she applies it. This does not facilitate communication.

But she has known the privilege of privileges: coherence.

A Second Nobel Prize

At the end of the same year, 1911, it is the jury of the Swedish Academy that gives itself the pleasure of bestowing on her the Nobel Prize. In chemistry this time, and not shared.

But the news reaches her in the heart of a tempest next to which the academic eddies are a spring shower. In a word, due to her association with a certain married man, Langevin, Mme Curie has for a time ceased to be an honorable woman.

Conflict with the Workers in the Laboratory

Nor at work are things always smooth. There is a day, for instance, when the laboratory's head of works is raining blows on the woman's door and yelling:

"Camel! Camel!"

No doubt she can be.

She is capable of everything.

The Entr'acte

Thanks to Marthe Klein who has taken her there, she discovers the south of France, its splendor, its August nights in which one sleeps on the terrace, the warmth of the Mediterranean where she begins to swim again. Tourists are rare. Only, on the beach, a few English . . .

The passion for stones is the only one she is known to have where ownership is concerned, but this passion is lively: she will also buy a house in Brittany.

She is still slight, slender, supple, walks with bare legs, in espadrilles, with the manner of a young girl. According to the days, she carries ten years more or ten years less than her age.

For some time she has needed glasses, but what could be more natural?

In Quest of a Gram of Radium

The courage, the determination, the assurance that made her the twice-crowned queen of radioactivity are powerless before the evidence: Paris is a festival, but French science is anemic. Toward whom, toward what, should she turn?

Those who are most dynamic among the scientists will

try to sound the alarm, everywhere, with voice and with pen: whether it be prestige, industrial competition, or social progress, a nation that does not invest in research is a nation that declines.

This, everyone knows more or less—rather less than more—today.

Missy

And so, one May morning in 1920, Marie welcomes at her office at the Curie Pavilion Henri-Pierre Roché who accompanies a very little graying person with large black eyes, slightly limping: Mrs. Meloney Mattingley, whom her friends call Missy. The minuscule Missy is editor of a feminine magazine of good reputation.

And the unforeseeable is going to happen. One of those mysterious consonances, as frank as a C-Major chord. A friendship, whose consequences will be infinite.

Marie is charming, though who knows why, with this bizarre little creature.

In Quest of a Gram of Radium

Mme Curie is, in a word, poor. In a poor country.

Stupefying! Something to surprise the cottages lining Fifth Avenue, certainly.

Missy has a good nature. She loves to admire, and Marie seems to her admirable. This excellent disposition being accompanied by a vigorous practical sense, Missy, who compares herself to a locomotive, moves a series of railway cars if not mountains.

How much does a gram of radium cost? One million francs, or one hundred thousand dollars. One hundred thousand dollars for a noble cause attached to a grand name—this can be found. Missy believes she can collect it from several very rich compatriots.

She mobilizes the wife of the king of petrol, Mrs. John D. Rockefeller, that of the vice and future president, Mrs. Calvin Coolidge, and several other ladies of the same caliber.

She takes each bull by the horns—that is, each editor of each New York newspaper by his sentiments.

A Trip to the United States

Evidently, when Missy will have succeeded, Marie will have to come in person to get her gram of radium. In a parallel way, a well-launched autobiography can bring her substantial author's rights. What benefit will Missy draw personally from the operation? Purely moral.

Correct? Unquestionably.

Friendship

What remains of their correspondence, which is, at times, almost daily, attests to the permanence of the affection that binds these two warriors, equally lame, equally intrepid.

If anyone esteems herself at her true price, it is Marie. If anyone is prepared to pay it, it is Missy. But take care: on both sides, one must be "regular."

Marie has promised to come get her gram of radium herself. Does she confirm? She confirms. To write her autobiography. Does she confirm? She confirms. Good.

The king and queen of Belgium remained six weeks, says Missy. The queen of radium cannot make a less royal visit.

Health

She writes to Bronia: "My eyes are very weakened and probably not much can be done for them. As for my ears, an almost continual buzzing, often very intense, persecutes me. I worry about it very much: my work may be hampered—or even become impossible. Perhaps radium has something to do with my troubles, but one can't declare it with certainty." Radium guilty? It's the first time that she mentions the idea. She will soon have confirmation that she is suffering from a double cataract.

The Trip to America

Mme Curie is to receive from the hands of the president of the United States the miraculous product of a national collection, one gram of radium.

She shakes hands with a great many people until someone breaks her wrist.

That evening, Missy knows definitively who Marie really is. And reciprocally.

Fabulous razzia: Marie has pocketed in addition fifty thousand dollars' advance for her autobiography, though the book is to be insipid. Missy has at every point kept her promises, and well beyond.

Leavetaking

The crystalline lenses of the beautiful ash-gray eyes are becoming each day more opaque. She is convinced she will soon be blind. Marie and Missy embrace each other crying.

Let us say right away, however, that these two slender dying creatures will nevertheless meet again. It will be seven years later, again at the White House . . .

Missy and Marie certainly belong to the same race. That of the irreducibles.

Time Passing

And now the red curls of Perrin, discoverer of Brownian motion, have become white.

Scientific Conferences

These conferences to which she travels often weigh on her. She finds only one pleasure in them: still a devotee of excursions, she vanishes and goes off to discover a few of the splendors of the Earth. For over fifty years a recluse, she saw almost nothing.

From everywhere, she writes and describes to her daughters. The Southern Cross is "a very beautiful constellation." The Escurial is "very impressive" . . . The Arab palaces of Grenada are "very lovely" . . . The Danube is bordered with hills. But the Vistula . . . Ah! The Vistula! With its most adorable banks of sand, etc., etc.

The Illness of Marie

One afternoon in May 1934, at the laboratory where she has tried to come and work, Marie murmurs: "I have a fever, I'm going home . . ."

She walks around the garden, examines a rosebush that she herself has planted and that does not look well, asks that it be taken care of immediately . . . She will not return.

What is wrong with her? Apparently nothing. Yet she has no strength, she is feverish. She is transported to a clinic, then to a sanatorium in the mountains. The fever does not subside. Her lungs are intact. But her temperature rises. She has attained that moment of grace where even Marie Curie no longer wants to see the truth. And the truth is that she is dying.

The Death of Marie

She will have a last smile of joy when, consulting for the last time the thermometer she is holding in her little hand, she observes that her temperature has suddenly dropped. But she no longer has the strength to make a note of it, she from whom a number has never escaped being written down. This drop in temperature is the one that announces the end.

And when the doctor comes to give her a shot:

"I don't want it. I want to be left in peace."

It will require another sixteen hours for the heart to cease beating, of this woman who does not want, no, does not want to die. She is sixty-six years old.

Marie Curie-Sklodowska has ended her course.

On her coffin when it has descended into the grave, Bronia and their brother Jozéf throw a handful of earth. Earth of Poland.

Thus ends the story of an honorable woman.

Marie, we salute you . . .

Conclusion

She was of those who work one single furrow.

Postscript

Nevertheless, the quasi-totality of physicists and mathematicians will refuse fiercely and for a long time to open what Lamprin will call "a new window on eternity."

Mir the Hessian

Mir the Hessian regretted killing his dog, he wept even as he forced its head from its body, yet what had he to eat but the dog? Freezing in the hills, far away from everyone.

Mir the Hessian cursed as he knelt on the rocky ground, cursed his bad luck, cursed his company for being dead, cursed his country for being at war, cursed his countrymen for fighting, and cursed God for allowing it all to happen. Then he started to pray: it was the only thing left to do. Alone, in midwinter.

Mir the Hessian lay curled up among the rocks, his hands between his legs, his chin on his breast, beyond hunger, beyond fear. Abandoned by God.

The wolves had scattered the bones of Mir the Hessian, carried his skull to the edge of the water, left a tarsus on the hill, dragged a femur into the den. After the wolves came the crows, and after the crows the scarab beetles. And after the beetles, another soldier, alone in the hills, far away from everyone. For the war was not yet over.

My Neighbors in a Foreign Place

Directly across the courtyard from me lives a middle-aged woman, the ringleader of the building. Sometimes she and I open our windows simultaneously and look at each other for an instant in shocked surprise. When this happens, one of us looks up at the sky, as though to see what the weather is going to be, while the other looks down at the courtyard, as though watching for late visitors. Each is really trying to avoid the glance of the other. Then we move back from the windows to wait for a better moment.

Sometimes, however, neither of us is willing to retreat: we lower our eyes and for minutes on end remain standing there, almost close enough to hear each other breathing. I prune the plants in my windowbox as though I were alone in the world and she, with the same air of preoccupation, pinches the tomatoes that sit in a row on her windowsill and untangles a sprig of parsley from the bunch that stands yellowing in a jar of water. We are both so quiet that the scratching and fluttering of the pigeons in the eaves above seems very loud. Our hands tremble, and that is the only sign that we are aware of each other.

I know that my neighbor leads an utterly blameless life. She is orderly, consistent, and regular in her habits.

Nothing she does would set her apart from any other woman in the building. I have observed her and I know this is true.

She rises early, for example, and airs her bedroom; then, through the half-open shutters, I see what looks like a large white bird diving and soaring in the darkness of her room, and I know it is the quilt that she is throwing over her bed; late in the morning her strong, pale forearm flashes out of the living-room window several times and gives a shake to a clean dustrag; in housedress and apron she takes vegetables from her windowsill at noon, and soon after I smell a meal being cooked; at two o'clock she pins a dishcloth to the short line outside her kitchen window; and at dusk she closes all the shutters. Every second Sunday she has visitors during the afternoon. This much I know, and the rest is not hard to imagine.

I myself am not at all like her or like anyone else in the building, even though I make persistent efforts to follow their pattern and gain respect. My windows are not clean, and a lacy border of soot has gathered on my windowsill; I finish my washing late in the morning and hang it out just before a midday rainstorm breaks, when my neighbor's wash has long since been folded and put away; at nightfall, when I hear the clattering and banging of the shutters on all sides, I cannot bear to close my own, even though I think I should, and instead leave them open to catch the last of the daylight; I disturb the man and woman below me because I walk without pause over my creaking floorboards at midnight, when everyone else is asleep, and I do not carry my pail of garbage down to the courtyard until late at night, when the cans are full: then I look up and see the housefronts shuttered and bolted as if against an invasion, and only a few lights burning in the houses next door.

I am very much afraid that by now the woman opposite has observed all these things about me, has formed a notion of me that is not at all favorable, and is about to take action with her many friends in the building. Already I have seen them gather in the hallway and have heard their vehement whispers echoing through the stairwell, where they stop every morning on their way in from shopping to lean on the banisters and rest. Already they glance at me with open dislike and suspicion in their eyes, and any day now they will circulate a petition against me, as my neighbors have done in every building I have ever lived in. Then, I will once again have to look for another place to live, and take something worse than what I now have and in a poorer neighborhood, just so as to leave as quickly as possible. I will have to inform the landlord, who will pretend to know nothing about the activity of my neighbors, but who must know what goes on in his buildings, must have received and read the petition. I will have to pack my belongings into boxes once again and hire a van for the day of departure. And as I carry box after box down to the waiting van, as I struggle to open each of the many doors between this apartment and the street, taking care not to scratch the woodwork or break the glass panes, my neighbors will appear one by one to see me off, as they always have. They smile and hold the doors for me. They offer to carry my boxes and show a genuinely kind interest in me, as though all along, given the slightest excuse, they would have liked to be my friends. But at this point, things have gone too far and I cannot turn back, though I would like to. My neighbors would not understand why I had done it, and the wall of hatred would rise between us again.

But sometimes, when this building with its bitter

atmosphere becomes too oppressive for me to bear it any longer, I go outside into the city and wander back to the houses I used to live in. I stand in the sun talking to my old neighbors, and I find comfort and relief in their warm welcome.

Oral History (with Hiccups)

My sister died last year leaving two dau ghters. My husband and I have decided to ad opt the girls. The older one is thirty-three and a b uyer for a department store, and the yo unger one, who just turned thirty, works in the st ate budget office. We have one ch ild still living at home, and the house is not b ig, so it will be a tight fit, but we are willing to do this for their s ake. We will move our son, who is eleven, out of his ro om and into the small room I have been using as a s ewing room. I will set up my machine d ownstairs in the living room. We will put a bunk bed for the girls in my s on's old room. It is a fair-sized room with one cl oset and one window, and the bathroom is just down the h all. We will have to ask them not to bring all their th ings. I assume they will be willing to m ake that sacrifice in order to be part of this family. They will also have to w atch what they say at the d inner table. With our younger son present we don't want open c onflict. What I'm worried about is a c ouple of pol itical issues. My older niece is a f eminist, while my husband and I feel the tables have been turned against m ales nowadays. Also, my younger niece is probably more pro-g overnment than either my older niece or my h usband and me. But she will be away a good deal, traveling for her j ob. And we have d eveloped some negotiating skills with our own ch ildren, so we should be able to w ork things out with the two of them. We will try to be firm but f air, as we always were with our older b oy before he left h ome. If we can't w ork things out right away, they can always go to their r oom and c ool off until they're ready to come back out and be c ivil. Excuse me.

The Patient

The day after the patient was admitted to the hospital, the young doctor operated on her upper colon, where he felt sure the cause of her illness lay. But his medical training had not been good, the doctors who taught him were careless men, and he had been pushed through school quickly because he was clever and the country was desperate for doctors; the hospital was poorly staffed and the building itself was falling into ruin because of government mismanagement: piles of broken plaster choked the hallways. Because of all this, or for some other reason, the woman's condition did not improve, but grew rapidly worse. The young doctor tried everything. At last he admitted that there was nothing more he could do and that she was on the point of dying. He was overwhelmed by the grief and guilt that come with the first death of a patient. He was at the same time filled with strange excitement, and felt he had joined the ranks of serious men of the world, men who hold the lives of others in their hands and are like gods. Inexplicably, then, the woman did not die. She lay peacefully in a twilight coma. As each day passed with no change, the young doctor grew more and more maddened by her immobility. He could not sleep and his eyes became bloodshot. He had trouble eating and his face became gaunt. At last he could not contain his frustration any longer. He went to her bedside and drove his fist again and again into her pinched, yellow face until she did not look human anymore. One last breath leaked from her mouth and then, battered and bruised, she died.

Right and Wrong

She knows she is right, but to say she is right is wrong, in this case. To be correct and say so is wrong, in certain cases.

She may be correct, and she may say so, in certain cases. But if she insists too much, she becomes wrong, so wrong that even her correctness becomes wrong, by association.

It is right to believe in what she thinks is right, but to say what she thinks is right is wrong, in certain cases.

She is right to act on her beliefs, in her life. But she is wrong to report her right actions, in most cases. Then even her right actions become wrong, by association.

If she praises herself, she may be correct in what she says, but her saying it is wrong, in most cases, and thus cancels it, or reverses it, so that although she was for a particular act deserving of praise, she is no longer in general deserving of praise.

Alvin the Typesetter

Alvin and I worked together typesetting for a weekly newspaper in Brooklyn. We came in every Friday. This was the autumn that Reagan was elected president, and everyone at the newspaper suffered from a sense of foreboding and depression.

The old gray typesetting machines, with their scratches and scars, were set back to back in a tiny room next to the toilet. People raced in and out of the toilet all day long and the sound of flushing was always in our ears. Pinned to the corkboard walls around us as we bent over our keyboards was an ever-thickening forest of paper strips. The damp paper strips were covered with type, and when they had dried, they were taken away by the paste-up people to become columns on the newspaper page.

The work we had to do was not hard, but it required patience and care, and we were under constant pressure to work faster. I typed straight copy, and Alvin set ads. If the machines stopped rumbling for more than a few minutes, the boss would come downstairs to see what was holding us up. And so Alvin and I continued to type while we ate our lunch, and when we talked to each other, as we did from time to time, we talked surreptitiously, sticking our eyes up over the tops of the machines.

We were blue-collar workers. Every time I thought about how we were blue-collar workers, it surprised me, because we were also, with any luck, performing artists. I played the violin. As for Alvin, he was a stand-up comedian. Every Friday Alvin told me about his career and his life.

For seven months he had auditioned over and over again without success at a well-known club. At last the manager had relented and given him a spot. Every week now he came on in the dead early hours of Sunday morning for five minutes to close the show. Sometimes the audience liked him and sometimes it did not respond at all. If the manager occasionally left him onstage for ten minutes or gave him a spot earlier in the evening, at nine thirty, Alvin felt this was an important advance in his career.

Alvin could not describe his art except to say that he had no script, no routine, that he never knew just what would happen onstage, and that this lack of preparation was part of his act. From the snatches of monologue he spoke for me, however, I could see that some of his patter was about sex—he made jokes about cream and sperm—and that some of his patter was about politics, and that he also liked to do impersonations.

He usually worked without any props. In the week of Election Day, in November, he carried to the nightclub a special patriotic kerchief covered with red, white, and blue American symbols to wear over his head. Most often, though, what he took out onstage was only himself, as though his long, solemn face were a mask, or his body a marionette that he controlled with strings from above, slim, loose-jointed, floating over the floor. He had his stance, his silences, his bald head, and his clothes. He wore the same clothes onstage that he wore to work: dark formal pants and often a shirt of cheap synthetic material covered with palm trees or pine trees on a white background.

When I arrived at the office, Alvin would be typing at his machine in his stocking feet, and his long, narrow shoes would be sitting next to my machine. If Alvin was glum, neither of us said much. If he was elated, he could not help standing up from his machine and talking. And on some days I would speak to him and he would look at me blankly. He would later admit that he had been smoking hash for days on end.

Over the clicking of the machines Alvin told me that he lived apart from his wife and son. His son did not like Alvin's friends or the food Alvin ate, and made the same excuse over and over again not to see him. He told me about his circle of friends—a group of Brooklyn vegetarians. He was planning to eat Thanksgiving dinner with these vegetarians and he was planning to spend the Christmas holiday sleeping at the YMCA. He told me about his travels—to Boston and places in New Jersey. He asked me many times to go out on a date with him. We went once to the circus.

He told me about the typesetters' agency that never found him any work. "Don't I seem ambitious to you?" he asked. He complained to me about the lack of order in our office, and about the poor writing in the pieces we were given to typeset. He said it was not part of his job to correct spelling and grammar. He told me with indignation that he would not do more than should be expected of him. He and I had a sense of our superiority to those in charge of us, and this was only aggravated by the fact that we were so often treated as though we had no education.

Because Alvin was good-natured and presented himself to the rest of the newspaper staff without reservation, because his whole art consisted of isolating and exposing himself as a figure of fun, he was well liked by many of them but also became a natural victim of some: the manager of the production department, for instance, kept pushing him to work faster and often asked him to do his ads over again, and talked against Alvin behind his back. Alvin responded to this goading with injured pride. But worse than the production manager was the owner of the paper, who worked most of the week upstairs in his office but on press day came down to the production department and sat on a stool alongside the others.

He was a little man with a red mustache and glasses who wore his flannel shirts tucked into his blue jeans and smelled of deodorant when he became excited. He never walked slowly and he was in and out of the toilet faster than anyone else: no sooner had the door shut behind him than we would hear the thunderous flush from the tank overhead and he would spring out the door again. For much of the week he talked to his employees with good humor, though not to us, the typesetters, and tolerated the caricatures of his face posted all over the room and the remarks about him written on the toilet wall. On press day, however, and when things were going badly at the paper, his sense of catastrophe would drive him to turn on us one by one and dress us down publicly in a way that was humiliating and surrounded by silence. What made this treatment especially hard to accept was that our pay was low and our paychecks bounced regularly. The accountant upstairs could not keep track of where the newspaper's money was, and she added on her fingers.

Alvin received the worst of it and hardly defended himself at all: "I thought you said . . . I thought they told me to . . . I thought I was supposed to . . ." Any answer he made provoked another outburst from the boss, until Alvin retired in silence. I was embarrassed by his lack of pride. He was afraid of losing his job. But after Christmas his attitude changed.

Over the holidays, Alvin and I both performed. I played the violin in a concert of excerpts from *The Messiah.* Alvin's performance was to be an entire evening of monologues and songs at a local club run by a friend. Before the event Alvin handed out a Xeroxed flyer with crooked lettering and a picture of himself wearing a beret. In his text he called himself "the widely acclaimed." The tickets were five dollars. Our newspaper ran an ad for his performance and everyone who worked with us there showed great interest in the event, though when the evening came, no one from the newspaper actually went to see him.

When Alvin came in to work on the Friday following his performance, he was the center of attention for a few minutes and an aura of celebrity floated around him. But Alvin told a sad tale. There were only five people in the audience at his performance. Four were fellow comedians, and the fifth was Alvin's friend Ira, who talked throughout his monologues.

Alvin was eloquent about his failure. He described the room, his friend the owner, his friend Ira. He talked for five minutes. The boss, who had been listening with the others, grew restless and distracted and told Alvin there was work waiting for him. Alvin raised a hand in concession and went into the typesetting room. The production people returned to their stools and bent over their pages. Our machines began rumbling. The boss hurried upstairs.

Then Alvin stopped typing. His pupils were dilated and he looked particularly remote. He stood up and walked out. He said to the production room at large: "Listen: I have work to do. But I haven't started yet. I would like to perform for you first."

Most of the production people smiled because they liked Alvin.

"Now I'm going to impersonate a chicken," he said.

He climbed up on a stool and started flapping his arms and clucking. The room was quiet. The production people perched on their long-legged stools like a flock of resting egrets and stared at this bald chicken. When there was no applause, Alvin shrugged and climbed down and said, "Now I'm going to impersonate a duck," and waddled across the room with his knees bent and toes turned in. The production people glanced around the room at one another. Their looks darted and hopped like sparrows. They gave Alvin a spattering of applause. Then he said, "Now I'm going to do a pigeon." He shook his shoulders and jerked his head forward and back as he strutted in the circular patterns of a courting pigeon. He managed to convey something of the ostentation of a male pigeon. Abruptly he stopped and said to his audience, "Well, don't you have any work to do? What are you sitting around for? All this should have been done yesterday!" The little hair he had was poking straight out from his head as though he were full of electricity. He swallowed his saliva. "That's all we are," he said. "A bunch of dumb birds."

The smiles faded from the faces of his audience. The weariness of that leafless late December, our fear of our weakened government, our dread of its repressive spirit, descended on us once again.

Into the abrupt silence came the chiming of a church bell across the street. The production manager by reflex checked his watch. Alvin's body sagged. He turned and walked into our tiny room. The back of his head had its own expression of defeat.

For a moment everyone stared at him in amazement. He sat slumped over his machine, solitary, flooded by fluorescent light, exhausted by his performance. He had not been very funny, in fact he was a poor actor, and yet something about his act had been impressive: his grim determination, the violence of his feelings. One by one the production people went back to work: paper rustled, scissors clattered on the stone tabletop, murmurs passed back and forth over the sound of the radio. I sat down at my machine and Alvin looked up at me from under his heavy lids. His look carried all the hurt, the humiliation, the mockery of the past few months. He said without smiling, "They think I'm nothing. They can think what they like. I have my plans."

Special

We know we are very special. Yet we keep trying to find out in what way: not this way, not that way, then what way?

Selfish

The useful thing about being a selfish person is that when your children get hurt you don't mind so much because you yourself are all right. But it won't work if you are just a little selfish. You must be very selfish. This is the way it happens. If you are just a little selfish, you take some trouble over them, you pay some attention to them, they have clean clothes most of the time, a fresh haircut fairly often, though not all the supplies they need for school, or not when they need them; you enjoy them, you laugh at their jokes, though you have little patience when they are naughty, they annoy you when you have work to do, and when they are very naughty you become very angry; you understand some of what they should have, in their lives, you know some of what they are doing, with their friends, you ask questions, though not very many, and not beyond a certain point, because there is so little time; then the trouble begins and you don't notice signs of it because you are so busy: they steal, and you wonder how that thing came into the house; they show you what they have stolen, and when you ask questions, they lie; when they lie, you believe them, every time, because they seem so candid and it would take so long to find out the truth. Well, if you have been selfish, this is what sometimes happens, and if you have not been selfish enough, then later, when they are in serious trouble, you will suffer, though even as you suffer you will continue, from long habit, to be selfish, saying, I am so distraught, My life has ended, How can I go on? So if you are going to be selfish at all, you must be more selfish than that, so selfish that although you are sorry they're in trouble, sincerely and deeply sorry, as you will tell your friends and acquaintances and the rest of the family, you will be privately relieved, glad, even delighted, that it isn't happening to you.

My Husband and I

My husband and I are Siamese twins. We are joined at the forehead. Our mother feeds us. When we are moved to copulate we join lower down as well forming a loop like a certain espaliered tree. Time passes. I separate from my husband below and give birth to twins who are not joined together as we are. They squirm on the ground. Our mother cares for them. They are most often asymmetrical with each other, even in sleep when they lie still. Awake, they stay near each other, as though elastic bands held them, and near us and near our mother. At night the bond is even stronger and we snap together and lie in a heap, my husband's hard muscles against my soft muscles, against our mother's stringy old muscles, and our babies' feather muscles, our arms around one another like so many snakes, and distant thumping music in the fields behind us.

Spring Spleen

I am happy the leaves are growing large so quickly.
Soon they will hide the neighbor and her screaming child.

Her Damage

On the counter lay a pile of plastic packets of duck sauce, soy sauce, and mustard from their Chinese dinner. In her anger she was provoked by the smooth, slippery little bodies and slammed her fist down among them. Two or three exploded. She could not see through her tears. Her bathrobe cuff was drenched in mustard, and the next morning he discovered a spatter of soy sauce, or maybe duck sauce, over the ceiling, two windows, and one wall. She cleaned it off the windows, but it wouldn't come off the ceiling, where it had stained through the white paint, and then when she was done trying to get it off she saw that the drops of detergent and water falling on the wood floor had spotted the finish.

A few days later, carrying the baby, she stepped into a hole in the dining-room floor in the old house where a plank had been removed because of termites. She bruised her arm badly, though the baby was not hurt. Then she stopped up the coffeemaker with coffee grounds so that it overflowed onto the counter and floor when it went on in the morning. She sprayed the side of her face with the spray attachment at the sink. She burned her hand feeding the wood stove. The baby rolled off the side of their bed and fell onto the floor. She took the baby out for a walk late in the afternoon when the temperature was below freezing, its face turned red, and it started screaming with pain. This was the holiday season.

They sat talking peacefully before dinner. He said she probably needed to get more sleep. She was waiting for the oven to heat, but had forgotten to turn it on.

At dinner, he pointed out that the soy sauce had also spotted the apples in the fruit bowl and the lamp over the dining table. He went on to remind her of the toilet seat she had broken. It was an expensive red Swedish toilet seat. The lid had slipped out of her hand and dropped, cracking the seat. He had immediately taken the whole thing off and replaced it with a green one.

He had also replaced the plastic sheeting over the door to the deck because it had shattered when she left the door open in the cold. Then for the second time she disengaged the connection of a wire over the bedroom door. As he stood on a chair fixing it, she asked him if she could hold the light for him, but he said No, just don't slam the door anymore when you get mad.

The most recent thing was that she took a roll of photographs with no film in the camera, though this did not cost them any money or cause any damage, except for the baby's weariness in its many poses and her regret for the lost pictures, so many of which she remembered clearly, the last being a shot of an oil barge with a tugboat coming up the creek through the first winter ice toward her where she stood at the window, beginning to realize there was no film in the camera.

Workingmen

Now that we are living out here in the country the only people we see are workingmen who come to do jobs for us. They are independent and self-reliant, and they start work early in the day and they work hard without stopping. Last week it was Bill Bray, to install the washing machine. Next week it will be Jay Knickerbocker, to tear off the front of the porch. Today it is Tom Tatt. Tom Tatt is supposed to come disconnect some wires for us. Where is he? Early in the morning we stand in the kitchen together. Where is Tom Tatt? We walk outdoors. Here in the early sunshine is Tom Tatt. He has already finished the job, and is snubbing the cut ends of wire with little black snubs.

In a Northern Country

Magin was over seventy and not well. His right leg was lame and his lungs were weak. If his wife had been alive, she would not have let him go. As it was, his friends had told him to stay at home and wait for his brother Michael to come back. Yet he had never listened to anyone but his wife, and now he did not listen to anyone.

He was close to Silit, if the maps of the Trsk Land Office were correct. He had walked since early morning, very slowly, and his feet were sore. Just at noon, he came within sight of the town. His brother's postcard had been sent from here. Karsovy, therefore, should be only a few miles to the north.

He set down his bag on the snow and rubbed his cramped fingers. He looked up at Silit: the street was lined by narrow houses with shuttered windows. Many of the roofs had fallen in and tumbled over the doorsills. Down by the well at the end of the street, under a couple of pine trees, he saw two old women knitting on a bench. He picked up his bag and walked to them and they stopped knitting to stare at him.

Until he shouted his question, they did not understand him. Then one of them opened her mouth and pointed wordlessly across the street.

In the shadow of the eaves, a man sat combing his brown beard with a broken comb. His eyes were on Magin. A roofless car was parked in the lane beside him.

Magin crossed the street. "Can you take me to Karsovy?" he asked in Trsk. The man stopped moving.

"There's no such place," he said.

"There must be," said Magin. He pulled out the creased postcard from his brother and started to thrust it at the man.

"There is not. You are mistaken."

Magin dropped his bag and shook his fist in the man's face, crumpling the postcard. He would not argue. "I am not mistaken," he shouted. His voice broke.

The man was startled. "Well," he said, spitting on his palm and rubbing his boot with it, "I don't often go there."

Magin was trembling with anger and the blood at his temples throbbed. "How much?" he asked.

"I'll take fifty," the man said. Magin drew a purse from his back pocket and laid two coins on the man's palm.

Magin picked up his bag and followed the man to the car. The man pulled himself up into the driver's seat, looking straight ahead. Magin hoisted his bag onto the backseat and climbed in beside it. When he sat down, the springs gave way so far that he came to rest on something that felt like an iron rod. He did not move.

The engine turned over and the car jerked forward and threw Magin against the back of the seat. The car skidded into the snowy ruts of the road. Magin lurched from side to side as the trees veered at him around the bends of the road. Two doves flapped away as the car passed them.

The driver's hostility bewildered Magin. As an hour passed in the monotonous woods, he grew more and more uneasy. His search might be hopeless. There had been no word from his brother for weeks. And there was the question of how long he himself would last. "This is crazy," he said to himself suddenly. "Here I am with one foot in the grave, in a north country winter, and I expect something to come of it. Mary would have laughed." He pulled the collar of his overcoat up around his chin.

At last they reached Karsovy. As they drew up into a large clearing, Magin saw women in black crossing the drifts like shadows. Men crouched in front of their doorways.

Magin climbed down with his bag and rested against the car door. He looked up and saw that several people had gathered and were watching him. The women inched forward: their eyes flew from his face to his bag, but not a word passed their lips. Magin searched among the stony-faced men for the leader of the village, and the people became uneasy. They were puzzled by him.

"What?" said Magin to the driver, who had not moved from his seat. "What are they waiting for? Why are they staring at me? Why don't they say anything?"

"Why should they say anything?" the driver said finally. "Anyway, you wouldn't understand them. No one understands them. They don't even know how to speak Trsk." He smacked the wheel. "I brought another old man like you out this way. That was months ago and no one's heard of him since." He spat in the snow and glanced at the villagers with contempt. Before Magin could speak, he leaned on the horn, turned the car, and drove back into the woods.

Magin wondered what to do. One by one the villagers turned and went away, glancing back over their shoulders and stopping in midstep to stare at him again. Two women stayed behind. One was old, thin, and shabbily dressed. The other was younger, and more muscular. The old one started forward, tightening her kerchief and opening her toothless mouth in a smile. The other one caught her by the sleeve.

"Nininininini," the old one said, her tongue against the roof of her mouth, and her eyes glimmered from under the brow of her kerchief. She pulled away from the younger one and started forward again. The younger one cuffed her lightly on the shoulder and hissed at her. The old one turned and spat, and then walked away, her skirt trailing over the snow behind her.

The younger woman motioned to Magin to follow her. They turned up a small path, Magin favoring one leg. Under the trees he felt the cold close in on him like a vise. He coughed. His breath rattled in his throat.

The path wound among the stone huts. Heavily furred dogs lay before many of the doors and growled as Magin and the woman went by. At the end of the path lay the woman's hut. With one hand on the latch, she took a quick look back at Magin. Standing next to her, he caught a whiff of her fetid clothes. She opened the door and Magin followed her blindly. He was assaulted by the smell of unwashed linen. Slowly the air came in from the outside and he breathed more easily.

When his eyes grew accustomed to the pale light that fell over the back of the room from the small windows and the chinks in the stone, he saw that the hut was divided into two rooms by a thin wooden wall. To his left, in the larger room, he made out a table, a cupboard, some chairs, a bed, and on the far wall a framed photograph of the country's leader in military dress. To his right was a small room, doorless. He could see the end of a narrow cot, and nothing else. The woman, standing close beside him, pushed on his shoulder.

"Ehh, ehh," she said, and nodded. He went into the little room and dropped his bag by the bed. He was so tired that he could hardly bear the weight of his clothes. He wanted to lie down, but he was embarrassed by the woman behind him.

He looked out the window and then turned around. The woman had left. He lay down and closed his eyes tightly. He could not even remember why he was here. He began dreaming before he was fully asleep. He dreamt of the train ride through France, though that was already several days behind him. His wife, her hair slipping from its pins with the motion of the train, was reading aloud to him from a newspaper, like a child in her outmoded glasses and ill-fitting dress. Yet in the dream he felt that he was the one in the wrong place.

Less than two hours later, waking from his sleep, he saw his brother's tape recorder on a shelf in the corner of the room. He waited for this vision to fade.

It often happened, now, that his memory failed or that he re-created things he remembered and placed them where they did not actually exist.

The tape recorder remained, however, and beside it he now saw a neat pile of notebooks, some clothing, a sewing box, a pair of slippers, a pair of boots, and a knife. Was it possible that his brother had lived in this room? Magin did not move, for fear his brother's possessions would vanish.

After fifteen minutes or so, Magin was fully awake. He got up and went over to the shelf. Touching his brother's possessions, he felt reassured. This was his brother's room: he had often been in his brother's room when his brother was absent, though this was a different room from any of the others. Yet this was his brother's room, and that meant that though his brother was now gone from the room, he would return to it.

And yet why, in that case, had the woman allowed him to lie down and go to sleep here? Perhaps she had merely been showing him the room, and did not intend him to sleep here. Or perhaps she thought he would wait for his brother here. And, after all, that was what he was actually doing, now.

But there was a musty, disused smell about the clothes. And the notebooks stuck together, so that when Magin touched one, they all moved in a block. Perhaps his brother had been gone for a long time. He could not be dead, because in that case the woman would have put his possessions away somewhere. Unless this was where she had put them.

When he went out of the room, the woman was setting a meal on the table. Magin took her arm and led her into the small room. He pointed to his brother's possessions and asked her, "Where is the man who owns these things?"

She answered him only by gesturing toward the objects on the shelf in a way that Magin could not understand. She said one or two words only, and these he could not identify in any way with Trsk. Though this disappointed him, it did not surprise him. His brother had come here in order to record the language, after all. He had said it was on the point of dying out.

Magin gave up, not knowing what move to make, and followed the woman back to the table. Out the window, there were long violet shadows under the trees. He sat down, very hungry. He looked at the food. A cube of dry meat stood next to a heel of bread. He could see that the meat was too tough for his old teeth. He picked up the bread and ate it little by little, letting it soften before he chewed it. His hunger faded.

As the woman cleared the table, Magin lit a thin, cheap cigar and immediately started to cough. He felt a certain satisfaction in having come this far. However, he did not see how he was going to find out where his brother was: he was rather helpless, it turned out, because of the language. He stubbed his cigar and slipped what remained of it back in its box.

The woman put on her overcoat and gestured toward the door. Magin thought, with sudden hope, that now she was going to show him how to find Michael. In his excitement, he forgot where his room was, and stood still until the woman pushed him in the right direction. He put on his coat and followed her.

Outside the hut, the birds were now quiet; there was almost no light left in the sky, and the air was sharp. Magin, hurrying, stumbled over hidden roots. The dogs were gone from the doorways of the huts, which he and the woman passed quickly. When Magin thought they were still far away from the clearing, the sky widened. The windows of the largest hut glowed with orange firelight. Magin's mouth was dry. He swallowed and walked after the woman into the hut.

Before he could steady himself, the woman disappeared from his side. At first the firelight dazzled him. He looked down. A dog was snaking toward him with its belly to the ground. The room was dense with people. In perfect silence they watched him: near the fire, men squatted on low stools and benches digging rhythmically into the thick socks that covered their ankles and scratching their scalps and ears; farther away, in a disordered group, the women sat together hissing over their needlework, shrugging fitfully, and sucking their teeth.

The dog began snarling, and the silence exploded: a tall man with a hooked nose rushed toward the dog, who was crouching at Magin's feet with its teeth bared. A bench tumbled to the floor. The man kicked the dog in the ribs. The dog yelped and slipped away through legs and under stools. The men by the fire roared, and the women cried out strangely, themselves like animals. The dog squirmed into a corner. The man looked at Magin.

In Trsk, Magin said, "I came up here to look for my brother Michael, a scholar. My brother Michael came here to study your language." He stopped because the man obviously did not understand him and was turning away. The man looked among the women for the one who had brought Magin here, and pointed at her, pronouncing what to Magin was only a guttural noise. The woman rose and spoke long enough to explain everything she knew. The man took Magin by the sleeve and sat him down on a bench near the fire. He spoke to an old man who was bent over a checkerboard in one corner of the room, and then went away. The man had not responded.

Magin lit the butt of his cigar and sat still for some time, wondering what was going to happen. The women sewed placidly, murmuring to one another. The men passed a jug around. For Magin, they poured the liquor into an earthenware cup. They scratched and talked, smiling and nodding at Magin every so often. Occasionally a man would come to him and recite a few words in English, which startled Magin extremely. "No, no. Sky," one would say. Or another would say, "No, yes, here. Tape two."

Magin threw the end of his cigar into the fire and kept an eye on the old man in the corner. The game was nearing its end. The long white hair of the old man grazed the scabbed pate of his opponent whenever they leaned over the board. Every time the white-haired one moved a piece, the other screwed up his nutlike face in anger. Magin lit another cigar and coughed. He was so tired that he could hardly sit straight. Suddenly the bald old man was on his feet, his skull gleaming in the firelight.

"Ruckuck," he cried and brought his fist down on the checkerboard. The pieces—red and black disks and a few fragments of stone and wood—flew through the air and fell on the floor like a shower of hail. The white-haired man smiled calmly, his nose nearly touching his chin.

Now at last he looked at Magin and reluctantly came and sat down beside him. Magin stubbed out his cigar and put the end back in the box.

"Seek old man?" asked the white-haired man in Trsk.

"I'm looking for my brother," said Magin.

"Brother here," said the man.

Magin became excited. "Here?" He pointed to the ground.

"No, no, no." The man held up his hand impatiently. "Brother here. Then: brother gone. Brother gone with man—north. Lost. Gone, lost. Gone, dead. Maybe." He sliced his throat with one finger.

"What man?" Magin asked.

"Leader, cousin." The man pointed to himself. "Gone to hunt." He made the motion of shooting a rifle.

"How long?" Magin asked. He was lighting the butt of his cigar, though he did not know it. The people were all quiet, though they could not understand anything.

"Gone two day, two night. Then very cold, snow fall. Gone five week." He held up his hand, fingers spread. He pointed to himself. "I leader, soon." He smiled.

Magin started coughing and the old man left to get a drink. Magin could not catch his breath, and his eyes watered. Then he began to cry without control. He had drunk too much.

Later, the women put away their work and pulled on

their coats and shawls by the light of a few stuttering candles. The men knocked the ashes from their pipes, smacked each other across the back, and walked to the door. The women followed. When they had all gone, Magin sat for a few minutes in the dark and smelly room, trying to collect his thoughts. It was not easy. He believed, for some time, that he was in the Smoking Room of the Engineers Club. He was waiting for Harry to come out of the cloakroom. His head swam. He remembered where he was and got up hastily, afraid of losing track again.

Outside he looked over the dim snow to the trees. He did not remember which direction to take. He searched for something familiar in the dark landscape. Hearing a faint noise, he turned and saw small shadows moving over the snow. The first to reach him was a thin white dog, who paused and stiffened, its nose pointed up at him. It was joined by a larger dog, who walked with difficulty and whose stomach was distended, stretching its worn black skin like a drum. One by one they came up, until a small pack had formed around him. He had nothing to offer them. He leaned down and smoothed the white dog's head. The bones of the skull were round under his palm. The dog did not move. Fearing the sudden snarl and bite, Magin drew back his hand and walked cautiously away. His heart was jolting. He saw a twisted pine tree at the edge of the open space, and recognized it. Near it he found the path.

The dogs walked a few feet behind him, their footsteps muffled by the snow. He was uncomfortable. When the hut came in sight, a dog growled behind him. As he turned, the white dog caught his pants leg between its teeth. The dog growled again and shook its head from side to side. The cloth ripped and Magin began running. His old legs did not move very fast. The dogs dashed back and forth and snapped at his ankles. He reached the hut. As he struggled with the latch, they fell back. Once inside, he stopped to catch his breath, which was raking his throat. Out the window, he saw the dogs circle among themselves, sniff at his footprints, and settle on their haunches, watching the door. Magin went to his cot and lit a fresh cigar. He sat down without undressing and smoked, trying to remain calm. Stubbing his cigar on the dirt floor, he wrapped himself in a thin blanket and lay back. He fell asleep only after a long time.

Most of the night, the cold kept waking him. Toward morning, he slept deeply at last, then lightly again, dreaming of pains in his chest. The dreams became more and more vivid until his eyes were open on a window of pink light and he knew that the violence in his left lung was not a dream. He could not leave the bed. He wanted to smoke, but did not dare. Lying still, staring straight up, he struggled with the pain, resisting every attack, and relaxing when the pain died.

Curiously, what he had learned the night before seemed less final in the daylight. The village leader was gone, with his brother. The people were choosing a new village leader, supposing that the other was dead. They supposed that his brother was dead too. Yet there were other possibilities: his brother might be ill, or injured; someone might be caring for him in a place where there was no way of sending word. Yet the thought haunted Magin that he might have made a foolish decision in coming, and that he could not escape the consequences. He tried to draw a breath and the pain stopped him. Fighting the pain, he then saw that he had had no choice. He could not have stayed at home. There was nothing for him at home. Everything, now, was where his brother was. The pain slowly diminished. After half an hour, as the room grew more and more yellow with the rising sun, Magin was able to sit up.

His wrinkled and sticky clothes clung to him. He had not taken them off since leaving the river three days before. He reached under the bed for his bag and opened it. Inside was a pile of fresh linen. He shut the bag again. He found a safety pin in his pocket and pinned together the bottom of his pants leg. He breathed in his own musty smell. He ran his fingers through his hair and stood up. The pain had perceptibly weakened him and his knees trembled as he walked into the other room.

The dogs were gone. The tracks in front of the door startled the woman. Magin pointed to his torn pants and tried to tell her what had happened. She took an old twig broom and swept away the tracks. The snow against the trees was stained yellow.

At breakfast, Magin ate even less bread than he had the night before. He craved coffee, but sipped cold tea. He lit a cigar and kept it between his fingers without daring to smoke it. Then he walked outdoors, leaving his overcoat behind. Blinking in the glare of the sunlight, he shaded his eyes, which were pale and sensitive. From among the trees he heard men's voices rise and break off. Birds twittered without pause, chipping away at the silence between the trees. He walked along the path, and the ground under his feet was smooth.

He reached the edge of the clearing in time to see two men struggling out of the underbrush on the opposite side, dragging behind them the corpse of a large deer that furrowed and reddened the snow. His throat tightened as he watched them slit the deer's belly and disembowel it. Dogs crouched on their haunches at a small distance, ready to spring forward. Women carried up pans and buckets to catch the blood and innards. A few other men gathered around the animal, and fingered its antlers and hefted its limbs. Magin went up to them and they turned their heads and smiled at him. The brown body was stretched out on the snow, its neck arched and its belly caved in. It was a young buck. The smallest man grabbed Magin's wrist with a soft, wet hand and pulled him over to feel the antlers. They were downy, and warm from the sun. Magin studied them and the pain began to grow again in his lung. The tall man with the hooked nose came up with a saw in his fist, and Magin moved back. The man kneeled to saw off the antlers. A thin stream of dust fell onto the snow. Magin grew dizzy as he watched them under the hot sun. His knees gave way and two men caught him and held him up. The man with the hooked nose let fall the deer's head, round and bare, and stood up with the antlers in one hand and the saw in the other. Magin sat down on a large rock.

A few men had lit a fire on the ground and were roasting the innards over it. The flames were hardly visible in the noon sun. Near the woods, the dogs fought over the deer's stomach and intestines. The old man came up to Magin's rock with a charred stick in his hand. On the end of the stick was one of the deer's kidneys. He sat down beside Magin, cut off a piece of kidney with a blunt knife, and held it out to Magin with his thumb clamped across it.

"Eat," he said in Trsk.

Magin took the meat, unwillingly, and ate it, though it sickened him. He wiped his fingers on the snow and dried them on his pants. The other men swallowed their meat as quickly as the dogs, stood up sleepily, and began to cut the deer into pieces.

The pain continued to grow in Magin's chest. When it

gave him a moment of respite, he asked the old man beside him, "What do you think I should do?"

The old man chewed steadily, looking away. When he answered, the pain had attacked Magin again and he could not hear him. When it stopped, he put his hand on the old man's arm. The old man pushed his meat into his cheek and said, "Wait, wait. Later will be news." He shifted the bolus of meat around with his tongue. "One month, two months."

Magin sat still in disappointment. The old man beside him swallowed his meat and fell into a doze. Magin then lit the stub of cigar that had gone out as he held it. With his first lungful of smoke, the pain became severe and he started coughing. The mucus in his handkerchief was pink. He became aware that he was quite sick. It did not occur to him that he might not leave with his brother, or that he might not leave at all. He had always been able to leave a place, and his brother had always been alive and in a place known to Magin. Only Magin's wife was gone when he expected her to remain.

When, later, the sound of a shotgun from deep in the woods roused him from his thoughts, there was a wide plate of shadow across the clearing. He had not noticed the old man leave. He was cold, but did not know it until he saw that his hands were as blue as the shadows on the snow. The air was sharp in his throat and he had very little strength left in his legs as he went up the path. He stopped now and then to rest. When he was nearly to the hut, he heard a thrashing in the brush nearby. Looking through the trees, he saw a doe on the ground. Her body was steaming in the air. In the snow under her heaving side, a large hole was opening where the blood from her wound melted it. Her eyes were moist. Curious, Magin left the path and pushed through the snow and branches to where she lay.

She was still. Only her eyelids moved. But when Magin came near her, she thrashed again, digging her hind legs into the brush and lunging forward with her head. The blood spurted from her side. Then she lay still again, panting, and Magin leaned over her, pitying her. Without warning, her hind leg drew back, trembling, and shot out, striking him in the ribs.

Magin fell backward into the snow, and was only half conscious of what had happened to him. The snow seeped through his hair.

After a long time, dim forms drew near him, circling around him. Hot breath washed over his ear and cheek, and the harsh stink of malnourished animals filled his nostrils. Then there were voices of men, and snarling and yelping. Someone moved him and the pain sharpened until he lost consciousness.

He woke late at night in his bed, remembering nothing. His body, sheathed in blankets, struggled against fever. Pain sat like a rock in his chest. The pillow was hard under his head and his bones ached. When he shivered in the heat, his skin prickled and stung under his damp clothes. His swollen eyes were dry in their sockets, and his chest labored for air. He fought against this weariness, afraid that if he slept, he would stop breathing. But his weariness overcame him little by little. The fever spread. His limbs shook until the bedframe itself trembled, and sweat ran from him until the mattress under him was damp.

A white snowfield blinded him. A cold north wind crossed it, opening small holes in the ground and leaving banks of steam in its wake. Out of the holes crawled many deer, no larger than mice. Blinking feebly in the light, they tapped the snow with their hooves. As one of them drew its body up out of a hole, a dog leaped on it and devoured it with a convulsive jerking motion. Magin ran at the dog to beat it off, and caught his foot in a hole. He fell forward, his sight clouded by the steam. The cold crept into his bones, and he shivered uncontrollably. In the gloaming that filled the room he groped for some covering. The blanket burned under his hand. He barely had the strength to grasp it and draw it up over his body.

His eyes rested on the pale window. A late-rising moon shone over the sill, casting a gray light on the floor. The rotten floorboards softened and began to cave in. As the wood crumbled, Magin saw, down in the darkness under the house, the face of a light-haired man. Magin saw that his skin was steely gray and mottled, as though he had been there a long time. Magin watched, and the dead man moved restlessly, then opened his eyes.

Magin woke, his heart thumping. He saw the large circle of the sun outside his window. Turning his face, looking for darkness, he saw, without recognizing her, the woman standing in the doorway. She backed away from him. Shadows moved in the hut. He smelled fear.

"Don't go," he said. From beyond the wall, whispered echoes of his words came back to confuse him.

"I'm here," he said.

The echoes died. White faces with hollow eyes passed his doorway, curious. Slender hands pointed to the pit in the floor and the stiff, ivory face of the man. The sun grew hotter, singing the wool of the blankets and suffocating him. Trying to free himself of the tangled blankets, he ripped his clothes and meshed his fingers in the tattered cloth. Groaning, he scratched at his own skin, trying to find a way out of his fevered body. The sun dimmed, leaving him exhausted. He slept deeply without dreaming.

When he opened his eyes, the room was again black.

He heard the sound of the woman snoring. He was thirsty. "Wake up," he said. His voice was too feeble. He drew a shallow breath and as the pain increased, spoke again. He coughed and choked on his mucus. The woman only shifted in her bed. He lay back to wait for dawn to draw her from her sleep. Slowly he worked the blankets off his burning legs. A cool breeze blew over his skin.

In the morning, the pain had climbed into his throat, so that he could not swallow without tears coming to his eyes. As though mocking his own darkness, the sun shone over the bed where his limbs gleamed through the rents in his clothes. He looked at his body and saw that it was wasted: the veins stood out over his arms where the flesh had shrunk, and his skin was like parchment. His lungs drew little air into his body; his chest rose and fell almost imperceptibly.

He listened to the early air, searching for some sound to root him in the world. Birdsong circled away through the woods and back again. A dog barked once. A man called out and another, nearby, answered. A footstep brushed the dirt close to Magin, and looking up he saw the woman's face in the doorway.

"Ning," she said, smiling.

Magin tried to raise himself from the bed, but had no strength in his arms.

"Oh no. No, no, no," the woman cried in English with a look of horror on her face, throwing back her head.

"Listen to me," said Magin.

The woman took a breath and rushed on.

"No: tk. Uurk, uursh."

Magin turned away from her. His pain deafened him.

The woman hobbled quickly to the door and called out: "Ruckuck. Tk! No, no!" Magin heard the sound of people coming: a soft rustling and then the ground shaking outside his door.

The people crowded into the hut, filling it with the smell of burning wood and tobacco.

"Tk. Pshsht uuril," said one man, softly.

Magin shrank from the crowd above him.

"Ning," said the woman.

"No, tk, no pshtu tori," said another man, bending over Magin and breathing on his face.

As each minute passed, Magin felt the need for silence more desperately, and his fear grew. He wanted to be alone, to think of Mary, to breathe, and to sleep.

There was almost no air left in the room. Magin's eyesight grew dim. With difficulty, he searched the faces above him for the white-haired old man and did not find him. The woman was smiling in a friendly way. He tried to lift his arm. It was too heavy. Fixing her with his eyes, he said in Trsk, "Bring me water."

She did not understand, and stopped smiling.

A black-bearded man, standing near the bed, puffed on his pipe in quiet contemplation of Magin. Magin hardly breathed. His throat was dry and he could not swallow.

"Water," he said again, hoarsely.

"Water," answered several voices.

Then the black-bearded man said a few guttural words and the people began talking vigorously. "Uurk," said a small man. "No, tsatet ruck!" shouted another. The dogs, who had come to the hut at the heels of the men, became excited and barked sharply, one after another, outside the door. Magin fainted.

When he regained consciousness the room was empty. He tried to think clearly, but his thoughts faded and slipped from his grasp. The pain had wrapped around him tightly. His throat burned. He looked across at the inner wall and followed the grain of the wood. It was dark and water-stained. He looked at the floor. Clumps of snow lay over the pocked dirt. His eyes turned up toward the ceiling, and found only deepening darkness over the beam. His eyes moved down over the outer wall, from stone to stone, until they fixed on the window. There, beyond the pane, was a crowd of faces, staring intently at him.

Startled, he turned away. He heard fingers moving over the sill. Snow rustled below the window. He tried to close his hands around the mattress, testing his strength, and waited for the voices to rise again.

Away from Home

It has been so long since she used a metaphor!

Company

I like the students. I like their company. I like them here—if only they would remain in the indefinite future. They must be somewhere in my future or they will not be here for me, for company, where I can talk to them sometimes all day long. But that future must never come. Because it is so hard to meet them in the class itself. The problem is that in order to have the company of them here, in my imagination, I must pay the price of that future arriving, as it does, with all the difficulty of that encounter.

Then there is another sort of company in the letters I have not answered. If I answer the letters, those patient or impatient people waiting for answers are no longer present to me. If I answer the letters, I suppose I may be in some cases present to them, then. But, though not telling myself this is the reason, I don't answer these letters. And yet this is selfish, and of course impolite. I answer some, in fact. But most go unanswered for weeks, months, more than a year, several years, or forever. Several times, I have waited so long to answer a letter that the person has moved away. Once, I waited so long to answer a postcard that my friend died.

But maybe these people are no longer waiting for

answers by now anyway; maybe their attention is no longer on me, and this company is only an illusion: the friendly or neutral words are still there on various sheets of paper in different envelopes, but in the minds of these people who wrote the unanswered letters the words for what they are thinking about me, if they think of me at all, are no longer friendly or neutral but unfriendly, dismissive, even disgusted. I believe I have this company, but I do not have it, unless believing this is enough, and I do in some form have this company, whatever they may be thinking.

When I answer one of these letters, true, sometimes all I receive in return, weeks later, is a brief, tired reply. But more often the reply comes quickly and is full, warm, even delighted; and then, just because it is so generous and such wonderful company, it may sit again on my bedside, or on my desk, or on my pile of correspondence, for weeks or months or longer before I answer it.

Finances

If they try to add and subtract to see whether the relationship is equal, it won't work. On his side, he is giving $50,000, she says. No, $70,000, he says. It doesn't matter, she says. It matters to me, he says. What she is giving is a half-grown child. Is that an asset or a liability? Now, is she supposed to feel grateful to him? She can feel grateful, but not indebted, not that she owes him something. There has to be a sense of equality. I just love to be with you, she says, and you love to be with me. I'm grateful to you for providing for us, and I know my child is sometimes a trouble to you, though you say he is a good child. But I don't know how to figure it. If I give all I have and you give all you have, isn't that a kind of equality? No, he says.

The Transformation

It was not possible, and yet it happened; and not suddenly, but very slowly, not a miracle, but a very natural thing, though it was impossible. A girl in our town turned into a stone. But it is true that she had not been the usual sort of girl even before that: she had been a tree. Now a tree moves in the wind. But sometime near the end of September she began not to move in the wind anymore. For weeks she moved less and less. Then she never moved. When her leaves fell they fell suddenly and with a terrible noise. They crashed onto the cobblestones and sometimes broke into fragments and sometimes remained whole. There would be a spark where they fell and a little white powder lying beside them. People, though I did not, collected her leaves and put them on the mantelpiece. There never was such a town, with stone leaves on every mantelpiece. Then she began to turn gray: at first we thought it was the light. With wrinkled foreheads, twenty of us at a time would stand in a circle around her shading our eyes, dropping our jaws—and so few teeth we had among us it was something to see—and say it was the time of day or the changing season that made her look gray. But soon it was clear that she was simply gray now, just that, the way years ago we had to admit that she was simply a tree now, and no longer a girl. But a tree is one thing and a stone is another. There are limits to what you can accept, even of impossible things.

Two Sisters (II)

1

The younger sister is bored in the shop and rings the bell. The older sister comes slowly down the stairs and asks the younger sister why she rang the bell.

The reason is simple: to see her come down. Because she is so fat and moves so slowly; the stairs buckle and creak under her, she has trouble breathing, she holds the banister as if it were still her father's hand, her plump knees knock against each other. It is very amusing to the younger sister and breaks the tedium of the morning.

She says none of this out loud. Out loud she says, "There has been a mistake in yesterday's figures." But of course the older sister cannot find the mistake, though she goes over the figures many times. Her dress is tight under her arms and her ankles are swollen from standing so long.

The younger sister cannot play this trick very often, or she would be found out. But that makes it all the more exciting to her.

2

The two sisters, no longer young, are forced to sleep in the same bed. They dream of different things and carefully hide their dreams from each other in the morning. Sometimes they touch by accident in the bed and fly apart as though they had been burned. They do not sleep well and are not refreshed in the morning. One wakes early, goes to the toilet, and would like to resume sleeping. But there is no joy in going back to bed when her sister lies there already sweating like a sow in the early heat.

3

My sister with thighs like pillars. She eats her potatoes as though she would make a revolution among them, as though they were the People. No, then what is this passion of hers? It is terrifying to see her cloudy eyes become sharp when my dinner is put on the table. I am afraid she will devour not only the dinner but me and my poor life too. Beside her laughter, mine is like the cheeping of a bird in the ivy. No, she never laughs. I never laugh. Her silence, though, is so much greater than mine that mine is like a wisp of smoke in a rain cloud.

4

One day the younger sister smacked the older sister in the face. She did it out of frustration and boredom with her life. She regretted it immediately. Not because she had hurt her sister, who stood paralyzed, her hand to her cheek and her hat rolling over the floor, but because now her sister would weep and moan and speak of the incident for months, to the younger sister's shame and anger. She had wanted to diminish her sister in some way, even destroy her, but instead she had given her new dignity.

5

Two sisters, like stone, who do not speak to each other. They have nothing in common but their parentage. One rises early and the other late; one will not eat animal products and the other will not eat whole grains; one has a rash in the summertime and the other cannot wear wool; one will not go to the movies for fear of strange men and the other will not watch television; in every election their votes cancel each other, and they are as no one. Only in their mutual distrust are they alike.

The Furnace

My father has trouble with his hearing and does not like to talk on the phone, so I talk on the phone mainly to my mother. Sometimes she abruptly stops what she is saying to me, I hear a noise in the background, she says my name, and waits. Then I know my father has come into the room during her conversation and asked who she is talking to. Sometimes, at that point, he interjects a question for me, but often he asks her something that has nothing to do with me, while I wait at the other end of the phone. After she and I have gone on talking, he may come into the room again, having thought of something else he wants to say. When I hear his voice in the background I stop whatever I am saying to my mother and wait.

Sometimes she forces him to get on the phone. "Tell her yourself," she says. He gets on the phone and without saying hello tells me what it is he wants me to know and then gets off without saying goodbye. Back on the phone, she says, "He's gone."

Although he has never liked to talk on the phone, he has always liked to write letters. He usually prefers to write a letter that includes some kind of instruction, or at least a transmission of what he thinks will be new information. For a while, we carried on a correspondence whose regularity was unusual for my family, in which very little has ever been regular or systematic. Then I didn't hear from him for some weeks. Maybe I was the one who did not answer his last letter. I told my mother to tell him I would like to hear from him, and he then sent me some clippings from the Crime Beat section of their local paper. In the top margin he had written: "The underside of Cambridge life." Some entries he had marked with a dark line of ink down the side margin.

> . . . A Jefferson Park man entered the dispute, slashing the teen just below the right eye with an unidentified weapon. While this happened, the Jackson Circle man stole the bike. Later, police found a Jackson Street man riding the bike. Police arrested the Jackson Circle man, Jackson Street man, and Jefferson Park man and charged them with assault with a dangerous weapon (knife) and armed robbery.

On another clipping he had underlined certain sentences:

> Police officers recovered two martial arts swords and a meat cleaver.

> At 10 p.m. an employee of the Cantab Lounge reported that a suspect who had been shut off at the bar assaulted her by throwing a glass at her.

> A Cambridge resident reported that he was assaulted with a fingernail clipper by a suspect who

> was throwing trash around the doorway at Eddy's Place.
>
> A Rindge Avenue resident reported that her daughter hit her over the head with a glass.
>
> A Rindge Avenue resident reported that she was assaulted with a large pin by two other neighborhood residents.

In the top margin of this clipping he had written: "Strange weapons dept."

After this he sent me an article he had written. He occasionally wrote an article or a letter to a newspaper about something that had come up in connection with the Bible or some other religious topic. The articles and letters were clever, and by now I was interested in the Bible and religious topics myself.

This one, on circumcision, was called "The Unkindest Cut" and opened with a sentence about the "male organ." In his thin, shaky handwriting, he had noted in the margin at the top of the article that I shouldn't feel I had to read this, nor should my husband feel he had to read it. He was sincere, but he often attached disclaimers to the articles and letters he sent and I generally disregarded them.

Yet when I tried to read the article, I found it hard to read so much about the male organ as written by my father. I asked my husband if he would read it and tell me the gist of it but he did not really want to read it either. I did not know what to do about this situation, since it would have been awkward even to mention it to my father, but in time, as I took no action, I began to forget it. My father had probably forgotten it long before, since his memory has become more and more undependable, as he and my mother both point out.

But the letters he was sending me for a while were about the household he grew up in: besides his mother and father, there were two grandmothers and a grandfather who was slightly mad, maids, cooks, and cleaning women who came and went, and his grandmothers' female nurse-companions and his grandfather's male nurse-companions, who also came and went. His father's mother owned the house and dominated it, to his mother's annoyance. I have seen this house, which still stands in a street not far from where they live, and it looks to me surprisingly modest to have held such a number and variety of people. The last time it was sold, he read about the sale in the paper and wrote to the new owners, explaining that he had been born in the upstairs front room and had played in the hayloft of the small barn. The new owners were pleased to hear from him and sent him photographs of the house.

He would write to me in some detail and in the midst of it apologize, saying that what lay immediately ahead would be tedious and that I could read fast or skim if I liked. He said he was trying to recover facts that he had not thought of for most of a century. But I would write back asking for even more detail, because I wanted to come as close as I could to a way of life that seemed to me precious for several reasons, one being simply that even the memory of it was slipping away, because fewer and fewer people were alive who had experienced it.

Most recently we had gotten into a correspondence about the furnace in the house where he grew up. He said that while he lived there, changes had occurred, but they were all additions, and what was there to begin with remained. For instance, a gas stove was installed in the kitchen alongside the coal stove. His grandmother felt that for certain things the coal stove was more economical. A new oil furnace was added in the basement, but the huge old coal furnace remained. At some point electricity was added to gas for lighting. His grandmother kept both because in a storm, she warned them, the electricity might fail.

He remembered how one of the cleaning women used to comb her long hair in the kitchen at the end of the day, so that she could go forth suitably neat. She would then extract the hairs from the comb and put them not in the stove, which required the effort of lifting one of the iron covers, but on top of the stove, where they burned to an ash that remained visible until someone thought to remove it.

In the early days, he said, a "furnaceman" would come at about seven in the morning to shake down the big furnace, remove ashes and clinkers, and shovel more coal in from one of the two big bins whose board sides projected into the cellar, resting on the cellar floor. An early furnaceman was named Frank and his grandmother continued to call subsequent ones "Frank" as her memory for names weakened. The furnace was a matter of constant concern in very cold weather. Even when his father was home, his grandmother would go down to investigate, and then, in order to force his father to act, would do something deliberately noisy to it. He would shout, "Mother, Mother," pounding on the floor with his foot, and rush down the cellar stairs. She was not supposed to go down them, for they had no banisters, and there was a drop on either side to the cellar floor below. The only lighting came from the open door of the kitchen, from tiny dirty outdoor windows at ground level, and from a gas pipe that came down from the ceiling and supplied the same kind of feeble, naked flame that his mother used in her room to heat her curling iron.

On ash collection days the furnaceman lifted the barrels up the steps of the bulkhead. In winter, a boardwalk was put down from the street in front to the bulkhead. Along this, or in the soft gravel when the walk was not in place, the furnaceman, on the days of the city collection, rotated the tilted ash barrels. To bring the coal in, along the same boardwalk, required a two-man team: one man would shovel the coal into a container on the back of the second man, who would carry it into the yard, unshoulder it with a twist of his body, and dump it down the chute. Coal delivery was by horse and wagon when my father was a child. He said on a normal working day there would be at least three horses and wagons on his street, delivering ice, coal, milk, groceries, fruits and vegetables, or express packages, or peddling, or buying old newspapers or old iron. There was also a horse-drawn hurdy-gurdy.

What he said about his furnace and all the trappings of the furnace made me go down and look more carefully at our own furnace. Our house is either a hundred years old or a hundred and fifty, depending on which town historical document we believe. This furnace was converted to gas from coal probably forty years ago. The trappings were still there, a coal hod on the floor of the coal bin and, hanging on the wall, pronged iron bars for opening the hatches. I looked up and saw two long, stout boards stowed above the coal bin. Now that I had read what my father wrote about the men bringing the coal in across the snow, I had no doubt these boards were put down for the coal delivery here too. I was excited to discover this.

I wrote back to my father about what I had discovered,

knowing that for several reasons he would be less interested in my coal furnace than his memories of his own. It is natural for an old man to be engrossed in his memories and less interested in the present. But he has always been more interested in his own ideas than anyone else's.

Although he likes to have conversations with other people and hear what they say, he does not know what to do with an idea of someone else's except to use it as a starting point from which to produce an even better idea of his own. His own ideas are certainly interesting, often the most interesting in a given situation. He has always been interesting at a dinner party, even though as he aged, a time came when he would have to leave the table part of the way through and go lie down for a while.

Dinner parties were an important part of the life my mother and father had together from the very beginning. There was a skill to taking part in a dinner party, and a technique to giving one, especially to guiding the conversation at the table. There was an art to encouraging a shy guest, or subduing a noisy one. My mother and father are still sociable, but they are handicapped by their age now and limit what they do. Now they have people in for tea more often than dinner, and at a certain point during the tea, also, my father leaves the room to go lie down.

Though my mother still goes out to concerts and lectures, my father rarely does. One of the last events they went to together was a grand birthday party held in a public library. Four hundred guests were invited, coming from around the world. My mother told me about it, including the fact that during the party my father fell down. He was not hurt. She was not in the same room with him when he fell.

He is unsteady on his feet, and has fallen or come close

to falling quite often in the last few years. I was present when a health technician came to give advice about re-arranging the apartment so that it would be safer for the two of them. The health technician observed my father there in the apartment for a while. My father's head is large and heavy and his body is thin and frail. The technician said he noticed that my father tended to toss his head back, and this threw him off balance. The technician said he should try to change that habit and also use his walker in the house. Although the technician was friendly and helpful, he was very energetic and spoke in a loud voice, and toward the end of the visit my father became too agitated to stay in his company any longer and left to go lie down. After that visit, my mother told me, my father tried to remember to use his walker but tended to leave it here and there in the apartment and then had to walk around without it to find it again.

If I ask my mother, on the telephone, how my father is, she often lowers her voice to answer. She often says she is worried about him. She has been worried for years. She is always worried about some recent or new behavior of his. She does not seem to realize that this behavior is not always recent or new, or that she is always worried about something. Sometimes she is worried because he is de-pressed. For a while she was worried because he so often became hysterically angry. Not long ago she said he seemed to take an unnatural interest in their Scrabble games. After that she said he was losing his memory, did not remember incidents from their life together, kept referring to one family member by the name of another, and sometimes did not recognize a name at all.

He had to stay in a rehabilitation hospital for a while after his last fall, to have some physical therapy. To my mother's astonishment, he did not mind playing catch with the other patients in the physical therapy group, or tossing a beanbag in a contest. She said this was not like him: she wondered if he was regressing to a childish state. She suspected that he had enjoyed the attention there, and the food. Since his return home, she told me, he had not been eating very well. She was upset because he did not seem to like her cooking anymore. On the other hand he did finish a piece of writing he was working on.

A year ago, when my mother herself was in the hospital with a serious illness, he and I went out to look for a restaurant where we could have supper before going back to sit with my mother. It was a cold, windy night in May. We were downtown in the city, in a neighborhood of hospitals, tall, well-lighted buildings all around us. There were walkways over our heads, and underground garages opening on all sides, but no restaurants that I could see. Stores were closed, not many cars went by on the streets, and almost no people walked on the sidewalk. My father was unsteady on his feet and I was watching for every curb and uneven piece of pavement. He was determined to find a restaurant where he could have an alcoholic drink. At last, we entered a passageway in one of the tall buildings, walking into what looked from the outside to be a deserted mall. Going down an empty corridor and past some empty store windows and up some steps, we found a restaurant with a bar and an amount of good cheer and number of lively customers surprising after the empty streets outside. We sat down at a table and talked a little, but my father's mind was on his drink and he kept looking for the waiter, who was too busy to come to our table. I was thinking that this dinner was likely to be the last one I would have in a restaurant with my father, and certainly the least festive.

In an upper floor of one of the tall buildings nearby, my mother lay suffering from a rare blood disorder and all the other ills that came one after another because of the treatment itself. We thought she might be dying, though my father seemed to forget this at times, or rather, if she seemed better one day, he cheered up completely and began making jokes again, as though she would certainly get well. The next day he might arrive at the hospital to find one of us crying and his face would fall.

My father grew so impatient for his drink that he stood up on his unsteady legs, bracing himself with his cane. The waiter came. My father ordered his drink. What he wanted so much was a Perfect Rob Roy.

His hearing is not good, and his eyesight is not very good either, and for a while, if I asked him how he was, he would say that except for his eyes and his ears, his balance, his memory, and his teeth, he was doing reasonably well. In order to read certain sizes of print he has to take off his glasses and hold the text within an inch or two of his nose. It used to be that sometimes, when I asked my mother how my father was, she would answer: "He was well enough to go to the Theological Library today." Then he stopped going to any library because it was so hard for him to see the titles of the books and to bend down to the lower shelves. Then his balance became so bad it was very risky for him to go out by himself at all. Once he fell in the street and hit the back of his head. A stranger passing in a car called an ambulance on his cell phone. It was after that fall that he went into the hospital for physical therapy and after he returned home did not go out by himself anymore. On one of my last visits, at Christmas, he said he needed a magnifying light for the large dictionary in the living room.

He has always enjoyed looking things up in the dictionary, particularly word histories. Now my mother says she is worried about him because he is no longer merely interested in word histories but obsessed by them. He will get up from a conversation with a guest at tea and go look up a word she has used. He will interrupt the conversation to report the etymology. He has always preferred an illustrated dictionary. He likes to study the pictures, particularly the pictures of handsome women. At Christmas, he showed me one of his favorites, the president of Iceland.

I have gone down to look at the furnace again because in a few days it will be removed and a new one put in its place. The dust is deep and gray in the old coal bin. The wooden planks that form the sides are rich in color and smoothly fitted together. Tossed in the dust and half buried are the old coal hod and some metal parts of the coal chute. I ask my husband if the men who come to install the new furnace will have to remove the walls of the coal bin and he says he thinks they will not.

After I wrote to my father about my discovery of the boards, he answered my letter with another about his childhood and also another memory of coal men, this one dating from when he was grown up. He said he was out driving with my sister next to him in the car when he happened upon an accident that had just occurred. He said that two men had been delivering coal. The delivery truck had been parked at an angle in a driveway. The driver was talking to the owner of the house, presumably about the delivery. The second man, his assistant, was standing at the end of the driveway with his back to the truck, looking out at the street. The truck's brakes were apparently faulty and the truck rolled backward down the driveway. Either no one saw this or no one cried out in time, the coal man's assistant was struck by the truck and run over, and his head was crushed. My father said he drove some distance past the accident, parked his car and, instructing my sister to stay where she was, went back to look. A short way beyond the man's crushed head, he saw the man's brains on the pavement.

My father said he knew he was wrong to go and look, he should have driven on. Then he began to talk about the anatomy of the brain, that the incident dramatized a conviction he had always had. He had always believed that consciousness was so dependent on the physical brain that the continuation of consciousness and one's identity after death was inconceivable. He admitted that this conviction was probably metaphysically naïve, but added that it had been strengthened by a lifetime's observation of many insane and manic-depressive types, some in his own family. Among the manic-depressive types, he said, he included himself. Then he went on to talk about the mind of God, whom he described as a Being with presumably no neurons.

Now the new furnace is installed and working but the house does not seem any warmer. The rooms that were always chilly before are still chilly. There is still a perceptible change in temperature as we go up to the second floor. The only difference is that because this new furnace works with fans, we can hear it while it is on. It is much smaller than the old one, and shiny. It makes a better impression on anyone visiting the basement, which was one reason to get it, I realize now, since we may one day want to sell this house. I have cleaned out the coal bin, at last, preserving the coal hod and the sections of chute and storing them in another wooden stall in a part of the cellar we haven't touched yet that contains an old pump, among other things.

My correspondence with my father about the furnace seems to have ended, as has our correspondence about his family. His letters, in fact, have shrunk to small scrawled notes attached to more clippings from the local paper.

Twice he has sent my husband and me the same "Ask Marjorie" column, one that discusses the shape of the earth and points out that the ancients knew perfectly well that the earth was round. Both times he wrote a message on the back of the envelope asking my husband and me if we were taught that in ancient times people believed the earth was flat.

He has also sent me more items from the Crime Beat section.

> At 10:30 p.m. a Putnam Avenue resident said an unknown person broke into the home by pushing in the rear door. A dollar bill was taken.
>
> At 9:12 a.m. a North Cambridge man from Mass. Ave. said someone had broken in but nothing was missing.
>
> A Belmont resident working at a Mass. Ave. address stated that another employee told her that she had been fired and then proceeded to scratch the victim in the neck.

By this one he wrote in the margin: "Why? What is the connection?"

> Friday, March 11. At 11:30 p.m., a Concord Avenue woman was walking down Garden Street near Mass. Ave. when a man asked her, "Are you smiling?" The woman said yes, so the man punched

> her in the mouth, causing her lip to bleed and swell. No arrests were made.

> Three men were arrested for assault and battery on Third Street near Gore Street at 2:50 a.m. Two men are Cambridge residents, both charged with assault and battery with a dangerous weapon, a shod foot. A Billerica man received the same charge, but with a hammer.

My father put an X in the margin beside the grammar mistake.

> Tuesday, June 13. A Rhode Island resident reported that between 8:45 a.m. and 10 a.m., at an address on Garden St., an unknown person took her purse with $180 and credit cards. A male was witnessed under the table but the victim believed that it was someone from the power company.

On my last visit, my father seemed in worse condition than I had seen him before. When I asked him if he was working on anything in particular now, he said no and then turned his head slowly to my mother and looked at her in bewilderment, his mouth hanging open. There was an expression of pain or agony on his face that seemed habitual. She looked back at him, waited a moment, impassive, and then said: "Yes, you are. You're writing about the Bible and anti-Semitism." He continued to stare at her.

Later that evening, before he went to bed, he said: "This is symptomatic of my condition: You're my daughter, and I'm proud of you, but I have nothing to say to you."

He left to get ready for bed, and then came back into

the room wearing dazzling white pajamas. My mother asked me to admire his pajamas, and he stood quietly while I did. Then he said: "I don't know what I will be like in the morning."

After he went to bed, my mother showed me a picture of him forty years before sitting at a seminar table surrounded by students. "Just look at him there!" she said in distress, as though it were some sort of punishment that he had become what he was now—an old man with a beaked profile like a nutcracker.

Saying goodbye, I held his hand longer than usual. He may not have liked it. It is impossible to tell what he is feeling, often, but physical contact has always been difficult for him, and he has always been awkward about it. Whether out of embarrassment or absentmindedness, he kept shaking his hand and mine up and down slightly, as though palsied.

Recently, my mother said he was still worse. He had fallen again, and he was having trouble with his bladder. Can he still work? I asked her. To me, it seemed that if he could still work, then he was all right, no matter what else was going wrong with him. Not really, she said. "He has been writing letters, but there are odd things in some of them. It may not matter, since they're mostly to old friends." She said maybe she should be checking them, though, before he sent them.

It was a phone conversation with another old woman that reminded me of a name I had forgotten for this time of life. After telling me about her angioplasty and her diabetes, she said: "Well, this is what you can expect when you enter the twilight years." But it is hard not to think that my father's bewilderment is only temporary, and that behind it, his sharp critical mind is still alive and well. With this younger, firmer mind he will continue to read the letters I send him and write back—our correspondence is only temporarily interrupted.

The latest letter I have seen from him was written not to me but to one of his grandsons. My mother thought I should see it before she sent it. The envelope was taped shut with strong packing tape. The entire letter concerns a mathematical rhyme he copied from the newspaper. It begins:

"A dozen, a gross and a score
plus three times the square root of four
divide it by seven plus five times eleven
equals nine to the square and not more."

Then he explains mathematical terms and the solution of this problem. Because he changed the margins of his page to type the poem, and did not reset them, the whole letter is written in short lines like a poem:

"The total to be divided by 7 consists
of the following:
12 plus 144 plus 20 plus 3 times
the square root of 4.
These are the numerals above the line
over the divisor 7. They add up to 182,
which divided by seven equals 26.
26 plus 11 times 5 (55) is 81.
81 is 9 squared. A number squared
is a number multiplied by itself.
The square of 9 is nine times nine or 81."

He goes on to explain the concept of squaring numbers, and of the cube, along the way giving the etymologies of certain words, including *dozen*, *score*, and *scoreboard*. He talks about the sign for square root being related to the form of a tree.

I tell my mother the letter seems a little strange to me. She protests, saying that it is quite correct. I don't argue, but say he can certainly send it. The end of the letter is less strange, except for the line breaks:

"For me memory and balance fail rapidly.
You are young and have a university library
system for your use. I, who have
a good home reference collection,
sometimes can get other people to
look up things for me, but it is not the same.
I have to explain that I have increasingly
lost my memory and sense of balance,
I can't go anywhere, not the libraries
or the bookstores to browse. We have to pay
a young woman to walk out with me
and prevent me from falling
though I take a mechanical walker with me.
I don't mean it has an engine that propels it.
I do the propelling, but that it is
shiny and metal and has wheels."

Young and Poor

I like working near the baby, here at my desk by lamplight. The baby sleeps.

As though I were young and poor again, I was going to say.

But I am still young and poor.

The Silence of Mrs. Iln

Her children found it impossible to understand old Mrs. Iln now. They were forced to call her senile. But if they had paused a moment from their wild activities and tried to imagine her state of mind, they would have known that this was not the case.

Decades before, when her recent marriage had cast a pleasant light over her otherwise homely features, she had been as articulate as any other woman, perhaps even more articulate than was necessary. If her husband asked her where his cuff links were, she might answer, "I think they are in the top drawer of your bureau, though it could be that you took them off in the dining room and they are still there, on the table, or perhaps they have fallen onto the floor by now, in all this confusion; if they got stepped on I don't know what I would do, I just don't know . . ." When she had had a little wine and felt moved to give her opinion of the political situation, she would burst out with, "You know what I think? I think it's a case of collective madness: I think they're all insane, we're all insane, but it isn't our fault, and it isn't the fault of our parents, and it isn't the fault of our parents' parents. I don't know whose fault it is, but I would like to know . . ."

A few years later, she and her husband understood each other too well to need long explanations. Her opinions did not change over time, but hardened into obsessive and monotonous responses, and remained thoroughly familiar to her husband. She began to curtail her sentences, and her meaning was always clear to her husband and to her children, as they grew up. When her children left home, one by one, Mrs. Iln was gradually overcome by the feeling that she had no purpose in the world and no reason to be alive. She lost sight of herself completely. Her husband had grown into her until she hardly distinguished him from herself, and now her sentences were reduced to a few words: "Dresser drawer in your bedroom," she would say, or "completely insane." Since her husband knew what she was going to say before she said it, even those few words were unnecessary and in time were left unspoken. "I wonder where my cuff links are," her husband would say softly, more to himself than to her. And even before she wagged her head toward the bureau, he would be there rummaging among his handkerchiefs and foreign coins. Or when he read aloud to her from the morning paper she would purse her lips and give him a certain stormy look and he would hear the "insane" of a few years before echoing in the air. He too might have stopped speaking, if he had not grown to like the constant murmur from his own lips.

Since nothing happened in her house that had not happened before, since her children, who found her silence unnerving after the din of their own homes, rarely visited her, Mrs. Iln no longer had any reason to speak, and silence became a deeply rooted habit. When her husband fell gravely ill, she tended him silently; when he died, she had no words for her grief; when her oldest children asked her to live with them, she shook her head and went home.

Sometimes she felt the need to give a word or two of explanation especially to her grandchildren, as she watched them from beyond her wall of silence; sometimes her children begged her to speak, as though it would prove something to them. And at these times she struggled as though in a nightmare to bring out one sound, and could not. It was as if by speaking she would have damaged something inside herself.

More and more often in her loneliness, thoughts would come to her as they had never come before, not even in her youth. They were thoughts more complex than "insanity," and she would hear the words mounting in turmoil within her. But when her children came at the weekend to sit with her for an hour or two, it was hard to find the right moment to begin speaking of all she had thought, and if the moment came, when their restless chatter stopped and their eyes fell on her old pitted face, then she could rarely summon the words that had flown hither and thither in her head all week. And if she managed to summon the words to her mind, then she could never, never break through the last barrier and free herself from the constriction of her speechlessness.

At last she stopped trying, and when her children came they saw an expression on her face that had not been there before—a stiff, dead look, a look of blankness and defeat that reflected her hopelessness. They immediately seized upon this expression as evidence of senility. She was astonished and hurt by their reaction. If they had been more patient with her, if they had stayed with her for longer periods of time, they would have seen something in her that was not senility. Yet they clung to the idea of senility and registered her name in a nursing home.

At first she was horrified, and everything in her cried

out against the coming change. With renewed vigor she frowned at them and sent them a look that her husband had well understood. But they were not moved. In their eyes, her every gesture could now be called senile. Even quite normal behavior seemed mad to them, and nothing she did could reach them.

But once she was actually living in the nursing home, she made peace with her surroundings. During the day she sat in the library reading and thinking. She read very slowly and spent many more hours staring at the wall than at the book. She tested her mind against what she read and it grew stronger. Only the nurses were not quite real to her and puzzled her: she thought their brittle good humor was not honest. They did not like her, because her lucid eye made them uneasy. But she moved comfortably among her bloodless, wrinkled companions, more comfortably than she had ever moved among the vigorous people of her former life. She found the silence in the crowded dining room appropriate. She understood very well the morose men and women who struggled along the garden paths in the afternoon or sat staring through the porch railings at the street during the long summer twilight. Tentatively at first, and with growing wonder, she realized that she had been nearly dead among the living. Among the nearly dead, she was at last beginning to live.

Almost Over: Separate Bedrooms

They have moved into separate bedrooms now.
That night she dreams she is holding him in her arms. He dreams he is having dinner with Ben Jonson.

Money

I don't want any more gifts, cards, phone calls, prizes, clothes, friends, letters, books, souvenirs, pets, magazines, land, machines, houses, entertainments, honors, good news, dinners, jewels, vacations, flowers, or telegrams. I just want money.

Acknowledgment

I have only to add
that the plates in the present volume
have been carefully re-etched
by Mr. Cuff.

VARIETIES OF DISTURBANCE

(2007)

A Man from Her Past

I think Mother is flirting with a man from her past who is not Father. I say to myself: Mother ought not to have improper relations with this man "Franz"! "Franz" is a European. I say she should not see this man improperly while Father is away! But I am confusing an old reality with a new reality: Father will not be returning home. He will be staying on at Vernon Hall. As for Mother, she is ninety-four years old. How can there be improper relations with a woman of ninety-four? Yet my confusion must be this: though her body is old, her capacity for betrayal is still young and fresh.

Dog and Me

An ant can look up at you, too, and even threaten you with its arms. Of course, my dog does not know I am human, he sees me as dog, though I do not leap up at a fence. I am a strong dog. But I do not leave my mouth hanging open when I walk along. Even on a hot day, I do not leave my tongue hanging out. But I bark at him: "No! No!"

Enlightened

I don't know if I can remain friends with her. I've thought and thought about it—she'll never know how much. I gave it one last try. I called her, after a year. But I didn't like the way the conversation went. The problem is that she is not very enlightened. Or I should say, she is not enlightened enough for me. She is nearly fifty years old and no more enlightened, as far as I can see, than when I first knew her twenty years ago, when we talked mainly about men. I did not mind how unenlightened she was then, maybe because I was not so enlightened myself. I believe I am more enlightened now, and certainly more enlightened than she is, although I know it's not very enlightened to say that. But I want to say it, so I am willing to postpone being more enlightened myself so that I can still say a thing like that about a friend.

The Good Taste Contest

The husband and wife were competing in a Good Taste Contest judged by a jury of their peers, men and women of good taste, including a fabric designer, a rare-book dealer, a pastry cook, and a librarian. The wife was judged to have better taste in furniture, especially antique furniture. The husband was judged to have overall poor taste in lighting fixtures, tableware, and glassware. The wife was judged to have indifferent taste in window treatments, but the husband and wife both were judged to have good taste in floor coverings, bed linen, bath linen, large appliances, and small appliances. The husband was felt to have good taste in carpets, but only fair taste in upholstery fabrics. The husband was felt to have very good taste in both food and alcoholic beverages, while the wife had inconsistently good to poor taste in food. The husband had better taste in clothes than the wife though inconsistent taste in perfumes and colognes. While both husband and wife were judged to have no more than fair taste in garden design, they were judged to have good taste in number and variety of evergreens. The husband was felt to have excellent taste in roses but poor taste in bulbs. The wife was felt to have better taste in bulbs and generally good taste in shade plantings with the exception of hostas. The husband's taste was felt to be good in garden furniture but only fair in ornamental planters. The wife's taste was judged consistently poor in garden statuary. After a brief discussion, the judges gave the decision to the husband for his higher overall points score.

Collaboration with Fly

I put that word on the page,
but he added the apostrophe.

Kafka Cooks Dinner

I am filled with despair as the day approaches when my dear Milena will come. I have hardly begun to decide what to offer her. I have hardly confronted the thought yet, only flown around it the way a fly circles a lamp, burning my head over it.

I am so afraid I will be left with no other idea but potato salad, and it's no surprise to her anymore. I mustn't.

The thought of this dinner has been with me constantly all week, weighing on me in the same way that in the deep sea there is no place that is not under the greatest pressure. Now and then I summon all my energy and work at the menu as if I were being forced to hammer a nail into a stone, as if I were both the one hammering and also the nail. But at other times, I sit here reading in the afternoon, a myrtle in my buttonhole, and there are such beautiful passages in the book that I think I have become beautiful myself.

I might as well be sitting in the garden of the insane asylum staring into space like an idiot. And yet I know I will eventually settle on a menu, buy the food, and prepare the meal. In this, I suppose I am like a butterfly: its zigzagging flight is so irregular, it flutters so much it is painful to watch, it flies in what is the very opposite of a straight line, and yet it successfully covers miles and miles to reach its final destination, so it must be more efficient or at least more determined than it seems.

To torture myself is pathetic, too, of course. After all, Alexander didn't torture the Gordian knot when it wouldn't come untied. I feel I am being buried alive under all these thoughts, though at the same time I feel compelled to lie still, since perhaps I am actually dead after all.

This morning, for instance, shortly before waking up, which was also shortly after falling asleep, I had a dream that has not left me yet: I had caught a mole and carried it into the hops field, where it dove into the earth as though into water and disappeared. When I contemplate this dinner, I would like to disappear into the earth like that mole. I would like to stuff myself into the drawer of the laundry chest, and open the drawer from time to time to see if I have suffocated yet. It's so much more surprising that one gets up every morning at all.

I know beet salad would be better. I could give her beets and potatoes both, and a slice of beef, if I include meat. Yet a good slice of beef does not require any side dish, it is best tasted alone, so the side dish could come before, in which case it would not be a side dish but an appetizer. Whatever I do, perhaps she will not think very highly of my effort, or perhaps she will be feeling a little ill to begin with and not stimulated by the sight of those beets. In the case of the first, I would be dreadfully ashamed, and in the case of the second, I would have no advice—how could I?—but just a simple question: would she want me to remove all the food from the table?

Not that this dinner alarms me, exactly. I do after all

have some imagination and energy, so perhaps I will be able to make a dinner that she will like. There have been other, passable dinners since the meal I cooked for Felice that was so unfortunate—though perhaps more good than bad came of that one.

It was last week that I invited Milena. She was with a friend. We met by accident on the street and I spoke impulsively. The man with her had a kind, friendly, fat face—a very correct face, as only Germans have. After making the invitation, for a long time I walked through the city as though it were a cemetery, I was so at peace.

Then I began to torment myself, like a flower in a flower box that is thrashed by the wind but loses not a single petal.

Like a letter covered with corrective pencil marks, I have my defects. After all, I am not strong to begin with, and I believe even Hercules fainted once. I attempt all day, at work, not to think about what lies ahead, but this costs me so much effort that there is nothing left for my work. I handle telephone calls so badly that after a while the switchboard operator refuses to connect me. So I had better say to myself, Go ahead and polish the silverware beautifully, then lay it out ready on the sideboard and be done with it. Because I polish it in my mind all day long—this is what torments me (and doesn't clean the silver).

I love German potato salad made with good, old potatoes and vinegar, even though it is so heavy, so coercive, almost, that I feel a little nauseated even before I taste it—I might be embracing an oppressive and alien culture. If I offer this to Milena I may be exposing a gross part of myself to her that I should spare her above all, a part of myself that she has not yet encountered. A French dish, however, even if more agreeable, would be less true to myself, and perhaps this would be an unpardonable betrayal.

I am full of good intentions and yet inactive, just as I was that day last summer when I sat on my balcony watching a beetle on its back waving its legs in the air, unable to right itself. I felt great sympathy for it, yet I would not leave my chair to help it. It stopped moving and was still for so long I thought it had died. Then a lizard walked over it, slid off it, and tipped it upright, and it ran up the wall as though nothing had happened.

I bought the tablecloth on the street yesterday from a man with a cart. The man was small, almost tiny, weak, and bearded, with one eye. I borrowed the candlesticks from a neighbor, or I should say, she lent them to me.

I will offer her espresso after dinner. As I plan this meal I feel a little the way Napoleon would have felt while designing the Russian campaign, if he had known exactly what the outcome would be.

I long to be with Milena, not just now but all the time. Why am I a human being? I ask myself—what an extremely vague condition! Why can't I be the happy wardrobe in her room?

Before I knew my dear Milena, I thought life itself was unbearable. Then she came into my life and showed me that that was not so. True, our first meeting was not auspicious, for her mother answered the door, and what a strong forehead the woman had, with an inscription on it that read: "I am dead, and I despise anyone who is not." Milena seemed pleased that I had come, but much more pleased when I left. That day, I happened to look at a map of the city. For a moment it seemed incomprehensible to me that anyone would build a whole city when all that was needed was a room for her.

•

Perhaps, in the end, the simplest thing would be to make for her exactly what I made for Felice, but with more care, so that nothing goes wrong, and without the snails or the mushrooms. I could even include the sauerbraten, though when I cooked it for Felice, I was still eating meat. At that time I was not bothered by the thought that an animal, too, has a right to a good life and perhaps even more important a good death. Now I can't even eat snails. My father's father was a butcher and I vowed that the same quantity of meat he butchered in his lifetime was the quantity I would not eat in my own lifetime. For a long time now I have not tasted meat, though I eat milk and butter, but for Milena, I would make sauerbraten again.

My own appetite is never large. I am thinner than I should be, but I have been thin for a long time. Some years ago, for instance, I often went rowing on the Moldau in a small boat. I would row upriver and then lie on my back in the bottom of the boat and drift back down with the current. A friend once happened to be crossing a bridge and saw me floating along under it. He said it was as if Judgment Day had arrived and my coffin had been opened. But then he himself had grown almost fat by then, massive, and knew little about thin people except that they were thin. At least this weight on my feet is really my own property.

She may not even want to come anymore, not because she is fickle, but because she is exhausted, which is understandable. If she does not come it would be wrong to say I will miss her, because she is always so present in my imagination. Yet she will be at a different address and I will be sitting at the kitchen table with my face in my hands.

If she comes, I will smile and smile, I have inherited this

from an old aunt of mine who also used to smile incessantly, but both of us out of embarrassment rather than good humor or compassion. I won't be able to speak, I won't even be happy, because after the preparation of the meal I won't have the strength. And if, with my sorry excuse for a first course resting in a bowl in my hands, I hesitate to leave the kitchen and enter the dining room, and if she, at the same time, feeling my embarrassment, hesitates to leave the living room and enter the dining room from the other side, then for that long interval the beautiful room will be empty.

Ah, well—one man fights at Marathon, the other in the kitchen.

Still, I have decided on nearly all the menu now and I have begun to prepare it by imagining our dinner, every detail of it, from beginning to end. I repeat this sentence to myself senselessly, my teeth chattering: "Then we'll run into the forest." Senselessly, because there is no forest here, and there would be no question of running in any case.

I have faith that she will come, though along with my faith is the same fear that always accompanies my faith, the fear that has been inherent in all faith, anyway, since the beginning of time.

Felice and I were not engaged at the time of that unfortunate dinner, though we had been engaged three years before and were to be engaged again one week later—surely not as a result of the dinner, unless Felice's compassion for me was further aroused by the futility of my efforts to make a good kasha varnishke, potato pancakes, and sauerbraten. Our eventual breakup, on the other hand, probably has more explanations than it really needs—this is ridiculous, but certain experts maintain that even the air here in this city may encourage inconstancy.

I was excited as one always is by something new. I was naturally somewhat frightened as well. I thought a traditional German or Czech meal might be best, even if rather heavy for July. I remained for some time undecided even in my dreams. At one point I simply gave up and contemplated leaving the city. Then I decided to stay, although simply lying around on the balcony may not really deserve to be called a decision. At these times I appear to be paralyzed with indecision while my thoughts are beating furiously within my head, just as a dragonfly appears to hang motionless in midair while its wings are beating furiously against the steady breeze. At last I jumped up like a stranger pulling another stranger out of bed.

The fact that I planned the meal carefully was probably insignificant. I wanted to prepare something wholesome, since she needed to build up her strength. I remember gathering the mushrooms in the early morning, creeping among the trees in plain sight of two elderly sisters—who appeared to disapprove deeply of me or my basket. Or perhaps of the fact that I was wearing a good suit in the forest. But their approval would have been more or less the same thing.

As the hour approached, I was afraid, for a little while, that she would not come, instead of being afraid, as I should have been, that she would in fact come. At first she had said she might not come. It was strange of her to do that. I was like an errand boy who could no longer run errands but still hoped for some kind of employment.

Just as a very small animal in the woods makes a disproportionate amount of noise and disturbance among the leaves and twigs on the ground when it is frightened and rushes to its hole, or even when it is not frightened but merely hunting for nuts, so that one thinks a bear is about to burst into the clearing, whereas it is only a mouse—this is what my emotion was like, so small and yet so noisy. I asked her please not to come to dinner, but then I asked her please not to listen to me but to come anyway. Our words are so often those of some unknown, alien being. I don't believe any speeches anymore. Even the most beautiful speech contains a worm.

Once, when we ate together in a restaurant, I was as ashamed of the dinner as though I had made it myself. The very first thing they brought to the table ruined our appetite for the rest, even if it had been any good: fat white *Leberknödeln* floating in a thin broth whose surface was dotted with oil. The dish was clearly German, rather than Czech. But why should anything be more complicated between us than if we were to sit quietly in a park and watch a hummingbird fly up from the petunias to rest at the top of a birch tree?

The night of our dinner, I told myself that if she did not come, I would enjoy the empty apartment, for if being alone in a room is necessary for life itself, being alone in an apartment is necessary if one is to be happy. I had borrowed the apartment for the occasion. But I had not been enjoying the happiness of the empty apartment. Or perhaps it wasn't the empty apartment that should have made me happy, but having two apartments. She did come, but she was late. She told me she had been delayed because she had had to wait to speak to a man who had himself been waiting, impatiently, for the outcome of a discussion concerning the opening of a new cabaret. I did not believe her.

When she walked in the door I was almost disappointed. She would have been so much happier dining with another man. She was going to bring me a flower, but appeared without it. Yet I was filled with such elation just to be with her, because of her love, and her kindness, as bright as the buzzing of a fly on a lime twig.

Despite our discomfort we proceeded with our dinner. As I gazed at the finished dish I lamented my waning strength, I lamented being born, I lamented the light of the sun. We ate something that unfortunately would not disappear from our plates unless we swallowed it. I was both moved and ashamed, happy and sad, that she ate with apparent enjoyment—ashamed and sad only that I did not have something better to offer her, moved and happy that it appeared to be enough, at least on this one occasion. It was only the grace with which she ate each part of the meal and the delicacy of her compliments that gave it any value—it was abysmally bad. She really deserved, instead, something like a baked sole or a breast of pheasant, with water ice and fruit from Spain. Couldn't I have provided this, somehow?

And when her compliments faltered, the language itself became pliant just for her, and more beautiful than one had any right to expect. If an uninformed stranger had heard Felice he would have thought, What a man! He must have moved mountains!—whereas I did almost nothing but mix the kasha as instructed by Ottla. I hoped that after she went away she would find a cool place like a garden in which to lie down on a deck chair and rest. As for myself, this pitcher was broken long before it went to the well.

There was the accident, too. I realized I was kneeling only when I saw her feet directly in front of my eyes. Snails were everywhere on the carpet, and the smell of garlic.

Perhaps, even so, once the meal was behind us, we did arithmetic tricks at the table, I don't remember, short sums, and then long sums while I gazed out the window at the building opposite. Perhaps we would have played music together instead, but I am not musical.

Our conversation was halting and awkward. I kept digressing senselessly, out of nervousness. Finally I told her I was losing my way, but it didn't matter because if she had come that far with me then we were both lost. There were so many misunderstandings, even when I did stay on the subject. And yet she shouldn't have been afraid that I was angry at her, but the opposite, that I wasn't.

She thought I had an Aunt Klara. It is true that I have an Aunt Klara, every Jew has an Aunt Klara. But mine died long ago. She said her own was quite peculiar, and inclined to make pronouncements, such as that one should stamp one's letters properly and not throw things out the window, both of which are true, of course, but not easy. We talked about the Germans. She hates the Germans so much, but I told her she shouldn't, because the Germans are wonderful. Perhaps my mistake was to boast that I had recently chopped wood for over an hour. I thought she should be grateful to me—after all, I was overcoming the temptation to say something unkind.

One more misunderstanding and she was ready to leave. We tried different ways of saying what we meant, but we weren't really lovers at that moment, just grammarians. Even animals, when they're quarreling, lose all caution: squirrels race back and forth across a lawn or a road and forget that there may be predators watching. I told her that if she were to leave, the only thing I would like about it would be the kiss before she left. She assured me that although we were parting in anger, it would not be long before we saw each other again, but to my mind "sooner" rather than "never" was still just "never." Then she left.

With that loss I was more in the situation of Robinson Crusoe even than Robinson Crusoe himself—he at least still had the island, Friday, his supplies, his goats, the ship that took him away, his name. But as for me, I imagined some doctor with carbolic fingers taking my head between his knees and stuffing meat into my mouth and down my throat until I choked.

The evening was over. A goddess had walked out of the movie theater and a small porter was left standing by the tracks—and that was our dinner? I am so filthy—this is why I am always screaming about purity. No one sings as purely as those who inhabit the deepest hell—you think you're hearing the song of angels but it is that other song. Yet I decided to keep on living a little while longer, at least through the night.

After all, I am not graceful. Someone once said that I swim like a swan, but it was not a compliment.

Tropical Storm

Like a tropical storm,
I, too, may one day become "better organized."

Good Times

What was happening to them was that every bad time produced a bad feeling that in turn produced several more bad times and several more bad feelings, so that their life together became crowded with bad times and bad feelings, so crowded that almost nothing else could grow in that dark field. But then she had a feeling of peace one morning that lingered from the evening before spent sewing while he sat reading in the next room. And a day or two later, she had a feeling of contentment that lingered in the morning from the evening before when he kept her company in the kitchen while she washed the dinner dishes. If the good times increased, she thought, each good time might produce a good feeling that would in turn produce several more good times that would produce several more good feelings. What she meant was that the good times might multiply perhaps as rapidly as the square of the square, or perhaps more rapidly, like mice, or like mushrooms springing up overnight from the scattered spore of a parent mushroom that in turn had sprung up overnight with a crowd of others from the scattered spore of a parent, until her life with him would be so crowded with good times that the good times might crowd out the bad as the bad times had by now almost crowded out the good.

Idea for a Short Documentary Film

Representatives of different food products manufacturers try to open their own packaging.

Forbidden Subjects

Soon almost every subject they might want to talk about is associated with yet another unpleasant scene and becomes a subject they can't talk about, so that as time goes by there is less and less they can safely talk about, and eventually little else but the news and what they're reading, though not all of what they're reading. They can't talk about certain members of her family, his working hours, her working hours, rabbits, mice, dogs, certain foods, certain universities, hot weather, hot and cold room temperatures at night and in the day, lights on and lights off in the evening in summer, the piano, music in general, how much money he earns, what she earns, what she spends, etc. But one day, after they have been talking about a forbidden subject, though not the most dangerous of the forbidden subjects, she realizes it may be possible, sometimes, to say something calm and careful about a forbidden subject, so that it may once again become a subject that can be talked about, and then to say something calm and careful about another forbidden subject, so that there will be another subject that can be talked about once again, and that as more subjects can be talked about once again there will be, gradually, more talk between them, and that as there is more talk there will be more trust, and that when there is enough trust, they may dare to approach even the most dangerous of the forbidden subjects.

Two Types

Excitable

A woman was depressed and distraught for days after losing her pen.

Then she became so excited about an ad for a shoe sale that she drove three hours to a shoe store in Chicago.

Phlegmatic

A man spotted a fire in a dormitory one evening, and walked away to look for an extinguisher in another building. He found the extinguisher, and walked back to the fire with it.

The Senses

Many people treat their five senses with a certain respect and consideration. They take their eyes to a museum, their nose to a flower show, their hands to a fabric store for the velvet and silk; they surprise their ears with a concert, and excite their mouth with a restaurant meal.

But most people make their senses work hard for them day after day: Read me this newspaper! Pay attention, nose, in case the food is burning! Ears!—get together now and listen for a knock at the door!

Their senses have jobs to do and they do them, mostly—the ears of the deaf won't, and the eyes of the blind won't.

The senses get tired. Sometimes, long before the end, they say, I'm quitting—I'm getting out of this *now.*

And then the person is less prepared to meet the world, and stays at home more, without some of what he needs if he is to go on.

If it all quits on him, he is really alone: in the dark, in silence, numb hands, nothing in his mouth, nothing in his nostrils. He asks himself, Did I treat them wrong? Didn't I show them a good time?

Grammar Questions

Now, during the time he is dying, can I say, "This is where he lives"?

If someone asks me, "Where does he live?" should I answer, "Well, right now he is not living, he is dying"?

If someone asks me, "Where does he live?" can I say, "He lives in Vernon Hall"? Or should I say, "He is dying in Vernon Hall"?

When he is dead, I will be able to say, in the past tense, "He lived in Vernon Hall." I will also be able to say, "He died in Vernon Hall."

When he is dead, everything to do with him will be in the past tense. Or rather, the sentence "He is dead" will be in the present tense, and also questions such as "Where are they taking him?" or "Where is he now?"

But then I won't know if the words *he* and *him* are correct, in the present tense. Is he, once he is dead, still "he," and if so, for how long is he still "he"?

People may say "the body" and then call it "it." I will not be able to say "the body" in relation to him because to me he is still not something you would call "the body."

People may say "his body," but that does not seem right either. It is not "his" body because he does not own it, if he is no longer active or capable of owning anything.

•

I don't know if there is a "he," even though people will say "He is dead." But it does seem correct to say "He is dead." This may be the last time he will still be "he" in the present tense. Or it will not be the last time, because I will also say, "He is lying in his coffin." I will not say, and no one will say, "It is lying in the coffin," or "It is lying in its coffin."

I will continue to say "my father" in relation to him, after he dies, but will I say it only in the past tense, or also in the present tense?

He will be put in a box, not a coffin. Then, when he is in that box, will I say, "That is my father in that box," or "That was my father in that box," or will I say, "That, in the box, was my father"?

I will still say "my father," but maybe I will say it only as long as he looks like my father, or approximately like my father. Then, when he is in the form of ashes, will I point to the ashes and say, "That is my father"? Or will I say, "That was my father"? Or "Those ashes were my father"? Or "Those ashes are what was my father"?

When I later visit the graveyard, will I point and say, "My father is buried there," or will I say, "My father's ashes are buried there"? But the ashes will not belong to my father, he will not own them. They will be "the ashes that were my father."

In the phrase "he is dying," the words *he is* with the present participle suggest that he is actively doing something. But he is not actively dying. The only thing he is still actively doing is breathing. He looks as if he is breathing on purpose, because he is working hard at it, and frowning slightly. He is working at it, but surely he has no choice. Sometimes his frown deepens for just an instant, as though something is hurting him, or as though he is concentrating harder. Even though I can guess that he is frowning because of some pain inside him, or some other change, he still looks as though he is puzzled, or dislikes or disapproves of something. I've seen this expression on his face often in my life, though never before combined with these half-open eyes and this open mouth.

"He is dying" sounds more active than "He will be dead soon." That is probably because of the word *be*—we can "be" something whether we choose to or not. Whether he likes it or not, he "will be" dead soon. He is not eating.

"He is not eating" sounds active, too. But it is not his choice. He is not conscious that he is not eating. He is not conscious at all. But "is not eating" sounds more correct for him than "is dying" because of the negative. "Is not" seems correct for him, at the moment anyway, because he looks as though he is refusing something, because he is frowning.

Hand

Beyond the hand holding this book that I'm reading, I see another hand lying idle and slightly out of focus—my extra hand.

The Caterpillar

I find a small caterpillar in my bed in the morning. There is no good window to throw him from and I don't crush or kill a living thing if I don't have to. I will go to the trouble of carrying this thin, dark, hairless little caterpillar down the stairs and out to the garden.

He is not an inchworm, though he is the size of an inchworm. He does not hump up in the middle but travels steadily along on his many pairs of legs. As I leave the bedroom, he is quite speedily walking around the slopes of my hand.

But halfway down the stairs, he is gone—my hand is blank on every side. The caterpillar must have let go and dropped. I can't see him. The stairwell is dim and the stairs are painted dark brown. I could get a flashlight and search for this tiny thing, in order to save his life. But I will not go that far—he will have to do the best he can. Yet how can he make his way down to the back door and out into the garden?

I go on about my business. I think I've forgotten him, but I haven't. Every time I go upstairs or down, I avoid his side of the stairs. I am sure he is there trying to get down.

At last I give in. I get the flashlight. Now the trouble is

that the stairs are so dirty. I don't clean them because no one ever sees them here in the dark. And the caterpillar is, or was, so small. Many things under the beam of the flashlight look rather like him—a very slim splinter of wood or a thick piece of thread. But when I poke them, they don't move.

I look on every step on his side of the stairs, and then on both sides. You get somewhat attached to any living thing once you try to help it. But he is nowhere. There is so much dust and dog hair on the steps. The dust may have stuck to his little body and made it hard for him to move or at least to go in the direction he wanted to go in. It may have dried him out. But why would he even go down instead of up? I haven't looked on the landing above where he disappeared. I will not go that far.

I go back to my work. Then I begin to forget the caterpillar. I forget him for as long as one hour, until I happen to go to the stairs again. This time I see that there is something just the right size, shape, and color on one of the steps. But it is flat and dry. It can't have started out as him. It must be a short pine needle or some other plant part.

The next time I think of him, I see that I have forgotten him for several hours. I think of him only when I go up or down the stairs. After all, he is really there somewhere, trying to find his way to a green leaf, or dying. But already I don't care as much. Soon, I'm sure, I will forget him entirely.

Later there is an unpleasant animal smell lingering about the stairwell, but it can't be him. He is too small to have any smell. He has probably died by now. He is simply too small, really, for me to go on thinking about him.

Child Care

It's his turn to take care of the baby. He is cross.

He says, "I never get enough done."

The baby is in a bad mood, too.

He gives the baby a bottle of juice and sits him well back in a big armchair.

He sits himself down in another chair and turns on the television.

Together they watch *The Odd Couple.*

We Miss You: A Study of Get-Well Letters from a Class of Fourth-Graders

The following is a study of twenty-seven get-well letters written by a class of fourth-graders to their classmate Stephen, when he was in the hospital recovering from a serious case of osteomyelitis.

The disease set in after a rather mysterious accident involving a car. Young Stephen, according to his own later report and a brief notice in the local newspaper, was returning home by himself at dusk one day in early December. He stepped into the street, preparing to cross, and was hit obliquely by a slow-moving car, not with great force, but with enough force to knock him to the ground. The driver of the car, a man of indeterminate age, stopped and got out to see if the boy was all right. Ascertaining that no great harm had been done, the man drove on. In fact, the boy had hurt his knee but said nothing about the accident at home, out of embarrassment or a perception that he was somehow to blame. The knee, untreated, became infected; the osteomyelitis bacteria entering the wound; the boy became seriously ill and was hospitalized. After some weeks, and worry on the part of his doctors, family, and friends, he recovered, thanks in part to the recently developed drug penicillin, and was discharged.

At the time of Stephen's hospitalization, his parents put the following notice in the local paper in an attempt to locate the driver of the car. The notice was headlined PARENTS SEEK TO TALK TO DRIVER OF CAR IN ACCIDENT. It read:

> About the first week of December, Stephen, son of Mr. and Mrs. B. of 94 N. Rd., at the corner of Elm and Crescent Streets in the late afternoon, was struck very lightly by a car whose driver got out and looked the boy over and discussed it with him. Then each went on his way.
>
> The parents of the boy would like to get in touch with the driver of the vehicle and are appealing to him to communicate with them.

There was no response to the notice.

After the Christmas holidays were over and his classmates returned to school, the children's teacher, Miss F., assigned them to write Stephen a get-well letter. She then corrected the letters sparingly but precisely and sent them in a packet to Stephen. This was a school exercise clearly intended, if we may judge from the number of consistent features, to teach certain letter-writing skills.

The School

The school in which these letters were written was a large brick building dedicated to use by classes from kindergarten through eighth grade and situated in the heart of a pleasant residential neighborhood. The streets were lined with mature shade trees, and the houses were for the most part roomy and comfortable but unostentatious middle-class homes with modest or, occasionally, generous yards planted with lawns and a variety of trees, shrubs, and flowers. Most of the children lived in the immediate neighborhood of the school and walked to and from school by themselves or with friends on sidewalks that were well maintained but here and there cracked or buckled by the roots of the large trees. Stephen himself, along with his neighbors Carol and Jonathan, lived one street over from the school. At the corner of the street on which the school stood was a small store owned and presided over by a matronly woman with a rather forbidding manner. It sold candy and a limited range of groceries, and was heavily patronized by the children after school. Across from this store, a street descended steeply toward a broad, shallow river in which the children were not allowed to swim because of effluents from the factories upstream. The school building was surrounded by a large asphalt playground lacking climbing or swinging equipment. The classrooms were well lighted, with natural daylight coming in through large windows.

General Appearance and Form of the Letters

The letters are written on lined exercise paper of two different sizes, most of them on the smaller, 7″ by 8½″, four of them on the larger, 8″ by 10½″. Although the paper is of a low grade and was manufactured nearly sixty years ago, it has remained supple and smooth in texture, and the letters are still clearly legible, some students in particular having borne down heavily to make very dark and distinct lines. They are all written in ink, though the ink varies, some blue and some black, some dark and some light, some lines thin and some thick.

The penmanship is for the most part quite good, i.e., the script slopes at a fairly consistent angle to the right, most letters touch the line, the letters are evenly spaced, the uprights of the letters do not touch the line above, etc., though the variations in thickness of line and formation of letters, as well as the wavering lines, betray the tremulous hands and labored efforts of the novice script users. Some of the capitals, however, are very elegantly formed, with a handsome flourish.

There are twenty-seven letters altogether, written by thirteen girls and fourteen boys. Twenty-four of the children's letters are dated January 4, evidently the day on which the teacher set them to work as a group; two are dated January 5, and one January 8, implying that these children were absent on the day the exercise was initiated.

The letters all carry the same heading, obviously prescribed by the teacher, on three lines in the upper-right-hand corner: the name of the school; the town and state; and the date. They are ruled by hand in pencil down the left margin to provide a uniform indented guide for the beginning of each line, with the exception of the January 8 letter—this latecomer evidently was not given the instruction or did not hear it—and those written on the larger sheets of paper, which bear a printed rule down the left margin. The hand-ruled lines vary: some are thin and straight, others thick and slanted, and one trails off at an angle at the bottom, the pupil having evidently reached the end of his ruler before he reached the bottom of the page.

The salutations are all the same: "Dear Stephen." The closings vary within a narrow range: "Your friend" (5 boys and 10 girls); "Your classmate" (3 girls and 2 boys); "Your pal" (4 boys); "Sincerely yours" (1 boy); "Love" (1 boy); and "Your pal of pals" (1 boy: this was Jonathan, a close friend). It should be noted that only the boys use the colloquial *pal*, whereas nearly twice as many girls as boys use the more formal *friend*.

The teacher has inked in corrections on some of the letters, in the darkest ink and a smaller hand. She has added commas where missing (most frequently after the salutation, "Dear Stephen," the closing, e.g. "Your friend," and between the name of the town and the state) and question marks where required. She has corrected some misspellings ("happey," "sleding," "throught," "brouther," and "We are mississ you very much"). In one case she has, surprisingly, had to correct the spelling of a child's name, reducing "Arilene" to "Arlene." She has supplied two missing words. Several errors have escaped her notice. On the whole, the letters are spelled and punctuated correctly; the teacher makes, on average, only about one correction per page, and most of these are punctuation corrections. Either the students have learned their lessons very well or, perhaps more likely, these are fair copies of rough, corrected drafts.

Twenty-two children sign their full names, first and last. One signs "Billy J." and the remaining four sign only their first names. (For reasons of confidentiality, only the initial letter of the children's last names will be retained here.)

Length

Excluding the salutation and closing, the letters range in length from three to eight lines and from two to eight sentences. None of the boys' letters is longer than five sentences, whereas, of the girls, one each has a letter containing six, seven, and eight sentences. Although the girls number one fewer than the boys, they are overall more communicative, contributing 84 lines versus the boys' 66, and 61 sentences versus the boys' 53.

Not all of the girls, however, are communicative. Two write letters containing only three lines and three sentences. One is the gloomy letter by Sally quoted below. The second brief letter, by Susan B., includes what may be an envious reference to a box of candy. In general, the length and content of the shortest letters appear to connote depressive or apathetic states of mind in their authors, while the content and length of the longest give the impression of being the products of the more cheerful and outgoing temperaments. Those in the midlength range variously express stout realism (broken branches and fallen snowmen), bland formulae (see Maureen's letter below), or strong feelings and personality (Scott's "I'd yank you out of bed").

Overall Coherence

There is a tendency toward non sequiturs in the letters: one sentence often has little to do with the sentence that follows or precedes it (e.g., "The temperature keeps on changing. I can't wait until you come back to school").

Some letters, however, develop one idea with perfect cogency throughout: e.g., Sally's grim letter, Scott's enthusiastic, somewhat violent letter threatening to "yank" Stephen out of bed, and Alex's informative letter about sledding, which names the location of the sledding and notes progress from last year—"We had some fun over at Hospital Hill. We went over a big bump and went flying through the air. This year I went on a higher part than I used to."

Sentence Structures

The letters overall contain a predominance of simple sentences (e.g., "There was a big snowball fight outside"), with now and then a compound, complex, or compound-complex sentence.

Compound Sentences

The shortest letter (two sentences) is written by Peter. He is the same boy whose ruled line is thick, slanted, and bent at the bottom. However, he is also one of the few students to form a compound sentence, and in so doing uses the rarer and more interesting conjunction *but*: "We are having a very happy time but we miss you."

Another who uses *but* is Cynthia, one of the realists in the class: "I have made snowmen but they have fallen down."

Susan A., another realist, uses *but* to modify her description of fairyland, as quoted below.

Other conjunctions used in the letters are: *until* (2), *because* (2), and the most common and inexpressive or neutral: *and* (7).

One girl, Carol, using the conjunction *because*, forms two compound sentences in a letter that is only three sentences long: "I hope you will be back to school very soon because it is lonesome without you" and "New Year's Eve your [little] Sister slept at our house because your Mother and Father and [older] Sister went to a party." Because she employs more elaborate sentence structures, her letter is one of those containing the most lines (8) yet the fewest sentences (3).

The most common, and least expressive, conjunction is *and* (7 occurrences), as in Alex's sentence: "We went over a big bump and went flying through the air." One girl, Diane, forms a compound sentence out of two imperatives: "Hurry up and come back."

Complex Sentences

Aside from the frequent formulaic complex sentences beginning with "I hope" (e.g., "I hope you get better") and "I wish" (e.g., "I wish you saw it"), there are relatively few instances of complex sentences:

Fred: "Well I guess this is all I have to tell you."

Theodore: "I beat the boys who were against me."

Alex: "This year I went on a higher part than I used to."

Susan B.: "Jonathan A. told me that he send [*sic*] you a big box of candy."

Kingsley has two complex sentences in succession: "What do you think you are going to get for Christmas?" and "I got every thing I wanted to get."

Compound-Complex Sentences

Van, the boy who admits to being uninspired and writes one of the briefest letters, is also, however, one of the few pupils to construct a compound-complex sentence, though he omits two words and contradicts himself (see his use of *think*): "I think that is all to say [*sic*] because I just can't think."

Jonathan also constructs a compound-complex sentence. His is more cheerful but uses a less expressive conjunction: "I hope you liked my box of candy, and I can hardly wait until you will be home again."

Susan A. uses the more loaded conjunction *but*: "When it was over everything looked like a fairyland but some trees were bent and broken." She follows this sentence with another compound-complex sentence, using the strong conjunction *so* and including an imperative: "We are very sorry that you are in the hospital, so get well quick."

Verbs

Some of the children's verb tenses are unclear.

Apropos a movie, Theodore writes: "I wish you saw it." It is unclear whether he means "I wish you could see it" or "I wish you had seen it."

Billy T. writes: "I hope you will eat well." It is not clear when or where Stephen should eat well.

Joseph A. writes: "I hope you have fun." It is not clear when or where Stephen should have fun. Both Billy and Joseph probably intended the meaning conveyed by the present participle forms "are eating well" and "are having fun." It may be noted that Joseph is the only child to associate Stephen's stay in the hospital with having fun.

The most vivid verb is Scott's Anglo-Saxon *yank*.

Imperatives

The only instances of use of the imperative (4, one softened by "Please") are found in the letters of girls. This may imply a greater inclination to "command" or "boss" on the part of the girls than the boys, but may also be statistically insignificant, given the small number of letters in the sample.

Style

The style of the letters is for the most part informal, i.e., neither excessively formal nor extremely casual or colloquial. Occasionally, the diction becomes conversational: there are two instances of *Well* as openings of sentences (both omit the comma that should follow). There is a vivid conversational verb, *yank*, in Scott's letter. It is worth noting, however, a conspicuous formality common to most of the children on at least one point: given a choice, as they seem to have been, most of the children sign their full names to their letters. Also, in the two instances in which children refer to other children by name, they use the full name, even though Stephen would have known perfectly well from the context which child they were talking about. It may be that in the school setting, first and last names were so commonly used inseparably by the teacher in calling the roll or in reprimanding, that when writing in school, in any case, the children profoundly identified one another and themselves by first and last names both.

Two of the children achieve moments of stylistic eloquence. One, Susan A., creates a vivid concrete image that is enhanced by her use of alliteration and a forceful rhythm: "some trees were bent and broken." The other, Sally, opens with a powerful specific image—"Your seat is empty"—and then reinforces it with parallel structure: "Your stocking is not finished."

It could be argued that Scott, too, achieves a certain pleasing balance with his alternation, in the four sentences of his cogent letter, between "over there" and "here where we are," "up there" and "back here again," in fact creating a seesaw motion and thereby tying Stephen more closely to the class than any of the other children.

Content

Some of the letters are bland and/or inexpressive, while others are more informative and more colorful, and/or express their writers' personalities more vividly.

Probably the blandest letter, in that it includes all the most commonly expressed formulaic sentiments and only the most general "news," with no departures from convention in content or style that would express an individual personality, is Maureen's. Although it is undeniably friendly and cheerful, the friendliness and cheerfulness seem somewhat rote: "How are you feeling? I miss you very much. I hope that you will be back in school soon. I like school very much. I had a very nice time in the snow." Her handwriting is round and slants consistently to the right with one notable exception: the word *I*, which is vertical. It may not be going too far to suggest that these markedly contrasting *I*'s express a sublimated rebelliousness, a suppressed desire to be less conformist and obedient than she evidently is.

Another fairly bland letter, in a small, round script, is Mary's, although she is slightly more emphatic than Maureen—"We all miss you very much"—and adds one specific: "I have had lots of fun playing with my sled in the snow."

The content can be generally summarized as falling under the following headings, within the two more general categories of expressions of sympathy and "news":

Formulaic Expressions of Sympathy

come back soon/wish you were here
(17 occurrences in 27 letters)
how are you/hope you are feeling better (16)
miss you (9)
experience in hospital/food (4)
empathy: I know how it feels (2)

News

playing in snow (9)
Christmas/Christmas presents (7)
school/schoolwork (4)
eating/food (4)
weather (3)
shopping with parent (2)

movies (2)
pets (1)
New Year's Eve (1)
Stephen's family (1)
party (1)

FORMULAIC EXPRESSIONS OF SYMPATHY

Miss You

Many of the children's letters include the standard "We [or I] miss you" or "We [or I] miss you very much," often paired with "We [or I] hope you will be back soon."

Van opens with those two sentiments and then finds himself at a loss: in thin, tremulous handwriting, with so little space between the words that they almost touch, he closes with "I think that is all to say [*sic*] because I just can't think." Some of Van's letters sit nicely on the line, some float up above it, and some sink below it. It is possible, in his case—as in others in which the child betrays some anxiety—that the letters do not sit on the line because the child is overcompensating: for fear of letting his letters sink below the line, he keeps them up off the line; for fear of letting them float up off the line, he forces them down below it. We must remember, when imagining these children learning to write neat script, that a line is not an actual resting place for a letter. It is a conceptual mark, and a very thin one, and a beginning writer finds it difficult to touch that line exactly with each letter. There is thus a certain amount of anxiety, for some children, even in the act of writing script, regardless of what they are trying to express.

Joan is more specific, and thus more poignant, immediately evoking the classroom: "I miss you in our row in school." She conveys, in addition, a sense of solidarity among the children in that particular row—"our row."

Sally is even more specific, and her letter, though one of the briefest, carries the most powerful, and the darkest, emotional burden: "Hope you are feeling better. Your seat is empty. Your stocking is not finished." This last sentence is followed by a period, but then, ambiguously, by a lowercase *b*, so that we cannot be sure whether Sally meant to continue the sentence or begin a new one when she goes on to say, again dwelling on darker possibilities: "but I don't think it will be finished." The function of the *but* is also unclear. Sally's handwriting is faint and thin, and the letters extremely small, except when, as she has evidently mistaken the teacher's instructions, the tall letters such as *f* and *l* extend hesitantly all the way up to touch the line above. The content, along with the brevity of the letter and Sally's small handwriting, would seem to indicate either an innate pessimism or a low self-esteem, despite the quite exceptional exuberance and panache of her capital *H*.

How Are You/Hope You Are Feeling Better

Another commonly expressed sentiment is: "We [or I] hope you are feeling well/will feel better soon/will get well soon/how are you feeling?"

Billy J. opens with "I hope you are feeling well," closes with "I hope you will be back soon," and adds only one sentence in between: "We are not doing much." The words *not doing much* are smaller and more compact than the rest, perhaps reflecting the content of the remark. Billy's letters also tend to sink below the line, according well in spirit with his only news—that not much is being accomplished.

Lois strikes a conversational note that is stylistically unusual among the letters when she writes, in bold black script that sits squarely on the line but sometimes disappears off the right side of the page: "How are you feeling now? Better, I hope."

Joseph A., instead of writing "How are you?" writes "How do you?" The teacher does not notice this.

Come Back Soon/Wish You Were Here

Lois, who manages eight sentences within the space of her six lines, expresses this sentiment twice, once at the beginning—"When will you be back?"—and once, employing a courteous command, at the end—"Please try to come back soon."

Carol's letter, as quoted above, adds the intensifying explanation "because it is lonesome without you"—either quite sincere, since she lives next door to Stephen and may be a close friend, or at least polite. It should be noted that Carol stands in a privileged relationship to Stephen, since their families are also friends, as her letter clearly indicates.

The enthusiastic Joseph goes farther, expressing impatience: "I can't wait until you come back to school."

Stephen's friend Jonathan, whose handwriting is well rounded and upright, each letter sitting firmly on the line, uses almost the same words: "I can hardly wait until you will be home again." Presumably, Jonathan replaces the more common "back to school" with "home again" because he is not only a good friend but a neighbor.

One girl, Diane, expresses the same sentiment in almost the same words—"I can hardly wait for you to come back to school"—and then reinforces it with a second sentence that employs two imperatives: "Hurry up and come back."

Her friend Mary K. expresses it more precisely and rather severely, hoping that Stephen "will be back in school in a very short time."

Billy T. emphasizes Stephen's discharge from the hospital rather than his return to school. He also devotes two of the three sentences of his brief letter to this idea: "When will you be out? I hope you will be out soon."

Another boy, Scott, expresses this sentiment in one of the most cogent letters, in which each sentence follows logically from the one preceding. He begins with empathy, "I know how it feels over there," and then develops his idea, first repeating his expression of empathy (unusual among the letters): "I think you would like to be here where we are." Now he adds a note of drama, along with a rare use of the subjunctive: "And if I were up there I'd yank you out of bed." Finally he completes his back-and-forth structure with another reference to the school and the logical—"Then"—result of his imagined action: "Then you could be back here again." (Scott's phrases "over there" and "up there" signal his awareness that the hospital is some distance from the town and on an elevated site, a fact supported by Jonathan's identical use of "up there" and a third child's reference to "Hospital Hill" in a description of sledding.)

One girl, Susan B., in one of the briefer letters (three lines, three sentences), expresses only the common sentiments and then adds the wistful secondhand report: "Jonathan A. told me that he send [*sic*] you a big box of candy." Her handwriting changes noticeably in the latter part of this sentence: dark, upright, and confident at the start of her letter, the words become increasingly faint and slant more and more to the right until the word *candy*, thin and delicate, is lying almost on its side.

Experience in Hospital/Food

Only a few children express curiosity about Stephen's experience in the hospital.

Kingsley asks: "Do you like it at the hospital?"

Stephen's good friend Jonathan, too, is interested: "How is it up there?"

Stephen's next-door neighbor, Carol, is more specific: "Do you have good meals there?"

Billy T. is also concerned about Stephen's food, presumably in the hospital, although his use of the future tense makes this somewhat unclear: "I hope you will eat well."

Arlene, who was evidently not sure how to spell her own name, or perhaps chose to decorate it with the added *i*, brings a tone of urgency or even peremptoriness to her letter, with her two brief but exact questions: "Who is your nurse? Who is your doctor?" We understand, however, when we come to the last sentence in her letter, that her interest may be "professional": "I got a nurse kit for Christmas."

Empathy: I Know How It Feels

Scott opens with a display of empathy—"I know how it feels over there"—before threatening to visit Stephen.

Joseph O. also opens with what seems to be generous empathy: "I know how you feel." But he then continues with an apparent non sequitur: "I am going to get a new coat with a hood."

News

Weather

A few children mention the weather.

Joseph A. says, laconically or reasonably: "The temperature keeps on changing."

Cynthia, who has a good understanding of the importance of accuracy and detail (see below), writes: "It's very icey [*sic*] out today."

Another girl, Susan A., is more poetical about the

weather, deploying the only metaphor in the entire sample of letters. Although the metaphor is a hackneyed one, she immediately afterward improves on it with a more powerful realistic description: "A week ago we had a sleet storm. When it was over everything looked like a fairyland but some trees were bent and broken." Her ultimately matter-of-fact and realistic approach to her surroundings is reflected in handwriting that is quite regular, except for some tremulous lines in the taller letters.

Eating/Food

Aside from the two mentions of eating in relation to Stephen's hospital experience, the only mentions of food are the two references to Jonathan's gift of the box of candy, one by Jonathan himself ("I hope you liked my box of candy") and the other by the perhaps envious Susan B.

School/Schoolwork

Aside from the commonly expressed wish that Stephen would return to school soon, school and schoolwork are not mentioned by many of the students, perhaps because they are sitting in school as they write.

Diane is the only student to mention a textbook: "We are reading in Singing Wheels." We may even posit, on the basis of her exceptional interest in this text, along with her subsequent mention of receiving a Victrola for Christmas, implying an interest in music, together with her inconsistent handwriting (letters sometimes slanted and sometimes upright, sometimes sinking below the line, etc.), that Diane is rather intellectually and artistically inclined, and "creative." At the same time, given her inclusion of her siblings in her letter (see below), as well as her friendship with Mary, and Mary's mention of their skiing, she appears to be outgoing, sociable, family-oriented, and physically active.

The above-mentioned friend, Mary K., after she describes skiing with Diane, closes her letter: "Well we are starting reading now so I will have to say, 'Good-by.' " (The teacher, although she inserted the hyphen in "Good-by," has not supplied the missing comma after "Well.") Mary is the only one to evoke the classroom at the moment the children are writing, by mentioning an imminent classroom activity. She evidently shares Diane's interest in, or enjoyment of, the class's activity of reading.

A third mention of school, but in the most general terms, is the bland remark by Maureen quoted earlier: "I like school very much." As we observed earlier, however, Maureen may not like school as much as she says she does.

A fourth girl, Lois, mentions another area of study, perhaps one that interests her more than reading: "We are still on tables." She precedes this, however, by the disclaimer: "We are not doing very much work." (It should be pointed out that despite the evident care with which the teacher has conducted this exercise, two students comment that they are "not doing much/not doing very much work." This is either true or, more likely, merely the perception of these particular students, who may, if such is the case, be either brighter and quicker to finish their work than some of the others or simply less interested. Whatever the case, the teacher has allowed these remarks to stand.)

Shopping with Parent

The children go downtown to shop, they shop for winter clothes, and they go with their mothers.

Fred writes: "My Mother and I are going downtown to get a stormcoat. My Sister is going to get a new skisuit and a hat." This is the entire content of the letter, aside from his closing sentence: "Well I guess this is all I have to tell you." (Again, the teacher has failed to supply the missing comma after "Well.")

Playing in Snow

The children are generally more expressive about their play in the snow than any other subject, sometimes providing place-names and other details.

Alex writes: "We had some fun over at Hospital Hill. We went over a big bump and went flying through the air. This year I went on a higher part than I used to." His handwriting, perhaps in keeping with his sense of adventure, is inconsistent, the letters sometimes on the line and sometimes above or below it, the ink laid down sometimes in a thin, elegant stroke, sometimes a thick, awkward one.

Two boys describe fights. John W. writes, "There was a big snowball fight outside. Almost all of the groups were fighting." Since any snowball fight would necessarily take place outside, his use of *outside* must be local and specific, indicating the school grounds, especially since only there would "almost all of the groups" be present. Stephen was evidently expected to know exactly who constituted "all of the groups."

Theodore writes: "I had a snowball fight with some boys down at my house. I beat the boys who were against me."

The realist Cynthia, not as combative as the boys, writes in firm dark ink, "I have been sliding once and I had fun. I have made snowmen but they have fallen down." The consistent slope of her letters, her sensitive use of parallel structure, and her precision as to the frequency and results of her activities suggest that she may be a good student.

Mary K. is one of only two to mention another child by name: "Last Monday Diane T. and I went skiing. There is a small jump in the hill and we had a hard time jumping it." Her somewhat stern "I hope you . . . will be back in school in a very short time," in addition to the specificity of "small jump" and "hard time," may lead us to posit that she demands a fairly high standard of performance from herself as well as from others.

Janet adds an unexpected element: "I have been sledding and skiing and the cats go with me." This may be one of the few instances, among the letters, of objectively interesting information. Before signing off, she notes, less interestingly, "They sleep with me, too."

Lois's reference to the snow is general, and therefore less interesting, but she is the only one, kindly, to include mention of Stephen in the activity: "Sorry you can't be with us in the snow."

Movies

Stephen is also included in Theodore's report of going to the movies: "A few days ago I went to see Marine Raiders and Stagecoach Kid. I wish you saw it."

John C. also writes about going to the movies and names not only the movies but the town, though his use of *And* is unclear: "I went to P. [a nearby town]. And I went to the movies once in P. I saw Branded." His script is gracefully formed but unusually consistent in sinking down slightly below the line. This may indicate a desire for more stability on his part, a fear of imagination, or, on the contrary, an unusually firmly grounded personality. His mention of the movie, however, may allow us to posit that he is attracted to works of the imagination, but at the same time reacts against their inherently unsettling presentation of an alternate reality by attempting to ground himself more firmly in his own reality.

It is notable that whereas the children are not always specific about other subjects in their letters, they take pains to supply the titles of the movies they have seen.

Christmas/Christmas Presents

Some of the children list their Christmas presents without comment. Others offer a general comment without specifying what they received.

Diane includes her siblings' presents, too: "I got a victrola for Christmas. My sister got a doll carriage. My brother got a football." It is unclear whether these were their only presents, or merely the most noteworthy.

John C., on the other hand, appears to be giving a complete list, and displays a nice sense of order in progressing from the greatest to the smallest number in his enumeration: "I got three cowboy books, two games, and a flashlight for Christmas."

Joan is not specific, but she mentions a sibling and introduces her sentence about Christmas presents with a general statement: "I had a nice Christmas. My brother and I have very nice Christmas presents."

Jonathan is one of three who ask about Stephen's presents: "Did you get alot of toys for Christmas?"

Janet is less interested in quantity and wants specifics: "What did you get for Christmas?" She follows up with a second question that could refer to both quality and quantity: "Was Santa good to you?"

Kingsley is the only one to assume, rightly or wrongly, that because Stephen is in the hospital, he has not yet celebrated Christmas: "What do you think you are going to get for Christmas?" In keeping, perhaps, with the tentative nature of his question, the word *think* rises off the line and then returns to it. He follows this question with a general statement of satisfaction: "I got every thing I wanted to get." Some of his letters are much larger than others, e.g., the *b* in *better* and the *C* in *Christmas*—both of which may have been especially significant words for this boy.

Conclusion: The Daily Lives of the Children, Their Awareness of Space and Time, and Their Characters and States of Mind

We may confidently form some idea of the children's daily lives, characters, and moods from these letters, as well as their perceptions of space and time, even though the letters may to some extent misrepresent the truth because of the circumstances under which they were written: the teacher may have limited their choices as to appropriate subjects, and was surely present at the front of the room overseeing the exercise; the children did not choose to write the letters, but were compelled to write them; they were also aware that they had only a limited amount of time in which to write them and that the next subject loomed ("Well we are starting reading now").

Daily Lives

If we are to believe most of the information contained in the letters, we may ascertain at least the following about the children: Their possessions are relatively few—in any case, they are satisfied with as few as five fairly modest Christmas presents (see John C.), although quantity is clearly of interest to them (see Jonathan). They spend time with family members and classmates. Their activities include playing in the snow (both sledding and skiing), going to the movies, shopping downtown, and occasionally traveling out of town. Some have pets and strong friendships, and some have an interest in schoolwork. Some of the boys are interested in cowboys, reading, football, and the movies; some of the girls in music, dolls, and nursing. Both boys and girls like to play outdoors.

Time

In general, the children's sense of time and place is well developed. The letters overall contain a clear sense of the past (e.g., what they got for Christmas), the present ("Your seat is empty"), and the future ("My Sister is going to get a new skisuit"). Some of the children anticipate Stephen's return in the future. Only Jonathan promises further communication: "I will send you more letters soon."

The immediate future at the time of the writing is evoked, exceptionally, by Mary K. ("Well we are starting reading now").

Place

The letters also show that the children have a clear and accurate sense of where they are in space. As they sit in their schoolroom writing, they are in fact on a higher elevation than the center of town, which they not only colloquially but also correctly refer to as "down town." They are closer to the center of town, however, than is the hospital, which they locate "over there." Their plateau is also lower than the elevation on which the hospital sits, which they refer to as "up there." "Up there" may also indicate their awareness of the fact that the hospital lies slightly to the north of the town.

It may also be pertinent to suggest that in the phrase "over there" we see a rare coincidence of actual and psychological space, in that their use of the phrase quite possibly signals an attempt on their part to distance themselves firmly from the hospital and its implied threat of death and disease.

The immediate space of the classroom is evoked by Joan and by Susan B. with their respective references to "in our row" and "Your seat is empty."

It should be noted, in addition, that some children are more preoccupied generally by the outdoors ("we went skiing") while some are more concerned with interior spaces (the classroom, row or seat; the hospital). There is also, besides the distancing "over there," a general, perhaps anxious, identification of the hospital with the direction "out" (Billy T.'s "When will you be out?") in contrast to the reassuring identification of the school with "in" and "back in" (Mary K.).

Characters and States of Mind

The teacher, though carefully controlling the form and general content of the letters, seems to have allowed the students to follow their own desires as to specific content and style, perhaps within certain limits. This being the case, the children's choices of subject matter, along with their treatment of it, may give us clues as to their different characters and temperaments.

Some children indicate a high degree of self-sufficiency, entertaining themselves (outdoor play), while others reveal some dependence on "packaged" or "ready-made" entertainment (two instances of trips to the movies). Some reveal more inclination toward activity in general, whether physical or cultural (outdoor play, movies), while others are more concerned with material acquisition (Christmas presents, shopping trips); and finally, a majority of the children focus on outer-directed or interactive activities of one kind or another (play, shopping), while a small percentage seem preoccupied by certain ideas or mental states (you are gone, your seat is empty, "I just can't think").

Some show an inclination toward an interactive social world outside the family ("Diane T. and I"), while others are oriented more toward a domestic or familial world (shopping with Mother). Including siblings in accounts of the Christmas holiday ("My sister got a doll carriage. My brother got a football") may reveal feelings of insecurity and a need to identify with the large family unit.

Some children display boldness ("I'd yank you out of bed"); or a quest for adventure ("This year I went on a higher part than I used to"); while others dwell on absence and lack ("I just can't think"; and the refrain of "I miss you" and "We miss you"). Some strike a sad note (Carol's "lonesome"; Sally's "Your seat is empty"); or hint at a feeling of failure and/or defeat (fallen snowman, bent and broken branches); or of jealousy/envy/deprivation (another child received the box of candy). Some are peremptory in their tone (the girls' use of the imperative) and some are loving (Janet's obvious fondness for her pets). Some of the children are more sensitive to difficulty and loneliness than others. But all the children are capable of expressing friendly feelings toward a classmate in an unfortunate situation, at least when they are assigned to do so.

Some of the children display contradictory traits or inner conflict, as noted in the case of Maureen above. Another case is that of Arlene: although she is eminently practical, and seems sincere in her choice of nursing as a profession, she may betray a degree of suppressed romanticism (and thus an attraction toward a less practical vocation) in her highly unusual alteration of her own name from the more down-to-earth "Arlene" to the prettier and more fanciful "Arilene."

Although the dominant mood expressed by the letters appears to be positive and optimistic, some of the children's choices of subject matter and style betray a certain fear or uneasiness, or an awareness of the darker side of their lives (snowball fight, difficulty with jump), and this generalized fear may be present in all the children to some extent (e.g., the anxious repetition of "I hope . . . I hope . . .").

In fact, although theirs would appear to have been a relatively safe world—including sledding, Christmas presents, shopping with Mother—it had its darker side: bent and broken branches, fallen snowmen, the empty seat and the unfinished stocking, the box of candy that went to another child. What did they feel as they played on Hospital Hill, with the hospital itself looming over them? Were they aware of Stephen, alone, perhaps looking out at them? Were they perhaps always half conscious that Stephen's sudden accident might equally well have happened to them? The children were, it should be kept in mind, already deeply familiar with an environment that was confusingly paradoxical and vaguely threatening: the outdoor fun of sledding and skiing could take place only within sight of the grim façade of the hospital above them; their after-school treats could be gained only through an encounter with the hostile proprietor of the corner store, and would then be unwrapped within sight of the steep drop toward the slow-moving but dangerous river. More generally, in fact, one might say that these children, caught between the implicit threat of the hospital on the hill and the more explicit threat of the river down below, may indeed have wished to slip away, as they often enough did, out of reach of both these menaces, toward "down town" with its offerings of tempting merchandise in Mother's company, or even out of town altogether (a trip to P.), or into the fictional world offered by the movie theaters, the cowboy books, and their own imaginations ("fairyland").

Addendum

Of interest, for comparison, may be a letter in Stephen's own handwriting, on an unlined page, written after he returned home, in which he thanks a former teacher for a gift evidently received during his convalescence. His letter is a rough draft, including one misspelling and one usage error, and lacking certain punctuation marks, and may closely resemble the rough drafts of his classmates' letters, if such existed. It is dated "Feb. 20 1951" and reads: "Dear Miss R., Thank you for the book. I am out of the hospital and I dont have to wear krutchs anymore Love Stephen."

Passing Wind

She didn't know if it was him or the dog. It wasn't her. The dog was lying there on the living-room rug between them, she was on the sofa, and her visitor, rather tense, was sunk deep in a low armchair, and the smell, rather gentle, came into the air. She thought at first that it was him and she was surprised, because people don't pass wind in company very often, or at least not in a noticeable way. As they went on talking, she went on thinking it was him. She felt a little sorry for him, because she thought he was embarrassed and nervous to be with her and that was why he had passed wind. Then it occurred to her very suddenly that it might not have been him at all, it might have been the dog, and worse, if it had been the dog, he might think it had been her. It was true that the dog had stolen an entire loaf of bread that morning, and eaten it, and might now be passing wind, something he did not do otherwise. She wanted immediately to let him know, somehow, that at least it was not her. Of course there was a chance that he had not noticed, but he was smart and alert, and since she had noticed, he probably had, too, unless he was too nervous to have noticed. The problem was how to tell him. She could say something about the dog, to excuse it. But it might not have been the dog, it might have been him. She could not be direct and simply say, "Look, if you just farted, that's all right; I just want to be clear that it wasn't me." She could say, "The dog ate a whole loaf of bread this morning, and I think he's farting." But if it was him, and not the dog, this would embarrass him. Although maybe it wouldn't. Maybe he was already embarrassed, if it was him, and this would give him a way out of his embarrassment. But by now the smell was long gone. Maybe the dog would fart again, if it was the dog. That was the only thing she could think of—the dog would fart again, if it was the dog, and then she would simply apologize for the dog, whether or not it was the dog, and that would relieve him of his embarrassment, if it was him.

Television

1

We have all these favorite shows coming on every evening. They say it will be exciting and it always is.

They give us hints of what is to come and then it comes and it is exciting.

If dead people walked outside our windows we would be no more excited.

We want to be part of it all.

We want to be the people they talk to when they tell what is to come later in the evening and later in the week.

We listen to the ads until we are exhausted, punished with lists: they want us to buy so much, and we try, but we don't have a lot of money. Yet we can't help admiring the science of it all.

How can we ever be as sure as these people are sure? These women are women in control, as the women in my family are not.

Yet we believe in this world.

We believe these people are speaking to us.

Mother, for example, is in love with an anchorman. And my husband sits with his eyes on a certain young reporter and waits for the camera to draw back and reveal her breasts.

After the news we pick out a quiz show to watch and then a story of detective investigation.

The hours pass. Our hearts go on beating, now slow, now faster.

There is one quiz show that is particularly good. Each week the same man is there in the audience with his mouth tightly closed and tears in his eyes. His son is coming back on stage to answer more questions. The boy stands there blinking at the television camera. They will not let him go on answering questions if he wins the final sum of $128,000. We don't care much about the boy and we don't like the mother, who smiles and shows her bad teeth, but we are moved by the father: his heavy lips, his wet eyes.

And so we turn off the telephone during this program and do not answer the knock at the door that rarely comes. We watch closely, and my husband now presses his lips together and then smiles so broadly that his eyes disappear, and as for me, I sit back like the mother with a sharp gaze, my mouth full of gold.

2

It's not that I really think this show about Hawaiian policemen is very good, it's just that it seems more real than my own life.

Different routes through the evening: Channels 2, 2, 4, 7, 9, or channels 13, 13, 13, 2, 2, 4, etc. Sometimes it's the police dramas I want to see, other times the public television documentaries, such as one called *Swamp Critturs.*

•

It's partly my isolation at night, the darkness outside, the silence outside, the increasing lateness of the hour, that makes the story on television seem so interesting. But the plot, too, has something to do with it: tonight a son comes back after many years and marries his father's wife. (She is not his mother.)

We pay a good deal of attention because these shows seem to be the work of so many smart and fashionable people.

I think it is a television sound beyond the wall, but it's the honking of wild geese flying south in the first dark of the evening.

You watch a young woman named Susan Smith with pearls around her neck sing the Canadian National Anthem before a hockey game. You listen to the end of the song, then you change the channel.

Or you watch Pete Seeger's legs bounce up and down in time to his "Reuben E. Lee" song, then change the channel.

It is not what you want to be doing. It is that you are passing the time.

You are waiting until it is a certain hour and you are in a certain condition so that you can go to sleep.

There is some real satisfaction in getting this information about the next day's weather—how fast the wind might blow and from what direction, when the rain might come, when the skies might clear—and the exact science of it is indicated by the words "40 percent" in "40 percent chance."

•

It all begins with the blue dot in the center of the dark screen, and this is when you can sense that these pictures will be coming to you from a long way off.

3

Often, at the end of the day, when I am tired, my life seems to turn into a movie. I mean my real day moves into my real evening, but also moves away from me enough to be strange and a movie. It has by then become so complicated, so hard to understand, that I want to watch a different movie. I want to watch a movie made for TV, which will be simple and easy to understand, even if it involves disaster or disability or disease. It will skip over so much, it will skip over all the complications, knowing we will understand, so that major events will happen abruptly: a man may change his mind though it was firmly made up, and he may also fall in love suddenly. It will skip all the complications because there is not enough time to prepare for major events in the space of only one hour and twenty minutes, which also has to include commercial breaks, and we want major events.

One movie was about a woman professor with Alzheimer's disease; one was about an Olympic skier who lost a leg but learned to ski again. Tonight it was about a deaf man who fell in love with his speech therapist, as I knew he would because she was pretty, though not a good actress, and he was handsome, though deaf. He was deaf at the beginning of the movie and deaf again at the end, while in the middle he heard and learned to speak with a definite regional accent. In the space of one hour and twenty minutes, this man not only heard and fell deaf again but created a successful business through his own talent, was robbed of it through a company man's treachery, fell in love, kept his woman as far as the end of the movie, and lost his virginity, which seemed to be hard to lose if one was deaf and easier once one could hear.

All this was compressed into the very end of a day in my life that as the evening advanced had already moved away from me . . .

Jane and the Cane

Mother could not find her cane. She had a cane, but she could not find her special cane. Her special cane had a handle that was the head of a dog. Then she remembered: Jane had her cane. Jane had come to visit. Jane had needed a cane to get back home. That was two years ago. Mother called Jane. She told Jane she needed her cane. Jane came with a cane. When Jane came, Mother was tired. She was in bed. She did not look at the cane. Jane went back home. Mother got out of bed. She looked at the cane. She saw that it was not the same cane. It was a plain cane. She called Jane and told her: it was not the same cane. But Jane was tired. She was too tired to talk. She was going to bed. The next morning she came with the cane. Mother got out of bed. She looked at the cane. It was the right cane. It had the head of a dog on it, brown and white. Jane went home with the other cane, the plain cane. After Jane was gone, Mother complained, she complained on the phone: Why did Jane not bring back the cane? Why did Jane bring the wrong cane? Mother was tired. Oh, Mother was so tired of Jane and the cane.

Getting to Know Your Body

If your eyeballs move, this means that you're thinking, or about to start thinking.

If you don't want to be thinking at this particular moment, try to keep your eyeballs still.

Absentminded

The cat is crying at the window. It wants to come in. You think about how living with a cat and the demands of a cat make you think about simple things, like a cat's need to come indoors, and how good that is. You think about this and you are too busy thinking about this to let the cat in, so you forget to let the cat in, and it is still at the window crying. You see that you haven't let the cat in, and you think about how odd it is that while you were thinking about the cat's needs and how good it is to live with the simple needs of a cat, you were not letting the cat in but letting it go on crying at the window. Then while you're thinking about this and how odd it is, you let the cat in without knowing you're letting the cat in. Now the cat jumps up on the counter and cries for food. You see that the cat is crying for food but you don't think of feeding it because you are thinking how odd it is that you have let the cat in without knowing it. Then you see that it's crying for food while you're not feeding it, and as you see this and think it's odd that you have not heard it cry, you feed the cat without knowing that you're feeding it.

Southward Bound, Reads
Worstward Ho

Sun in eyes, faces east, waits for van bound for south meeting plane from west. Carries book, *Worstward Ho.**

In van, heading south, sits on right or west side, sun in through windows from east. Highway crosses and recrosses meandering stream passing now northeast and now northwest under. Reads *Worstward Ho*: On. Say on. Be said on. Somehow on. Till nohow on. Said nohow on.†

---

*She waits near the highway before the entrance of HoJo's for the van going south. She is going south to meet a plane coming from the west. Waiting with her is a thin, dark-haired young woman who does not stop walking back and forth restlessly near her luggage. They are both early and wait for some time. In her purse she has two books, *Worstward Ho* and *West with the Night*. If it is quiet and she reads *Worstward Ho* on the way south, when she is fresh, she can read *West with the Night* on the way back up north, when it will be later and she will be tired.

†The van arrives and she takes care to sit on the right side, so that as they travel south the sun will not come in through her window but through the windows across the aisle from her. It is early morning, and the sun shines in through the windows from the east. Later in the day, as she returns north, she thinks, it may be late enough so that the sun will come through the windows from the west.

The highway she travels crosses and recrosses a meandering stream that passes now northeast and now northwest under her. As long as she is alone, sitting in the back of the van, she does not read but looks out the window.

Road turning and van turning east and then north of east, sun in eyes, stops reading *Worstward Ho.*[*]

Road turning and van turning east again and south, shadow on page, reads: As now by way of somehow on where in the nowhere all together?[†]

Road and van turning briefly north, sun at right shoulder, light not in eyes but flickering on page of *Worstward Ho*, reads: What when words gone? None for what then.[‡]

Van turning off highway, sun behind, sun around and in window and onto page, does not read.

Soon the van pulls up in front of a shopping mall. The restless young woman with the dark hair immediately stands up and remains standing in the aisle looking at the other passengers and out the windows. Two women board the van. They smell heavily of face powder as they walk past her to sit in the back near her. Now, since she is no longer alone, she begins to read.

The van is quiet, so she reads *Worstward Ho.* The first words are: "On. Say on. Be said on. Somehow on. Till nohow on. Said nohow on." She is not very pleased by these words.

[*]But soon after, she reads a sentence she likes better: "Whither once whence no return." After that, for a while, some sentences are pleasing and some are not.

The van travels almost due south down the highway. Sometimes it leaves the highway, the sunlight circling around behind all of them, to make a stop and pick up more passengers. At each stop, the restless young woman stands up and looks around in a commanding way. The passengers who get on to the van are mostly women.

She reads on comfortably for some miles, but when the road turns, and the van turns with it, east and then north of east, the sun is in her eyes and she cannot read *Worstward Ho.*

[†]She waits, and when the road turns east again and then south, a shadow falls on the page and she can read. With difficulty, though the light is good, she reads such words as "As now by way of somehow on where in the nowhere all together?"

[‡]If the van turns briefly north, so that the sun is at her right shoulder, the light is no longer in her eyes but flickering on the page of the book, illuminating but further confusing such already confusing words as "What when words gone? None for what then."

Van pointing east motionless in station, in shadow of tree, reads: But say by way of somehow on somehow with sight to do.*

Van pointing south and moving, reads: So leastness on.

Van turning off highway, sun behind, sun around and in window and onto page, does not read.

Van pointing east then north of east motionless, in treeless station not in shadow, sun in face, does not read.†

Van turning, sun ahead, sun around and in opposite window, shadow on page, van pointing south and moving, reads: Longing the so-said mind long lost to longing. Dint of long longing lost to longing. Said is missaid. Whenever said said said missaid.‡

---

*Now the shade of a tree by a small gas station allows her to go on to read: "But say by way of somehow on somehow with sight to do." While the driver makes a phone call, one woman leaves the van to try to find a working bathroom, fails, and returns to the van.

The van resumes going south and she reads with pleasure and some understanding: "Now for to say as worst they may only they only they." And then with more pleasure: "With leastening words say least best worse. For want of worser worst. Unlessenable least best worse." And then soon there is something a little different: "So leastward on. So long as dim still. Dim undimmed. Or dimmed to dimmer still. To dimmost dim. Leastmost in dimmost dim. Utmost dim. Leastmost in utmost dim. Unworsenable worst."

The sun in another small gas station stops her from reading, heat and brightness coming in her window, what was the west window when the van was heading south but probably must be considered the east window just at this moment. While the driver makes another phone call, two women, now, leave the van to try to find a working bathroom, fail, and return to the bus.

†The van heads south again.

‡Though she is several pages farther along, some of the words are the same again: "Next fail see say how dim undimmed to worsen. How nohow save to dimmer still. But but a shade so as when after nohow somehow on to dimmer still."

Then there is something new at the bottom of the page: "Longing

Van turning off highway, sun behind, sun around and in window and onto page, does not read.*

Van turning last time back onto highway, sun ahead, sun around and in opposite window, shadow on page, reads: No once. No once in pastless now.

Van turning last time off highway, sun ahead, sun around and in window, does not read.†

Van farthest south motionless in shadow, pointing north, reads last words: Said nohow on.‡

---

the so-said mind long lost to longing. The so-missaid. So far so-missaid. Dint of long longing lost to longing."

Then a combination: "Longing that all go. Dim go."

Soon after, with confusion, she reads: "Said is missaid. Whenever said said said missaid." She misunderstands and reads again: "Whenever said said said missaid." Then a third time, and when she imagines a pause in the middle of it, she understands better.

*At the next stop, the van driver calls out for "folks Benson and Goodwin." The Benson couple and the single Goodwin, sitting forward in the van, identify themselves as "Two Benson and one Goodwin." It takes the driver a very long time to find their papers. While he is searching, three women, now, leave the van, find a working bathroom, and return to the van.

Now each time the van stops, it stops with the sun coming in what was the west window but is now the east window, preparing to turn right and head south into the sun again. Now she has grown used to waiting with the sun on her face and on the page and watching the asphalt outside and the other passengers inside until the van turns and goes on south.

†Near the end of the book, she reads: "No once. No once in pastless now," and just now the van passes a cemetery near the airport and she sees many white stone angels, their wings raised.

‡By the time she reaches the end of her trip south, the southernmost point in the van's route, from which it will head north again, she has finished the book, which is not long. Although she has liked many of the words that came in between, its last words, "Said nohow on," say as little to her as its first, "On. Say on. Be said on."

The Walk

A translator and a critic happened to be together in the great university town of Oxford, having been invited to take part in a conference on translation. The conference occupied all of one Saturday, and that evening they had dinner alone together, though not entirely by choice. Everyone else who had participated in the conference or attended it had departed, even the organizers. Only they had chosen to stay a second night in the rooms provided for them in the college in which the conference had taken place, a down-at-heels building with stained carpets in the hallways, a smell of mildew in the guest rooms, and creaking iron bedsteads.

The restaurant was light and airy, entirely enclosed in glass like a greenhouse. The meal was good and most of the time their conversation was lively. She asked him many questions and he talked a good deal about himself. She knew something about him, since they had corresponded now and then over the years—she had asked his help on one or two points; he had admired an essay of hers; she had praised a reminiscence of his; he had courteously included an excerpt from her latest translation in an anthology. He had a certain almost obsequious charm. He liked talking about himself, and did not ask many questions of her. She noticed the imbalance but did not mind. There was some goodwill between them, though also an underlying tension because of his negative reaction to her translation.

He felt that she kept too close to the original text. He preferred the studied cadences of an earlier version and had said so in person and in print. She felt that he admired lyricism and empty rhetorical flourishes at the expense of accuracy and faithfulness to the style of the original, which was far plainer and clearer, she said, than the flowery and obfuscating earlier version. During the conference, she had given a formal presentation of her approach and he had said nothing in response, though from her lectern she could see by the expression on his face, half amused and half scornful, and by the occasional wince, as he shifted in his seat, that his feelings were strong. For his own presentation he had chosen to discuss the language of translation criticism, including his own, mischievously—or malevolently—taking as his examples the reviews of the translations of the participants in this conference. He had caused almost all of them discomfort and embarrassment, and stung their pride, for only one of them had received no bad reviews.

When they had finished their dinner, it was still light out, since the summer solstice was only a few days away. As the sky would be light for several more hours and they had been shut up in the conference room all day, suffering some tedium at various points and some tension at others, much of it caused by him, and as they were, to some extent, anyway, enjoying each other's company, they agreed that a walk would be pleasant.

The college where the conference had been held, and the restaurant, which was near it, were a good ten minutes on foot from the center of town, and their plan was to walk into town, stroll up and down the streets a bit, and then walk back out. He had not been there for many years and was curious to see it again. She had explored it on her own for the first time when she arrived the day before, but not very thoroughly or satisfactorily, since it had been crowded with tourists and too hot under the midday sun to be comfortable. She had taken the circular tour bus twice, or rather, she had made two full circuits and one half circuit, going down the main street twice, past the botanical gardens twice, to the outlying colleges twice and in again, and out to the outlying colleges one more time in order to return to where she was staying, and so she was more familiar with the town than he was. By tacit agreement she became the guide. They both felt like the colonials they were, in the mother country, she with one accent displeasing to native ears and he with another that they would not have been able to place.

They talked steadily as they walked into town, still mostly about him, his academic position, his students, his children and how he was bringing them up, and his wife, whom he missed. He and his wife had attempted a separation, but after some weeks she had returned to him. He had, during those weeks, he said, sunk into despair. When there were two of you, you decided so many little things together, such as which room to sit in with your morning coffee. When you were alone, he said, it was so miserably difficult to make those little choices.

The streets were relatively empty, though it was a Saturday night. There were not many tourists, only a few families and couples. The pavements were clear, as though they had been swept clean of the crowds. Now and then, undergraduates in formal evening dress rushed past in a cluster or singly, on the way to a university function. He and she had the curious sense that the town was full of people, but that the people were all attending events behind closed doors and out of sight. The streets were theirs for the moment. The sun hovered low in the sky, hanging above the horizon, descending so slowly that its descent was barely perceptible, and bathing the yellow stones of the old buildings in a honey-colored light. The sky above the rooftops was vast, a pale painted blue.

At the end of a long pedestrian street paved in cobblestones, they heard a full chorus of voices traveling out on the quiet evening air. The concert was taking place in a circular, rose-colored hall. They climbed the steps to a side entrance, thinking they might slip in for the remainder of the concert. He, a cosseted youngest child, was not one to obey regulations, and although she felt in this hour somewhat like a kindly aunt indulging him and his outrageous statements, she was by habit no more law-abiding than he was. Especially here, in the mother country, feeling they were less proper than the native citizens, they would be tempted to behave less properly.

But blocking the entryway were two middle-aged, heavyset women in long skirts and stout-heeled shoes chatting and laughing together, one of whom turned to them and told them civilly but firmly that they could not enter. He and she stood still for some time next to the women, enjoying the rising and falling song while they gazed down into what had been the heart of the original university, a small, centuries-old courtyard fronted by the modest façade of the first university library.

Each of the short neighboring streets, as they continued their walk, offered the surprise of another old college, often with its own gate and spiked fence and courtyard, or some tracery or corbel or bell tower to be admired. Sometimes they both wanted to go up the same street, sometimes only one of them, when the other politely went along. She found it an interesting exercise to explore a place with a person she did not know well, following not only her own impulses but also his.

Since they had both been married for many years, strolling together like this had some of the comfortable familiarity of long habit, yet it also had some of the awkwardness of a first date, since, after all, they did not really know each other very well. He was a small man, and delicate in his motions and gestures. She took care not to walk too close to him, and thought from his slight unsteadiness now and then that he was probably taking the same care to keep a certain distance from her.

When more than an hour had passed, they decided to return to their college. Now she volunteered to lead them by a different way, for the interest of it, along a street that ran parallel to the one they had come in on and would then connect to it near their destination. She did not explain all this to him, but simply assured him that the street they were about to enter would take them back to their college. He entrusted himself to her and paid little attention to where they were going, as he continued to talk.

He spoke emphatically, using strong adverbs, often expressing indignation, and admitting that some of his opinions were, as he put it, virally jaundiced: Certain things, according to him, were flagrantly obvious, or embarrassingly inaccurate, or patently ridiculous; others, of course, were magnificent, delightful, or entrancing. Condemning a certain publishing house, he remarked—although he was not old enough to have experienced the Second World War—that in its front line, incompetence and dishonesty pullulated like trench lice among infantrymen, and that the upper-level administrators should be taken out of the trenches every so often and given something restfully self-restoring to do, like sewing pages. She was content to listen, and several times thought how perfectly suitable was this conclusion—her own relative passivity, and the mild physical exertion—to the long, trying day.

Much of the street was familiar to her from passing it three times before, when the circular tour had headed out of town, but she became a little worried ten minutes into their walk back, when she was not sure which left turn to make. After all, things had flown by relatively quickly out the window of the bus. He questioned her mildly twice and she admitted her uncertainty the second time. But when they took what turned out to be the correct left turn and correctly rejoined their original road nearly opposite the restaurant where they had had dinner, and she was enjoying a feeling of satisfaction, he did not notice where they were, and simply walked on by her side, across the street from the restaurant, until she pointed it out to him. Then he was truly astonished, as though he had imagined they were far away from that corner and she had produced it out of her jacket pocket.

Now she thought he would recognize a parallel with a scene in the book she had translated, but he did not; she thought perhaps he was too occupied with reorienting himself. In the version he preferred, the passage read:

> We would return by the Boulevard de la Gare, which contained the most attractive villas in the town. In each of their gardens the moonlight, copying the art of Hubert Robert, scattered its broken staircases of white marble, its fountains, its iron

gates temptingly ajar. Its beams had swept away the telegraph office. All that was left of it was a column, half shattered but preserving the beauty of a ruin which endures for all time. I would by now be dragging my weary limbs and ready to drop with sleep; the balmy scent of the lime-trees seemed a reward that could be won only at the price of great fatigue and was not worth the effort. From gates far apart the watchdogs, awakened by our steps in the silence, would set up an antiphonal barking such as I still hear at times of an evening, and among which the Boulevard de la Gare (when the public gardens of Combray were constructed on its site) must have taken refuge, for wherever I may be, as soon as they begin their alternate challenge and response, I can see it again with its lime-trees, and its pavement glistening beneath the moon.

Suddenly my father would bring us to a standstill and ask my mother—"Where are we?" Exhausted by the walk but still proud of her husband, she would lovingly confess that she had not the least idea. He would shrug his shoulders and laugh. And then, as though he had produced it with his latchkey from his waistcoat pocket, he would point out to us, where it stood before our eyes, the backgate of our own garden, which had come, hand-in-hand with the familiar corner of the Rue du Saint-Esprit, to greet us at the end of our wanderings over paths unknown.

Since he had not noticed, she intended to mention it soon, but was at the moment more interested in pointing out to him a house they were about to pass. It had once been the home of Charles Murray, the great editor of *The Oxford English Dictionary.*

When she had arrived in this town the day before, her strongest desire had been to see, not the more famous sights, but the house in which this editor had lived while doing the better part of his work, a personal account of which she had read by his granddaughter. She had taken pains to ask each person she met if he or she knew where this house might be. No one had been able to tell her, and as she ran out of time, she had given up the idea of finding it. Then, at the end of her day of touring, just as the tour bus had reached her street for the third time and stopped to let her off by the porter's lodge of the college, the guide had said something about this same editor and his house. She was already climbing down the steps and half off the bus when she heard it, and could not question the guide further. She could not believe the house was right here, in this neighborhood where she was staying, and the next day she continued to ask each person she met where the house might be.

After she had given her talk at the conference, she was approached by a short, stout man with a preoccupied, almost angry expression who concentrated his attention on her alone, ignoring everyone around them, and asked several pertinent questions and made several concise remarks about her talk. He was modest enough not to identify himself, and when she asked him who he was, he said he had just retired as librarian of this college and would be pleased, in fact, to give her a tour of the library. Since he seemed to be a highly competent person with many facts at his disposal, she thought to ask him the question she had been asking everyone else since the day before. The librarian said that of course he knew the house—it was right across the street. And he immediately led her out to the corner and pointed. There it was, its upper story and roof showing above its brick wall, as though the librarian had taken it from his jacket pocket and set it there just to please her.

The situation was not exactly the same, of course, since the librarian had not magically brought her home but had instead produced the very house she had been looking for. But now she told the story to the critic, with whom she felt a closer companionship after walking so far with him and bringing him safely back. She thought that now he would recognize the situation, and think of their walk and the passage from the book he knew so well.

In her version, the scene read:

> We would return by way of the station boulevard, which was lined by the most pleasant houses in the parish. In each garden the moonlight, like Hubert Robert, scattered its broken staircases of white marble, its fountains, its half-open gates. Its light had destroyed the Telegraph Office. All that remained was one column, half shattered but still retaining the beauty of an immortal ruin. I was dragging my feet, I was ready to drop with sleep, the fragrance of the lindens that perfumed the air seemed to me a reward that one could win only at the cost of the greatest fatigue and that was not worth the trouble. From gates far apart, dogs awakened by our solitary steps would send forth alternating volleys of barks such as I still hear at times in the evening and among which the station boulevard (when the public garden of Combray was created on its site) must have come to take refuge, for, wherever I find

myself, as soon as they begin resounding and replying, I see it again, with its lindens and its pavement lit by the moon.

Suddenly my father would stop us and ask my mother: "Where are we?" Exhausted from walking but proud of him, she would tenderly admit that she had absolutely no idea. He would shrug his shoulders and laugh. Then, as if he had taken it out of his jacket pocket along with his key, he would show us the little back gate of our own garden, which stood there before us, having come, along with the corner of the rue du Saint-Esprit, to wait for us at the end of those unfamiliar streets.

But he was more interested in the great editor, and the house, and the mailbox directly in front of the house, which had been put there especially for the editor's use and from which so many of the requests for quotations had been mailed. She thought she would comment to him on the parallel at some other time, in a letter, and then perhaps he would be amused.

It was late. The sun had at last gone down, though the sky was still filled with the lingering cool light of the solstice. After he had with some difficulty opened the front door with the unfamiliar key, they said good night inside the entrance to the college and went their separate ways, he up the stairs and she down the corridor, to their musty rooms.

It was too late for her to enjoy sitting alone in the room after the long day, as she generally liked to do; she had to be up early. But then, it was not in any case the sort of room in which to enjoy silence and rest, being so meagerly appointed, with its small, frail wardrobe, whose door kept swinging open, its inconvenient lamp, its hard, flat pillows, and that persistent smell of mold. True, the bathroom, by contrast, was fitted with old marble and porcelain, and its one narrow window looked out on a handsome garden, though even it had lacked certain necessary supplies: Soon after he arrived, the day before, while she was away touring the town, he had left a panicked note on her door, though they had not yet met, inquiring about soap.

She was not disappointed by the whole experience, she decided, as her thoughts sorted themselves out. She was in bed now, with a book open in front of her, trying to read by the inadequate lamp, but each time she returned her eyes to the page, another insistent thought occurred to her and stopped her. She would have been disappointed if she had not, in the end, seen Murray's house, or if she had not seen the library, whose alarm she nearly triggered by walking across a perfectly open space at the top of an ancient staircase. She would have been disappointed in this building if the conference room had not been so gracious, with its high ceiling and dark oak beams, and she would perhaps have been disappointed in the conference itself if one of the speakers had not shown such interesting examples of the great writer's rough drafts. She was disappointed that some of the other participants had not stayed on afterward for at least a little while, that they had, in fact, seemed to be in such a hurry to leave.

But then there was the long walk, and her changing impressions of the town, which had been so crowded, hot, and oppressive at midday the day before and was this evening so serene, with its empty streets, the hollow spaces of its courtyards and back gardens, the darkness, against the sky, of its church steeples and clock towers, with its short alleys and narrow lanes, and its soft stones that, in her memory, had reflected the sky in tints of coral, growing just a few shades dimmer, as the hours passed, in the cool night.

The peace and emptiness of the town in the evening had seemed fragile and temporary; the next day it would be submerged once again in the hot crowd. And because she had made so many circuits out of the town, by bus and then on foot, it seemed to her, too, that the weight of her experience of the town was here, at this distance from it, as though the town were always to be experienced from a distance exactly the length of those two streets which, arising here, and diverging, made their way to it.

At last her thoughts came at longer intervals and she read more than she stopped to think. She then read later than she meant to, gradually forgetting the lamp, the room, and the conference, though the walk remained, as a presence, somewhere behind or beneath her reading, until she relaxed completely and slept, no longer bothered by the hard pillow.

The next morning, when she came out with her suitcase, he was there, too, in a white summer suit slightly too ample for his small frame, standing by the porter's lodge. He and she had ordered taxis for the same hour, the day before, and the two drivers were standing by the curb chatting in the early sunlight. He was, in fact, going to the same part of town, though not to the train station, but neither of them had suggested sharing a taxi. She waited while he talked on, for a few minutes, to the porter, and then they took leave of each other again before setting off in their separate taxis. As he stepped neatly into his, his last words to her, solemn and rather portentous, she thought, were ones that nobody, as it happened, had ever spoken to her before, but that she judged were likely to be correct, since he lived on the other side of the globe: "We will probably not meet again." He then made a graceful gesture of the hand that she later could not remember exactly, and whose meaning she could not quite grasp, though it seemed to combine a farewell with a concession to some sort of inevitability, and his cab moved slowly down the street, followed, soon, by her own.

Varieties of Disturbance

I have been hearing what my mother says for over forty years and I have been hearing what my husband says for only about five years, and I have often thought she was right and he was not right, but now more often I think he is right, especially on a day like today when I have just had a long conversation on the phone with my mother about my brother and my father and then a shorter conversation on the phone with my husband about the conversation I had with my mother.

My mother was worried because she hurt my brother's feelings when he told her over the phone that he wanted to take some of his vacation time to come help them since my mother had just gotten out of the hospital. She said, though she was not telling the truth, that he shouldn't come because she couldn't really have anyone in the house since she would feel she had to prepare meals, for instance, though having difficulty enough with her crutches. He argued against that, saying "That wouldn't be the *point*!" and now he doesn't answer his phone. She's afraid something has happened to him and I tell her I don't believe that. He has probably taken the vacation time he had set aside for them and gone away for a few days by himself.

She forgets he is a man of nearly fifty, though I'm sorry they had to hurt his feelings like that. A short time after she hangs up I call my husband and repeat all this to him.

My mother hurt my brother's feelings while protecting certain particular feelings of my father's by claiming certain other feelings of her own, and while it was hard for me to deny my father's particular feelings, which are well known to me, it was also hard for me not to think there was not a way to do things differently so that my brother's offer of help would not be declined and he would not be hurt.

She hurt my brother's feelings as she was protecting my father from certain feelings of disturbance anticipated by him if my brother were to come, by claiming to my brother certain feelings of disturbance of her own, slightly different. Now my brother, by not answering his phone, has caused new feelings of disturbance in my mother and father both, feelings that are the same or close to the same in them but different from the feelings of disturbance anticipated by my father and those falsely claimed by my mother to my brother. Now in her disturbance my mother has called to tell me of her and my father's feelings of disturbance over my brother, and in doing this she has caused in me feelings of disturbance also, though fainter than and different from the feelings experienced now by her and my father and those anticipated by my father and falsely claimed by my mother.

When I describe this conversation to my husband, I cause in him feelings of disturbance also, stronger than mine and different in kind from those in my mother, in my father, and respectively claimed and anticipated by them. My husband is disturbed by my mother's refusing my brother's help and thus causing disturbance in him, and by her telling me of her disturbance and thus causing disturbance in me greater, he says, than I realize, but also more generally by the disturbance caused more generally not only in my brother by her but also in me by her greater than I realize, and more often than I realize, and when he points this out, it causes in me yet another disturbance different in kind and in degree from that caused in me by what my mother has told me, for this disturbance is not only for myself and my brother, and not only for my father in his anticipated and his present disturbance, but also and most of all for my mother herself, who has now, and has generally, caused so much disturbance, as my husband rightly says, but is herself disturbed by only a small part of it.

Lonely

No one is calling me. I can't check the answering machine because I have been here all this time. If I go out, someone may call while I'm out. Then I can check the answering machine when I come back in.

Mrs. D and Her Maids

Names of Some Early Maids, with Identifying Characteristics

Cora, who misses them all
Nellie Bingo: our darling, but she disappeared into a sanatorium
Anna the Grump
Virginia York: not a whirlwind
Birdell Moore: old-fashioned, with warm Southern sweetness
Lillian Savage: not insulted by drunks
Gertrude Hockaday: pleasant, but a perfidious hypochondriac
Ann Carberry: feeble, old, and deaf
The "Brava": came irregularly, not to be considered a Negro
High school girl: worse than nothing
Mrs. Langley: English, and exactly what we need
Our Splendid Marion
Minnie Treadway: briefly a possibility
Anna Slocum: wished it had all been a bad dream
Shirley: like a member of the family
Joan Brown: philosopher of the condition

Mrs. D

Before she is Mrs. D, she lives in the city with her little daughter and her maid, Cora. The daughter is four years old. She goes to nursery school and when at home is taken care of mainly by Cora. This leaves Mrs. D free to write and also to go out in the evenings.

Mrs. D writes short stories, some good, some less good, which she places mostly in ladies' magazines. She likes to speak of "selling" a story, and she counts on earning a little money from it to supplement her salary. She will publish a story in one of the best magazines just before she is married. The story is called "Real Romance."

Marriage to Mr. D

When Mrs. D's little daughter is six, Mrs. D marries again, and becomes Mrs. D. The ceremony takes place in the country at a friend's house. It is a small wedding and the reception is out on the lawn under the trees. The season is early fall, but the women are still wearing summer dresses. The little daughter's blond hair is now cut short. Cora is not at the wedding. She no longer works for Mrs. D, but they write letters to each other.

Housekeeping

Mr. and Mrs. D set up house in a college town, where Mr. D has a job teaching. Mr. D gives his stepdaughter breakfast every morning and walks her to school. Mrs. D lingers in bed before beginning her day at the typewriter.

Mrs. D Has A Baby

After a year of marriage, Mrs. D becomes pregnant. A baby boy is born in the fall, at the Lying-In Hospital. He is strong and healthy. Mr. D is very moved. He will write a short story about a father and his small son.

Cora Still Misses Them All

Cora writes:

Ge; Was I glade to hear from you all I would had writting you but I misslayed your address I can tell by the exsplaination that you all are fine I would love to come out and see you all expecilly the new one I know my little girl is lovely as ever all way will be Yes I am Working, but I hafter to make up mine whether I will stay here ore go back with my one should I had said the other people did I ever write you about them well they was very nice from England a lawyer ore laywer whitch ever you spell it Oh, I know you will be suprise who I am working for Now you jest; I will tell you later on I had a little accident this summer I fell and crack my knee broke a Fibula whitch I has been layed up for 2 month but I am up and working now when are you coming to the city again when you do please try to bring the children when every you move drop me a line let me know I dont care how nice other people are I still think about you I wish you all could come to the city to stay Mr D could get a job Easyer than Alphonso could out there we have a nice house out here in the Country you know how I am about the Country well we are doing fine did you ever meet Mike Mrs. F boy he is nice but I know your new one is much more nicer My greatest Love to you all

Why Mrs. D Needs a Maid

Mrs. D wants a family, but she also wants to write, so she needs a maid to keep the house clean, cook and serve meals, and help care for the children. The expense of keeping a maid will be compensated by the money Mrs. D will earn writing.

One of the Earliest Maids Is One of the Best

Our darling Nellie. All I had to struggle to attain was a perfect maid, which is our most phenomenal achievement. We can't get over our luck as she moves like a dainty angel about the house doing her duties with absolute perfection.

But Nellie's Health Is Not Good

We are still having maid trouble because our very sweet maid is not really strong enough for the job and is constantly out sick, which makes it quite a problem to know what to do. We have had her examined by the doctor and he has told her to get X-rays taken of her lungs so we will know by the end of this week whether we can even hope to have her any more at all.

Nellie Writes from the Sanatorium

I hope you will forgive me for not writing to you and tell you that I am sick in the hospital. I didn't want you to worry I hope you will forgive me.

I've been in the hospital 8 months And I miss home and every one.

Im in the ward with 8 girls and like it very much we get along swell.

In December Walter father had a x ray taken and the doctor said he have Tuberculosis so I had my taken and he said I have it. Oh I wish you cold see me the first two months all I did was cry.

I am coming along fine. If you see me you wont know me. I will send you a snapshot in my next letter. I have gas on my left side.

I dont know how long I have to stay here. I hope it wont be long cause it's lonsome.

I'm dying to see the baby.

I re'cd your Card and thanks a lot I will never forget you you been so good to me.
I dont think I will work any more not for a long time any way.
Doctor said I have to be quiet when I go home.
Give my love to the baby.
I really miss you All. Love to All. Nellie Bingo.

Mrs. D Answers an Ad

I am writing in response to your advertisement in today's Traveler, since I shall be hiring a maid very soon. I should be glad to have you telephone me at Kirkland 0524 if the following details about the job are of interest to you.

We are a family of four. I must spend all my mornings at my work of writing. We live in a modern, convenient house.

The job is not an easy one, since there is all the housework to be done. I like to care for the baby as much as possible myself. We all regard that as a family pleasure as well as a duty, but of course he adds greatly to the washing. We enjoy eating, and we would hope that you like to cook and know how to use leftovers in appetizing and flavorsome dishes. But we do not require fancy cooking.

Anyone who works for us will have the chance to earn regular increases as long as she continues to make the house run so smoothly that my own work is in turn made more profitable.

We need someone who has the kind of temperament to fit into our house, of course. She should be cooperative, willing to accept and put into practice new ideas, especially in handling the baby, and calm, patient, and firm in dealing with him. Meals should be prompt.

I should be glad to hear from you, and the sooner the better.

Yours very sincerely.

The Impression She Gives

Mrs. D gives the impression, in her letter, that she is sensible, efficient, and well organized, and that her family life is orderly.

She likes a clean house, but she herself is casual in caring for her things—after removing a sweater, she will drop it in a heap. But she has acquired for the house, often at low prices, well-made, handsome furniture and rugs, and when she and the maid have given the house some attention it looks attractive to outsiders.

She herself is only sometimes calm, patient, and firm, but it is true that the family enjoys eating.

A Bad Experience Follows

I have finally got rid of Anna the Grump.

Mrs. D Publishes a Story

The story is called "Wonderful Visit."

Time Goes By

The family are now living at their third address in this college town. Mrs. D composes an ad herself, with several false starts and extensive revisions before she is satisfied with the result:

Writer couple with well-trained schoolgirl daughter and year-old baby

Writer couple who must have harmonious household with wife free for morning work

Woman writer who must be free of household problems every morning requires helper able to do all housework including personal laundry and part care baby; must be cooperative, like to cook, have high standards of cleanliness, willing to accept new ideas, calm and firm in dealing with baby. We should wish to have dinner guests about once a week and at that time have good table service. Job is not easy but return will be fair treatment

Return for heavy job will be fair dealing, definite time off, wages $16 per week to start and chance to earn quarterly increases. Kirkland 0524

The Well-Trained Schoolgirl

It is true that Mrs. D's daughter is well trained, though not in all respects. She is polite and sensitive to the feelings of others. She works hard in school and earns high grades. She is not very tidy in her habits, however, and does not keep her room very neat.

She is rather beautiful, according to Mrs. D, and remarkably graceful, but not phenomenally intelligent. Mrs. D describes her to friends as a tall, tense young child, and complains that she is subject to enthusiasms and anxieties that she herself finds "very wearing." She complains about her daughter's high voice. A speech therapist may help.

She remarks that sometimes, when the child is with her, she herself "cannot behave like a civilized being."

Fair Treatment, Cleanliness, and New Ideas

It is true that Mrs. D is fair in her treatment of her maids. She also tends to develop intensely personal relationships with them. She is inquisitive as to their lives and thoughts. This can inspire affection on the part of the maid, or resentment, depending on the maid's personality. It can lead to complicated patterns of vulnerability and subsequent ill will not always comfortable for maid or employer. Mrs. D tends to be highly critical of her maids, as she is of herself and her family.

At First Mrs. D Is Pleased with the Results

Mrs. D confides to a friend:

The best thing about it, the really unbelievable thing, is that she can be an excellent maid and at the same time a person capable of appreciating the kind of qualities such families as yours and ours have.

A Family Like Hers

Mrs. D sees her family, and the families of her friends, as enlightened and sympathetic to the working classes, as well as stylish, smart, witty, and cultured as regards literature, art, music, and food. In the area of music, for instance, she and her family enjoy certain pieces by the classical composers, although they also favor the more popular musicals and, over the years, will spend Sunday afternoons listening to recordings of *Oklahoma!*, *Finian's Rainbow*, *South Pacific*, and *Annie Get Your Gun.*

Soon There Are Problems, However

Just when I run into the most marvelous dream of a maid that won't happen again in a century, we sublet our apartment for six weeks and this maid doesn't want to leave town. She may be influenced by her boyfriend, a twenty-four-year-old who is somehow intellectual-looking despite his position as driver of a florist wagon.

Mrs. D Tries to Be Honest in Recommending Her to Others

Our maid's name is Virginia. She may not turn out to be the gem for temporary work that I had hoped I was sending you.

She is not the sort who starts out like a whirlwind.

She has a sort of nervous shyness.

She is extremely slow on laundry, but it probably wouldn't matter so much in your case since you send out more things.

She can't catch up with the ironing. But if you take a firm hand it ought not to be a problem. Also, you ought to make out a schedule for her.

Mrs. D Reflects on Her Experience of Virginia After Letting Her Go

Mrs. D writes a long description of Virginia:

When she came to see me for her first interview she sat sideways on the chair not looking at me. Sometimes she looked directly at me and smiled, and then she looked intelligent and sweet, but much of the time she had a hangdog heavy dull look to her face. Her voice was slow, rough, and hesitant, though her sentences were well formulated. She talked to me about her other job. She said to me, "Maybe I'm too conscientious, I don't know. I never seem to catch up with the ironing, I don't know. The man changes his underwear every day."

When she spoke of desserts, her eyes lit up. "I know thousands of desserts I like to make," she said.

She said she had been left alone very early and hadn't had much schooling and that was why she had happened to get into domestic service.

She and I tried to work out a good schedule. She did not want to work after putting the dinner on the table at six, but she wanted to have her own dinner before leaving, otherwise she would have to eat in a restaurant. So we tried that, but there is something extraordinarily prickly about waiting on yourself, going in and out of the kitchen, when a servant is sitting there eating. And she did eat an enormous meal.

She had a pathological interest in her own diet. She was

a fiend about salads and milk and fruit, all the things that cost the most.

I missed one of the baby's blankets, the best one, which I had crocheted a border for, all around. Then one day I left the iron on all afternoon on the back porch and that's when I found the baby's blanket. She had used it to cover the ironing board. What else might she do? Too soon after, the baby's playpen came apart in her hands.

Now my distrust was deepened to a certainty: she was not the person on whom to base any permanent plans. It was also obvious that she could not keep up with the ironing or anything else.

She acted dissatisfied and glum if she stayed beyond two o'clock. I had to sympathize, because what she wanted to do was go to the YWCA, where she and a few of the other domestics were taking some very improving courses.

All her friends were urging her to get a job in a defense plant. I asked her about it and she said, "The girls all say I'm wrong, but I just don't think I'd like factory work."

I was rushing around most of the morning when I should have been at the typewriter. I offered her the full-time position because the one time we had company she did such a fine job. She put on a beautiful dinner, exquisitely arranged and well cooked and perfectly served. The whole thing went off exceedingly well. But she calculated that the full-time job wouldn't be worth it to her. She also told me that if she took the full-time job she didn't see how she could get her Christmas shopping done. That was the crowning remark.

Her experience of our household was not at its easiest. We were moving at the time, and we were still not settled before I had to rush to finish a story. But she could not see that this was a chance to make herself useful to a coming writer who could thereafter afford to pay her better.

Mrs. D, the "Coming Writer"

It is not clear what Mrs. D's ambitions are. She writes easily and fluently, and has no difficulty conceiving plots for her stories. Over lunch she and Mr. D often exchange ideas for stories or characters, though Mr. D rarely has time now to write fiction. Mrs. D's plots often involve domestic situations like her own. The characters, usually including a husband and wife, are skillfully and sympathetically drawn; they have complex relationships with recognizable small frictions, hurts, and forgiveness. She is particularly good with the speech of young children. However, the stories often have a vein of wistful sentimentality that works to their detriment.

Her approach to writing is practical. She will "capture" certain qualities in a character, a change will take place, there will be small epiphanies. When the story is done, she will try to sell it to the highest class of magazine, or the one with the best rates. The cash often makes a difference in the family's economy.

Mrs. D's Creativity

Mrs. D spends her energies on many other creative projects besides writing. She sews clothes for the children, knits sweaters, bakes bread, devises unusual Christmas cards, and plans and oversees the children's craft projects. She takes pleasure in this creativity, but her pleasure itself is rather intense and driven.

Hope for Better Things to Come

Mrs. D writes:

Now we are looking forward to the new maid, Birdell, who will be starting Saturday. She promises to have all the warm Southern sweetness and flexibility of the old-fashioned Negro servant.

Birdell Does Not Work Out. Another Prospect Is Lillian

According to herself, Lillian Savage can do anything from picking up after the children to setting out a tasty snack to "swanky" stuff like typewriting and answering the phone or even taking dictation. She says: "You have to be good-natured to take a domestic job. Nothing flusters me. You'd be surprised at what I've taken from men that get to drinking, and I know how to handle it; I don't get insulted."

Perfidy

Lillian seems like a good possibility, but then an old employer wants her back. Gertrude is going to help out and fix it so that Lillian can come anyway, but then she doesn't call and Lillian doesn't call. After the matter of Ann Carberry, neither one of them ever calls Mrs. D again.

Mrs. D Reflects on Gertrude, Who Didn't Work Out

She was always pleasant, but was often home with various diseases—colds, etc. Once, she stayed home because, thinking she was getting a cold, she took a heavy dose of physic and it gave her cramps in the stomach and brought on her "sickness" two weeks early. The next time she had an inflammation of the eye; she thought maybe it was a stye. It was terribly inflamed. The doctor put drops on it that stung terribly but helped. The doctor said not to go to her job for fear of infection. She felt fine but supposed she'd have to do what the doctor said.

Her husband had health problems, too. She talked a lot about his bad physical condition and his stopped-up bowels.

Then he got drafted. Well, that was that for her—she wouldn't be working for me any more. He was set on making her stay with his relatives while he was gone and she was not strong enough to resist. She would just have to work for nothing in the boarding house and be part of family quarrels, which she hated and which made her ill. She was a very attractive and interesting personality. Any attractive white girl who was willing to do other people's housework at a time like this was bound to be interesting for some reason.

Further Reflections, Including Annoying Things About Gertrude

She would leave the house in terrible shape: diapers on the floor, the bathroom strewn with everything, all the baby's clothes, wet diapers, socks and shoes and unwashed rubber pants. The tub was dirty, the towels and washcloths and the baby's playthings were all over, the soap was in the water, and the water was even still standing in the tub. She left thick cold soapy water in the washing machine and tubs, diapers out of the water, and the bucket was never upstairs.

She would make pudding using good eggs, when we were out of freshly made cookies.

She was always grabbing dish towels for everything, throwing them toward the cellar door when they were too dirty, along with others that had been used maybe once. She left ashes around in all sorts of dishes, such as the salt dishes.

Then she went and recommended a maid who was too old, feeble, and deaf for the job.

Mrs. D's Work Habits

Mrs. D likes to start work as early in the morning as she can. Once the children are taken care of, she sits down at her typewriter and begins to type. She types fast and steadily, and the sound is loud, the table rattling and the carriage bell ringing at the end of every line. There is only an occasional silence when she pauses to read over what she has just written. She makes many changes, which involve moving the carriage back a little, x-ing out the word or phrase, rolling the carriage down a little, and inserting an emendation above the line.

She makes a carbon copy of each page, and she types both her first drafts and the copies on cheap yellow paper, aligning a piece of yellow paper, a piece of carbon paper, and another piece of yellow paper, and rolling them together into the carriage. Her fingers, with their carefully applied clear nail polish, sometimes become smudged with ink from the typewriter ribbon or with carbon from the carbon paper.

Mrs. D sits at her worktable with good upright posture. She has full, dark-brown, medium-length hair with gentle curls in it and combed to one side. She has dark eyes, round and naturally rosy cheeks, an upturned nose, and nicely shaped lips to which she applies lipstick. She wears no other makeup except, occasionally, some powder when she goes out. She looks younger than she is. She dresses nicely, usually in a skirt, blouse, and cardigan, even when alone at the typewriter.

Mrs. D Makes Another Attempt

Mrs. D writes:

We are in the throes of trying to get a maid to take with us to the summer cottage.

The Summer Cottage

Mrs. D has found a reasonably cheap cottage close to the sea where they can spend the summer. It is not a very long drive from the college town. Mrs. D goes out to the place ahead of time and puts in a good-size garden. Because of the garden, they are allowed extra gas for the move out there. Gas has been rationed because of the war.

Once they are settled, Mrs. D urges friends to come stay with them. But these friends will probably take the train: there is now a ban on pleasure driving because of the shortage of gas. They are allowed to use the car if they are going to buy food, so they may plan a food-shopping trip around picking up a friend at the station. They are also allowed to use the car if they are going clamming.

Later in the summer, the ban on pleasure driving will be lifted and they will immediately drive to the ocean for a swim.

Drafts of a Letter to an Agency, Written from the Seaside

My dear Miss McAllister,

I find it impossible to keep Ann Carberry whom you sent me through Gertrude Hockaday last week. She has tried, and in many ways she is quite satisfactory. She keeps the kitchen in fine condition and enjoys figuring out ways to use the available food to make tasty meals. But this about uses up all her time and energy; she does not step out of the kitchen on some days except to take her afternoon rest.

Which leaves, of course, the main need unsatisfied: the care of the baby.

It has been necessary for me to do all the washing, and all of his care except for giving him his meals. And she is seventy years old.

Her age, her feebleness, and her deafness combine to make her quite unsuitable for this job

•

nor did she ever notice a full wastebasket standing at the head of the stairs.

She is a very sweet person, very eager to please. She seems to enjoy cooking. She likes to cook her specialties, such as Parker House rolls, and I think she would suit an elderly family who could afford to pay a high wage for the light work of which she

and in a place where there were no other more pressing duties

would be very welcome in a house where other pressing duties need not be neglected to make these treats, such as Parker House rolls. Because of these weaknesses, which made her obviously very fluttery and apprehensive, I had not the heart to break the news to her suddenly. I thank you for your kind cooperation with Gertrude in finding me any maid at all.

Two Weeks

Ann works for one week and is then given a week's notice.

Some Other Annoying Things About Ann

She became dizzy-headed if she kept going all day.

She snored.

She panted when serving at the table.

Ann's Parting Wisdom

Ann comes in with a very small tray and remarks: "They say an ounce of help is worth a pound of pity."

The Brava

Mrs. D writes:

We now have a little Brava girl aged fourteen. She is colored, but not regarded as Negro—she must be treated as Portuguese.

She is wonderful with the baby and can do dishes and other simple things. So far, however, she has been very irregular in her comings.

But After the Brava

Mrs. D is distressed. She has no help. She cannot write. Her family requires a great deal of work, and she is with them too much. She confides to a friend:

I am without a smitch of hired help. I cannot even behave myself like a civilized being, much less do any writing. The main reason of course is overwork on my part.

And to another:

I am in a complete state of jitters, due to the search for a maid.

And to another:

We have been intending to get in touch with your friend but haven't had company for quite a while because of our maid crisis. I should improve greatly this next year if I can only get some help. I am not too sanguine about that.

Family Finances

Mr. and Mrs. D, always short of money, have debts they must pay. One of their debts is to a friend named Bill. Bill himself is now in straitened circumstances and politely tells them that he must have the money back.

The two children are now enrolled in the same private school, one in fifth grade and the other in nursery school. Mrs. D asks the director for a tuition reduction, and he grants the children half scholarships.

Mrs. D Tries a High School Girl

Mrs. D writes:

We got a little high school girl but she was worse than nothing.

Mr. D Does Not Have Time to Write

Mr. D teaches three days a week, and on each day he teaches three classes. He has 150 themes to correct each week. His students are very bright.

The Englishwoman

One of Mr. D's colleagues recommends a cleaning woman. Mrs. D writes:

With his tips as to her temperament, I was able to apply the right pressure when I called up, and now she is with us. Our fingers are crossed as we say it. She is—if I can believe my luck—exactly what we need. She likes to go ahead without any instruction and she adores to work for disorderly people because, as she says, "they appreciate coming in and finding things clean and neat." She is English, experienced, quick, and able. Her name is Mrs. Langley.

All Goes Well, for a Time

Mrs. Langley is downstairs in the playroom ironing.

But Mrs. Langley Will Not Stay

Mrs. Langley has left us.

Miscarriage

Mrs. D has been trying to have another baby, but she miscarries early in the pregnancy. It is her third miscarriage. But she will not give up.

Our Splendid Marion

For a time they are joined by what Mrs. D considers a wonderful girl, a nineteen-year-old commercial-college student. She lifts an enormous load from their shoulders, but they worry because she seems to have a life of all work and no play and never sees boys.

Then she, too, goes on her way.

Mrs. D Sees a Doctor

Mrs. D consults a doctor about her trouble conceiving. She tells him that an earlier doctor had helped her to conceive by blowing some sort of gas into her.

Mr. and Mrs. D Are Both Writing

Mrs. D will be having a story published soon, and she has just finished writing another one, after working every day from nine thirty to three. As for Mr. D, he is not writing stories anymore, but he has begun writing articles.

They hope her latest story will sell, too, because they find themselves without much money.

Mrs. D Is Pregnant Again

Again Mrs. D places an ad, shorter this time:

> COOK-HOUSEKEEPER—12 noon to early dinner, in considerate home. No washing, no Sunday work. $20 week. Tel. 2997.

Minnie Answers in Flowery Handwriting

Regarding the enclosed "ad" does it mean I may have a room in your house, or does it refer to one who has a home, and who would come in each week day to fill your needs? I did not just understand from the wording of the "ad" just the conditions so thought I'd inquire and if interested I'd like to hear from you if the position has not been taken and details of duties.

Minnie Will Be Given a Chance. She Writes to Accept

Your gracious letter at hand and I hope my earnest efforts may prove satisfactory, and of course I expect to consult with you as to your wishes regarding all things pertaining to your home management. My idea, after I become familiar with things, is to relieve you as much as I can, so you may have more freedom to care for your health, and other duties of your own. I very much appreciate the fact that you have not asked for references etc. as I prefer to come on my own merits, yet it is a gracious gesture on your part to receive into your home an entire stranger, with no introduction except our correspondence. I hope I may prove worthy of your confidence and that I may soon adjust myself to your house hold.

Minnie Does Not Work Out, and Soon Thereafter Mrs. D Decides to Hire a Girl from a Residential School for Delinquent Children

Mrs. D receives a letter from the field worker, Miss Anderson:

There are many matters to be considered before we could place a girl permanently in your home, and at the present time I do not have a suitable girl available.

Mrs. D Persists in Asking for One in Particular. Miss Anderson Answers

Anna would be glad to stay with you permanently. But I am afraid you would find that adequate supervision would be a bigger problem than you realize. I could tell you more about Anna's very poor background, and her mentality, which we have studied over a period of years, and you would then realize why our rules have to be rather severe.

For instance, there is the question of the hour she is to get in when she goes to the movies one night a week. I set this at 10:30 rather than 11:30, thinking that she should be able to go to the first show, in which case 10:30 seems late enough. She has also asked if she may attend the New Year's Dance at the White Eagle Dance Hall with her girl friend and their escorts. Knowing nothing of the type of dance this will be, I hesitate to grant this privilege. These requests are just a sample of the problems which would increase as time went on. We want our girls to be contented and lead as normal a life as possible, but they must be protected.

Mrs. D Persists. Miss Anderson Yields

As soon as I hear that a definite transfer has been accomplished I will send you a contract, and will contact the Welfare Department.

After discussing matters in detail we can probably be a bit more lenient, but success depends a great deal on her outside contacts, and she will need a great deal of guidance, as is the case with many of our state's unfortunate girls.

Despite High Hopes on the Part of All Concerned, Anna's Employment Is Not a Success

Mrs. D writes:

It is so hard to keep Anna in bounds, for even under this watching she managed to connive with a taxi driver and take our youngest out to visit friends of hers at a long distance and feed him Lord knows what.

She may also have been making indiscreet gestures downtown.

Back at the School

Anna writes:

Sorry not to have answered long before now, but we can write only one letter a week which is on Sundays.

How is everyone down that way. It sure is quite a lost to me.

The snow storm we had a week ago, didn't have too much effect on our trip here. There was 2–4 inches of snow in Some places. Miss Anderson wished she had some chains that day. Cars slid from one side of the road to the other, and one car went off on the wrong side of the road into a ditch. Several had to get out of the car to clean off windshiels and I don't know what. We stopped at the Rutland Dairy Bar for lunch, and then from there we had good weather.

Hope your trip was as successful as that of ours.

The points of view which you had mentioned in your letter are all very true and I only wished it had been a bad dream myself.

Glad to know you called Evelyn and Mrs. Warner. I can imagine how they felt and by all means Evelyn. She and I thought quite a lot of each other and I sure miss her. I miss church chior and M. Y. F. very much.

Close now with best wishes.

Mrs. D Finds Another Girl She Likes from the School and Receives a Contract for Her Hire and Supervision

Unless wages for your present girl are paid in full to date of return or transfer no other girl will be placed with you until full settlement of all accounts is made.

You will not hire this girl out to any other party.

You are to exercise parental supervision with due consideration for physical health and cleanliness, moral training, improvement of mind, and wise use of leisure time.

If girl does not prove satisfactory you will notify the school at once and she will be returned. The school also reserves the right to return the she any time the school sees fit.

You will promptly advise the Priest or Minister of the Church with which she is affiliated, as to her arrival in your community.

You will supervise the buying of her clothing and all other necessary articles and you will allow her a small amount of spending money, not more than $1.00 cents per week. Her wages will be $15 per week.

Mrs. D Gives Birth to a Healthy, Full-Term Baby. She Sends the School a Good Report of Shirley

Shirley has been wonderful all through my hospitalization and since my return home. Thanks to her I have had a good rest and shall be able to pick up my various responsibilities eagerly as soon as we get a little cool weather.

We have managed to get Shirley into a swimming hole for most of the hot afternoons.

Mrs. D Supervises as Shirley Buys Clothes

On the July 31 bill: raincoat, hairbrush, suit, skirt, jacket, underpants, gym suit.

On the August 31 bill: sweater, dickey, wool skirt, blouses, sneakers, blue jeans.

Meanwhile, Anna Writes from Her New Position in Connecticut

I said I would write and let you know where I went, when I got a new job, so here I am. I am working in Conn. They are lovely people and they take me with them most every place they go. I have a very nice room with a little radio, electric fan, private bath room with hot and cold water, and etc.

We are near the salt water beach, and go swimming 2 or 3 times a week, and we sure injoy it, as it's so hot every day here, that we can hardly breath, and the humidity very heavy with out any stirring in the air that we all lie around like sticks.

Last Sunday, there was 8,500 people and children at the beach. What do you think of that.

I walk nearly 4 to 6 miles when I go shopping or movies, etc., both ways altogether. Except when they go in by the car.

I am partly on my own here, and next month I will be having all my own money. I don't have to send any of my mail back to the school. The last letter I got from home was about a month ago saying that they were having nothing more to do with me because I wouldn't stop writting letters to my brother in the service. I just couldn't stop that for anyone as I think too much of that brother. I have written home to them twice with in the last 3 weeks and no answer. They won't even let my sisters write to me any more.

Well I am so glad to think that I am out again and hope to hold it out.

I am so glad to know that you are adoring your little

baby girl. I can see your reason if you take to them the way I do.

Write soon.

After a Year, Shirley Is Still with Mrs. D

It is an entirely satisfactory situation.

But Mrs. D Worries About Shirley's Sensitivity and Her Family Back Home

Life isn't easy for a girl like Shirley, sensitive and loving and having to give up a family whom it is natural for her to care about.

The Field Worker Is Not Sure Shirley Should Take On an Additional Job

Shirley requests permission to work Sunday afternoons in a luncheonette as waitress. Without knowing more particulars concerning the reputation of the luncheonette, the clientele, etc., I hesitate to give her permission. However if all is in order in that respect, and if such work would not interfere with her duties in your home and with her school work, I have no objection to her earning a little extra money in this way. However she must remember that her first obligation is to you.

Trouble: Shirley Explains to Mrs. D

Mrs. D; I lied to you about the Sunday night altogether. I was with Dixie, Dolores, & a soldier named Jimmie who I met before we left for the Cape. I didn't think it would sound so suspicious to be out to dinner with Dixie, but I guess it sounded worse. You would probably think it was a pick-up, so I'm not going to try to argue out of it. As far as doing anything else underhanded, I've only been out once a week, so I don't see how I could possibly do anything so terrible. I have missed Church about 3 times, maybe 4. Only two of the times I have helped out at the Maples. The other times I have waited for Tootsie & Ralph to come after me when they got out of Church. One of the days that I said I had to stay after school I didn't. I went riding with Judy.

Mr. Russell talked to me about it. He said to be "above board" with you, so I'm telling you everything. I can't think of anything else I have done underhanded. Since last Thurs. I've tried to be very nice & happy with everyone but I'm not at all. If I can't even go home to see my mother & family things must be in pretty bad shape. I haven't been home since the last of Dec. I would like to see everybody.

I have learned a lesson Mrs. D and I'll never lie to you again. I would be the happiest person, if you would give me another chance to work at the Maples. I want to very much because you wouldn't have to give me any money then. I hate to ask you for it, and I do need it. I don't like you to have to pay my cleaning bills, & money for the bus & things like that, that I have to ask you for all the time. You wouldn't even have to give me an allowance. I promise you with my whole heart that you wouldn't regret it. If you say be home at six thirty I'd be home if I had to leave everything in a mess. Ray told me when he called today that the girls who work there said they never missed anyone as they missed me sunday. I couldn't get a job anywhere and make as good money as I do there, one day a week. I only want to work on Sundays, & no other place would want a person who could work just that time. Beckmann's only pay 45 ¢ an hr. & the Walkers pay 60 ¢ besides the tips. Lots of the kids from high school came down that sunday, because I was working & it certainly helps the business. It is hard work but I love it, and would never complain about being tired. Ray also told me that Dixie wasn't putting anyone on steady for Sundays, because he was waiting to see if I could come back. Dixie knows why I can't do it anyway, because I told him why I'm here. He would be willing to help me, I know. I'm begging you for this one chance, and if it doesn't work, I'll go back to the school. I'd hate to but I would be willing to go if I knew I did something wrong.

Shirley

Shirley Is Forgiven, but Eventually Leaves Mrs. D of Her Own Accord. After Shirley, There Is Joan Brown, Though Not for Long

From her new job, Joan sends a note to Mrs. D's little boy:

Everyone has their ups and downs. At our house, they are nearly all downs. I guess its the same at yours.

I really enjoyed working at your house, and I didn't really understand myself, for more or less wanting to leave. But it is much more pleasant working at a store.

You shall never know how I feel about doing housework all the time, as you shall probably never experience it.

How Many Maids Will Mrs. D Have in Her Lifetime?

Mrs. D will have at least one hundred maids in her lifetime. At a certain point she stops calling them maids and begins to call them cleaning women. They don't live in her house, but come in from outside.

After Joan Is Long Gone, Mrs. D Writes to a Friend

What I am doing is trying to start a new cleaning woman digging out some of the accumulations of this and that.

Names of Some Later Maids, with Characteristics
Ingrid from Austria, with them for a year: moved to Switzerland
Doris: came to clean twice a week
Mrs. Tuit, pronounced "Toot": was hit on the head by a music stand
Anne Foster: lost a ring at the beach
Mrs. Bushey: deaf as a doorpost

20 Sculptures in One Hour

1

The problem is to see 20 sculptures in one hour. An hour seems like a long time. But 20 sculptures are a lot of sculptures. Yet an hour still seems like a long time. When we calculate, we discover that one hour divided by 20 sculptures gives us three minutes a sculpture. But though the calculation is correct, this seems wrong to us: three minutes is far too little time in which to see a sculpture, and it is also far too little to be left with, after starting with a whole hour. The trouble, we suppose, is that there are so many sculptures. Yet however many sculptures there are, we still feel we ought to have enough time if we have an hour. It must be that although the calculation is correct, it does not represent the situation correctly, though how to represent the situation correctly in terms of a calculation, and why this calculation does not really represent it, we can't yet discover.

2

The answer may be this: one hour is really much shorter than we have become accustomed to believe, and three minutes much longer, so that we may eventually reverse our problem and say that we start with a fairly short period of time, one hour, in which to see 20 sculptures, and find after calculation that we will have a surprisingly long period of time, three minutes, in which to look at each sculpture, although at this point it may begin to seem wrong that so many periods lasting so long, three minutes each, can all be contained in so short a period, one hour.

Nietszche

Oh, poor Dad. I'm sorry I made fun of you.
Now I'm spelling Nietszche wrong, too.

What You Learn About the Baby

Idle

You learn how to be idle, how to do nothing. That is the new thing in your life—to do nothing. To do nothing and not be impatient about doing nothing. It is easy to do nothing and become impatient. It is not easy to do nothing and not mind it, not mind the hours passing, the hours of the morning passing and then the hours of the afternoon, and one day passing and the next passing, while you do nothing.

What You Can Count On

You learn never to count on anything being the same from day to day, that he will fall asleep at a certain hour, or sleep for a certain length of time. Some days he sleeps for several hours at a stretch, other days he sleeps no more than half an hour.

Sometimes he will wake suddenly, crying hard, when you were prepared to go on working for another hour. Now you prepare to stop. But as it takes you a few minutes to end your work for the day, and you cannot go to him immediately, he stops crying and continues quiet. Now, though you have prepared to end work for the day, you prepare to resume working.

Don't Expect to Finish Anything

You learn never to expect to finish anything. For example, the baby is staring at a red ball. You are cleaning some large radishes. The baby will begin to fuss when you have cleaned four and there are eight left to clean.

You Will Not Know What Is Wrong

The baby is on his back in his cradle crying. His legs are slightly lifted from the surface of his mattress in the effort of his crying. His head is so heavy and his legs so light and his muscles so hard that his legs fly up easily from the mattress when he tenses, as now.

Often, you will wonder what is wrong, why he is crying, and it would help, it would save you much disturbance, to know what is wrong, whether he is hungry, or tired, or bored, or cold, or hot, or uncomfortable in his clothes, or in pain in his stomach or bowels. But you will not know, or not when it would help to know, at the time, but only later, when you have guessed correctly or many times incorrectly. And it will not help to know afterwards, or it will not help unless you have learned from the experience to identify a particular cry that means hunger, or pain, etc. But the memory of a cry is a difficult one to fix in your mind.

What Exhausts You

You must think and feel for him as well as for yourself—that he is tired, or bored, or uncomfortable.

Sitting Still

You learn to sit still. You learn to stare as he stares, to stare up at the rafters as long as he stares up at the rafters, sitting still in a large space.

Entertainment

For him, though not usually for you, merely to look at a thing is an entertainment.

Then, there are some things that not just you, and not just he, but both of you like to do, such as lie in the hammock, or take a walk, or take a bath.

Renunciation

You give up, or postpone, for his sake, many of the pleasures you once enjoyed, such as eating meals when you are hungry, eating as much as you want, watching a movie all the way through from beginning to end, reading as much of a book as you want to at one sitting, going to sleep when you are tired, sleeping until you have had enough sleep.

You look forward to a party as you never used to look forward to a party, now that you are at home alone with him so much. But at this party you will not be able to talk to anyone for more than a few minutes, because he cries so constantly, and in the end he will be your only company, in a back bedroom.

Questions

How do his eyes know to seek out your eyes? How does his mouth know it is a mouth, when it imitates yours?

His Perceptions

You learn from reading it in a book that he recognizes you not by the appearance of your face but by your smell and the way you hold him, that he focuses clearly on an object only when it is held a certain distance from him, and that he can see only in shades of gray. Even what is white or black to you is only a shade of gray to him.

The Difficulty of a Shadow

He reaches to grasp the shadow of his spoon, but the shadow reappears on the back of his hand.

His Sounds

You discover that he makes many sounds in his throat to accompany what is happening to him: sounds in the form of grunts, air expelled in small gusts. Then sometimes high squeaks, and then sometimes, when he has learned to smile at you, high coos.

Priority

It should be very simple: while he is awake, you care for him. As soon as he goes to sleep, you do the most important thing you have to do, and do it as long as you can, either until it is done or until he wakes up. If he wakes up before it is done, you care for him until he sleeps again, and then you continue to work on the most important thing. In this way, you should learn to recognize which thing is the most important and to work on it as soon as you have the opportunity.

Odd Things You Notice About Him

The dark gray lint that collects in the lines of his palm.

The white fuzz that collects in his armpit.

The black under the tips of his fingernails. You have let his nails get too long, because it is hard to make a precise cut on such a small thing constantly moving. Now it would take a very small nailbrush to clean them.

The colors of his face: his pink forehead, his bluish eyelids, his reddish-gold eyebrows. And the tiny beads of sweat standing out from the tiny pores of his skin.

When he yawns, how the wings of his nostrils turn yellow.

When he holds his breath and pushes down on his diaphragm, how quickly his face turns red.

His uneven breath: how his breath changes in response to his motion, and to his curiosity.

How his bent arms and legs, when he is asleep on his stomach, take the shape of an hourglass.

When he lies against your chest, how he lifts his head to look around like a turtle and drops it again because it is so heavy.

How his hands move slowly through the air like crabs or other sea creatures before closing on a toy.

How, bottom up, folded, he looks as though he were going away, or as though he were upside down.

Connected by a Single Nipple

You are lying on the bed nursing him, but you are not holding on to him with your arms or hands and he is not holding on to you. He is connected to you by a single nipple.

Disorder

You learn that there is less order in your life now. Or if there is to be order, you must work hard at maintaining it. For instance, it is evening and you are lying on the bed with the baby half asleep beside you. You are watching *Gaslight.* Suddenly a thunderstorm breaks and the rain comes down hard. You remember the baby's clothes out on the line, and you get up from the bed and run outdoors. The baby begins crying at being left so abruptly half asleep on the bed. *Gaslight* continues, the baby screams now, and you are out in the hard rainfall in your white bathrobe.

Protocol

There are so many occasions for greetings in the course of his day. Upon each waking, a greeting. Each time you enter the room, a greeting. And in each greeting there is real enthusiasm.

Distraction

You decide you must attend some public event, say a concert, despite the difficulty of arranging such a thing. You make elaborate preparations to leave the baby with a babysitter, taking a bag full of equipment, a folding bed, a folding stroller, and so on. Now, as the concert proceeds, you sit thinking not about the concert but only about the elaborate preparations and whether they have been adequate, and no matter how often you try to listen to the concert, you will hear only a few minutes of it before thinking again about those elaborate preparations and whether they have been adequate to the comfort of the baby and the convenience of the babysitter.

Henri Bergson

He demonstrates to you what you learned long ago from reading Henri Bergson—that laughter is always preceded by surprise.

You Do Not Know When He Will Fall Asleep

If his eyes are wide open staring at a light, it does not mean that he will not be asleep within minutes.

If he cries with a squeaky cry and squirms with wiry strength against your chest, digging his sharp little fingernails into your shoulder, or raking your neck, or pushing his face into your shirt, it does not mean he will not relax in five minutes and grow heavy. But five minutes is a very long time when you are caring for a baby.

What Resembles His Cry

Listening for his cry, you mistake, for his cry, the wind, seagulls, and police sirens.

Time

It is not that five minutes is always a very long time when you are caring for a baby but that time passes very slowly when you are waiting for a baby to go to sleep, when you are listening to him cry alone in his bed or whimper close to your ear.

Then time passes very quickly once the baby is asleep. The things you have to do have always taken this long to do, but before the baby was born it did not matter, because there were many such hours in the day to do these things. Now there is only one hour, and again later, on some days, one hour, and again, very late in the day, on some days, one last hour.

Order

You cannot think clearly or remain calm in such disorder. And so you learn to wash a dish as soon as you use it, otherwise it may not be washed for a very long time. You learn to make your bed immediately because there may be no time to do it later. And then you begin to worry regularly, if not constantly, about how to save time. You learn to prepare for the baby's waking as soon as the baby sleeps. You learn to prepare everything hours in advance. Then your conception of time begins to change. The future collapses into the present.

Other Days

There are other days, despite what you have learned about saving time, and preparing ahead, when something in you relaxes, or you are simply tired. You do not mind if the house is untidy. You do not mind if you do nothing but care for the baby. You do not mind if time goes by while you lie in the hammock and read a magazine.

Why He Smiles

He looks at a window with serious interest. He looks at a painting and smiles. It is hard to know what that smile means. Is he pleased by the painting? Is the painting funny to him? No, soon you understand that he smiles at the painting for the same reason he smiles at you: because the painting is looking at him.

A Problem of Balance

A problem of balance: if he yawns, he falls over backward.

Moving Forward

You worry about moving forward, or about the difference between moving forward and staying in one place. You begin to notice which things have to be done over and over again in one day, and which things have to be done once every day, and which things have to be done every few days, and so on, and all these things only cause you to mark time, stay in one place, rather than move forward, or, rather, keep you from slipping backward, whereas certain other things are done only once. A job to earn money is done only once, a letter is written saying a thing only once and never again, an event is planned that will happen only once, news is received or news passed along only once, and if, in this way, something happens that will happen only once, this day is different from other days, and on this day your life seems to move forward, and it is easier to sit still holding the baby and staring at the wall knowing that on this day, at least, your life has moved forward; there has been a change, however small.

A Small Thing with Another Thing, Even Smaller

Asleep in his carriage, he is woken by a fly.

Patience

You try to understand why on some days you have no patience and on others your patience is limitless and you will stand over him for a long time where he lies on his back waving his arms, kicking his legs, or looking up at the painting on the wall. Why on some days it is limitless and on others, or at other times, late in a day when you have been patient, you cannot bear his crying and want to threaten to put him away in his bed to cry alone if he does not stop crying in your arms, and sometimes you do put him away in his bed to cry alone.

Impatience

You learn about patience. You discover patience. Or you discover how patience extends up to a certain point and then it ends and impatience begins. Or rather, impatience was there all along, underneath a light, surface kind of patience, and at a certain point the light kind of patience wears away and all that's left is the impatience. Then the impatience grows.

Paradox

You begin to understand paradox: lying on the bed next to him, you are deeply interested, watching his face and holding his hands, and yet at the same time you are deeply bored, wishing you were somewhere else doing something else.

Regression

Although he is at such an early stage in his development, he regresses, when he is hungry or tired, to an earlier stage, still, of noncommunication, self-absorption, and spastic motion.

Between Human and Animal

How he is somewhere between human and animal. While he can't see well, while he looks blindly toward the brightest light, and can't see you, or can't see your features but more clearly the edge of your face, the edge of your head; and while his movements are more chaotic; and while he is more subject to the needs of his body, and can't be distracted, by intellectual curiosity, from his hunger or loneliness or exhaustion, then he seems to you more animal than human.

How Parts of Him Are Not Connected

He does not know what his hand is doing: it curls around the iron rod of your chair and holds it fast. Then, while he is looking elsewhere, it curls around the narrow black foot of a strange frog.

Admiration

He is filled with such courage, goodwill, curiosity, and self-reliance that you admire him for it. But then you realize he was born with these qualities: now what do you do with your admiration?

Responsibility

How responsible he is, to the limits of his capacity, for his own body, for his own safety. He holds his breath when a cloth covers his face. He widens his eyes in the dark. When he loses his balance, his hands curl around whatever comes under them, and he clutches the stuff of your shirt.

Within His Limits

How he is curious, to the limits of his understanding; how he attempts to approach what arouses his curiosity, to the limits of his motion; how confident he is, to the limits of his knowledge; how masterful he is, to the limits of his competence; how he derives satisfaction from another face before him, to the limits of his attention; how he asserts his needs, to the limits of his force.

Her Mother's Mother

1

There are times when she is gentle, but there are also times when she is not gentle, when she is fierce and unrelenting toward him or them all, and she knows it is the strange spirit of her mother in her then. For there were times when her mother was gentle, but there were also times when she was fierce and unrelenting toward her or them all, and she knows it was the spirit of her mother's mother in her mother then. For her mother's mother had been gentle sometimes, her mother said, and teased her or them all, but she had also been fierce and unrelenting, and accused her of lying, and perhaps them all.

2

In the night, late at night, her mother's mother used to weep and implore her husband, as her mother, still a girl, lay in bed listening. Her mother, when she was grown, did not weep and implore her husband in the night, or not where her daughter could hear her, as she lay in bed listening. Her mother later could not know, since she could not hear, whether her daughter, when she was grown, wept and implored her husband in the night, late at night, like her mother's mother.

How It Is Done

There is a description in a child's science book of the act of love that makes it all quite clear and helps when one begins to forget. It starts with affection between a man and a woman. The blood goes to their genitals as they kiss and caress each other, this swelling creates a desire in these parts to be touched further, the man's penis becomes larger and quite stiff and the woman's vagina moist and slippery. The penis can now be pushed into the woman's vagina and the parts move "comfortably and pleasantly" together until the man and woman reach orgasm, "not necessarily at the same time." The article ends, however, with a cautionary emendation of the opening statement about affection: nowadays many people make love, it says, who do not love each other, or even have any affection for each other, and whether or not this is a good thing we do not yet know.

Insomnia

My body aches so—
It must be this heavy bed pressing up against me.

Burning Family Members

First they burned her—that was last month. Actually just two weeks ago. Now they're starving him. When he's dead, they'll burn him, too.

Oh, how jolly. All this burning of family members in the summertime.

It isn't the same "they," of course. "They" burned her thousands of miles away from here. The "they" that are starving him here are different.

Wait. They were supposed to starve him, but now they're feeding him.

They're feeding him, against doctor's orders?

Yes. We had said, All right, let him die. The doctors advised it.

He was sick?

He wasn't really sick.

He wasn't sick, but they wanted to let him die?

He had just been sick, he had had pneumonia, and he was better.

So he was better and that was when they decided to let him die?

Well, he was old, and they didn't want to treat him for pneumonia again.

They thought it was better for him to die than get sick again?

Yes. Then, at the rest home, they made a mistake and gave him his breakfast. They must not have had the doctor's orders. They told us, "He's had a good breakfast!" Just when we were prepared for him to start dying.

All right. Now they've got it right. They're not feeding him anymore.

Things are back on schedule.

He'll have to die sooner or later.

He's taking a few days to do it.

It wasn't certain he would die before, when they gave him breakfast. He ate it. They said he enjoyed it! But he's beyond eating now. He doesn't even wake up.

So he's asleep?

Well, not exactly. His eyes are open, a little. But he doesn't see anything—his eyes don't move. And he won't answer if you speak to him.

But you don't know how long it will take.

A few days after that, they'll burn him.

After what?

After he dies.

You'll let them burn him.

We'll ask them to burn him. In fact, we'll pay them to burn him.

Why not burn him right away?

Before he dies?

No, no. Why did you say "a few days after that"?

According to the law, we have to wait at least forty-eight hours.

Even in the case of an innocent old accountant?

He wasn't so innocent. Think of the testimony he gave.

You mean, if he dies on a Thursday, he won't be burned until Monday.

They take him away, once he's dead. They keep him somewhere, and then they take him to where he'll be burned.

Who goes with him and keeps him company once he's dead?

No one, actually.

No one goes with him?

Well, someone will take him away, but we don't know the person.

You don't know the person?

It will be an employee.

Probably in the middle of the night?

Yes.

And you probably don't know where they'll take him either?

No.

And then no one will keep him company?

Well, he won't be alive anymore.

So you don't think it matters.

They will put him in a coffin?

No, it's actually a cardboard box.

A cardboard box?

Yes, a small one. Narrow and small. It didn't weigh much, even with him in it.

Was he a small man?

No. But as he got older he got smaller. And lighter. But still, it should have been bigger than that.

Are you sure he was in the box?

Yes.

Did you look?

No.

Why not?

They don't really give you an opportunity.

So they burned something in a cardboard box that you *trust* was your father?

Yes.

How long did it take?

Hours and hours.

Burn the accountant! What a festival!

We didn't know it would be cardboard. We didn't know it would be so small or so light.

You were "surprised."

I don't know where he has gone now that he's dead. I wonder where he is.

You're asking that now? Why didn't you ask that before?

Well, I did. I didn't have an answer. It's more urgent now.

"Urgent."

I wanted to think he was still nearby, I really wanted to believe that. If he was nearby, I thought he would be hovering.

Hovering?

I don't see him walking. I see him floating a few feet off the ground.

You say "I see him"—you can sit in a comfortable chair and say that you "see him." Where do you think he is?

But if he's nearby, hovering, is he the way he used to be, or is he the way he was at the end? He used to have all his memory. Does he get it back before he returns? Or is he the way he was near the end, with a lot of his memory gone?

What are you talking about?

At first I used to ask him a question and he would say, "No, I don't remember." Then he would just shake his head if I asked. But he had a little smile on his face, as though he didn't mind not remembering. He looked as if he thought it was interesting. He seemed to be enjoying the attention. At that time he still liked to watch things. One rainy day we sat together outside the front entrance of the home, under a sort of roof.

Wait a minute. What are you calling "the home"?

The old people's home, where he lived at the end.

That is not a home.

He watched the sparrows hopping around on the wet asphalt. Then a boy rode by on a bicycle. Then a woman walked by with a brightly colored umbrella. He pointed to these things. The sparrows, the boy on the bicycle, the woman with the colorful umbrella in the rain.

No, of course. You want to think he's still hovering nearby.

No, I don't think he's there anymore.

You may as well add that he still has his memory. He would have to. If he didn't, he would lose interest and just drift away.

I do think he was there for three days afterwards, anyway. I do think that.

Why three?

The Way to Perfection

Practicing at the piano:
My Alberti basses were not even.
But did my movement float this morning?
Yes!

The Fellowship

1

It is not that you are not qualified to receive the fellowship, it is that each year your application is not good enough. When at last your application is perfect, then you will receive the fellowship.

2

It is not that you are not qualified to receive the fellowship, it is that your patience must be tested first. Each year, you are patient, but not patient enough. When you have truly learned what it is to be patient, so much so that you forget all about the fellowship, then you will receive the fellowship.

Helen and Vi: A Study in Health and Vitality

Introduction

The following study presents the lives of two elderly women still thriving in their eighties and nineties. Although the account will necessarily be incomplete, depending as it does in part on the subjects' memories, it will be offered in detail whenever possible. Our hope is that, through this close description, some notion may be formed as to which aspects of the subjects' behaviors and life histories have produced such all-around physical, mental, emotional, and spiritual health.

Both women were born in America, one of African-American parents and one of immigrants from Sweden. The first, Vi, is eighty-five years old, currently still in very good health, working four days a week as a house- and office cleaner, and active in her church. The other, Helen, ninety-two, is in good health apart from her weakened sight and hearing, and though she now resides in a nursing home, she lived alone and independently until one year ago, caring for herself and her large house and yard with minimal help. She still looks after her own hygiene and tidies her room.

Background

Both Vi and Helen grew up in intact families with other children and two caregivers (in Vi's case these were her grandparents, for many years). Both were close to their siblings (in Vi's case there were also cousins in the immediate family) and remained in close touch with them throughout their lives. Both have outlived all of them: Helen was predeceased by an older brother who reached the age of ninety and an older sister who died at seventy-eight; Vi by seven brothers, sisters, and cousins, all but one of whom lived into their eighties and nineties. Her last remaining cousin died at the age of ninety-four, still going out to work as a cook.

Vi spent most of her childhood in Virginia on her grandparents' farm. She was one of eight siblings and cousins, all of whom lived with the grandparents and were raised by them up to a certain age. Her grandfather's farm was surrounded by fields and woods. The children went barefoot most of the time, so their physical contact with the land was constant, and intimate.

The children never saw a doctor. If one of them was sick, Vi's grandmother would go out into the fields or woods and find a particular kind of bark or leaf, and "boil it up." Her grandfather taught the children to recognize certain healthful wild plants, and in particular to tell the male from the female of certain flowers, since each had different properties; then they would be sent to gather the plants themselves. As a regular preventive health measure, at the beginning of each season, the grandmother would give them an infusion to "clean them out"; this would, among other benefits, rid them of the parasitic worms that were a common hazard of rural life at that time. When Vi moved up to Poughkeepsie to live with her mother, the home treatments ceased: when she had even a mild cold, her mother would take her to the doctor and he would give her medicines.

Vi's grandparents were both hard workers. For instance, in addition to her regular work, her grandmother also made quilts for all eight of the children. She would sew after breakfast and again in the afternoon. She enjoyed it, Vi says: she would use every bit of material, including the smallest scraps. Her grandmother's hands were nice, "straighter than mine," says Vi. Her grandmother would also sew clothes for the children out of the printed cotton fabric of flour sacks. On the first day of school, says Vi, she and her girl cousins would be wearing "such pretty dresses."

Her grandmother was a kind woman. Her grandfather, also kind, was stricter. When he said something, he meant it, says Vi. The kids listened to both, but waited until their grandfather was out of the house to make their special requests, because their grandmother was more likely to give them what they wanted.

Her grandfather raised all his own meat and vegetables. He built a house for them all with his own hands. She says her grandfather's hands were very bent and crooked.

The family slept on straw mattresses. Once a year her grandmother would have the children empty out the old straw and fill them with new. The kids would roll around on the newly filled mattresses to hear them crackle. The mattresses were stuffed so full that before the straw settled, the kids would keep sliding off. The pillows were stuffed with chicken feathers. Once a year, the grandmother would have the children empty out the old feathers and fill them with new feathers she had saved for the purpose.

The children were expected to do their chores without being reminded. If not, they suffered the consequences. Once, Vi says, she forgot to bring water from the spring. When her grandfather, resting from his day's work, asked for a drink, she admitted that she had forgotten, and he sent her out to fetch it, even though night had fallen. The way to the spring led past the small burial ground where some of the family rested, and she was frightened to walk by it in the dark. The children believed that ghosts roamed around after the sun was down. She had no choice, however, and she crept past the graveyard and down the hill to the spring, filled the bucket, and then ran all the way home again. She says that by the time she was back at the house, the bucket was half empty. She never forgot that chore again.

All the children grew up to be hard workers except the youngest, she says, who was the baby of the family and spoiled, and who did nothing when she grew up but have babies of her own. And, Vi is quick to point out, this sister died at the earliest age of them all, only seventy-two.

Eventually Vi moved north to live with her mother, who had a dairy farm. She continued going to school, in a two-room schoolhouse where the boys sat on one side of the room and the girls on the other. She attended up to the tenth grade. She took piano lessons for a while, and now wishes she had gone on with them, but she was a child who needed to be "pushed," she says, and her mother did not push her, being too busy. Besides running the farm, her mother worked for a local family for thirty years, mainly cooking.

Vi was married twice. Her first husband was "no good," she says: he ran after other women. Her second husband was a good man. She wishes she had met him first.

The many affectionate stories she tells about him and their life together indicate that their relationship was full of love, mutual appreciation, and good fun. "When I was a Standish," Vi will say, meaning when she was married to her first husband and bore his name. She will also express it another way: "Before I was a Harriman."

She had only one child, a daughter by her first husband, but she helped to raise her two granddaughters, who lived with her for a number of years.

Helen, too, grew up on a farm in her early childhood. Her father, soon after coming over from Sweden, acquired several hundred acres of farmland on the outskirts of a Connecticut village on an elevated plateau of land. Below, in the river valley, was a large thread-manufacturing town. He owned a small herd of cows and sold milk to neighboring families. He also raised chickens and bred the cows. He owned a team of horses for plowing, and the family used to go down the long hill into town in a wagon drawn by the two horses, who would be given a rest and a drink halfway down. Her family lived on the farm until Helen was seven, when they moved into town so that her older brother could go to the local high school.

While Helen's father worked the farm, her mother kept a kitchen garden and a poultry yard, and looked after the family. After they moved into town, Helen's father worked as custodian at the high school and later at the local college. In town, Helen's father, like Vi's grandfather, built a house with his own hands. It stood on a piece of land behind the house the family occupied. When he eventually sold both houses, her father was able to afford the larger house in which she raised her own family and lived most of her life.

Helen married when she was twenty. Her husband

played the saxophone and the clarinet in a dance band. Though his first love was music, he took a job in a bank to support the family, and over the years played less and less. Helen had two children born close together, both boys, and when they were still quite small, the family moved back into what was now Helen's parents' home, a large, though plain, white house in a neighborhood of roomy Victorian houses and mature shade trees on the side of the hill overlooking the river valley and the mills. A self-contained apartment was created for them on the second and third floors. For the rest of their lives, Helen took care of her parents as well as her own family. Her mother was ill and bedridden for the last thirteen years of her life.

After her parents were both gone, the house also sheltered, for a few years following the end of World War II, a succession of displaced families from refugee camps in Germany sponsored by Helen and her husband, some of whom still send her cards in the nursing home. Helen's sons left home and started families of their own, her husband eventually died, and Helen remained alone in the large house. For a brief time, she rented the second-floor apartment. The tenants were an elderly man and his teenage granddaughter. They left after the granddaughter became pregnant, and Helen did not rent the apartment again, but used the rooms for her sons and their families when they came to visit, and for storage. Now that Helen is gone, the house stands empty.

Employment

Both Vi and Helen began working at an early age, either helping their families or earning money outside the family.

Vi first worked outside the family at age nine, earning

five cents for fetching water "for a woman." One of Vi's later jobs, with her first husband, was woodcutting: they would use a two-handled saw to cut up "pulp wood" to fill a boxcar, for which they would earn $500. If they "skinned the bark" off each tree, the load would earn them $600. Later, she worked as a laundress in a nursing home, and still later took jobs cleaning houses and offices.

Vi teases the girls in the office who say they are tired—they've been sitting in a chair all day!

At her current housecleaning jobs, Vi works steadily from nine a.m. until four or five p.m., rarely stopping, though she will occasionally pause to talk, standing where she is, for as long as ten minutes at a stretch. When she is working she does not like to eat lunch, but she will also, usually, stop once during the day to sit down at the kitchen table and eat a piece of fruit—a banana, a pear, or an apple. If she has not had a piece of fruit by the end of the day, she will take a banana, hold it up in the air with a questioning look, and then sit down sideways at the kitchen table to peel and eat it quietly, or she will take the piece of fruit home with her. In the warm and hot weather she likes to have a tall glass of cold water with an ice cube in it. The heat does not particularly bother her, though, even on days when the mercury is in the nineties.

She works steadily, but she does not hurry. She says her grandmother taught them to take their time doing a job and to be thorough. She will, as she says, "put the night and the day on it," dusting every bar of a wooden chair and every spindle of a banister.

Vi's employers value her work and are loyal to her. After her eighty-fifth-birthday party, she went down to Washington to visit her granddaughter and stayed away far longer than she had planned. She was having work done on her teeth that extended week after week. Several months went by without a word from her, her bills piled up, and the telephone company threatened to cut off her phone service. She eventually made a visit back home to pay bills and contact employers, but in all this time no one made a move to replace her. Everyone simply got along as best they could until she was back again. She has been cleaning for the same office, a law office, for thirty years.

One of her longtime employers, an elderly woman, finally entered a nursing home. She complained to Vi that the people there did not know how to make a bed properly or to bathe her. She asked Vi if she would come to the home and continue to take care of her. Vi said she would do it in a minute, but she knew that the people who worked there would not let her.

Another employer moved to Washington and asked Vi please to move there with her and continue to work for her, but Vi would not consider moving from her home and community.

Helen helped her mother, who took in laundry, by delivering and picking up the clothes. One of her mother's customers then employed Helen for a time in her own home, to sweep and serve meals. To earn pocket money, Helen would go out into the countryside, collect wildflowers, and sell them to craft hobbyists who pressed the flowers and used them to decorate trays.

Hope, who, at age 100, would be the third case in an expanded version of this study, used to bake her own bread as a child growing up on the edge of a small town in Iowa. She would sell it to her neighbors in order to pay the costs of supporting her pony. The pony was not her own, but was lent to her for the summer in exchange for the work she would do to gentle and train it.

After her children entered school, Helen took a job doing alterations at a small, family-owned women's clothing store on Main Street. She would walk down to work and walk home again. Subsequently, she worked in the city of Hartford, also as a seamstress. To go there, she took a slow local train that wound its way through woods and past cemeteries and small towns.

Helen worked for four years for the clothing shop. The owner of this business and his wife looked after their employees, became friends with many of them, and continued some friendships long after the employment had ended. Helen's working environment was, therefore, an emotionally sustaining one. After she had been in the nursing home a year, her old boss was admitted following a stroke. He lingered for a couple of weeks, and Helen would make her way slowly, with her walker, into his room to visit him. A tall, handsome man with a smooth, pale face, he lay back on his pillow staring at her with his bright eyes, but he did not know her. His wife, often there beside him, visiting, would try to remind him, but he would shake his head.

Physical Activity: Work and Play

Both Helen and Vi have had lives filled with physical activity, most consistently walking, including long distance, and both spent significant amounts of time outdoors in the fresh air, especially as children, but also as adults. In both cases, once childhood was past, this activity principally consisted of work of one kind or another, either for themselves or for pay. But their leisure pursuits have often been active as well. Neither Vi nor Helen ever played a sport, but both danced regularly, and Vi's travels have often included a fair amount of walking.

When Vi was a child, she walked into town for errands and to attend school. Apart from her mealtimes and the hours spent in school, she was physically active the entire day, at her chores and at play—principally outdoors—with her siblings, cousins, and friends. As a young and middle-aged adult, too, she was physically active all day, her time divided between work for her own or her family's maintenance and work for pay, in both cases physical and active.

In these, her late years, Vi continues to do all her housework and yard work herself, with occasional help from family or friends if they are visiting. She will also, from time to time, clean her granddaughter's house, or a friend's house. She cooks, gardens, and rearranges her furniture. "I was always moving things," she says; "my second husband used to call me 'the moving van.' " Her second husband used to clean the kitchen when she was out working, keeping the stove and oven spotless. He would clip the hedge. Now she does it herself, but thinks she does a pretty poor job of it. Her husband also planted and tended all the rose shrubs, most of which are now gone. After a full day's work housecleaning, she will take home some plants and immediately put them in the ground. She says she likes to get her hands in the dirt.

After the working day is over, she will not only go on to tend her garden but, on certain days, leave the house after supper and spend the evening at choir practice. At a party just recently, she was one of the models in a fashion show, which required her to change into and out of eight different outfits. She admits to being tired afterwards ("I was so tired, I can't tell you; my bed said to me, 'I'm waitin' for you' "). But after going to bed early that night, she rose early the next day, Sunday, baked a pan full of macaroni and cheese for the church dinner, went out and worked in the yard, worked in the house, and after resting went off to the church dinner. After the dinner, because almost everyone else had left, she stayed behind to wash the dishes with a couple of friends, also elderly. They were at the church working until midnight.

Vi washes her clothes in a washing machine but hangs them to dry on a line outdoors or in the basement, as did Helen when she lived at home; neither owns a dryer, though both could afford it. Their caregivers, as they were growing up, no doubt taught them to take advantage of a "good drying day." It should be noted that hanging clothes out and taking them in again expends considerably more energy than transferring them to a dryer, and also involves exposure to the outside air and sunlight, thus no doubt adding another small measure to Vi's and Helen's well-being.

Hope, by contrast, has avoided housework as much as possible all her adult life, having felt she had better things to do.

As Helen was growing up, she, like Vi, would walk considerable distances almost every day. When she lived outside of town, up on the farm, she walked to school, besides helping with housework and farmwork and playing outdoors. When she moved into town, she continued to walk to school, a distance of seven or eight blocks each way. Her recreations as a teenager, besides dancing, included such group physical activities as scavenger hunts, then called "mystery hunts," that involved roaming the town for several hours.

When she was a young mother, she would take her small sons out into the countryside onto friends' farmland to pick berries, which she would then bake into a pie.

Helen walked wherever she needed to go. Her house was four blocks up from the main street, the last block very steep. She walked down to the shop where she worked, and walked home again. When she went into the city to work or to shop at G. Fox's department store, she would walk to and from the train station, a distance of at least six blocks. In her later years, when she no longer went down to Main Street, she would still walk half a block up the hill and then several blocks over to her church on Sunday and, unless a friend gave her a lift, back home again.

Besides this lifetime—more than eighty years—of walking up and down the long hill, there was the work in and around the house. Like Vi, Helen, when she lived in her house, did all the housework and yard work herself. In the course of her day, it was not unusual for her to go down into the basement several times to fetch something or to hang out some wet clothes, and to climb, more than once, one flight to the second floor or two flights to the attic to find a piece of clothing or put a photograph away.

Even after her eyesight went, Helen continued to look after the house without regular help, tidying and cleaning, watering the African violets on the dining-room windowsills and the Christmas cactuses upstairs in the sunny front room. The house was still perfectly neat, though not quite as clean, since she could not see that the ruffled yellow curtains in the kitchen were becoming dingy or that there were fingermarks on the woodwork by the downstairs bathroom where she rested her hand going in. She worked slowly and meticulously. She had such a habit of neatness, and was so attentive, that even with her advanced macular degeneration she would find, in tidying the house after the family had departed, a single small jigsaw puzzle piece on the porch floor. She was so patient that although she could not see more than light and shadows, she would slowly peel the potatoes for dinner, feeling for the eyes with her fingertips and digging each one out with the tip of the peeler. She would gently but firmly insist on doing the dishes herself, though she would sometimes lie down and rest first.

In the yard, she would rake the leaves and pick up the sticks that dropped from the many overhanging trees; in winter, she shoveled at least some of the snow. Family would help only with the heavier jobs: a visiting son would trim the hedge, bring the porch furniture up from the basement, put on or take off storm windows. A grandchild would sometimes help with the leaves or the sticks. If there was an unusual problem she could not handle, such as squirrels in the attic, one of her sons would help. If there was an emergency, such as a fire in the chimney, she would call her next-door neighbors.

All these various activities continued until she entered the nursing home at age ninety-one.

Whereas Vi is still active, Helen now spends the better part of her day sitting in a chair by her bed. She must deliberately seek exercise: with a nursing home aide or volunteer, or a family member, she walks all the way around the nursing home, which is laid out in the shape of a diamond surrounding an open-air courtyard. Leaning on her walker, she heads off in one direction or the other, past the residents' rooms, most of them doubles, past the hairdressing salon (hours posted on the door), past the doors out to the courtyard, the front lobby and the stained-glass swinging doors into the chapel, a lounge with a large-screen television and a card table, a nurses' station, another passage leading to the courtyard, the recreation room, the residents' showers, the dining room, another nurses' station, the staff lounge with its locked door and its snack and soda machines visible through a window, another residents' lounge with a smaller television and a bookcase, the kitchen, and more residents' rooms, until she reaches her own room again. Here she parks her walker, backs up to her chair, bends to grip its arms, and sinks down into it saying "Ah" with a smile, relieved that the walk is done.

Hope, too, deliberately seeks her exercise: she takes her walker out into the long hall of her apartment building with its smell of fresh plaster; and with a friend, a family member, or her paid companion by her side, she walks a set number of times to the windowed door at the far end and back to the identical windowed door at the near end, sometimes encountering a neighbor along the way. She then returns to her apartment, lies back on her old blue sleigh bed with its litter of books and magazines, papers and notebooks, purse, tray table, and ragged cloth napkin, and rests for a moment before continuing her exercise with a set number of arm and leg lifts. When she is done, she asks for her water to be refilled; she must have water in two glasses by her bedside, one half full, next to her, the other full, at arm's length.

Present Living Situation

Helen's house is a large one, with four floors that were once in constant use: a basement for storage and laundry, a ground floor with kitchen, dining room, two parlors, a small bathroom, and Helen's bedroom; a second floor with another kitchen, a large front room, two bedrooms, and a larger bathroom; and an attic floor containing one bedroom and one storeroom.

Though Vi's house is smaller than Helen's, it, too, has a basement, a ground floor, a second floor, and an attic. And like Helen's, it has a second kitchen on the second floor, part of a self-contained apartment created for rental. Three generations of a family lived there at one time: a grandfather, granddaughter, and the granddaughter's child.

Vi's house is in a pleasant, integrated neighborhood of modest but attractive and generally well-cared-for older houses that sits high above the confluence of a wide creek and an estuary, though most of the houses do not have a view of the water. Many are single-family houses, with their own well-tended yards. Many, like Vi's, are of brick, since the manufacture of bricks was once a dominant industry of the region, while some are of clapboard. Vi's house is painted white, and the eave of her enclosed front porch is lined by a black-and-white-striped metal awning. Her yard contains a small patch of lawn in front and a larger square of lawn in back by the garage. It is bordered by a low hedge along the driveway, and is ornamented by a variety of perennial plantings, including several clumps of phlox, a few hostas, and one rosebush.

Vi's house and Helen's are both clean and tidy, but whereas Helen's rooms are, some of them, remarkably empty, Vi's are crowded. One upstairs bedroom in Helen's house, for instance, contains nothing but a single bed, a folding wooden chair, and a lamp; the closet is empty, the windows curtainless, and the floor and the walls bare. Even in the reception rooms downstairs, very few decorative objects are in evidence. In the back parlor, the end tables by the sofa display only two: one a delicate Venetian glass vase brought back to her from Italy by her younger son; the other of unknown provenance and harder to classify—a teacup and saucer knitted from blue and white cotton. Every room in Vi's house, on the other hand, is filled with knickknacks, whatnot tables, easy chairs, heavy rugs and drapes, lamps, stacks of storage boxes, and vases of artificial flowers.

Whereas Vi's walls are covered with photographs and plaques awarded to her by her church, Helen has only three or four photos on display in each of her two parlors, her bedroom, and the upstairs guest room; she possesses many more, but keeps them in albums or boxes in bureau drawers. Vi has perhaps seventy to eighty photos hanging on the walls or standing on the surfaces of, particularly, her living and dining rooms. Both Vi and Helen display pictures of grandparents, parents, brothers and sisters, husbands, children, grandchildren, and friends. In addition, Vi likes to display pictures of her employers' pets, though not her employers themselves. Because one of Helen's sons is an artist, her parlor walls are hung with his paintings, the earlier ones figurative and the later ones abstract. These contrast noticeably in spirit with such odd, occasional knickknacks as the knitted cup and saucer.

Vi's closets are packed with clothes, some of which she has not worn in years. (When she wants to describe a closet full of clothes all in a mess, she says they "walk out of the closet and say how de do!") The organizer of a recent church fashion show made a visit to Vi's house to search these closets and created a good number of outfits from them. Helen's closets, on the other hand, are spare and reduced to the essentials, containing mostly just a few simple, functional, everyday clothes: cardigans, blouses, shirtwaist dresses, skirts, and housecoats. Some of these clothes came as gifts from her family at Christmas and birthdays, but often they are clothes that she has worn for years, sometimes passed on to her long ago by a friend, her sister, or her sister-in-law. She can afford to buy new clothes, but a long habit of thrift makes her see such expenditure as rarely necessary. She seems perfectly content with what she has.

Unused clothing is stored in the spare rooms of Helen's

house. In a bureau drawer in a guest room is a box containing a bed jacket or nightie that she has been given as a gift. A closet in one upstairs bedroom and a rack in the attic contain a small number of seasonal outfits that she is not wearing at the moment. When the season changed, she used to bring these down to replace the clothes in her bedroom closet; now she asks someone else to bring the clothes to her in the nursing home. When she still lived at home, she was continually sorting through what she had and reducing it further. She would come down with her slight stoop and her small steps from an upstairs room or the attic carrying an item of clothing or a piece of table linen or a brooch: "Could you use this?" she would ask.

Helen's house was always tidy, because she cleaned up right away. She had a place for each thing and she put it away in its place as soon as she was finished using it. There was one exception to this practice: instead of carrying an empty cardboard box down to the cellar and putting it away immediately, she would toss it down the cellar stairs and put it away the next time she went down—in this one case valuing economy of motion over tidiness. Tidiness is her habit, but she does not preach it, whereas Vi readily tells a child or young person that it is important to put his or her things away in order to know where to find them again. Vi's house is so much more crowded than Helen's that it does not look as obviously tidy as Helen's.

Both Vi and Helen have mottoes on the walls of the kitchen, but Vi's tend to be purely humorous while Helen's—in Swedish, English, or both—are either religious ("God Bless This House") or sentimental ("Home Sweet Home" and *"Hem kära hem"*) or moralistic (*"Den som vinner tid, vinner allt"*) or humorous with a moral message ("The hurrieder I go, the behinder I get") or simply friendly (*"Välkommen"*). Also hanging in Helen's kitchen are several pictures intended to charm or entertain, such as a photograph of a frightened kitten clinging by its front paws to a thin branch.

Though she goes back to visit her house from time to time, Helen now lives in a shared room in a pleasant nursing home. Her half of the room is on the hall side rather than the window side, and is therefore darker, but she prefers not to be moved. She has had two roommates so far. The first was bedridden and mentally incompetent, emitting only groans and shouts except for the one intermittent phrase "Oh boy oh boy." This woman died after a year, and the space is now occupied by an active woman in her forties with chronic progressive dementia. She is in the early stages of the disease and currently functions very well, caring for the cats and birds that live in the nursing home and giving Helen whatever help she can, as with the telephone, with selecting food choices from the daily menu offerings, and with many other necessary tasks. Helen and she have become fond of each other, and Helen's only difficulty with her is that the roommate, whether because of her disease or her medication, talks perhaps twice as fast as the average person, so that Helen, with her impaired hearing, cannot always understand her.

Because the nursing home is located in the town in which Helen has lived all her life, she regularly discovers, among the other residents, old friends or acquaintances who are in the home either for a short rehabilitation or, more usually, for permanent care. She had not been living there long, for instance, when one of her sons read off to her the names of the two women who lived directly across the hall. To her astonishment, one was Ruth, a close friend from her childhood with whom she had lost touch. Helen immediately went across the hall to visit her friend. The woman, however, was mentally incapacitated and, though Helen spent some time talking to her and recalling events from their youth, did not recognize her. Later, Helen showed her son a photograph in which she, in the front row, and Ruth, in the second, stood among ten or twelve other girls in their white confirmation dresses and curled hair, holding flowers.

Recreation

Although Vi sings in church, she does not sing while she works, or at other times.

Helen sang in church regularly as part of the congregation. She also sang Swedish songs with her family when she was growing up. When she still lived at home, she would sometimes hum softly along with the hymns that were chimed by a nearby church every evening at six o'clock. In the nursing home, she has occasionally been induced to sing a few carols with the other residents during a Christmas sing-along. She sings tremulously and so faintly as to be almost inaudible, her expression vacant and her eyes, behind their wide bifocal lenses, directed into the vague distance.

Every evening before bedtime, however, she goes across the hall to sing a Swedish children's prayer to her old friend Ruth.

When Vi's granddaughters lived with her, she used to come home in the evening exhausted after working sometimes not just one but two jobs, and the little girls would want to teach her a new dance. "Come on, Gramma," they would say, "come on, dance with us." She would say, "No, I'm tired, I'm too tired." They would say, "Come on, Gramma, come on, dance with us—it's good exercise!"

and she would give in and dance with them before she went to lie down.

Helen danced as a teenager, as often as once a week. Later, she would go to the dances where her husband was playing in the band, and still later, she and her husband would go out dancing together. When she still lived at home and her balance was good, she would occasionally catch hold of a grandchild's hands and dance with him for a moment by the kitchen door, singing a little tune to go along with the dance.

Activities with other people have been both Vi's and Helen's main forms of recreation all their lives. For Vi, most recently, these have taken the form of church activities, dinners with family or friends in her home, and travel. For Helen, they have been mostly confined to visits from family and friends and occasional scheduled events in the nursing home. Earlier in her married life, besides dancing with her husband, Helen liked to give card parties at home. She also put on regular dinners with friends and family, often including such characteristically Swedish dishes as pickled herring, pickled beets, meatballs, and limpa.

Reading was a form of recreation for Helen before her eyes went, but not for Vi. When Vi reads, it is the Bible. Helen used to read the Bible and other Christian books, such as *The Good Christian Wife*, but also magazines and the romantic novels of popular women authors like Judith Krantz.

Vi watches some television, but not much. She has a set in her kitchen that is on most of the time, especially when her daughter is visiting, but she is often busy cooking, talking on the telephone, or visiting with friends, and only intermittently pays attention to it. She is shocked by the low level of many of the programs.

At home, Helen had a console television set in the corner of her living room and used to watch game shows and one soap opera in particular, *As the World Turns.* After her eyesight became so poor, she would still listen to the programs, but then she abandoned television altogether. She also listened to the radio that she kept in the kitchen on a shelf over the sink, not only the Sunday sermons and inspirational talks, but also the women's basketball games, which she followed with some ardor: a tense moment in a game was one of the rare occasions when she was, in her own gentle way, assertive with another person, asking by the most delicate of gestures—an upraised hand and a tilt of the head—for a pause in the conversation so that she could hear the outcome of the play. She is still a fan of the UConn team. Vi does not seem to follow sports at all.

Neither Vi nor Helen is very interested in world or national news in areas such as economics, politics, literature, or art. They are both keenly interested in news of disasters and in human interest stories involving a universal theme in a particularly dramatic form—love, loss, betrayal, perversion, gross injury or disability, death. They may also, exceptionally, comment on some recent legislation that will affect them directly. But the news that engages them most is strictly local, concerning those close to them—and this includes not only their immediate friends and family but also their friends' extended family; in these areas they are quite up-to-date on the latest information, most often remembering all names and ages and relationships of those involved.

Now that Helen spends so many hours sitting in her chair by her bed, unable to read or watch television, she confides that her main leisure activity, when she is alone, is to remember and relive incidents and episodes from her past life.

Travel

Vi learned to drive at the age of sixty. Her last surviving cousin never drove a car, and it didn't do her any good, Vi says, always to be standing on street corners in all types of weather waiting for a bus or a taxi. Certain friends of Vi's will drive around town but will not drive to any other town, but Vi is not afraid to drive a fair distance.

She drives a large car that was her second husband's particular pride: he always kept it perfectly cleaned and shined. She says he would be so ashamed to see how she takes care of it, although it looks fairly clean and tidy to anyone else. True, she does allow dust to gather on the dashboard and tiny scraps of litter on the floor.

The fact that Helen never drove a car meant that in later life she and two of her friends shared their weekly trip out for groceries; thus, the necessary chore became a pleasant social occasion.

Vi travels regularly within the country and occasionally out of the country, whereas Helen no longer travels and rarely did.

Vi goes to Washington to visit her granddaughter, and sometimes farther south to attend a wedding or funeral. She either drives with her daughter or takes the bus with a friend. Other, local trips are either by car, when she drives herself, or in the church van, when the choir is going off somewhere to sing.

Helen has traveled very little in her life, though members of her extended family have gone to Sweden to visit historical family sites. She took several vacations in New England with her husband and sons and, after she was widowed, two trips to Florida with her brother. In all of her life, she has lived away from her hometown only once: after she graduated from high school, her brother drove her down to New York City, where she settled in Brooklyn and studied dressmaking for one year at the Pratt Institute. After she was married and raising her two sons, she rarely went farther from home than to Hartford by train.

For many years now, travel for Helen has been limited to drives around town and into the countryside as a passenger. She looks out the window, and despite her near blindness manages to identify old landmarks from her younger years: a friend's farm, the group home where her friend Robert lives with his large collection of first-edition books, the house where she once worked as a maid, her friends' florist shop, the house on Oak Street where her family first lived after they left the farm, and the house in back of it that her father built.

Pets and Other Animals

Both Helen and Vi are very fond of animals and have had pets and domestic animals in their lives from early childhood.

Vi is more partial to dogs; she has more stories about them, and photographs of them. But she is also amused by cats, especially one small black cat that tries to grab the dust cloth out of her hand where she works—helping her to clean, she says. Her backyard is full of strays and neighborhood cats, though she does not feed them. The old woman next door feeds them, she says, and although some of the other neighbors object, Vi sees no harm in it, since this is one of the old woman's few pleasures and she will be gone from this world soon enough. When Vi talks about this old woman, she seems to forget that she herself, being eighty-five, is also an old woman.

In Helen's early life, there were the two horses, as well as the cows, calves, cats and kittens, and a large flock of chickens. In her adult life, she has almost always had a cat as a pet. She used to feed strays at her back door, and one winter arranged a cardboard box shelter for one of them under the outside staircase. She would walk out over the ice with small, careful steps just before dark to set his evening meal down in the snow. There are cats in the nursing home, and one in particular, a large Persian, will occasionally wander in to visit her. She speaks to him, smiles, and reaches her hand down to him, though in her eyes he is only an orange blur.

Hope kept an overweight female cat throughout her later years, with sometimes harmony between them and sometimes ill will. She was sure the cat harbored resentments and indulged in some calculated bad behavior. When, eventually, she was advised by a home health expert that the cat posed a certain hazard to her by crouching in dark corners, getting underfoot, and occasionally attacking her ankles, she immediately arranged for it to be put down by the local vet before her family could intervene.

Although Helen, when she lived at home, kept a bird feeder well supplied outside the kitchen window where she could watch it over her morning coffee, she had no great love of, or interest in, other sorts of wild creatures.

Vi, the same in this respect, particularly dislikes snakes and often repeats a long story about finding one in her yard and going after it with a shovel. When she was a child in Virginia, the windows were kept open in the summertime and lizards would climb up to sun themselves on the windowsills. The children were scared of the lizards and wanted to kill them. But Vi's grandmother told them the lizards would not hurt them, to let the lizards stay there and enjoy the sun, and they would go away when they were ready.

Neither Helen nor Vi is particularly interested in the natural world beyond the confines of the garden. Nature for Helen, when she still lived at home, manifested itself either as a practical problem—trees shading the house, the lawn that did not grow well, the hedge that needed clipping, acorns in the driveway—or a domesticated thing of beauty like her favorite, the azalea shrub, or the dogwood in blossom. Her work in the yard was caretaking work rather than designing and planting, with the exception of the geraniums, which she liked to see set out in the spring in a row by the front porch. Every spring, too, she looked for the first blooms of the flowering bulbs.

She also enjoyed nature in the form of the landscape as seen from the car window on a Sunday drive.

Religion

Both Helen and Vi have maintained close involvement with their churches all their lives, although the church has loomed larger in Vi's life than in Helen's. Their churches have constituted their most important larger community, both social and spiritual.

In youth and middle age, Helen participated in the church's ladies' auxiliary group and helped out with such projects as bake sales for fund-raising. Every summer her family attended the church picnics. She said grace before every meal while she still lived at home. It is important to her that every family member be baptized, although her gentle insistence about this has sometimes had no effect. Her religious beliefs do not explicitly enter or color her conversation. She now rarely goes to a church service because the chapel in her nursing home is Catholic.

Vi's strong faith occasionally enters her conversation, when she refers to "God's will" or, more jocularly, describes what God might have in mind for her future. When she used to visit the local prison, she would incorporate some Christian teaching in her conversations with the prisoners. She likes to spend time at Bible study with her best friend on a warm Saturday evening in summer. They take chairs out into the backyard, and as it grows dark they read aloud to each other from Scripture, discussing each passage in preparation for the following day's Bible class.

Hope reacted against her mother's strong religious convictions by rejecting all organized religions and in fact all forms of spirituality, as well as, though indirectly, by joining, at one stage, the Communist Party.

Vi spends most of every weekend on church activities. She was for a time president of an official churchwomen's group, the Deaconesses. She sings in the choir, which involves going to choir rehearsals as well as occasionally traveling to other churches, often in distant towns, to give performances. Congregations of different churches also visit each other: often her church will visit another for a supper, or her church will prepare a supper to host another church, when she will bake and help wash up afterwards. She will exclaim later over the quantity of food consumed by the other congregation.

In her walk around the nursing home, Helen will sometimes ask family members to look for the names of acquaintances. She will always stop in front of the chapel. Here, next to the open stained-glass doors, a signboard with a black background and removable white letters bears the names of those residents who are in the hospital or recently deceased and in need of a candle and/or a prayer. She will ask to have the names read to her in case they include someone she knows.

Personal Habits

Both Vi's and Helen's eating habits are sensible, Vi's diet marginally more balanced since she includes more fresh fruits and vegetables. Neither is particularly health-conscious; their good habits are also the habits of their families of origin.

Both have always practiced moderation, eaten regular meals, and enjoyed food and the preparation of food, although Vi has been more explicitly enthusiastic about food than Helen. Both have eaten predominantly home cooking (including baking) all their lives, and although they enjoy restaurant meals have tended to eat very little food that could be called convenience, junk, or fast food, with the exception of sandwiches and pastries. When they were children, of course, neither one ever ate in a restaurant.

When Vi was growing up on the farm in Virginia, the family ate their own fruits and vegetables—fresh in season and home-canned in winter—and the animals they raised themselves. They bought almost nothing but sugar in a sack, which the children would carry home—and on the way, Vi says, being mischievous and fun-loving, they would sneak a taste by sucking a corner of the sack.

In contrast to her light lunch when she is working at a cleaning job, Vi has a hearty breakfast and dinner. For breakfast she has a glass of milk, a glass of juice, cereal, eggs, bacon, and toast. With her second husband she used to have pancakes on Sundays, with coffee. She drinks quite a lot of milk now, but did not when she was younger. When she goes home after a day of work, she says, she makes herself a nice dinner. In the cold weather she likes to start with a bowl of soup. "A little bowl?" "No, a medium-sized bowl." Then she has some meat, perhaps meatballs, pork chops, or chicken and vegetables. She makes the soup and the meatballs herself. She likes her own cooking. She does not care for meat now, though, as much as she used to; she likes vegetables and fruit more.

Helen used to order a Reuben sandwich when she went out to lunch: corned beef and cheese on rye bread. She would, however, eat only half the sandwich, taking the other half home for her next day's lunch. She liked to go out for doughnuts after church with her friends. They would also have breakfast together in a restaurant every Wednesday, before they did their grocery shopping. In her later years, her cupboards used to contain a good deal of canned food as well as Lipton tea, Sanka, boxes of pastries and cookies, and spices, flour, and sugar for baking. She liked sweets, but ate them in small quantities. She would have a piece of fruit during the day. She would buy prepared seafood salad for sandwiches. For family dinners, she regularly made mashed potatoes and what she called a "salad," which consisted of an aspic mold containing grated carrots, Jell-O, and pineapple. Earlier in her life, she would bake pastries and breads for her family, setting the dough to rise on the radiators in winter.

Both Vi and Helen like rhubarb and welcome a chance to have it fresh out of a friend's or family's garden and eat it stewed. Vi bends down herself and gives each stalk a vigorous twist at the base to break it off, collecting half a dozen to take home with her. In Helen's case, her family brings it to her already stewed and ready to eat, but there is always the danger that a member of the nursing home staff will remove the tub of slimy-looking fruit and throw it out, as happened once, before Helen has a chance to enjoy it.

Hope has been adamant, all her life, in planning a healthy food program for herself. Now, every day, under her instruction, her live-in companion prepares for her, for lunch, a bean soup, a small salad, and a small bowl of popcorn, followed by a fruit and yogurt dessert. She sometimes calls out to her companion several times to see if lunch is ready yet or to request additional services that delay the preparation of the meal. When the time comes, she makes her way slowly to the dining area via the kitchen, where she may give a few more instructions. While she eats, she wears a cracked green plastic tennis visor over her eyes to shade them from the overhead chandelier and watches a book program on the television.

Neither Helen nor Vi ever smoked. When she was small, Vi and her cousin Joe had tried smoking their grandmother's pipe when she was away. There wasn't much tobacco in it, but Vi became very sick. Later, she didn't dare tell her grandmother why she was so sick. If her grandparents had found out what she had done, she says, "I woulda had some sores *now*" from it. This bad experience discouraged her from ever wanting to smoke again.

Hope had the occasional cigarette in her twenties, during the years when, stylish and attractive, she also tended to form various short-lived attachments to, often, wealthy and well-born lovers and traveled abroad, sometimes at their expense. However, smoking did not agree with her and she did not continue.

Vi does not habitually drink alcohol at all. She says she likes her Manischewitz, but the last time she drank any, in fact, was many years ago: an employer used to invite her to breakfast and offer her a small glass, but that employer is long gone. Helen, before she moved into the nursing home, would occasionally be persuaded to have a little sweet wine after a holiday meal: seated in her customary place at one end of the dining table, in front of a glass-fronted cupboard containing sets of delicate sherry glasses and some commemoration plates and mugs, she would sip it slowly and thoughtfully. Now she does not have wine or any other alcohol.

Hope, by contrast, has drunk wine and mixed drinks all her life, enjoying an altered state of mind in which she is more apt to make risqué or tactless remarks, and whether or not company is present, she often has a glass of wine with her dinner.

For guests, she likes to open a bottle of champagne: When they arrive at the door, she is immediately distracted by the thought of the champagne and barely greets them before sending them to find it in the refrigerator. After the champagne has been drunk, she will sometimes have her guests bring out a leftover bottle of wine from the refrigerator, though it is ice-cold and may be sour.

Both Helen and Vi are thrifty by habit. Vi's second husband would look out for sales and buy, for instance, ten large bottles of bleach for thirty-nine cents a bottle. Vi, too, buys in quantity. She keeps these extra supplies on her small enclosed side porch.

Helen has a metal serving spoon that she used to stir things on the stove for so long that it is worn down nearly straight on one side.

When her daughter was a child, Vi was given nice hand-me-down children's clothes, including party dresses, by her employers. She would pack them carefully away until her daughter was the right size for them, then wrap them festively and present them for birthdays and Christmases as though they were new. Her daughter never suspected. Now Vi's daughter in turn brings her good clothing from yard sales. Vi rarely buys a piece of new clothing for herself.

Vi does not buy more food than she needs, and she does not let it spoil. The same was true of Helen when she lived at home and cooked for herself. Vi drinks Lipton tea, and she uses each teabag twice, sometimes three times.

Helen, by now, in the restricted space of the nursing home, feels somewhat oppressed and burdened by her possessions, though she has so few. More inclined to give than receive, she resists offers of presents, though she sometimes appears secretly pleased by them; "No, no," she will say gently, "don't bring me anything. I don't need *anything*!" Sometimes, only, she may ask for a bag of cough drops or a bar of soap.

Vi is quite open about liking to receive presents. She appreciates framed photographs, plants, and boxes of chocolates. At the end of her day's work, she likes to take home, in the growing season, either produce from an employer's vegetable patch or a perennial plant dug up out of the ground. But she likes gifts of money more than anything else. On the occasion of her eighty-fifth birthday, not only her employers but most of her friends gave her money.

Whether in order to make an economical choice or, more likely, to save trouble for her family, Helen, some years ago, went with her older son to a local funeral parlor, chose a casket, and paid in advance for the casket and funeral arrangements. With the same foresight, she had already chosen the nursing home in which she now lives.

Health

Vi is rarely ill, having only the occasional cold in her head and chest. She has some arthritis in her left shoulder, which prevents her raising her left arm above shoulder height. She has to compensate when working by using her other arm for some things. For a time she was given physical therapy for it, but it didn't get much better. She believes, though, that if you have arthritis, you have to use the affected limb, otherwise it will get worse and worse. She will cite the examples of several friends who moved less and less until they could not move at all. She has no other physical problems and takes no medication.

Although Helen's eyesight and hearing are poor, she takes no prescription medications, her only pills being vitamins and an occasional aspirin. She had no medical problems until the age of eighty, when she began to develop macular degeneration, which has grown progressively worse. Sometime after she turned ninety, a friend of hers noticed, on their weekly grocery shopping trip, that her ankles were badly swollen. Helen went to the doctor and it was discovered that her heart had begun to beat more slowly and erratically. She was fitted with a pacemaker. Following insertion of the pacemaker, medical problems began that appeared to have been caused by the medical interventions themselves. For instance, a heart medication upset her stomach. This in turn caused her to lose weight and weaken, making her more prone to falling. One fall resulted in a broken hip. She entered her present nursing home on a temporary basis for treatment and then arranged to stay there permanently. In the nursing home, a treatment with a medicated shampoo led to a chronic and persistent skin irritation that she will apparently never be free of. Two of her medical problems, then—her macular degeneration and her erratic heartbeat—occurred naturally and spontaneously, whereas the others—the weight loss with resultant weakness, the fall and fracture, and the skin condition—resulted from medical intervention.

Helen's well-being is dependent, now, on the environment of the nursing home and the treatment she receives there.

Physical Appearance

Both Helen and Vi take pride in their appearance. Both, *like Hope,* were attractive and popular with boys and men when they were younger. Their figures are strong, slender, and youthful. They have smooth, clear skin, Helen's pale but with a diffused rosy color and Vi's a rich, even brown.

Vi's face is round, her eyes are dark brown and sparkling and slant upward a little at the outer edges. Her eyebrows are straight and thick. Her lips are often parted, as though she is about to speak or smile, and then her lower lip curves downward. Helen's blue eyes are dim now, the whites yellowish. Both Helen and Vi wear large glasses, though Vi often removes hers for a photograph. Vi's hands are shapely and dark brown. Her fingers are slim and fairly straight; only the last joint of the index finger is a little bent and swollen. Helen's fingers are quite crooked.

A photograph of Helen taken when she was about twenty years old shows her leaning against the front porch of the large white house, her hands behind her back. Her head is tilted to one side, and she is smiling. Her black dress is low-waisted, with a V-neck, a loosely knotted black tie at the V, and a flared, pleated, knee-length skirt. She wears clear stockings and black heeled pumps with ankle straps. She has a string of pearls around her neck. Her long, dark hair is parted and tied back.

Both Vi and Helen pay attention to their clothes and enjoy dressing nicely. As a teenager, Vi wore a variety of handsome, but conservative, tailored clothes—blouses, suits, coats—of interesting fabrics, with detailed buttons and belts. She is pictured in one photograph wearing a wide-lapeled camel coat, a black beret, and a black scarf. In another, she is shown with a much older boyfriend who appears to be in his thirties and is dressed in a double-breasted suit, bicolored handkerchief folded into a triangle in his breast pocket, a tie with tiepin, and a hat, a cigar clamped in his mouth—but, as Vi points out, his pants have no crease. Here, she is wearing a pale blue dress with white buttons and a round white collar under a dark coat with a small white fur collar, and lavender heeled pumps with straps. In another photograph, with another boyfriend, this one her own age, she is wearing a dress with full cream-colored blouse and sleeves and broad swathes of lace down the front and around the neck. Her hair is simply arranged with a part down the middle, she is wearing her glasses, and, as in all her photographs, she has a relaxed, happy smile.

For a housecleaning job, Vi often goes out dressed in clean and pressed blue jeans, sneakers, and a sweatshirt or a sweater or, in warm weather, a T-shirt. Dressed in this way, she appears as athletic as a young girl. Very rarely, her head is wrapped in a kerchief tied in back; more usually, she is bareheaded, her hair braided in one of a variety of different styles. Her hair is still mostly dark, with only a little gray in it. When she dresses up for a party or church function, however, she wears a wig of smooth, waved, and styled black hair streaked with silver and a fancy dress of shiny material, sometimes with bouffant sleeves and a wide skirt, sometimes more streamlined. The change in her appearance is startling: she looks younger than her age, but also more formal, losing her youthful or tomboyish vivaciousness. In this guise she is known to most of the other church members not as Vi or Viola but as Mother Harriman.

When Helen still lived at home, she would have breakfast—often just a piece of toast and a cup of instant coffee—in her nightgown, housecoat, and slippers. Then, after washing the breakfast dishes, she would wash herself and dress in stockings, low-heeled pumps, a skirt, a blouse with a pin, or a dress, and sometimes a cardigan. She was always well groomed and her colors were pleasing in combination, if muted. Her gray hair was styled in a permanent wave. When she moved into the nursing home she immediately abandoned the permanent wave, and now her hair is straight and cut fairly short, a shiny silver, usually pinned to the side with a bobby pin. She now wears kneesocks instead of stockings, and athletic shoes because they have good support and traction.

Both Vi and Helen are graceful. They stand and move in an economical, balanced way, Helen more slowly and deliberately now than Vi. Neither one has ever been awkward, clumsy, or hasty. They know the importance of not rushing. If an employer or a friend has to go out on an errand, Vi will say, with a pleasant lilt to her words, "Take your time!"

Helen has always thought and planned ahead, and has been prepared for what she will do next. This is one of the reasons she is not clumsy and does not hurry. Only once did her younger son ever see her moving fast, and that was during an emergency: a little girl had fallen into a neighbor's well and was drowning.

Vi's posture is fully upright; she stands poised and balanced on her feet with her shoulders back and her head up, facing the person she is talking to and looking him or her directly in the eye. Helen has a slight stoop in her back and shoulders, and when she is seated, she tends to be rather graciously inclined toward the person she is talking to, this tendency no doubt exacerbated by her weak hearing. While she still lived in her own house, this forward inclination, as she peeled a potato or climbed the stairs with something in her arms, was expressive of her general state of readiness and activity, and even of her generosity, as she reached out a crooked hand to touch a grandchild or show a photograph.

Personality and Temperament

Both Vi and Helen are polite and gracious in their actions and responses, and appreciative and thoughtful of others. But beyond these good manners, both have a good deal of personal charm. This expresses itself in their voices, facial expressions, bearing, wit, and alertness of response. They maintain steady eye contact; their expressions are relaxed and smiling, their voices are well inflected, rising and falling pleasantly; they are closely attentive to the conversation in progress and quick to respond with a thoughtful remark.

Both Vi and Helen are so friendly and charming that they consistently elicit positive reactions from others—their friends, employers, doctors, nurses, church congregation members, children and grandchildren—and therefore in turn receive, from these others, the sustenance of friendliness, consideration, and wit.

At present, although, inevitably, certain of the staff at the nursing home are by nature unresponsive, cold in manner, or bad-tempered, most have become very fond of Helen and describe her modest and generous personality either directly—"She'll never tell you if she needs something"—or with gentle irony: "Oh, Helen—she's such a complainer!"

Vi appears to be happy, at times exuberant, often vivacious. By contrast, Helen is more subdued. Perhaps because of her infirmities and her permanent residence in the nursing home, she sometimes indicates quite directly, though with a resigned smile, that she will not mind when the time comes for her to die, or even that she will welcome it. If Vi, on the other hand, mentions her own "passing," it is in a humorous context.

Both rebound from difficulties, Vi often seeing the lighter side of a situation, Helen tending to accept the inevitable—"Well," she will say with a shrug and a smile, "what can you do?"

Both display enthusiasm, though Vi's is more vocal and louder than Helen's. If Helen enjoys competitive sports on the radio, Vi enjoys a good meal, a good story, and even a new broom.

Both abide firmly by their long-established habits and are reluctant or unwilling to try a novel way of doing something, or even to hear about it.

Hope, by contrast, still as mentally sharp as she ever has been, appreciates any form of ingenuity, especially her own. She will report her bold ideas and her clever solutions to practical problems with a relish that she expects to be shared.

Both Helen and Vi will express disapproval of certain things, such as the manners, behavior, or work ethic of young people, but Helen will often, after a brief pause, gently append some remark indicating understanding, such as "They do their best," or "They try," whereas Vi will not soften her criticism. Helen does not like most of the changes that have occurred in her hometown over the years, such as the intrusion of a gaudy Chinese restaurant on Main Street or the closing of the old movie theater and the YMCA. Both marvel—disapprovingly—over excessive weight in others. Along with such disapproval comes a certain degree of self-approbation in both. Vi will boast outright, with a chuckle of pleasure, and tell stories to her credit, such as how she outwalked all the other church members on a recent trip to Jerusalem. Helen will not boast, but will occasionally imply, by her mild criticism, that her own way is a better way.

Both Helen and Vi give generously to their friends and family, materially and in time and attention. When Helen still lived at home, she kept boxes of cookies and pastries on a lower shelf of a dish cupboard in the kitchen; when family or friends were leaving, she would take a selection or a whole box out of the cupboard and urge it on the departing travelers. She does the same now in the nursing home. Visitors have brought her so many gift boxes of cookies, candies, and fruit that she has a large store of them in her bedside cabinet. "Would you like these ginger cookies?" she will ask. "Take this banana," she will say.

Helen calls friends regularly to see how they are. She shows her concern and interest in the questions she asks her visitors. She remembers the names of all their family members and asks after these family members, too. When she still lived at home and had the use of her eyes, she would send a card on each birthday or anniversary. For a child, she would often enclose money. She would always telephone some hours after a visit to make sure her family had gotten home safely.

In those days, Helen's form of giving was in service as well as in conversation. Besides her church activities, she would visit friends in the hospital and in nursing homes. When she still could, she would walk many blocks from her house to the rather grim nursing home where various women she knew, including her sister-in-law and her old English teacher, were living out their days. When she could no longer walk the distance, she found a ride with a friend. She often came as a visitor to the same nursing home where she is now a resident.

If a friend of Vi's is in the hospital for an extended time, she will go over to her house and clean it for her. If a friend does not drive, Vi will drive her where she needs to go. When there is a death in the family of one of Vi's friends, relatives often come from far away, usually the South, but also the Midwest and the West Coast, to attend the funeral; Vi thinks nothing of accommodating these travelers for several days, giving them beds and meals. She will report this activity and how busy she has been, commenting, "I don't know my head from my heels!" or "I been jumpin'!"

In addition to her work for the church and for friends, Vi used to pay regular visits to inmates of a local prison. There she would, in particular, scold one young man whose family she knew: "Your mother died without ever seeing you any better than you are now," she would tell him. "How could you do that to your mother? Aren't you shamed?"

Conversational Manner

Helen is more of a listener, Vi more of a talker. Vi is quite willing to express strong opinions about how things ought to be and how people ought to behave, whereas Helen is less prescriptive or assertive. Sometimes, only, she will be gently insistent when the subject is one she feels strongly about, such as baptism.

Helen answers questions about herself in just a few words and reluctantly or hesitantly, only occasionally volunteering some memory she likes to recall. She does not talk at length about herself, but she will recall the past in brief increments, as, on an outing in the car: "We used to come down this hill in a wagon with Kate and Fanny pulling it." Or she will comment wistfully on her present situation: "I haven't been shopping in so long . . . I miss some of it."

Vi and Helen are both likely to ask questions in a conversation, but sparingly, and Helen more than Vi. Helen asks for news and listens attentively. Her questions are general inquiries, such as "How are the cats?" or "Are you going to stay home for a while now?"

Vi tends to do most of the talking, but if the person she is talking to makes a remark, she will respond with "Is that so?" or "Is that right?" with mild surprise and sudden seriousness that is sometimes genuine and sometimes merely polite. Sometimes her questions are more specific, as in "Oh, is he moving?" or "How old is he now?" but her intention is never to draw the other out at any great length. Both Helen and Vi are reserved about probing very deeply into another person's life or opinions, no doubt restrained by courtesy rather than lack of interest.

Hope, by contrast, has no reserve in this area, and asks detailed questions about even the most personal subjects. She enjoys fostering a degree of dependence in her family and friends and has no doubt about the powerful influence of her opinions and advice.

Vi often enjoys good times with her friends, and she likes to report the funny things that happen to them. She says, over and over: "Oh, I had some fun with them about that," or "Oh, we laughed a lot."

She is more interested in her own stories than those of the person she is talking to. Almost everything that has happened to her in her life can be turned into a funny story. The humor in these stories is mild, having to do with the foibles of human and animal behaviors and interactions. For instance, Vi's best friend hated dogs. This woman told the woman she worked for at her cleaning job that she wouldn't work there anymore if the employer got a dog. The employer thought Vi's friend didn't mean it, because she had worked for her so long, but she did mean it, and when the employer got a dog, Vi's friend said, "You won't be seeing any more of *me*!" and never returned. Vi's facial expressions and intonations enliven the story as she tells it, and she laughs at the end.

However difficult the situation, for Vi there is always a funny side to it. Her husband was ill in the hospital; she had just come from her night job to see him; when she left him she would have to walk two or three miles through the darkened city to get home. But the doctor said something that made her laugh and it is part of a funny story she tells. Another time, her best friend collapsed on the living-room floor at three in the morning and Vi was summoned by the family. Although they were all terrified, Vi laughs as she describes how she was down on the floor trying to help her friend when the firemen came, and what a time they had getting her out of the way so they could do their work. "Oh, it was funny." A patient in a nursing home where she worked refused to let Vi touch him because of her black skin; her sister, who also worked there, calmly advised her to ignore the insult and leave him alone, because some people were like that; but when the patient, one day, insulted Vi's sister in the same terms, Vi said, her sister was so mad she was ready to "slug" him! Oh, it was funny.

Helen does not tell stories the way Vi does, but she relays news of family, friends, and the families of friends that make up a longer ongoing story, and this story is deeply absorbing to her. Her group of friends is shrinking year by year, as those her own age die, but a good number still visit her regularly in the nursing home, or send cards on her birthday and at Christmas, and their children, too, remain in touch.

Helen speaks Standard English that includes certain regional or ethnic expressions such as "come to find out," meaning "then we found out," and "Lebanon way," meaning "in the vicinity of Lebanon"; to her, a window shade is a "curtain," and sometimes, a magazine is a "book"; she will use slang expressions such as "a live wire" and sometimes include a colorful, incongruous metaphor in her conversation, as when she remarks, apropos of how many of her friends are gone, that she is "the last of the Mohicans—as they say." She will punctuate her conversation with phrases or remarks expressive of resignation, such as "Well, anyway . . ." and "I've lived a pretty long life as it is . . ." She knows a little Swedish, from having grown up with Swedish-speaking parents and relatives. She says that just recently she suddenly recalled a Swedish prayer she had said as a child; after years in which she had not remembered it, it came back into her mind complete and intact.

Vi speaks a mixture of Standard English and her own variety of Standard Black English (sometimes she will say "he doesn't" and sometimes "he don't") sprinkled with Southern idioms ("white as cotton," "burying ground" for cemetery), old-time rural locutions ("grease" for hand lotion), and unusual, perhaps unique expressions acquired from her grandparents, particularly her grandmother, who may have made some of them up ("We had a bamboo time!"). In any single conversation, at least one or two rare, vivid phrases will occur. She is aware of how interesting these expressions are and enjoys using them. As a natural storyteller, she relishes the effect not only of the plots of her stories but also of the language she uses in telling them.

Conclusion

Although genetic inheritance surely plays a part in an individual's health and longevity, it is not unreasonable to conclude that certain shared traits in Vi's and Helen's life histories, personalities, and habits have been conducive to their longevity and good health.

Their eating habits have probably been an important factor, although, since Helen's diet has been fair but not optimal for many years, we may postulate that the fresh and unadulterated produce and animal protein of her early years on the farm established her good health and that the lifelong moderation and regularity of her meals thereafter were more important than what she actually ate. Alternatively, we may conclude that in Helen's case, eating habits may have been less important than her vigorous and constant exercise and the other factors contributing to her well-being.

Vigorous physical exercise initiated in childhood would establish good development of heart, lungs, and other muscles early in life. Exercise outdoors, earlier in the twentieth century, when air quality was better than it is now, would have provided excellent oxygenation of Vi's and Helen's developing bodies. *Hope, too, was physically active as a child, racing her ponies, canoeing with the Girl Scouts, and, as shortstop and captain, leading her softball team to victory in high school.* The fact that their figures were slender reduced stress on their bones and inner organs, and made them more likely to remain active, which in turn kept them slender. There is no doubt that abstinence from smoking and drinking alcohol would be likely to reduce stress on their livers and lungs, and promote good oxygenation of their bodily tissues.

Regular lifelong physical exercise would also act to relieve psychological stress, which would help to explain the lack of tension in both Helen and Vi; and this lack of tension would surely also be conducive to good health and longevity. Physical exercise in general would be helpful, but especially helpful would be the particular exercise provided by dancing, since it is rhythmical, cardiovascular, communal, and emotionally expressive.

Although it is harder to measure the effects of pride in their appearance; enjoyment of life, especially friends, family, food, work, and leisure activities; contentment with, or acceptance of, their situations; curiosity about the news of their friends and family; uncomplaining, cheerful temperaments; optimism; and a capacity for enthusiasm and amazement, a positive outlook may be assumed to promote a sense of well-being, good health, and, in turn, a longer life.

The sense of humor that they share so generously with others, Vi's ready laughter and Helen's gentle smile, no doubt provides another form of release, both physical and emotional, along with a strengthening of their supportive community, while their storytelling, however abbreviated in Helen's case, reinforces their firm sense of identity.

The loving, but strict, upbringing by their families of origin, with its strongly inculcated work ethic, would provide at least three major benefits: a steady emotional support, a reinforcement of identity, and training in the self-discipline that would encourage Vi and Helen to maintain good habits and find satisfaction in industry. Their close involvement with their families of origin would in turn encourage them to form close ties within their own created families and their circles of friends, these in turn providing a steady support for them. It may also be argued that the habit of orderliness that was taught them as children would be conducive to their creating and maintaining a healthy environment and thus to lessening the likelihood of their suffering a disabling or fatal accident.

Their close involvement with their church communities yields a complex of benefits, arising not only from the rituals and spiritual beliefs of the church but also from the social activities surrounding them.

Lastly, a love of domestic animals involves an interaction with a positively disposed or needy creature that generally reciprocates one's affection and provides yet another form of release from stress.

Many of the positive elements in Vi's and Helen's lives are, of course, part of a reciprocal pattern: for instance, the work Vi and Helen have done, whether at home or on a job, has provided them with a positive sense of satisfaction; or their generosity toward another person has yielded generosity in return; or their kindness to a pet has inspired affection on the part of the pet. The positive effects of their actions induce them, in turn, to repeat the actions; in other words, a positively reinforcing cycle is created that constantly perpetuates the well-being of the initiator, Vi or Helen.

November 2002

Update: In the three years since this study was written, there have been some relatively minor changes in the situations of Vi and Helen, now respectively eighty-nine and ninety-six, but their health and vitality remain very much the same.

Helen's house was sold and its contents dispersed. This meant that she could no longer ask her family to bring her something from home, for instance some piece of clothing from a certain closet. Most of her clothing was given away, as were her furniture, books, kitchenware, and linens. She did not want to move anything into the nursing home because of the lack of space. She consented only to have a single oil painting from the house to hang above her chair. It is a very early one by her son that depicts her Bible lying open on a table by a window next to a potted geranium.

The selling of the house also meant that she could no longer go back and visit it, as she used to do on excursions from the nursing home. Now her family drives past it on their way to see her, and reports to her on its condition: the new owners have rebuilt the front porch; the plantings have not changed; yesterday there was a car in the driveway; today there was a Christmas tree upstairs.

Vi now has two more great-grandchildren, or a total of four. The older ones tell the little ones they must mind her because she "belongs to the old school," as she reports with delight. Her house was badly flooded one winter when the pipes burst while she was away. It had to be completely gutted, and while Vi was waiting for the insurance company to come forward with more money for the repair work, she lived either with her granddaughter in Washington or with her best friend down the hill from her house—the same friend with whom she had studied the Bible on Saturday evenings and who had had a frightening attack at three in the morning.

When surprised by a visit at ten in the morning a year or so ago, the two companionable women, both in their eighties but looking twenty years younger, were still in their immaculately clean house robes, one hanging out a load of wash in the sunshine on a square laundry tree in the backyard and the other sitting at the gleaming formica table in the kitchen. Vi had no immediate plans to go back to work, but also no plans to give notice to any of her employers. Later, she quit her office-cleaning job, but she does continue, though now eighty-nine years old, to clean house for at least two families.

Vi is still in good health, and active in church. She has recently taken a much-anticipated trip to Alaska that was not as successful as it might have been, since one member of the group had to go home halfway through due to a death in the family. "They never should have told her," Vi says.

Helen's health, too, is reasonably good. Now ninety-six, she takes only one prescription medication, for high blood pressure. Her balance has worsened, and her hearing has deteriorated slightly. But she is mentally alert, with an excellent memory, and her sense of humor is still lively, as is her interest in the activities of her family and friends. After several years of a successful companionship, Helen's young roommate was removed to another facility. The roommate who succeeded her was an old woman of a sour temperament, active enough to propel herself around in a wheelchair, but a constant grumbler. She died not long after arriving; Helen did not know the cause. The current roommate is a kindly Ukrainian woman with a large circle of friends and family: Helen mentions the noise produced by the long, frequent visits, though she does not explicitly complain.

Helen maintains the same rather limited physical activity as when she entered the nursing home. Since she has fallen several times, however, she is no longer allowed to move about on her own but is connected to an alarm on the back of her chair by a wire clipped to the shoulder of her blouse; the alarm will sound if she stands up. She still takes a daily walk around the nursing home when there is a volunteer or family member available to accompany her. She moves at a fairly brisk pace, leaning forward on her walker, and quietly nods or says hello to almost everyone she meets, though many residents are unaware of the meaning of her greeting and respond with a blank stare—which of course she can't see. One section of the hallway, near the entrance lobby, displays greatly enlarged framed vintage photographs, in color, of features of the town as it used to be, such as the footbridge over the river, the old shopping street with its awnings and horse-drawn carriages, the great limestone buildings of the thread mill, and the legendary frog pond of Revolutionary War fame. She calls this part of the walk "going down Main Street" and likes to stop in front of each photograph and ask questions about it. She is still reluctant to join in any of the planned activities of the home, but she will, if pressed by family members, attend a Christmas concert or "Piano with Bob" in the Recreation Room, politely staying until the very end of what may be a tedious hour-long performance.

January 2006

Reducing Expenses

This is a problem you might have someday. It's the problem of a couple I know. He's a doctor, I'm not sure what she does. I don't actually know them very well. In fact, I don't know them anymore. This was years ago. I was bothered by a bulldozer coming and going next door, so I found out what was happening. Their problem was that their fire insurance was very expensive. They wanted to try to lower the insurance premiums. That was a good idea. You don't want any of your regular payments to be too high, or higher than they have to be. For example, you don't want to buy a property with very high taxes, since there will be nothing you can do to lower them and you will always have to pay them. I try to keep that in mind. You could understand this couple's problem even if you didn't have high fire insurance. If you did not have exactly the same problem, someday you might have a similar problem, of regular payments that were going to be too high. Their insurance was high because they owned a large collection of very good wine. The problem was not so much the collection per se but where they were keeping it. They had, actually, thousands of bottles of very good and excellent wine. They were keeping it in their cellar, which was certainly the right thing to do. They had an actual wine cellar. But the problem was, this wine cellar wasn't good enough or big enough. I never saw it, though I once saw another one, which was very small. It was the size of a closet, but I was still impressed. But I did taste some of their wine one time. I can't really tell the difference, though, between a bottle of wine that costs $100, or even $30, and a bottle that costs $500. At that dinner they might have been serving wine that cost even more than that. Not for me, especially, but for some of the other guests. I'm sure that very expensive wines are really wasted on most people, including myself. I was quite young at the time, but even now a very expensive wine would be wasted on me, probably. This couple learned that if they enlarged the wine cellar and improved it in certain other specific ways, their insurance premiums would be lower. They thought this was a good idea, even though it would cost something, initially, to make these improvements. The bulldozer and other machinery and labor that I saw out the window of the place where I was living at the time, which was a house borrowed from a friend who was also a friend of theirs, must have been costing them in the thousands, but I'm sure the money they spent on it was earned back within a few years or even one year by their savings on the premiums. So I can see this was a prudent move on their part. It was a move that anyone could make concerning some other thing, not necessarily a wine cellar. The point is that any improvement that will eventually save money is a good idea. This is long in the past by now. They must have saved quite a lot altogether, over the years, from the changes they made. So many years have gone by, though, that they have probably sold the house by now. Maybe the improved wine cellar raised the price of the house and they earned back even more money. I was not just young but very young when I watched the bulldozer out my window. The noise did not really bother me very much, because there were so many other things bothering me when I tried to work. In fact, I probably welcomed the sight of the bulldozer. I was impressed by their wine, and by the good paintings they also owned. They were nice, friendly people, but I didn't think much of their clothes or furniture. I spent a lot of time looking out the window and thinking about them. I don't know what that was worth. It was probably a waste of my time. Now I'm a lot older. But here I am, still thinking about them. There are a lot of other things that I've forgotten, but I haven't forgotten them or their fire insurance. I must have thought I could learn something from them.

Mother's Reaction to My Travel Plans

Gainesville! It's too bad your *cousin* is dead!

For Sixty Cents

You are in a Brooklyn coffee shop, you have ordered only one cup of coffee, and the coffee is sixty cents, which seems expensive to you. But it is not so expensive when you consider that for this same sixty cents you are renting the use of one cup and saucer, one metal cream pitcher, one plastic glass, one small table, and two small benches. Then, to consume if you want to, besides the coffee and the cream, you have water with ice cubes and, in their own dispensers, sugar, salt, pepper, napkins, and ketchup. In addition, you can enjoy, for an indefinite length of time, the air-conditioning that keeps the room at a perfectly cool temperature, the powerful white electric light that lights every corner of the room so that there are no shadows anywhere, the view of the people passing outside on the sidewalk in the hot sunlight and wind, and the company of the people inside, who are laughing and turning endless variations on one rather cruel joke at the expense of a little balding red-headed woman sitting at the counter and dangling her crossed feet from the stool, who tries to reach out with her short, white arm and slap the face of the man standing nearest to her.

How Shall I Mourn Them?

Shall I keep a tidy house, like L.?
Shall I develop an unsanitary habit, like K.?
Shall I sway from side to side a little as I walk, like C.?
Shall I write letters to the editor, like R.?
Shall I retire to my room often during the day, like R.?
Shall I live alone in a large house, like B.?
Shall I treat my husband coldly, like K.?
Shall I give piano lessons, like M.?
Shall I leave the butter out all day to soften, like C.?
Shall I have problems with typewriter ribbons, like K.?
Shall I have a strong objection to the drinking of juice,
  like K.?
Shall I hold many grudges, like B.?
Shall I buy large loaves of white bread from the baker,
  like C.?
Shall I keep tubs of clams in my freezer, like C.?
Shall I make a bad pun at the wrong moment, like R.?
Shall I read detective novels in bed at night, like C.?
Shall I take beautiful care of my own person, like L.?
Shall I smoke and drink heavily, like K.?
Shall I drink heavily and smoke sometimes, like C.?

Shall I welcome people into my house to visit and to stay, like C.?
Shall I be well informed about many things, like K.?
Shall I know the classics, like K.?
Shall I write letters by hand, like B.?
Shall I write "Dearest Both," like C.?
Shall I use many exclamation marks and capitals, like C.?
Shall I include a poem in my letter, like B.?
Shall I often look up words in the dictionary, like R.?
Shall I admire the picture of the beautiful president of Iceland, like R.?
Shall I often look up etymologies, like R.?
Shall I bring a potted tulip to the back door as a gift, like L.?
Shall I give small dinner parties, like M.?
Shall I get a little arthritis in my hands, like C.?
Shall I keep a gray dove and a gray hound, like L.?
Shall I play the radio by my bed all night, like C.?
Shall I leave too much food in the rented house at the end of the summer, like C.?
Shall I often eat a single baked potato for my dinner, like Dr. S.?
Shall I have ice cream once a year, like Dr. S.?
Shall I swim in the bay alone, even in the worst weather, like C.?
Shall I drink vegetable cooking water, like C.?
Shall I label my folders in shaky handwriting, like R.?
Shall I chew my food slowly and thoroughly, like Dr. S.?
Shall I walk by the canal, like B.?
Shall I take my guests along the canal, like B.?
Shall I put daylily buds in the salad for my guests, like B.?
Shall I come out in the morning neatly dressed with my bed made, like R.?
Shall I have my first cup of coffee at eleven o'clock, like R.?

Shall I lay out the forks in a fan, and the napkins in a row,
for company, like L.?
Shall I make pancakes in the morning when traveling,
like C.?
Shall I carry liquor in the trunk of my car when on holiday,
like C.?
Shall I make an oyster stew on New Year's Eve that is full
of sand, like C.?
Shall I hand a knife carefully to another person handle first,
like R.?
Shall I speak against my husband to the grocer, like C.?
Shall I always read with a pencil in my hand, like R.?
Shall I hug my bereaved children too long and too often,
like C.?
Shall I ignore health warnings, like B.?
Shall I give gifts of money freely, like C.?
Shall I give gifts with animal themes, like C.?
Shall I keep a small plastic seal in my refrigerator, like C.?
Shall I have trouble sleeping on my arm, like R.?
Shall I take off my shirt just before I die, like B.?
Shall I wear only black and white, like M.?

A Strange Impulse

I looked down on the street from my window. The sun shone and the shopkeepers had come out to stand in the warmth and watch the people go by. But why were the shopkeepers covering their ears? And why were the people in the street running as if pursued by a terrible specter? Soon everything returned to normal: the incident had been no more than a moment of madness during which the people could not bear the frustration of their lives and had given way to a strange impulse.

How She Could Not Drive

She could not drive if there were too many clouds in the sky. Or rather, if she could drive with many clouds in the sky, she could not have music playing if there were also passengers in the car. If there were two passengers, as well as a small caged animal, and many clouds in the sky, she could listen but not speak. If a wind blew shavings from the small animal's cage over her shoulder and lap as well as the shoulder and lap of the man next to her, she could not speak to anyone or listen, even if there were very few clouds in the sky. If the small boy was quiet, reading his book in the backseat, but the man next to her opened his newspaper so wide that its edge touched the gearshift and the sunlight shone off its white page into her eyes, then she could not speak or listen while trying to enter a large highway full of fast-moving cars, even if there were no clouds in the sky.

Then, if it was night and the boy was not in the car, and the small caged animal was not in the car, and the car was empty of boxes and suitcases where before it had been full, and the man next to her was not reading a newspaper but looking out the window straight ahead, and the sky was dark so that she could see no clouds, she could listen but not talk, and she could have no music playing, if a motel brightly illuminated above her on a dark hill some distance ahead and to the left seemed to be floating across the highway in front as she drove at high speed between dotted lines with headlights coming at her on the left and up behind her in the rearview mirror and taillights ahead in a gentle curve around to the right underneath the massive airship of motel lights floating across the highway from left to right in front of her, or could talk, but only to say one thing, which went unanswered.

Suddenly Afraid

because she couldn't write the name of what she was: a wa
wam owm owamn womn

Getting Better

I slapped him again because when I was carrying him in my arms he tore my glasses off and hurled them at the grate in the hall. But he wouldn't have done it if I hadn't been so angry already. After that I put him to bed.

Downstairs, I sat on the sofa eating and reading a magazine. I fell asleep there for an hour. I woke up with crumbs on my chest. When I went into the bathroom, I could not look at myself in the mirror. I did the dishes and sat down again in the living room. Before I went to bed I told myself things were getting better. It was true: this day had been better than the day before, and the day before had been better than most of last week, though not much better.

Head, Heart

Heart weeps.

Head tries to help heart.

Head tells heart how it is, again:

You will lose the ones you love. They will all go. But even the earth will go, someday.

Heart feels better, then.

But the words of head do not remain long in the ears of heart.

Heart is so new to this.

I want them back, says heart.

Head is all heart has.

Help, head. Help heart.

The Strangers

My grandmother and I live among strangers. The house does not seem big enough to hold all the people who keep appearing in it at different times. They sit down to dinner as though they had been expected—and indeed there is always a place laid for them—or come into the drawing room out of the cold, rubbing their hands and exclaiming over the weather, settle by the fire and take up a book I had not noticed before, continuing to read from a place they had marked with a worn paper bookmark. As would be quite natural, some of them are bright and agreeable, while others are unpleasant—peevish or sly. I form immediate friendships with some—we understand each other perfectly from the moment we meet—and look forward to seeing them again at breakfast. But when I go down to breakfast they are not there; often I never see them again. All this is very unsettling. My grandmother and I never mention this coming and going of strangers in the house. But I watch her delicate pink face as she enters the dining room leaning on her cane and stops in surprise—she moves so slowly that this is barely perceptible. A young man rises from his place, clutching his napkin at his belt, and goes to help her into her chair. She adjusts to his presence with a nervous smile and a gracious nod, though I know she is as dismayed as I am that he was not here this morning and will not be here tomorrow and yet behaves as though this were all very natural. But often enough, of course, the person at the table is not a polite young man but a thin spinster who eats silently and quickly and leaves before we are done, or an old woman who scowls at the rest of us and spits the skin of her baked apple onto the edge of her plate. There is nothing we can do about this. How can we get rid of people we never invited who leave of their own accord anyway, sooner or later? Though we are of different generations, we were both brought up never to ask questions and only to smile at things we did not understand.

The Busy Road

I am so used to it by now
that when the traffic falls silent,
I think a storm is coming.

Order

All day long the old woman struggles with her house and the objects in it: the doors will not shut; the floorboards separate and the clay squeezes up between them; the plaster walls dampen with rain; bats fly down from the attic and invade her wardrobe; mice make nests in her shoes; her fragile dresses fall into tatters from their own weight on the hanger; she finds dead insects everywhere. In desperation she exhausts herself sweeping, dusting, mending, caulking, gluing, and at night sinks into bed holding her hands over her ears so as not to hear the house continue to subside into ruin around her.

The Fly

At the back of the bus,
inside the bathroom,
this very small illegal passenger,
on its way to Boston.

Traveling with Mother

1

The bus said "Buffalo" on the front, after all, not "Cleveland." The backpack was from the Sierra Club, not the Audubon Society.

They had said that the bus with "Cleveland" on the front would be the right bus, even though I wasn't going to Cleveland.

2

The backpack I had brought with me for this was a very sturdy one. It was even stronger than it needed to be.

I practiced many answers to their possible question about what I was carrying in my backpack. I was going to say, "It is sand for potting plants" or "It is for an aromatherapy cushion." I would also have told the truth. But they did not search the luggage this time.

3

In my rolling suitcase I had the metal container, well wrapped in clothes. That was now her home, or her bed.

I had not wanted to put her in the rolling suitcase. I thought that riding on my back she would at least be near my head.

4

We waited for the bus. I ate an apple so old it was nearly baked like a pie apple.

I don't know if she, too, heard and was bothered by the recorded announcement. It came over the loudspeaker every few minutes. The bad grammar in the beginning is what would have bothered her: "Due to security reasons . . ."

5

Leaving the city felt so final that I thought for a moment my money wouldn't be good where we were going.

Before, she could not leave her house. Now she is moving.

6

It has been so long since she and I traveled together.

There are so many places we could go.

Index Entry

Christian, I'm not a

My Son

This is my husband, and this tall woman with him in the doorway is his new wife. But if he is silly with his new wife, and younger, then I become older, and he is also my son, though he once was older than I, and was my brother, in a smaller family. She, being younger even than he, is now a daughter to me, or a daughter-in-law, though she is taller than I. But if she is smarter than a young woman, and wiser, she is no longer so young, and if wiser than I, she is my older sister, so that he, if still my son, must be her nephew. But if he, very tall though she even taller, has a child who is also my child, am I then not only a mother but also a grandmother and she a great-aunt, if my sister, or an aunt, if my daughter? And has my son then run off with his child's aunt or, worse, his own?

Example of the Continuing Past Tense in a Hotel Room

Your housekeeper ***has been*** Shelly.

Cape Cod Diary

I listen to the different boats' horns, hoping to learn what kind of boat I'm hearing and what the signal means: is the boat leaving or entering the harbor; is it the ferry, or a whale-watching boat, or a fishing boat? At 5:33 p.m. there is a blast of two deep, resonant notes a major third apart. On another day there is the same blast at 12:54 p.m. On another, at exactly 8:00 a.m.

The boats seem to come and go at all hours, and last night I could still hear their engines sounding well into the early morning. The pier is so far away, though, that the boats are the size of dominoes and their engines can be heard only when the town is quiet.

I am staying by the harbor in a damp little blue-and-white room that smells faintly of gas from the stove. The only people I see are an old couple who live just outside town. Sometimes they have visitors as old as they are, and then they invite me to have dinner or tea with them.

I work in the mornings and early afternoon, then I go out to get my mail. If I shop, I might buy a pencil sharpener, a folder, some paper, and a postcard. Another day, I might buy some fruit, some crackers, and a newspaper.

It is the beginning of August. I am not sure I should stay for the whole month. This may be a good place to work. My neighbors are quiet and I do not even have a telephone. Still, I'm not sure. I am trying to plan out how it would be. I can work most of the day. I can visit the two old people. I can write many letters. I can walk to the library. I can swim. What is missing?

A storm is coming, and the gulls cry over the streets. They have come over the land away from the storm. There is a heavy smell of fish in the air.

A short gust of wind, then calm, then the sea is dark gray and the rain comes down hard, and the wind blows against the awnings. My neighbor in the room above goes to his door, then begins walking around over my head.

To get to the beach from my room I go down the narrow boardwalk between two wooden buildings, mine and the motel next door. The two buildings lean together above me as I pass the windows of the motel apartments, waist high; at certain hours women are working in the kitchens, and there are snatches of conversations in the living rooms. These people seem louder and at the same time more stationary because they are idle and on vacation.

The different groups of people here: the year-round residents, who are sometimes artists and often shop owners; the tourists, who come in couples and families and are generally large, young, healthy, tanned, and polite; of these tourists, most are American, but some are French Canadian, and of these, some do not speak English; Portuguese fishermen, but they are harder to discover; some Portuguese who are not fishermen but whose fathers or grandfathers were fishermen; some fishermen who are not Portuguese.

I looked at whale jawbones in the museum this morning. Then I did some shopping. Whenever I go into the drugstore it seems that many people are buying condoms and motion sickness medicine.

Fog comes in over the next hill, foghorns sound, now and then boats whistle. Waves of mist blow like curtains, or smoke.

The noises here at different times of day: At five a.m., when sunlight pours into this room, there is relative quiet that continues until after eight thirty. Then there is increasing noise from the street: after ten a.m., a gentle Central American music, constant, inoffensive plucking and pinging, as well as the sound of passing cars, voices in conversation, the clatter of silverware from an upstairs terrace restaurant across the street, car engines turning over in the parking lot to one side of my room, people calling out to each other, laughing and talking, and all of this then continues through the day and the evening and past midnight.

I will probably not think about the whale jawbones once I am home again. I have noticed that it is only when I am at the seaside, for one short period of the year, though not every year, that the things of the sea become interesting to me—the shells, the creatures, even the seaweed; the boats and how they are built and what their functions are; and nautical history, including the history of whaling. Then, when my visit is over, I go away and I don't think about them.

•

For two days I did not speak to anyone, except to ask for my mail at the post office and say hello to the friendly checkout woman at the small supermarket.

When the storm began today I heard the footsteps of the man who lives above me going across to the door that leads out to his deck, pausing there for a while, and coming away again. The ceiling is low, and the sound of these footsteps is a very loud crunch, so that I feel they are almost on my head. When he comes home, first I hear the clanging of the street gate, then his brisk steps down the concrete walk of the alley, then the hollow wooden clatter as he climbs the stairs inside the building, then the loud crunch over my head. Steps in one direction, steps in another, then steps crisscrossing over my ceiling. Then there is silence—he may be reading or lying down. I know he also paints and sculpts, and when I hear the radio going I think that is what he is doing.

He is a friendly man in late middle age with a loyal group of friends. I discovered this one of the first nights I was here. He had been away in the city for a few days celebrating his aunt's hundredth birthday, as I heard him tell his friends, and was loudly welcomed back by a hoarse-voiced, middle-aged woman trailing a string of other people standing outside our building in the alley. They had come by to see if he was back. I know he is friendly because of a smile and greeting he gave me on his way into the building once, a greeting that lifted my spirits.

Sometimes there are loud thumps from above. At other times he seems to be standing still, and there is something a little mysterious and disturbing in the stillness, since I have trouble imagining what he is doing. Sometimes I hear just a few notes from a saxophone, the same notes repeated the same way a few times or just once before he stops and does not play again, as though something were wrong with the instrument.

There are two buildings on this property, one fronting the street and the other behind it, by the beach, with a small garden in between. My low, ground-floor room does not look out on the beach but on the damp garden. Each house is divided into apartments or rooms, maybe six in all. The landlady sells antique jewelry from a store in the building on the street. Most of the people who live in the buildings have seasonal work here and come to these rooms every summer. They are all quiet and sober, as the landlady made very clear before I moved in. She calls my room an apartment, even though it is just a room, as though there were something vulgar about the word *room*.

I was wrong about my neighbor upstairs. He is not the friendly man who once greeted me. He is barely polite. He has silver hair and a silver goatee and an unpleasant expression around his bulbous nose.

I was also wrong about the saxophone, which is not played by the man upstairs but by my neighbor across the patch of garden, a woman with a dog.

All week long I had heard people saying there would be a storm. I went out onto the beach, into its first fury, to see it hit the water. After I had stood for a while sheltering my face under my hand and watching the buildings on the piers in the distance vanish behind the curtains and sheets of rain, I went down to the water's edge, where the wind was much stronger, to see more closely how the rain hit the water. A man in a yellow slicker was dragging a rowboat up onto the sand. The wind came in so hard that it lifted the rowboat and turned it over. It lifted and flung the sand against my legs, stinging them. I took shelter under the motel deck next door, which is up on stilts off the beach. On the deck over my head, plastic chairs were being slung around and tumbled into corners by the wind.

Now the rain is coming down steadily, and the streets, which were empty at the beginning of the storm, are filling with people again, and there is, again, a heavy fish smell in the air. I have hung my clothes to dry from nails in the beams and posts of my room, so that it is a forest of damp garments swaying in the gusts of wind from the door and the windows.

The essay is taking shape now. As the time passes here, time is passing in the travels of the French historian. I trace and describe his itinerary through this country; he progresses, I progress in the essay, and the days pass. I am coming to feel that he is more my companion, in this room, than the live people in this town. This morning, for instance, because in my imagination I had been traveling with him ever since dawn, I felt I was not here in this seaside town but in a damp river valley some hundreds of miles to the west of here. I was in the previous century. This morning, the historian was watching fireworks from a boat in the middle of a broad river. For him it was evening.

It is not an easy piece of writing. I understand the information in the sources I am using, but I have no general background knowledge to draw on. I am afraid it will be very easy for me to make a mistake.

From within the town I look out at the harbor and across the harbor to the sea beyond. The horizon is very far away.

But that view itself, because it hardly changes, becomes a sort of confinement. The streets, too, teeming with people, seem always the same. I feel as though I were knocking up against myself at every turn. I am sometimes almost in a panic. That may be because I am also knocking up against the limits of what I can do with this work.

Yesterday I went a little way out of town, far enough to leave the houses behind. I walked past low hills covered with scrub brush and dead oaks, and dunes covered with dune grass, and then a marsh of bright green reeds cut through with channels of clear water.

But I can see that this, though it was so fresh to me today, and such a relief, would become dull, too, if I watched it from my window every day from a house outside town, and then I would need a glimpse of what I can see here: the stone breakwater, the two piers stretching out into the water, the small boats all pointing the same way, the one big, old hulk beached at low tide and leaning to one side; and in the streets the thick crowds constantly stopping at shop windows; the carriages and horses with women drivers wearing men's formal black suits, their blond hair in topknots; the motley people in a row on the bench before the town hall watching the others walk and drive by; the tall black transvestite who strides up the street in a sequin-covered red dress away from the Crown and Anchor Hotel; the tall white transvestite who stands next to the hotel with his dress open over one lean leg all the way up to his hip, a creased angry look about his long nose under his wig and above his red lips. They are advertising a show at the hotel.

The hotel is a large establishment almost directly across from the plain and tranquil old Unitarian Universalist Meeting House, which is set back from the busy street over an unadorned rectangle of lawn. The church was built in 1874 and is now being restored with the help of a fund raised by a group of painters here. The painters are the most famous inhabitants of this place, along with the writers. Earlier inhabitants were: the Portuguese fishermen and occasional Breton and English fishermen; the whalers; the Pilgrims who first landed here in 1620 and did not stay for three reasons, only two of which I can remember—the harbor was not deep enough and the Indians were not friendly; before them the Nauset and Pamet Indians themselves.

Today in the late afternoon I went to have a beer in the outdoor café next to the small public library, which is an old house shaded by an old oak with a circular wooden bench around its thick trunk. The waiter asked me, "Is there one in your party?" Edith Piaf was singing in the background. I said "Yes" and he brought my beer.

I am thinking about a recent mystery: On the day of the storm something washed ashore that was smooth, rubbery, and the size and shape of a dolphin's nose, though not the right color. It might have been the back of an upholstered plastic seat from a boat. For a day or two it remained there, moving as the water moved it, sometimes in the water and sometimes on the sand, always in about the same place. Then I didn't see it for a few days. Today as I was lying on the beach, a man in a ranger's uniform went under the deck of the motel, dragged the thing out, and methodically tore it to pieces, separating it into different layers. Some layers he left lying on the sand, the rest of it he folded and carried away with him.

•

The faces of the tourists here reflect what they see all day long, the harbor, the old buildings, the other people in the streets, with openness, even wonder. Only when they look in the shop windows, and seem to consider buying something, do they lose some of their ease and joy. Their faces close into expressions of intentness, care, even exhaustion.

I have been with the old people again. It is restful to me after I have been working, though if the work has not gone well I will not see them at all, preferring to sit with the difficulty than to leave it behind.

When I have made a little progress I am glad to leave it and have their company. In contrast to the work, to the denseness of all the information I am trying to put in some order, their conversation is undemanding. The old woman will talk endlessly if I ask her a question or two; the old man listens to her and sometimes adds a brief comment of his own. They do not seem to notice if I do not talk. Nothing at all is required of me when one says to the other, "Did you take your pills?"

The old man often sits in the passenger seat of the car waiting for his wife to return from doing an errand. He tells me he likes to watch the people going past. He will wait almost any length of time if he can watch the people and think his thoughts, which he finds interesting. Today he saw three women approach together, one of them feebleminded, as he called her, her head bobbing constantly. The leader of the group stopped by the hood of his car, set a pile of papers down on it, and began searching her purse for something. She took a long time searching and the old man sat there watching her directly in front of him and also watching the feebleminded woman, who stood at the edge of the sidewalk all that time, her head bobbing.

•

At the end of one pier tonight, two men were casting far out for bluefish. One remarked to the other that the slapping of the lure on the water over and over might be frightening the fish. At the other pier, fishing boats were lined up side by side, thick clumps of nets hanging from the masts, dinghies tied down onto the tops of cabins, stacks of new wooden crates on the decks, along with piles of baskets—only what was needed for the work.

From the beach, at dusk, I look back at the land and I see steeples against the sky, and, on a roof, what look like four white statues of women in robes against the sky, as in a cemetery, but then look more carefully and see that they are four white folded beach umbrellas with large knobs on top. In the water, small boats all point the same way on their moorings, only one suddenly will move independently, wandering a little and turning.

At night the Unitarian Universalist church burns a light in its steeple in remembrance of those lost at sea.

At the entrance of the alley, my alley, where it opens into the street, as at the mouth of a stream, there is the life of the street, turbulent, eddying, restlessly moving into the early hours of the morning.

At dawn I was woken by a thrashing in the patch of garden outside my door. It was a skunk caught in some brambles.

The travels of my French historian have taken him away from the damp river valley and out to the Midwest now. He is studying the structures of municipal governments in newly incorporated towns. This interests me only a little, but the historian himself is good company, and so his intelligence illuminates these subjects and they become tolerable.

Yesterday I took a walk in the rain and saw: tough-stemmed old stalks of Queen Anne's lace with their several heads waving in the wind and banging against a gravestone; the cemetery that has been allowed to go wild and is posted with signs prohibiting overnight camping; a woman awkwardly turning her car in a dead-end lane and crushing some tall stands of purple loosestrife outside a fenced garden; the man in the garden on his knees weeding a flower bed; a uniformed nurse in a small paddock talking over the fence about her horse to a neighbor in the road; the oldest house in town, built of wood from wrecked ships, with a plaque in front of it describing its circular brick cellar, whose technical name was included, though I now forget what it was; a street called Mechanic Street.

Last Sunday I decided to go to church. It didn't matter to me which one I went to. I was on my way to the Catholic church, St. Peter's, with its onion-shaped steeple of dark painted wood, when the bell began to toll in the belfry of the Unitarian Universalist church; I was walking slightly uphill in a narrow lane where I could see the belfry close at hand; I changed my mind and went back down the lane, into the yard past the flea market on the front lawn, into the church building, and upstairs to the chapel itself with its trompe l'oeil interior. Even the columns that looked so real were not real columns; the sparse congregation and the minister might have been trompe l'oeil, too.

But the minister was a young woman from the Harvard Divinity School, full of information, with an emphatic and direct manner; the music played on the organ was well chosen and performed; the soloist sang well from the organ loft; and the hymns were familiar old ones. Downstairs, after the service, sweet lemonade was served, with rounds of toast covered with sliced egg and olives laid out on a table that stood between the door to the musty basement thrift shop and the outer doorway with its rectangle of bright sunlight.

Later, on the street, I was thinking about a funny story the minister had told. A bronzed man on a motorcycle with impenetrable dark glasses and a bandanna around his forehead passed me and gave me a long dark look. I had been smiling, inadvertently, at him.

Recent dreams about animals: I was about to take an exam given by Z. when a small animal, a shrew or a mouse, escaped and I went off to help catch it. At that point I discovered other loose animals, larger ones. I alerted people and tried to get the animals back into their cages. This was taking place in a school, and the animals were probably connected with the exam.

On another night I was the one who let four animals loose in a field—a brown-and-white goat, a palomino horse, and two other large animals whose descriptions I was going to advertise so that they could be recovered. I stood watching the horse gallop into the field among other horses.

Yesterday I was sitting in the backseat of the old people's car. We were driving out to the ocean beach. The old man made a statement that shocked me, though neither he nor the old woman noticed it. I sat there shocked behind the old woman, who had great trouble driving straight into the setting sun.

•

I go for a long walk on a railroad track near the old people's house. The rails have been taken up, and the bed is straight and narrow and visible ahead of me for a great distance. A thin, bearded man dressed in layers of ragged clothing comes ambling along toward me with his black dog, which ranges around him nosing in the underbrush. The old people's cat, which has been walking with me, turns broadside to the dog and arches its back.

Last night, after midnight, walking barefoot near the kitchen sink, I stepped on something slippery and hard. On the mat lay what looked like some animal part, a glistening innard of uniform color and texture. I bent down to examine it: it was a slug. I was afraid I had killed it. I picked it up: it was cool and moist. As I held it in my palm, this dollop of glistening muscle, two bumps appeared at one end of it and then grew steadily into two long horns, as below them symmetrically two more bumps grew into slighter protrusions that I guessed were eyes, and at the same time the body thinned out and tensed, and then the slug set off and glided around my wrist and up my arm.

Tonight I heard the footsteps of a neighbor returning down the concrete path, then more footsteps, then many more all at once, and they continued so long and so steadily that I realized they were not footsteps: it was the rain. Heavy drops splashed on the leaves in the garden and on the planks of the wooden decks. Then, among the splashes of rain, I did hear the footsteps of a neighbor coming home, and it was the man above me, now walking over my ceiling.

•

Yesterday I rode a bicycle along a winding macadam trail past lily-choked ponds and through a thin forest of young beeches. On my way back, I stopped on the pier to watch fishermen mending their nets before they set out to sea. They pull large comblike implements through the squares of the net and tie knots in it. One man holds the net while the other does the mending with quick, economical motions. Small clusters of tourists stand on the pier above looking down at them respectfully where they work in the boats.

Not far away, three men fished off the pier for mackerel, casting again and again, pulling up silver fish that fought hard, all muscle, then unhooking them and slipping them carefully into a Styrofoam cooler where they flopped so violently that the cooler shook and thudded for a while after it was closed.

At the same time, a bright red oil truck was fueling the boats. It would stop next to them on the pier where they were tied two or three deep alongside and send the long hose down into one, over one into the next, and then into the third. At the same time, a steel cable that extended the length of the pier into what seemed to be a fish-packing shed was being wound mechanically onto a drum in one of the fishing boats. The winding went on and on. A group of tourists watched this carefully, too.

The tourists took pictures of the fishermen mending their nets. If a tourist asked a fisherman to smile, the fisherman would glance up soberly, with a neutral expression on his face, and keep still for the picture, but he would not smile.

I went out to eat recently with the two old people and two old friends of theirs. We sat in a room surrounded by water and they all ordered lobster. The plates came, and the red lobsters looked pretty lying on their lettuce leaves next to their little white cups of melted butter. Now the conversation died and the table was silent except for the furious cracking, pulling, and prying of those old people, who suddenly showed such competent physical strength, intent on destroying their lobsters.

People I see here: the clerk at the post office; the friendly checkout woman at the supermarket; my neighbors; my landlady; the woman across the garden, who once asked me in a neutral, curious tone what I was doing here; last night, a plump, gregarious off-duty bartender attending the free movie at the public library, though I did not speak to him. He wore a bandanna tied around his forehead and cowboy boots. He was there to see the 1954 movie, whose title I forget. Most of the small audience were old people calling back and forth to each other.

"Everybody's here!" someone cried.

I felt I was included in "everybody," though I was sitting by myself waiting for the movie to begin. I listened to the bartender talk to the other people. Then we all watched the movie.

A plumber came to my room yesterday to fix the shower. He told me his family had lived here for generations. He said that these days there isn't much cod or haddock and the fishermen are taking shellfish off the Great Bank about six miles west of the tip of the land; the beds there seem to be inexhaustible.

I have seen great crates of these shellfish, which I thought were quahogs, coming up onto the pier, hoisted by a small crane on a boat. The crates were stacked on the wharf while tractor trailers from Maryland with their engines running prepared to load them. Seagulls ran around on the asphalt with their wings raised threatening one another over the scraps. Only one gull sat on a crate at the top of a stack and pulled the slimy, elastic flesh of a quahog up through the slats, leaning back as he pulled, bending forward to get another grip, and leaning back again in the midst of a great noise from the boat's engines.

This was at twilight, and as the sky darkened, the lights on the boats grew brighter, and a handful of tourists watched, standing gingerly at the edge of the pier. The young fishermen, bare-chested, wearing shorts and high rubber boots, went about their work steadily, maneuvering hooks, hoisting a dredger, then a large piece of grating. The boat's engine throbbed, sometimes thundered.

On another night it was later. I was the only one watching. Sparks flew up into the darkness from a boat where something was being welded or soldered. Another boat set out to sea after blowing its whistle. A black fisherman ran to the stern of the boat as it pulled away. He looked up, smiled, and waved.

I have just come back from looking at the motorcycles on the pier. They are parked side by side in great numbers near the snack bars that sell such surprisingly good Portuguese fish soup. They are of all kinds, plain and fancy. The fancy ones are decorated with antlers, and with leopard skins.

More crickets are singing now as the air grows colder and colder. It is the last day of August and the season is changing suddenly. Just as it is time for me to leave, the historian, too, has finished his tour and will be returning to Europe.

Almost Over:
What's the Word?

He says,
"When I first met you
I didn't think you would turn out to be so
. . . strange."

A Different Man

At night he was a different man. If she knew him as he was in the morning, at night she hardly recognized him: a pale man, a gray man, a man in a brown sweater, a man with dark eyes who kept his distance from her, who took offense, who was not reasonable. In the morning, he was a rosy king, gleaming, smooth-cheeked and smooth-chinned, fragrant with perfumed talc, coming out into the sunlight with a wide embrace in his royal red plaid robe . . .